THE FRONTIER OVERLAND COMPANY

THE FRONTIER OVERLAND COMPANY

WILLIAM W. JOHNSTONE

AND J.A. JOHNSTONE

PINNACLE BOOKS

Kensington Publishing Corp.

www.kensingtonbooks.com

CHAPTER 1

North Branch, Wyoming
1866

Tucker Cobb was anxious to get the inaugural journey of the Frontier Overland Company on the road. It was just past dawn, but they had quite a bit of land to cover if they hoped to make Delaware Station by nightfall. Leo Burke's coach was scheduled to depart from North Branch the next day, and he did not want the two lines crossing each other.

But it appeared that young love had once again thrown a wrench into the driver's plans.

"I'd do anything to make you stay with me, Jane," the young cowboy pleaded with the lady about to board the stage. "I know I could make you happy if you'd just give me half a chance. I just know I could. You know my pa's got all the money we could ever spend even if things don't go well with the mine. I promise you'd never want for a single thing for the rest of your life."

Cobb could see the pretty woman was a good deal older than her beau and not just in years. He suspected the elegant veil she wore served to hide some of the effects of the hard road she had traveled thus far in life.

"It's not just about money," Jane assured him. "It's not about you and me, either. I have a chance at something better in Laramie, and I'd be a fool not to take it." She looked down at her gloved hands. "I'd hoped I'd made myself clear about that when we spoke last night."

Cobb watched the young man sag and, for a moment, thought he might throw himself at the woman's feet. "I never saw a problem money couldn't solve. You'll have to work for your money in Laramie, but if you stay here, all you have to do is love me."

She smiled up at him through her veil. "Love is hard work, too, if it's the real thing, Bart. It's best if I leave now, anyway. I've stayed here in town much longer than I'd planned to. The sooner I go, the sooner I can be settled in Laramie. That's where my future lies, but there's no reason to be sad about it. I'll be sure to write you as soon as I'm able. We can continue our friendship that way. Through correspondence. And once your mine starts showing a profit, you can come visit. Think of how romantic it'll be. Writing a letter, then checking with the mailman every day to see if you got a response back. It'll give us something to look forward to."

Bart stepped back from her as if she had slapped him. "That sounds a lot like friendship to me. Is that what you call this? We're a lot more than just friends, Jane. You're my girl. My woman. I want to take care of you, and I want to do it right here and now."

Cobb watched Jane as she tried to shy away toward the coach, only to have Bart grab hold of her arm with his left hand.

She tried to twist her arm from his grip. "We've talked about this until we were both blue in the face, and no good has ever come of it. I told you I'm nobody's girl. I don't belong to you or anyone else, and I never will. Now, let go of my arm."

But Bart's grip only tightened. "People don't say no to me."

At six feet tall and a solid two hundred pounds or so, Tucker Cobb was bigger than Bart by more than a head and had about fifty pounds on the boy. He stepped forward and said, "This woman is one of my passengers. You'd best let her go, son. She's had enough of your whimpering for one morning. Try to have some dignity."

Bart tore his eyes from the woman and glowered up at Cobb. "Dignity? What does a lousy coach driver know about dignity?"

Cobb grabbed Bart's left wrist and wrenched it, forcing him to break his hold on the woman's arm. He snatched Bart's right arm as Bart reached for the pistol on his hip and pushed the man back against the wall of the hotel.

As Bart struggled in vain to get free, Cobb looked back at his passenger. "You can board the coach, miss. This pup won't be bothering you anymore."

Jane brought a gloved hand to her mouth as she stepped up and into the coach before pulling the door closed behind her.

With the woman out of view, Cobb turned all of his attention to the lovestruck miner he had pinned against the wall. "Are you gonna behave yourself if I let you go?"

Bart continued to try to wriggle free. "You can't treat me like this! Don't you know who I am?"

"I surely do." Cobb delivered a sharp knee to Bart's stomach. The blow would have been hard enough to double him over if Cobb had not been holding him up. "You're a man too long on feelings and too short on sense. You're a man who's going to get himself hurt unless he can see reason. If I let go of you, are you going to make another play for that iron you're wearing?"

Bart did his best to push aside his pain as he glared up at Cobb. "My daddy's going to wipe the floor with you, you miserable—."

Cobb let go of the cowboy's left wrist and delivered a short right-handed jab to his jaw. Bart's knees buckled as Cobb twisted his right arm behind him, then he pulled Bart's pistol from its holster before kicking him in the seat of his pants. The blow sent him sprawling into the mud of the thoroughfare.

Never having much use for handguns, Cobb opened the cylinder, dumped out the bullets, and tossed the empty gun into the street. He saw five miners standing in front of a saloon across the thoroughfare and looking on. They seemed like they wanted to help Bart, but something was holding them back.

When Cobb looked to his right, he saw the reason for their hesitation. Butch Keeling, Cobb's partner, was leaning against the stagecoach. His Henry repeater was resting on his hip as he worked a toothpick around his mouth.

"A lot of help you were," Cobb chided him. "That young sprout almost killed me."

"Hardly." Keeling kept his eyes on the men across the street. "But those boys over there would've given it a go if I hadn't made them think otherwise."

Cobb knew his partner always had a knack for spotting danger before anyone else. He nodded down at Bart, who was beginning to get back on his feet. "That fella said he's somebody."

"You don't know who he is?"

Cobb did not. "All I know is he doesn't like to be refused by a pretty lady."

"That's Bart Hagen," Butch said. "King Hagen's boy."

Cobb might not have known much about the son, but he knew plenty about Charles Hagen. The rancher and financier had been called the king of the Wyoming Territory for a reason. He was said to be a frontier Midas, for everything he touched turned to gold.

Cobb said, "I'd have thought a boy with that kind of breeding would have better sense. He looks like a lousy cowpuncher to me."

Butch grinned. "The closest he's gotten to a cow is when it's sizzling on his plate. His daddy put him in charge of his family's mines in this part of the territory. And those friendly looking boys over there work for him. Since they knew better than to butt their noses into their boss's business, I'd say they have more brains than he does."

Cobb flexed the fingers in his right hand. He was coming up on forty-one years of age, and punching a man was not as easy as it used to be. "Who else are we waiting for?"

"The Right Reverend Earl Averill." Butch thumbed toward his right side. "Looks like he's coming this way."

Cobb looked beyond Keeling and saw a tall string of a man in a long, threadbare coat making his way toward the coach. He was carrying a heavy black satchel that looked like it weighed about as much as he did, if not more. The wind was not particularly strong that morning, but Averill looked like he was walking straight into a hurricane. It would not take much to knock him over.

Cobb moved around Butch to help his new customer. "Keep an eye on those boys over there. Make sure they don't do anything stupid."

"That's what I've been doing this whole time."

Cobb forced a smile as he greeted Reverend Averill in

the middle of the street. "I'm Tucker Cobb, Reverend. I'll be driving the stage today. Let me help you with your bag."

"Much obliged," the preacher said as he let Cobb take his burden. "I'm afraid I packed too much, but it was necessary."

Cobb was surprised by the weight of the bag. Having hauled freight for most of his life, he had a good sense of weight and measures and judged this bag to weigh closer to a hundred pounds. "What do you have in here?"

Reverend Averill held onto his black hat, though it was in no danger of blowing away. "A few items of clothing and my books for my congregation. The Word of the Lord is heavy in practice, but light in the heart to all willing to hear it."

Cobb had never been much for prayer, so he took his word for it. "I'll secure it up top with Miss Jane's luggage. You won't have to worry about it blowing off during the journey, though I might have to hitch up two more horses to haul it."

Cobb knew his feeble attempt at humor had fallen well short of its mark when the reverend said, "No need for that, Mr. Cobb." Averill surprised him when he reached the coach, opened the door for himself, and reached for the bag. "I'll be wanting to keep it in here with me at all times if it's all the same to you. It's a long journey to Laramie, and I'll want to keep up with my reading along the way."

Cobb knew it was bad business to argue with customers, especially before his first official trip, but it was necessary. "This bag takes up a fair bit of room, Reverend, and we're expecting a full coach by the time we reach Laramie."

"Then I'll be glad to keep it on my lap whenever space becomes a concern."

"Suit yourself." Cobb slid the heavy bag on the floor of the coach as the reverend took a seat by the door. He saw that Jane had moved to the far side of the bench and preferred to look out the window instead of greeting her fellow passenger. Cobb figured her run-in with the Hagen boy was still weighing heavy on her mind.

Cobb shut the door and, as he moved past Butch, saw Bart Hagen stagger toward his miners in front of the saloon. He had not picked up his empty pistol yet, which was fine by Cobb.

"Looks like you made quite an impression on that boy." Butch laughed. "He can barely stand up straight."

"Let's hope he stays like that until we're long gone," Cobb said. "Check the luggage up top to make sure it's steady and we'll get going. It's a long way to Bellwether, and I want to reach Delaware Station by dark. I've got a hankering for some of Ma's fine chili."

As Butch went to the wagon box to check the luggage, Cobb walked around to the other side of the coach and found Miss Jane still looking out the window, but too lost in her thoughts to see anything. Now that he was closer, he noticed a bruise under her left eye that had been covered by face powder. "I'm sorry things got rough just now, Miss Jane."

"No need to apologize for being a gentleman, Mr. Cobb. And call me Jane, please. There's no call for manners with a woman in my line of work."

Cobb would not hear of it. "You're my customer, which makes you something close to royalty as far as me and Butch are concerned. While I can't do much about what happens outside of this coach, everything that happens in and around it is my responsibility. My domain, you might say."

He patted the newly painted door as if the coach were a thoroughbred. "I know she might not look like much to you, but she's all mine. Mine and Butch's, I guess you could say. We pulled together every penny we had in the world and bought her last month. She's two-thousand pounds of wood, varnish, and dreams. Even had new cushions and springs put in to make the ride more pleasant for you folks back here. She's more than twenty feet long from the boot to the drawbar, and that's not including the six horses pulling her. On this trip, you'll be treated well, and anybody who thinks different is liable to find themselves on foot. You need anything, you just bang on the roof, and we'll tend to you directly. That sound good to you?"

"It sounds wonderful to me, Mr. Cobb." She smiled through the tears that streaked down her face. "And thank you." She seemed to remember something as she reached into the small bag on her lap and produced her ticket. "I forgot to give this to you."

He looked down at the ticket. It had been the first one he had printed up and the first one he had signed. He took it from her and tucked it into the pocket of his shirt. "I'm going to hang this on the wall of my office one day, as soon as I have call to have an office, that is."

Cobb knew he was likely only one in a long line of men who had been taken in by her smile, but he did not mind the company. "You can thank me tonight when we reach Delaware Station. You're in for a treat. Ma makes the best chili this side of Texas. And it's easy on the innards, too."

Averill handed over his ticket stub, too. "I trust we'll be getting underway soon, Mr. Cobb?"

Cobb took the ticket stub and pocketed it. Leave it to a preacher to ruin a nice moment between him and a pretty lady. "Your trust is well placed, Reverend. We'll get moving as soon as I get up top."

Cobb climbed up into the wagon box and took the reins of the six horses waiting to go. After Butch finished checking the luggage, he settled in beside Cobb with his Henry rifle across his lap. "All's secure, Boss. You may proceed."

Cobb saw no reason to remind Butch that they were partners in this enterprise. He had grown accustomed to being called the boss.

He released the brake and snapped the reins, sending the horses into a decent trot. The first journey of the Frontier Overland Company of Wyoming was finally underway.

In all of his years as a freighter, chuckwagon cook, and stagecoach driver, Tucker Cobb had learned how quickly the monotony of the endless miles could play tricks on a man. It was why he was glad Butch had decided to ride up here with him instead of back in the coach with the customers.

It not only allowed Butch to keep an eye on their surroundings but also gave Cobb a way to pass the time as they approached the tiny town of Bellwether.

"How many are we supposed to pick up in the next town?"

"Four," Butch told him without hesitation. "Edward Koppe, Joe Yost, Mrs. Kenneth Wagner, and Leon Hunt. We're supposed to pick up Lee Pearson and Albert Thomas at Delaware Station. Then it's a straight ride toward Ennisville and on to Laramie from there."

His partner's ability to remember names and details never ceased to amaze Cobb. "One day, you're gonna have to teach me that trick."

"What trick is that?"

"The one where you can call all those names to mind without looking at a telegram or a sheet of paper," Cobb explained. "You read or hear something once and remember it forever. I can hardly remember what I had for dinner last night."

"Biscuits and gravy," Butch reminded him. "Same as we had for breakfast." He shrugged off the compliment. "There's no trick to remembering things that I know of. It's just the way I was born, I guess. Remembering things isn't always a blessing. Sometimes, it's a curse. There's plenty I'd like to forget."

Cobb imagined there were plenty of events in every man's life he would like to forget. Butch Keeling was no different. Cobb had met his partner almost two years before, back when Cobb had been running the chuck-wagon for a cattle outfit out of Texas. The War between the States had just ended, and the weary nation sought to soothe its wounds with a nearly insatiable appetite for beef.

All Cobb knew about Butch was that he had once been a Texas Ranger before he had become a cowhand. He did not like to talk much about his past, which was fine as far as Cobb was concerned. He had never been one to enjoy looking backward, either.

He supposed that was why men like them always pre-ferred the rigors of the open road as opposed to the safety of civilization. The trail ahead always offered more pressing challenges and excitement than whatever they had done the day before. The past held no lien on them and neither did the future, for now was all they had.

The war had come and gone without taking much notice of Cobb and Butch. Neither man had seen fit to complain.

Cobb remembered the exact moment when he and the quiet former lawman had struck up their friendship. They could not have been more different in appearance. Where Cobb was tall and powerfully built, Butch was shorter, but lean and quick. Where Cobb preferred the bench of a chuckwagon or stagecoach, Butch was a horseman to his core. Where Cobb was quiet and introspective, Butch enjoyed trying to make people laugh with his tall tales from his time as a Texas Ranger. Cobb did not know how much truth there was in his friend's stories, but he knew Butch always found a way to make him laugh.

Cobb supposed they had become friends gradually somewhere along the many miles between Texas and the cattle markets in Nebraska. When the outfit dissolved after that final payday, the two men continued on together in the hopes of finding their fortunes somewhere in the wide expanse of a war-weary country.

While still in Nebraska, they had seen an advertisement in a newspaper about a man in Wyoming who had a small but profitable stagecoach line for sale and decided to see what they could make of the place. Both Cobb and Butch had been sensible with their money over the years. They had worked for others long enough to know the only way to get rich was to work for themselves.

Unfortunately, the stagecoach line had already been sold by the time they reached North Branch, but Bob Seary, the new owner, hired them on as drivers. They had spent the next year moving passengers and freight for him until Seary told them he had found himself a wealthy old widow to marry. He was looking to sell his business, which gave Cobb and Butch the inclination to buy it, including his team of horses. Out of such fortunes, the Frontier Overland Company of Wyoming had been born.

The old coach had seen many miles and needed a fair amount of work to make it presentable, but Cobb and Keeling had just enough money set aside to turn the wagon into a fine bit of carpentry. They had used the last bit of their combined resources to place an advertisement in the newspaper, promising a "rolling palace with every modern comfort" to prospective riders.

The idea had been Butch's, but the words had been Tucker Cobb's. He took a fair amount of pride in the fact that on this, their first trip, they were nearly sold out, with the prospect of picking up more business once they reached Laramie.

He watched Butch produce a small sack of chewing tobacco and bite off a mouthful of chaw. He did not bother to offer any to Cobb, who preferred a pipe with his coffee before bedtime.

His partner said, "That Miss Jane sure is easy on the eyes, ain't she?"

Cobb nodded. "She's got a real nice disposition, too."

"Disposition?" Butch laughed as he tucked his pouch away. "She's a woman, not a draft horse. No wonder you've never managed to find yourself a wife."

"That's because I never took the time to look for one," Cobb declared, as he kept the horses on a straight line across the flat land. "There was always something more important that needed to be done besides troubling myself with marriage."

"Like making money you don't spend except on something that means more work for us."

"Wives take money, too," Cobb answered. "Families take even more. What would I do with a family, anyway? I'm never in one place long enough to put down roots. And before you go teasing me about it, I haven't seen you going on bended knee before a lady."

"And deprive all the other women out here of my charming company? That wouldn't seem fair. These poor old gals out here in the wilderness need some excitement in their lives, and I aim to give it to them. You could call it a calling."

"Sounds closer to something else to me." Cobb had always enjoyed Keeling's overabundant confidence. They had never gotten around to discussing age, but during the course of their association, Cobb had figured Butch was about five years younger, putting him at around thirty-five. He was no longer a young man, but further away from a rocking chair on a porch than Cobb. Butch's wit and dark looks made him appealing to women and his Southern charm was often more than enough to secure their affections, at least for a few hours until it was time to leave.

Cobb kept the team moving at a steady pace. "Well, Miss Jane will be with us all the way to Laramie, which ought to give you plenty of time to get acquainted with her."

"I ain't like you, Cobb," Butch said, "and I've always been a touch impatient when it comes to love. I was fixing to try my luck with her tonight at the station."

Cobb glanced at him. "After a couple of plates of Ma's chili? Those beans don't exactly make for decent courting."

"Don't let it trouble you. I've got a way about me that the ladies find pleasing no matter my condition."

"Grass doesn't grow under your feet, does it?"

Butch settled back in the wagon box and hooked his boot on the edge. "Like my mama used to say, 'No time like the present.'"

"I'm sure your mama also warned you about women like Miss Jane," Cobb added. "And I'd advise you to hold off on doing anything until we get closer to Laramie. If she's the sort of woman you think she is, you'd do well to be within a day's ride of a doctor. I won't have any sympathy for you if you come down with a case of the scratches."

"You don't have sympathy for anything that doesn't have four hooves and can make you money. Don't hate me for knowing how to live."

"Live?" It was Cobb's turn to laugh. "Is that what they're calling it these days?"

"You're about as much fun as a wet blanket in a rainstorm." Butch pushed himself upright in the box and began to look around. He was almost as vigilant about watching their surroundings as Cobb was.

As he turned to look behind them, he said, "I can see some dust getting kicked up a good piece behind us. I think we might be expecting some company."

Cobb knew better than to question his partner's ability to gauge danger. For the moment, the best he could do was keep the team of horses running straight. "How many you figure?"

"They're still too far back for me to say for certain, but they're gaining on us. Faster than I'd like, too." Butch turned back around and lifted his rifle from the floor of the wagon box. "Their horses will be just about played out by the time they get here."

Since Cobb had been keeping the team moving at a steady pace, he knew there was a good chance they might be able to outrun them. "Seems like they're out of North Branch. I hope it's not who I think it is."

"Hope can get a man killed out here," Butch said. "I'd wager everything I own that it's Bart Hagen and his men come to fetch Miss Jane. Or to pay you back for hurting his pride like you did."

Sometimes, Cobb wished Butch was not always right. "I thought that boy's friends might've been able to talk some sense to him."

"Kind of hard to talk sense to the same man who's paying your wages," Butch observed. "How do you want to play this?"

Cobb knew their options were limited. They were too

far away from Bellwether to make a run for it. The horses had come with the coach, and none were in prime condition. He did not know how far he could push them before playing them out. It would not be long before the riders caught up to them and overtook them. Then, Cobb and Butch and their passengers would be at young Hagen's mercy. That did not sound like much of an idea to Cobb.

There was only one chance. The element of surprise. "You up for a fight?"

Butch rested the butt of his Henry repeater on his leg. "I was born ready. What did you have in mind?"

Cobb began to pull on the reins as the team crested a rise in the road, slowing the horses gradually. "The same thing we did in Abilene."

"I remember it well." Butch began to climb atop the stagecoach to take a position among the luggage. "The ground's about the same, too."

Cobb stood when the team came to a halt. He threw the brake and lifted the lid of his seat, where he stored the double-barreled shotgun. He hoped he was making the right choice. Getting killed on his first day would be bad for business.

CHAPTER 2

"What is it?" Reverend Averill asked through the open window. "What's happening?"

Cobb opened the breach of his gun to check the shells before closing it again. "Nothing to worry about. Just swatting at a couple of horseflies, Reverend. You and Miss Jane had best stay low for the duration. Things are liable to become awful lively in a minute."

Cobb watched the dirt cloud beyond the rise in the road grow as the riders quickly closed in on their position. He and Butch had survived many battles like this. Butch would fire from up top while Cobb remained on the ground and focused his fire on anyone unfortunate enough to get within range of his shotgun. It had always worked in the past, and he imagined now would be no different.

Cobb took a knee behind the rear wheel and trained his sights on the looming dust cloud. He could hear the thunder of the approaching riders and spotted the bowler hat of Bart Hagen in front of the five men racing behind him.

Cobb brought the stock of his shotgun against his shoulder and thumbed back both hammers.

As soon as they reached the top of the hill, Butch fired. The first shot hit the rider to Hagen's left. The impact of the bullet caused him to pull hard on the reins as he spilled back and out of the saddle. The horse screamed as it fell over on its rider before scrambling back to its feet and galloping away.

The blast caused the others to stop short, throwing even more dust into the air around them. Butch measured his second shot before firing into the middle of the group, then quickly followed that with a third.

Cobb held his ground, waiting for any rider who might break forward from the others. As he knelt beside the wheel, he saw the cloud grow thicker. When the dust had finally settled and he could see through it, no one was left on the road. Not even the horse and rider who had fallen.

"Looks like they've had enough of our company for today," Butch called out from the roof of the wagon. "They're turning tail and riding back to North Branch. Two of them are keeping their buddy upright on his horse. Some mighty articulate shooting, if I do say so myself."

Cobb heard the cartilage of his knees pop as he stood up and thumbed the hammers of his shotgun down. He knew that would be the end of it for now. Hagen had lost at least one man and had another wounded man to tend to. He would not want to have to explain to his father how he had lost a worker. The boy seemed smarter than Cobb had taken him for. Too bad he had not been smart enough to remain in North Branch where he belonged.

Cobb pounded the coach door before he began to climb back up into the box. "Everyone can get back in their seats. Trouble's over for now. Ought to be clear riding from here to Bellwether."

He was halfway up into the box when Miss Jane poked her head out from the window. "Was it Bart and his friends, Mr. Cobb. Was that them just now?"

"Don't know if they were friends," Cobb said, "but

there's fewer of them now than in the beginning. Might as well just settle in, miss. You've got nothing to fear from them now."

Cobb set the shotgun back in the cabinet beneath the seat before Butch came down from the roof. "I hope the rest of this trip is less interesting."

Cobb gathered up the reins as he released the break. "Here's hoping."

It was well before noon when Cobb pulled up his weary team in front of the Bellwether Hotel.

Had the town been situated anywhere else in the country, there would not have been much to say for the place. But as Bellwether was in the Wyoming Territory, it was considered a thriving and prosperous community. It sported a bank that owned the deed to most of the farms, ranches, and mines in the area. A general store carried all the goods one would expect to find at such a concern while also serving as the town's post office. Three saloons, not counting the one in the lobby of the hotel, catered to the thirst of the men who called the town home, and each place had its own loyal following. Ranchers and farmers preferred the Horse and Plow Saloon and Old Drover's Inn. Miners often frequented the Mother Lode.

The Bellwether Hotel served more as a rooming house for those who worked in town, though residents were told to double up during those rare occasions where the hotel had guests. The owner of the hotel, George Thomas, also served as the town constable and the source of what little gossip there was to be had there.

George ran his thumbs through his suspenders as he took in Cobb's rig when it pulled up in front of his place of business. "Well, would you look at that? Sporting a new coat of paint and all the trimmings. And I like that sign. 'Frontier Overland Company.' Sounds mighty official if you ask me."

"Nobody asked you." Butch jumped down onto the street and opened the coach door. "And it's as official as it gets, you old busybody. Old Cobb and me are respectable businessmen now, and it's time you treat us accordingly."

"Businessmen, maybe," George said. "As for the respectable part, that remains to be seen."

The hotel owner whisked off his faded slouch hat and swept the ground with it upon seeing Miss Jane about to step down from the coach. "Welcome to Bellwether, my good lady. I'm George Thomas, the owner and proprietor of this fine establishment. It's the best hotel within twenty miles because it also happens to be the only hotel for twenty miles. But we offer all our guests a clean and comfortable place to rest themselves before the next leg of their journey. My wife and I bid you a warm welcome."

Miss Jane offered a slight curtsy after Butch helped her down. "Pleased to make your acquaintance, Mr. Thomas."

"You'll find my wife inside at the desk," George told her. "She'll be more than happy to assist you." After she had gone into the hotel, Thomas said to Butch, "Is it me or is there something familiar about that gal."

"I'm sure she's familiar to a lot of men in town."

Cobb jumped down from the wagon box and hit Butch with his hat. "Enough of that kind of talk. She's a paying customer."

As Reverend Averill stepped off the stage, George Thomas bowed again and placed his hat over his heart. "Welcome to my humble hotel, Reverend. You'll be glad to find Bellwether to be a fine, God-fearing town."

The reverend pulled his heavy satchel from the coach and carried it in both hands. "I'm sure it is, but at the moment, I'm more interested in corporeal nourishment than spiritual."

"Mrs. Thomas will be happy to show you to our dining room, where you will find refreshment of all kinds. We aim to please."

After the reverend had gone inside the hotel, George Thomas dispensed with formality as he peered into the coach. "Only two of them, Cobb? Not much of a start for you boys, is it?"

Cobb was glad to disappoint him. "That shows how much you know. We're picking up four new customers right here in town. Isn't that right, Butch?"

Keeling said, "Edward Koppe, Joe Yost, Mrs. Kenneth Wagner, and Leon Hunt, if memory serves, which it often does."

George Thomas was clearly impressed. "Those are the Quakers looking to bring religion to Laramie. I told them they'd be better off sparing themselves the trouble by staying here or heading back East, but they're a determined bunch. Mrs. Wagner said the Almighty spoke to her in a vision and told her to press on to Laramie. The reverend will probably enjoy their company, seeing as they have so much in common."

Cobb was not so sure. "The only company the reverend seems to like is that heavy bag he's lugging around with him. I don't think he said a word to Miss Jane the whole ride from North Branch."

Butch said, "Guess the run-in we had with Hagen and his friends set him to praying harder than usual."

George perked up at the prospect of fresh gossip. "Trouble? What kind of trouble?"

Cobb was angry with himself for not asking Butch to keep his mouth shut about the incident. He did not want to risk a bad word spreading about their company before its first full day in operation, especially because it involved one of King Charles Hagen's sons.

"Just a young hothead out of North Branch looking to settle a score," Cobb said. "No real harm done."

"Hagen trouble is the kind of trouble I wouldn't wish on my worst enemy," George said. "Why, the devil himself would think twice before locking horns with the likes of King Charles."

Butch smiled. "We don't rank so high and mighty. It was his boy, Bart. A bunch of miners who rode out with him. Like Cobb said, no real bother at all." He patted the wagon. "They never got close enough to put a mark on her."

George did not look so sure. "Hagens have a way of leaving a mark long after a man thinks the battle's over. Since you said you're taking those Quakers on to Laramie, you'd do well to keep your heads down while you're in town. His Blackstone Ranch is only a few miles out of town."

Cobb knew where the Hagen ranch was located. "I aim to keep my head where it always is. High and in plain sight. It's an easy enough target for any man fool enough to try to take a shot at it."

"Truer words have never been spoken," Butch observed. "My partner here is a very proud man."

Mr. Thomas stepped aside and beckoned them to enter his hotel. "Guess the least I can do is offer you boys a last supper before your comeuppance."

Cobb saw no reason to tell the old busybody that they would be stopping at Delaware Station for the night before pressing on to Laramie. "I just hope your cook has stopped burning those biscuits. Felt like I was chewing adobe bricks the last time we stopped here."

"A bit of char is proven to be good for the condition,"

the hotelier said as he followed Cobb and Butch inside. "In your case, Cobb, I hope it does something for your sour disposition."

Cobb was glad the push toward Delaware Station was far less eventful than the stretch from North Branch. The team had held up well, all things considered, but he could sense they were beginning to tire. He would be glad to switch them out for new horses at the station. He hoped a fresh team might allow them to make better time in the morning, maybe arrive in Laramie ahead of schedule.

The coach had grown so quiet that Cobb had almost forgotten he had a nearly full wagon of passengers beneath him.

George Thomas had been right about the Quakers. They were a religious bunch who had barely greeted Cobb or Butch as they helped them with their baggage after lunch. Their belongings were as meager, as Cobb had expected, and their cases were light.

Edward Koppe was a pale mouse of a man who seemed content to follow Mrs. Wagner's lead. Joe Yost had the look of an underfed farmhand barely out of boyhood. Given his permanent look of wonderment at the spartan marvels of Bellwether, Cobb knew he would be in for quite a shock when he laid eyes on Laramie. Leon Hunt was the opposite of the Yost boy. He was far enough along into middle age that he was on the verge of becoming an old man. His sunken eyes had a darkness about him that led Cobb to believe he had seen a fair bit of life's horrors before he found comfort in religion.

There was no question in Cobb's mind that Mrs. Kenneth Wagner was the spiritual and actual leader of the group. She was a stout woman with a square jaw and small, cruel eyes that looked out disapprovingly on the world. Her prairie bonnet was as starched as the long blue dress she wore. She believed that every sinner she encountered could be saved by the words in the black Bible she kept clutched to her ample bosom.

Back when they had been preparing to get underway in front of the hotel, Butch had run afoul of the pious woman when he spat a stream of tobacco juice into the street.

"A foul habit, sir," Mrs. Wagner had said. "I detest the consumption of tobacco or spirits of any sort in a man. I hope my fellow pilgrims will not be subjected to such indecent behavior the entire trip to Laramie. My nephew Joe here is particularly susceptible to negative influences, given his tender age."

Cobb had forced an apology he did not mean. "I'll be sure to have a word with him, Mrs. Wagner."

She had remained in a huff as Cobb had helped her board the coach, and he imagined she had probably remained that way since leaving Bellwether.

Butch began to whistle through his teeth to break the monotony of the open road. "I can't wait to enjoy a good home-cooked meal at the station. I just hope Ma hasn't lost her touch with a skillet."

Any man who ate as much as Butch did should weigh four hundred pounds, yet he always managed to remain wiry. If Cobb looked at a glass of beer, his stomach swelled for days. "How can you think of dinner so soon after the size of the meal you just ate back at the hotel?"

"A good meal's always worth looking forward to," Butch said, "and in this line of work, a man has to eat when and where he can. There's no telling how long a meal might have to last him. Sleeping's the same way, come to think of it."

Cobb decided to concentrate on the team of horses instead of Butch's philosophical rantings. "You're sounding as dire as George Thomas back in town. Though I was glad he got himself a new cook. The biscuits were almost passable this time."

Butch sat back and rubbed his flat stomach. "Most peculiar meal I've had in a while. And the company didn't do much to help my digestion. Being surrounded by all those Holy Rollers made me feel like I was eating in church."

"Keep your voice down," Cobb barked. He doubted the passengers could hear them over the racket of the rattling coach, but talking ill about customers was a bad habit he did not wish to start. "One bad word from them and our business will dry up before it's had the chance to start. You're already on Mrs. Wagner's bad side with that juice spitting of yours. Don't do that when she's around, or at least not where she can see you."

"That woman's piety could cause a preacher to blanch," Butch observed. "Come to think of it, I think she managed to take a bite out of the poor reverend while we were there. Kept asking him about God and the Bible, but he had the good sense to ignore her and keep his eyes on his soup. What good is saying grace over a meal if you let it go cold before you eat it?"

Cobb had noticed that, too. He would have thought a man of the cloth would welcome conversation from the likes of Mrs. Wagner, but Averill had not. "He seems to be more of the bookish type of reverend to me. He was probably scared of her, not that I could blame him. Everyone else certainly was."

Butch grinned. "I wonder how she likes being in Miss Jane's company. Wonder if she's tried to convert her yet."

"You'll have a chance to find out for yourself in a bit. By my estimation, we're about a mile or so out from the station."

Butch rubbed his flat stomach. "That's good, because I'm starving."

CHAPTER 3

Cobb pulled back hard on the reins when he got close enough to see the wooden gate to Delaware Station swinging open on its hinges. Gene Bridges, the manager of the station, never forgot a task as important as leaving his gate open and unattended.

"Something must be wrong." Butch picked up his Henry rifle and jumped down. "Stay here. I'll go take a look."

Cobb threw the brake and rose as he took his shotgun from beneath his seat, then climbed down. He watched Butch approach the open gate. Since his first duty was the safety of his passengers, he remained with the coach.

Behind him, the coach door rattled as Mrs. Wagner looked outside. "This doesn't look like a proper stage station to me, Mr. Cobb. Why are we stopping?"

Cobb kept his voice down as he watched Butch pause outside the open gate. "Just stay in the coach, Mrs. Wagner. This might be nothing. It might be something. It'll be safer if you remain where you are. None of your people happened to be armed, are they?"

Mrs. Wagner was about to admonish him for thinking such a thing until Leon Hunt spoke over her. "I've got my pistol rig up top with my baggage if you think it can be useful."

Cobb did. "I'd be obliged to you if you could climb up and fetch it. It wouldn't hurt to have another gun around right about now."

Hunt pushed past Mrs. Wagner and her vocal objections to firearms, then went on top of the wagon to get his luggage. Cobb saw the look of concern on Miss Jane's face and offered a smile to calm her nerves. He must not have looked convincing as it did not have the desired effect.

Cobb walked to the front of the team of horses and listened for any signs of trouble now that Butch had slipped inside.

He did not have to wait long before Butch called out, "Cobb! Get in here. Gene's been hurt bad."

Cobb set to running and looked back up at Mr. Hunt, who was rummaging through his bag on top of the coach. "Stay here and keep an eye on the wagon. Shoot anyone who ain't us."

Cobb pushed the gate wide open and ran toward the station building. It was a sturdy fieldstone-and-mud structure that had withstood many seasons of harsh Wyoming weather.

He leapt up the steps and into the main body of the building, where he found Gene Bridges on the floor as Ma Bridges cradled her son's head in her lap. Her round face was streaked with tears as she looked up at Cobb. "Look at what they did to my poor Gene."

Cobb set his shotgun aside as he knelt beside the fallen station master. He had a nasty gash on the side of his head, but otherwise seemed unhurt. "What happened here?"

"Bandits," the older woman said. "They rode in here yesterday looking for a meal. They even paid their way.

Said they weren't looking for charity. But then, this afternoon, when it came time for them to leave, Gene caught them out by the corral, fixing to take our fresh horses. He tried to stop them, but they knocked him down and took them, anyway. Twenty horses, every one of them quality. Then, they came in here and took every cent we had, including what they'd just given me for their meals."

She choked back a sob as she stroked her unconscious son's head. "Gene cursed them for cowards as they held him at gunpoint. It wasn't until they cleaned us out that he got sick and fell right here where he is now. They must've hit him harder than we thought to make him like this."

Butch asked, "Where was Del when all of this was going on? Didn't he do anything?" Cobb knew Del Rice was the simpleton Gene paid to help care for the horses and visitors.

"I haven't seen him since this happened," Ma wept. "I fear the worst."

So did Cobb, but he kept his concerns to himself. He ran his fingers over Gene's skull and felt the bones give more than they should have. He had seen men with such injuries before. There was not much to be done for him now except to bandage it and hope he woke up.

He told Butch, "You stay here while I look for Del. Maybe see if you can't get him over to the bed."

"I will if you think it'll help."

Cobb was not sure that it would. "It can't hurt."

Cobb picked up his shotgun and went outside in the direction of the barn. There, both doors were closed when they were normally kept open. He took it as a bad sign but went toward it, anyway. He sensed the men who had descended on the tiny station were the worst sort and were liable to be capable of anything.

When he pulled open the doors, Cobb's worst fears were confirmed.

One glimpse at Del's remains caused his stomach to lurch. He managed to make it back outside before he got sick.

Cobb had just finished retching when he heard a man say, "The evil that men do lives after them."

Cobb raised his shotgun, only to find his passenger, Leon Hunt, standing before him. He was wearing a black leather gun belt with his hand flat against the holster that was slung low on his left leg.

Cobb did not like anyone seeing him get sick like this, much less one of his passengers. "I thought I told you to stay back with the wagon."

"They'll be fine." Hunt continued to look up at Del's remains hanging inside the barn. "No one's around. I checked carefully before I came in here. The men who did this rode off to the south. Almost twenty horses, maybe more, if I judge it right. They left a trail a blind man could follow in the dark. I guess they weren't expecting anyone to be coming after them so soon."

Cobb pulled off his hat and ran his hands through his graying hair. "You know a lot about this sort of thing for a churchman."

"I was many things before I threw my lot in with the Lord." He nodded toward Del's desecrated body. "I've seen this kind of thing a time or two. Men who are capable of something like this don't stop unless you make them stop."

Cobb wiped his mouth on his sleeve. "I care less about stopping them and more about my friends." Cobb could not bring himself to look inside the barn again. "The man who manages this place got his head broken for his trouble. He's inside with Butch now."

Hunt drew a knife from behind him and began to move

into the barn. "Go tend to your passengers and your friend, Mr. Cobb. I'll cut this man down. Doesn't seem right to keep him trussed up there like this. I'll see about having the boy help me dig a grave for him after we get the others settled."

Cobb did not know whether he should admire Leon Hunt for his calm in the face of such butchery or resent him for it, but he was in no position to question it. He went to help Butch and Ma with Gene before he could bring his passengers into the station.

After a quick meal of lukewarm beans and biscuits that he managed to heat up, Cobb took his pipe and sat alone on the steps of the station building. It had been far from the grand meal he and Butch had promised his passengers, but with Ma concerned about her son's condition, it was the best Cobb could manage under the circumstances.

Cobb filled his pipe and did his best to ignore Mrs. Wagner's endless rantings about the uncivilized men in this part of the country and how her ministry was their only hope for salvation.

Butch came outside and had the good sense to close the door behind him as he did. "I don't think that woman has quit talking since she set foot in there."

"She's just trying to cover up for being scared." He packed his pipe, thumbed a match alive, and lit the tobacco in the bowl. "Some people get drunk. Some cry. She talks. It's just her way, I guess."

"Wish her way was quieter is all." Butch placed a plug of tobacco in his mouth and nodded toward Hunt and Yost as they walked back from digging Del's grave beside the barn. "You and me should've been the ones who did that."

Normally, Cobb would have agreed. "Hunt insisted.

Said it was the least him and the boy could do, whatever that means."

"If it means you and me don't have to dig a grave, then I'm all for it." He cut loose with the first stream of his new chaw. "I've dug enough to last me a while."

"Me, too." Cobb drew deep on his pipe and allowed the smoke to drift out through his nose. The sight of Del's remains still haunted him, and he hoped the memory was carried away with the tobacco, but like the smoke from his pipe, it lingered.

"You want to talk about it?" Butch asked. "About finding Del like that, I mean."

He closed his eyes as he puffed on his pipe. "What makes you think I would?"

"On account of there not being anyone else here to listen to you. You're too proud to talk about it with our passengers, and Ma's got a world of concerns of her own with Gene being how he is. Given how quiet you've been since you found him, I imagine it wasn't pretty. I find it's better to give such things some air to forget about them quicker."

Cobb doubted anything would help him forget what he had found in that barn. He was glad Hunt and young Joe had drawn closer so he could put off talking about it a while longer.

"We set aside some beans and biscuits for you boys," Cobb told them. "You're welcome to whatever's left."

"No, thanks." Young Joe cradled his stomach. "I don't even want to think about food right now."

Leon Hunt patted the boy on the back. "Go inside and dunk your head in a bucket. It'll make you feel better."

"But that's the remedy for drinking sickness," Joe protested. "I ain't never touched a drop."

"Dunking your head in a bucket of cold water cures a

lot of ills," Hunt said. "Go do like I told you. You'll thank me later."

In the short amount of time that Joe had the door opened to step inside, Cobb heard Mrs. Wagner switch from blaming drink for Del's death to the influence of the "red heathens" in the area.

All three men looked relieved when Joe closed the door behind him.

"She's still going, isn't she?" Hunt noted as he sat beside Cobb.

"Hasn't stopped since before you boys started that grave," Cobb said. "Made me think about coming to see if you needed a hand."

Hunt patted some of the dirt from his black pants. "You were needed in there with the sick man and his wife. The dead don't need much from the living."

"Ma's his mother," Butch let loose with a stream of tobacco juice. "Gene's a bachelor, just like old Cobb here. He never took a wife. Now I don't think he'll ever have the chance, assuming he wakes up."

Cobb did not want to entertain such thoughts. "Butch and I are grateful to you and Joe for digging the grave. You didn't have to do that."

"No one should've had to do it except the men who did that to him," Hunt said. "The only question is, what do you two plan on doing about what they did to your friends?"

Cobb had hoped to be able to enjoy more of his pipe before he got around to considering such things. "I'll admit I haven't thought that far ahead. A little pipe smoke usually does wonders for limbering up my brain. It's not an easy undertaking no matter how you look at it. If it were just Butch and me, I'd be inclined to go after the men who did this, but we've got passengers to haul and a schedule to keep."

Hunt added, "And a team of half-dead nags who'll probably drop dead in a day or so. It's hard to pull a coach anywhere without good horses."

Cobb did not need one of his passengers to remind him of their circumstances. "There's that to mull over, too."

Butch hooked his thumbs in the gun belt he wore. "Sounds to me like you're looking for a fight, Mr. Hunt. Never knew a churchman such as yourself to be so . . . feisty."

"Mine is a masculine Christianity, Mr. Keeling," Hunt said, "and my path to salvation was a long and winding one." To Cobb, he said, "We've got to do something about these bandits. If we let them go, they'll only grow bolder. Next time, they're liable to do even worse than what they did to your friend here today. Men like this are like wolves. As I said, once they get the taste for it, they never lose it. Something tells me you both know I'm right."

"I don't hear anyone arguing with you." Cobb tucked the pipe into the corner of his mouth. He did not like anyone trying to buffalo his thinking. He liked to arrive at his own conclusions in his own way when time allowed, which it surely did now. "You act like you've got to talk me into something, Hunt. It's like you think I don't care about Del or Gene or those horses those murderers stole. I care deeply and more than you could know. The notion of letting these fellas get away with this never crossed my mind. In fact, Butch and me will be heading out after them at first light. The 'how' and 'who' of it is another matter entirely."

"Meaning?" Hunt asked.

The man's pushiness was beginning to gall him, so Cobb glanced at Butch to speak for him. Cobb often did this when he felt he was about to lose his temper.

Butch said, "The first question is about how we go after

them. We should've gone after them as soon as we got here but couldn't on account of our horses being the only horses in this station and they were already at their limit. They won't be much better come morning, but they should be rested enough by then for us to ride them. Seeing as how they're team horses, not saddle horses anymore, riding them will be an adventure unto itself."

Hunt slapped away some dirt from his boots. He had clearly not considered that.

Butch continued. "The 'who' of the matter is another problem. Ma told us there were five of them who did this. Me and Cobb have tangled with horse thieves before. I have a notion that you might've done so, as well."

"You'd be right," Hunt said.

"That's good because we'll need you," Butch went on, "but we're still outgunned by two. If we bring young Joe along, he's apt to be more trouble than the horses, so that idea is no good. The reverend is useless, and Mr. Koppe can barely stand up to Mrs. Wagner. I'd hate to think how he'd fare against a murderous horde."

Cobb removed the pipe from his mouth. "And there's Mr. Pearson and Mr. Thomas to consider."

Hunt stopped slapping the dirt from his boots. "Who are they?"

"The two men we were *supposed* to pick up here at the station," Cobb explained. "They're not here, which leads me to believe that they were two of the men who killed Del, busted Gene's head, and stole the horses. Their absence practically condemns them as such."

Hunt's eyebrows rose. "I didn't know about them."

Butch said, "There's lots of things you don't know, mister, but Cobb does, hence him coming out here to ponder matters over his pipe. Picking up Pearson and

Thomas was why we came to Delaware Station instead of pushing on a bit farther to Ennisville. It stands to reason Pearson and Thomas wanted us to come here, maybe to rob us or kill us, which means we might be a target at this very moment. That means we should leave you behind to fend off this bunch if they double back. That leaves us all outgunned no matter how you try to look at it."

All of this talk was beginning to give Cobb a headache and only increased the turmoil in his mind. He had always hated indecision in other men. Indecision often got people killed. It was time to make up his mind so at least they would have some kind of plan come the morning.

"How good are you on a horse, Hunt?"

"I would give a kingdom for a good one and, alas, some might say I have."

Cobb squinted at him through the pipe smoke. "What?"

Hunt waved away his confusion. "Don't mind me. Yes, I can ride and ride well."

"Good, because I've decided to leave Butch here to watch the station. He's been in scrapes like this before, haven't you, Butch?"

Butch spat a stream of tobacco juice. "I've seen my share."

"Then it's settled," Cobb declared. "Hunt, I'll need you ready to ride at first light. We're going to track the men and the horses and, with any luck, bring the stock back here so we can be on our way. I hope you've got plenty of bullets for that pistol you tote because Butch will need all he can spare right here."

"I usually make my shots count, Mr. Cobb. You need not give me a second thought."

The door to the station building opened, and Cobb did not have to turn around to know Mrs. Wagner was there.

The force of her personality filled the air like boiled cabbage.

She placed her fists on her wide hips. "I thought I smelled the stench of pipe smoke out here."

Cobb put the pipe back in his mouth. "You did, indeed."

"Need I remind you, Mr. Cobb, that we agreed there would be no consumption of tobacco or spirits of any kind for the duration of my charter?"

"You spoke out against it," Cobb said. "I don't recall any agreement on the subject. We're discussing matters of great importance out here, so I'd appreciate it if you'd let us get back to it."

Hunt stood and wiped his hands on his trousers. "I think I'll head inside and try some of those biscuits you were talking about."

Cobb would not look at him as he passed. He hoped the man showed more sand when he was faced with killers the next day.

Mrs. Wagner remained where she had planted herself. "There's also another matter I wish to discuss with you."

Cobb puffed on his pipe. "I'm sure there is."

She pulled the door closer, but not all the way shut, as she lowered her voice. "It concerns Miss Jane Duprey. Are you aware of her circumstances?"

Cobb closed his eyes. His pipe smoke, often his only refuge after a long day on the trail, began to taste sour to him. He imagined Mrs. Wagner could manage to spoil a sunrise. "I'm aware she paid her way in full, which are the only circumstances that concern me."

"She's a woman of ill repute." Mrs. Wagner's chins waggled in great indignance. "And since you've forced the issue, allow me to put a finer point on the matter. She's a harlot, sir. I didn't know such a woman would be on this trip, and I object to her presence here."

As was his custom, Butch Keeling could tell when his partner was about to reach his limit with someone, which was why he spoke up now. "You're out here on missionary work, aren't you, Mrs. Wagner?"

"I am, indeed."

"That's good to hear, because every missionary I've come across, and I've come across quite a few, are one of two types. They're either preachers or shepherds. If you're the latter, then it seems to me that Miss Jane ought to be someone you try to save. If you're the former, it'd be best if you saved all your hot air until we get to Laramie."

Mrs. Wagner gasped.

Cobb added, "If you don't like Miss Jane's company, I'll be happy to refund your money and leave you here until another stage arrives to bring you on to Laramie. Can't say as to when that'll be, but it's your decision. Now, leave me and Mr. Keeling here in peace. We'd like to finish our conversation."

Mrs. Wagner wheeled back inside and slammed the door behind her.

Butch laughed. "Good old Cobb. You always have a gentle touch with the ladies."

Cobb tapped his teeth with the stem of his pipe. "And you were wondering why I'm still a bachelor."

CHAPTER 4

Well before the first rays of the sun spread across the sky the next morning, Cobb stepped outside the station building with a mug of coffee. He found Hunt had already saddled two of the horses in the corral. He took it as a good start for the day ahead.

"You're up early," Cobb remarked as he slid through the corral's railings. "I was half-expecting to have to wake you."

"No need to wake me because I never went to sleep." Hunt finished tightening the cinch beneath the barrel of the second horse. "I saw these saddles in the barn yesterday and figured I might as well do something useful with my time."

"Anxious with anticipation, I see."

Hunt shook his head. "I had my coffee a bit later than usual and couldn't drop off. Guess it's a sign I'm getting old."

The thought of not drinking coffee was enough to send a shiver up Cobb's spine. He hoped he never got too old to enjoy his coffee at any time he saw fit.

He approached the horse and checked the saddle. He found it to his liking. "You weren't lying about knowing how to set a horse for the trail."

"I make it a practice to not lie," Hunt said. "At least, not anymore."

Cobb sensed there was quite a story behind Hunt's words, but it was none of his concern for the moment. "Let's just hope these old animals still have a few good miles left in them."

Hunt moved away from the horse and took down his coat from the top railing of the corral. "I had you pegged for a man who knew everything he could about his animals."

"I know as much as I can," Cobb said, "but we've switched teams so many times since working for the stage line that I can't keep track of them. It's not always easy to know how one will accept the bridle."

Cobb looked across the yard to his coach beside the barn. She was quite a sight. It was tough to see where the dark red and the black trim at the bottom met. It saddened him a bit to see it sitting there like that. Alone and out of use. Much had saddened him since coming to Delaware Station.

"You're a killer, aren't you, Hunt?"

The man stopped checking the saddle of the other horse for a moment before resuming his work. "What makes you say that?"

"The way you wear your gun," Cobb said. "The kind of rig you're sporting. I'm not accusing you of anything. I just like to know the sort I'm riding with is all."

Hunt reached beneath the barrel of his horse and pulled the cinch tighter. "I know how to ride and I know how to shoot. I'll be happy to give you a full list of my various careers as soon as we're underway if you think it'll make you feel any better about things."

"No need for that." Cobb finished his coffee. "Just making sure you'll stick if it comes down to a fight, which I believe it will."

"I'll stick long after you run off." Hunt stood up and flattened down the collar of his coat. "Never forget that 'Cowards die many times before their deaths; the valiant never taste of death but once.' "

That was the second time in as many days that Cobb had heard Hunt talk like that. "There you go quoting scripture again."

Hunt smiled. "Scripture of a kind, though not from the pen of a prophet but from the quill of the Bard himself."

"Bard?" The term meant nothing to Cobb. "That Old Testament or New?"

"It's literature," Hunt said. "The Bard is William Shakespeare. Once upon a time, I used to be an actor."

Cobb had never been one for plays and other such frivolities, though he often enjoyed a good piano player when a sour mood threatened to overtake him. "I just hope you're ready to sling more than words at those fellas if we find them. You'll need more than some fancy phrases to end this bunch."

Hunt opened the corral gate and led his horse out, then stepped back while Cobb led his through the opening.

Butch came outside, stifling a yawn. His gun belt was buckled and his Henry repeater was in one hand as he drank from a tin cup with the other.

"A man can't hardly expect to get any sleep around here with you two cackling around the yard like a couple of old hens."

Cobb knew his friend had been awake before him but enjoyed making people think he was lazy. It led some to underestimate him, which many had done at their own peril. "Have some respect, Butch. We're in refined company. It seems our Mr. Hunt here used to be an actor."

"That so?" Not much impressed Butch and he was not impressed now. "Maybe he could put on a mask and scare those boys into giving back our horses so we can get out of here."

Hunt climbed into the saddle. "Fear not, my frontier Falstaff. We'll be enough to do our country loss."

Butch yawned before taking another sip of coffee. "I'd better go back in and get some more. I wasn't counting on this fella putting me to sleep."

Cobb hauled himself up into the saddle. He was glad the horse accepted his weight. It must have been saddle broken before it had pulled a coach. "Where are you off to?"

Butch nodded toward the gate. "Figured I'd find myself a spot away from here where I could keep an eye out for trouble. You boys are apt to make those thieves scatter, and they might come back here looking for a place to hole up. I aim to be waiting for them if they do."

As was often the case, Cobb saw his partner was right. Butch could defend the station better outside the walls than within them.

Cobb said, "I figure they're bound to be less than a day's ride from here. Hunt and me will follow their tracks as long as we can and try to be back here by dark. If we're not, you'd best lock that gate and give young Joe your rifle. It promises to be a long evening for all concerned."

"You'll be back," Butch said as he walked back into the building for more coffee, "and we'll be expecting Mr. Hunt to entertain us when you do. Dance or sing or something to brighten everyone's mood."

Cobb looked back at Hunt as he dug his heels into the sides of his horse. "Mister, I sure hope you can ride and shoot as fancy as you talk."

Hunt followed close behind and had no trouble keeping up with him.

* * *

Butch Keeling may have been better with a gun than Tucker Cobb, but few had matched Cobb when it came to tracking. He imagined that being an orphan raised by a tribe of Omaha Indians had helped him understand the land. He had spent a fair part of his life running down what other people paid him to find. Renegade Indians. Cattle rustlers. Outlaws and lost army patrols. Even meat for men who were half-starved and desperate. He had learned how to listen to whatever the land told him instead of what he wanted to see and hear. It had saved his life many times.

He used that gift now to track the murderous men and stolen horses from Delaware Station. The land told him a great deal. The jumble of shod hooves in the dirt told him the five marauders had kept the horses herded close together as they brought them south, away from the wagon road. A man in front, two at the back, and a man serving as an outrider on each side. The animals had been used to living in corrals when they weren't pulling the burden of a heavy coach behind them. They had not been accustomed to running freely. Their pace was guarded at first, but as the miles stretched farther away from the scent of the station, they enjoyed their newfound freedom and ran flat out. He could tell by the tracks of the thieves that they had been forced to keep several of them from scattering.

Cobb took that as a good sign. After a day or so, the men and their own horses would be tired from the effort, making them easier to catch sooner rather than later.

Cobb was glad Hunt had not asked to stop to rest as they followed the trail south. His time with the talkative Butch had made him appreciate silence on those rare occasions when he found it, and Hunt was not much of a talker. He was content to follow as Cobb worked from the lead.

Cobb brought them to a stop when they reached a rocky cliff that afforded them a view of the valley below them. His eyesight had only just begun to trouble him when reading, but his vision at a distance was still as good as it had ever been.

He asked Hunt, "How far can you see?"

"As far as I need to," the former actor said, "but probably not as far as you. I noticed the tracks you've been following turned to the right back there."

Cobb pointed down at an expanse between two clumps of trees. "See that dark spot in the middle of the greenery? That's where they are. I can see smoke rising up from the cookfire they've built for themselves." He squinted into the distance to improve his range of vision. "That means they're relaxed, which is a good sign for us."

"But they'll see us coming if we approach across such open land, won't they?"

"Won't have any luck sneaking up on them, that much is for certain." Cobb began to doubt himself for bringing Hunt along. Butch would have been able to cut down at least two of them before the men could reach their horses.

Hunt was not wrong about being concerned about the open distance, but Cobb had an idea. "I say we stay here and wait for them to get underway again. If I read their trail sign right, and I think I have, then those boys have had a devil of a time keeping Gene's horses from scattering. Once they get moving again, we can ride up behind them and take them down one by one. We'll cut them down to size before the ones up front realize what's happening. They might even keep on running and let us take the horses." Now that he had said it, it made sense. It might work.

Hunt looked down at the herd he could not see. "You're

forgetting these horses of ours aren't up for that kind of pace. This one's got a knock in her lungs when she breathes, and yours seems to be favoring her hind left leg."

Cobb closed his eyes as his bright idea withered and died in front of him.

Hunt continued. "You ever get thrown from a tired horse? It's not a good feeling. It's even worse when men are shooting at you while it happens."

Hunt's fancy talk back at the station was mildly entertaining. His criticism out here flat out annoyed Cobb. "If you've got a better plan, now's the time to say it."

Hunt said, "There are five of them, right?"

Cobb did not have to think. He knew. "Yes."

"Good," Hunt said cheerfully, "because my pistol has six bullets. That makes it simple. I'm going to ride down there alone and kill them."

"Just like that? You think they're just gonna sit there and let you shoot them."

Hunt nodded. "They won't take an old man alone as much of a threat, but you won't get off that easy. Stay here until I get close to their camp. After I stop, you set to yelling and firing that shotgun in the air. Come toward their camp at a dead run after you reload. That ought to spook them, or at least give them something else to worry about. I'll even give you the same advice you gave me last night back at the station. Shoot everyone who's not me. It was good advice then and it's good advice now."

Hunt backed his horse away from the cliff. "Just make sure you don't get stage fright and run out there before I'm set. They're liable to scatter if you start your charge too early."

Cobb brought his horse around and watched Hunt ride off. "I don't like this idea of yours."

"It'll be fine," Hunt said over his shoulder as he continued down the incline to the valley. "Cry havoc, gentle Caesar, and let slip the dogs of war."

Cobb let his limping horse amble slowly behind Hunt. He hoped Hunt shot as fancy as he spoke.

CHAPTER 5

Leon Hunt kept his horse steady and his eyes on the disturbed ground as he slowly rode toward the camp of the murderers. He wanted them to see him first to avoid them going for their rifles. Distance was not his friend, but it might prove to be an ally if he played this right.

He had always been a left-handed shot, which often confused his opponents enough to give him the edge to be quicker on the draw. He could see he would need every advantage he could get. Each of the five men now around the campfire was probably young enough to have been his son. Horse stealing was not an old man's game.

He saw they had been looking at him for a while as he approached, but none went for their weapons. He hooked the reins on his right thumb and held up his empty hands as he used his stage voice to greet them. "Hail, fellows well met. What a beautiful start to the day we have. God be praised."

The man with the broadest shoulders among them spoke first. "Hail yourself. We ain't running a charity around here, old man. If you've come here for some grub, you're out of luck. You'd do well to just keep on riding."

Hunt heard the others with him laugh. Four others. Five

in total. Cobb had been right. He would be pleased about that. They did not see him as a threat. That was good.

Hunt decided to give Cobb a few more minutes to get into position. "I'm prepared to sing for my supper, or in this case, my breakfast, if you wish. I was, until quite recently, an actor."

The broad man set his tin plate on the ground in front of him. "I already told you to get."

But the killer to his right tried to settle down the burly man. "Hold off, Joe. I kinda want to see this. What'd you have in mind, mister? A song or a dance?"

"A recital," Hunt said as he held his right hand aloft. "One that I'm sure you'll find to be apt for this particular moment." He cleared his throat as he rested his right hand on his chest, while his left inched slowly down toward his pistol. "'When I do count the clock that tells the time, and see the brave day sunk in hideous night. When I behold the violet past prime, and sable curls all silvered over with white. When lofty trees I see barren of leaves which erst from heat did canopy the herd, and summer's green all girded up in sheaves, borne on the bier with white and bristly beard. Then of thy beauty do I question make, that thou among the wastes of time must go, since sweets and beauties do themselves forsake and die as fast as they see others grow. And nothing against Time's scythe can make defense, save breed, to brave him when he takes thee hence.'"

The five men traded glances when Hunt had finished,. and, as men often did when confronting something they did not understand, they laughed.

Hunt smiled down at them.

The man who had spoken up for Hunt said, "That was some speech, old-timer. You really are an actor, ain't you?"

"Alas, I'm the scythe."

Hunt drew and shot the broad man through the head. Hunt's defender dropped his tin plate and began to crawl away as Hunt shot a man to his left before he could draw his gun, then cut down a third who'd managed to pull his pistol clean. A fourth man hit the ground flat on his back as he rushed his pistol shot, but Hunt drilled him through the middle of the chest.

The man who'd defended Hunt got his feet under him and began to run away. Hunt had no trouble bringing the horse into a trot and easily ran the man down under hoof.

Hunt kept his gun trained down on the last killer as he asked, "You boys took these horses from Delaware Station, didn't you?"

The man stood. "Prove it."

Hunt shot him in the left thigh, causing him to cry out as he gripped his leg in pain.

"Proof is for a court of law," Hunt said over the sounds of the man's agony, "and I'm not that kind of judge." He heard a horse approaching at a hard gallop and knew it was Cobb racing toward him. "Answer my question before my friend gets here. He's in a mighty unforgiving mood."

"Yeah," the man said through gritted teeth. "We stole them horses. Already got a good buyer on his way here to take them. What's it to you?"

Hunt kept his horse steady. "That stable hand you left swinging in the barn. He was alive when you laid into him, wasn't he?"

"He was alive when the rest of us left with the horses," the wounded man said. "I can't speak to what Joe did after that."

Joe was what this man had called the first man Hunt had killed.

"You might not be able to speak for it, but you'll answer for it just the same."

"Wait!" The man threw up his left hand as if it would be enough to stop the bullet. "We ain't alone. We've got others coming. Men who are planning on buying those horses. They'll be here real soon, and they won't like seeing what happened to us."

Hunt enjoyed watching the man flinch as he thumbed back the hammer. "It's not your concern anymore."

Hunt shot the man between the eyes just as Cobb pulled his horse to a stop beside him. "What did he say?"

"Nothing important." Hunt holstered his almost empty pistol. "He said some men are on their way to buy these horses, but we'll be gone long before they get here." He gestured over to where the horses were gathered. They were too busy munching on the tall grass of the flat land to concern themselves with the affairs of men. He was glad his shots had not disturbed them. They would be easier to move in a bunch.

Cobb said, "Let's pull out two from the stock and put our saddles on them. The two we've got are about played out."

"You read my mind, Mr. Cobb." Hunt joined him in climbing down, then began to unbuckle his saddle from the horse. "But let's be quick about it in case our dead friend here was telling the truth about his visitors."

Cobb undid his saddle first and placed it on the ground. "I saw you kill those men like they were nothing to you, and you made it out without so much as a scratch."

Hunt wished it were only that simple. Not every wound a man bore was visible. "You saw much, Mr. Cobb, but not everything." He set his saddle aside and began to remove the bridle from his horse. "I'll feel better once we get this bunch back to the station. The sooner we're on our way, the better for all involved."

Butch Keeling had never been one to allow a good rest to go to waste. He had taught himself how to make the best of any given situation, even when nothing seemed to be happening around him.

He sat with his back against an old stone wall, surrounded by lush overgrowth, while he considered their current predicament. He was not concerned about what Cobb and Hunt were up to. Cobb was a lot tougher than he looked, and he looked plenty tough. He was one of the strongest men Butch had ever met—both in strength and in spirit—and he could lift more luggage and freight than ten men without getting tired. He was not one to allow being outnumbered to discourage him.

Tucker Cobb was even tougher in other ways. Butch had seen barroom chairs splinter across his back without so much as staggering him. He could knock a man out simply by backhanding him when his temper was up, which Butch was grateful was not often.

Butch had heard the stories of how he had killed two men in a bar fight in Abilene with only one punch apiece and how he had choked the life out of another in Amarillo with only one hand.

But it was his partner's toughness of spirit that Butch had been impressed with most. It took a while for Cobb to make up his mind, but once he got an idea in his head, it quickly took deep root, and it was nearly impossible to change it once it did. Butch had done well by following Cobb's instincts. His name would not be on a stagecoach now if it had not been for Cobb's stubbornness and clarity of purpose.

Butch wondered what his partner would do once he and Hunt returned with the horses. The notion of Cobb failing had never entered his mind. Butch knew Cobb would want to hitch up a team and continue on for Ennisville as soon as he could. They had a schedule to keep and were already well behind it. If the horses were strong enough, he might want to push past Ennisville all together and head straight for Laramie.

Butch knew how important being punctual was to his friend and their new stagecoach line, but doing right did not always follow a schedule. Gene Bridges had not woken up from his attack yet, and his mother was in a terrible state. With Del's body still warm in the ground, Butch hated the notion of leaving the old woman with a sick son and a station to run all by herself. The territory was full of vultures, and not all of them flew. She would be easy pickings for someone with dark intentions.

He had decided to tell Cobb he would be staying back to help her, at least until another stagecoach came along. New stage lines were springing up every day, and it would not be long before someone arrived to take over the duties. He hoped Cobb would not give him much of an argument on the subject but imagined he would. Butch would just have to deal with that when it happened.

He brought up his Henry repeater when he saw something moving past the station gate but lowered it when he saw it was just Jane. She had decided to take a stroll away from the others. She was wearing a pale blue dress today and had not put on her hat and veil. Her long golden hair hung straight behind her back and looked lovely in the new light of the morning.

She was not as young as she had first appeared back in North Branch, and he could see an ugly bruise marring her face. He wondered if that had been Bart Hagen's doing or one of her other admirers. He tried not to think about it, as it would only make him hate Hagen more than he already did.

Butch stood up and offered a wave. "Morning, Miss Jane."

She was not startled and, instead, offered a warm smile. "There you are, Mr. Keeling. We were wondering where you'd gone off to. Joe said you were out here somewhere protecting the station. I'd expected to find you in the courtyard, not all the way out here."

"I figured I could do that better if I was away from the place," Butch said. "Looks like you needed a walk. Mrs. Wagner can be a grind, can't she?"

Miss Jane glanced back at the gate before walking toward Butch. He found she had an elegant grace about her that most saloon girls he had known did not. "She's a woman of many fierce convictions, which can prove unpleasant at times. I've become her favorite target. She seems to think I'm in dire need of saving."

"If you are, then you've got plenty of company." He took his rifle with him as he stepped out from the overgrowth. "Looks like you're nursing quite a shiner there. Hagen give that to you?"

She brought her hand up to her wounded cheek. "You get right to the point, don't you?"

"Nothing delicate about a black eye," Butch said. "No shame in it, either. I've had a few dozen myself."

"Bart was begging me not to leave and lost his temper," Jane said. "He was sorry as soon as he did it. A man like him isn't used to being refused by a woman."

"A man who'd hit a woman isn't any kind of man at all," Butch said. "If I'd known what he'd done to you, I would've shot him when I had the chance."

That smile again. "Yes, I believe you would, Mr. Keeling."

"My friends call me Butch, ma'am. I'd appreciate it if you did, too."

"I think I'll stick with Mr. Keeling if it's all the same to you," she said. "I like a certain formality with people. I guess you think that makes me something of a hypocrite in my line of work."

Butch was not sure what a hypocrite was, but it did not sound flattering. "A body can't always help what they do in this world. Life has a way of making us do all sorts of things we didn't plan on. Me? I thought I'd be a lawman for the rest of my life. Now, here I am in Wyoming with fifty percent of a stagecoach line hauling old men and Bible-thumpers through the wilderness." He touched the brim of his hat. "Present company excluded, of course."

She offered a slight curtsy as she laughed. "Of course."

Butch liked her laugh. He had a feeling that she did not laugh often and that he had witnessed something both rare and genuine. "Sorry you have to be here for all this ugliness. When we were working the cattle drives, Cobb and me would go whole years without anyone getting a scratch. After this run, I'm beginning to wonder if that coach we spent all that money fixing up isn't cursed."

"Maybe you should have Reverend Averill say a prayer over it."

"I might if I could get him to look up from his prayer books long enough," Butch said. "He's a strange one for a preacher, ain't he?"

"I think Mrs. Wagner has him cowed." Jane took her time looking him over. "But she doesn't have you cowed, does she, Mr. Keeling? I have a feeling you were very brave during the war."

Butch shrugged. "I don't know. I wasn't in it. Neither was Cobb. We weren't Union men, but we weren't Confederates, either. We didn't see any point serving the South just because we happened to find ourselves there when the ball went up, and the North seemed to have more than its share of fighting men. We kept ourselves busy, though. There were always plenty of hungry people who needed beef."

"You were lucky," she said. "That war ruined a lot of good men."

"And made a lot of bad men worse."

She hugged herself as if a chill had gone through her, and Butch hated himself for not having a coat to offer her. "Have you known Tucker long?"

There was a way in which she had asked the question that made Butch think there was something more to it. That, and the fact that she had used his given name. "A few years now. We met on a cattle drive down in Texas. He ran the chuckwagon and I ran with the cattle. He's as steady a man as I've ever known. Rain or shine, tall grass or tumbleweeds, he always kept his head. He can cook, too. Yes, ma'am, he's gonna make a lucky woman a fine wife one day. Too bad he's so ugly."

She laughed again and Butch found himself laughing, too.

"I'm not so sure about that," she said. "About the ugly part, I mean. He certainly has his own charms, though I doubt he realizes it. He's not like some other men I've known. Bart always thought he was more than he was and got angry when he realized he was lying to himself. Tucker is different. Grounded in a way most men aren't. That's strange, seeing as how he seems to be moving around all the time."

"I've always said Tucker Cobb would be the same if

you plunked him down in a jungle, in New Orleans, or smack dab in the middle of Manhattan Island. He's a constant, like the rising of the sun or the changing of the seasons."

Butch watched her blush. He was sorry it was not on his account, but rather over what he had said about Cobb. "You're something of a poet, Mr. Keeling. You should write some of that down. Maybe have Mr. Hunt perform it for us tonight after supper when he returns."

Butch had been enjoying their conversation so much that he had almost forgotten about Cobb and Hunt. "I imagine there won't be any time for supper recitals tonight. Cobb will be anxious to get moving again once he gets back."

"He's a determined man, isn't he, Mr. Keeling."

"That's one way to put it," Butch said, "and he's not one to allow something as annoying as common sense get in his way."

She perked up and looked to the south, then brought her hands up to shield her eyes from the sun. "I see something, Mr. Keeling. I think they're back."

Butch joined her in looking and saw Cobb and Hunt bookending a herd of more than twenty horses toward the station.

Butch moved quickly to open the gate wide. "You'd better step aside, Miss Jane. Those horses are moving too fast to be too particular about where they step."

Butch ran into the courtyard and found young Joe milling around the corral. "Come help me get this gate open. Cobb's back with the horses."

Joe helped him get the corral's gate open, then Cobb moved the horses into the corral. Butch counted twenty-five head, which was more than Ma said the bandits had taken, before he and Joe closed the corral's gate behind them. He watched Miss Jane walking beside Cobb's horse as Hunt rode in front of them. Then both riders climbed down from their saddles.

Butch greeted Cobb with a handshake. "Looks like you brought back more than they took."

Hunt shook hands with Joe, too. "We didn't see any reason why we should've left them behind. Their previous owners have no further use for them, and Cobb thought they would fetch a handsome price in Ennisville or Laramie."

Hunt handed his horse's reins to Joe. "Bring this one and Cobb's horse back to the barn, take off their tack, then let them in with the others. He'll be looking to pick out the strongest for his team, so be ready when he does."

Joe led the horses to the barn while Butch counted five saddled horses in the corral. "Looks like you boys saw some action."

"Nothing to speak of," Hunt said. "Now, I'd like to avail myself of some eats if there's any left from breakfast."

"There's plenty," Butch said. "Ma was feeling better about Gene's condition since this morning, and she's been cooking up a storm."

Hunt moved inside the station building as Joe led both horses back to the barn. Cobb and Miss Jane walked together toward the corral, with Butch following close behind them.

Butch said, "I see you two have been busy. You and Hunt, I mean."

"Hunt did all the work," Cobb said. "Took each of them down like he was reading a newspaper. One of the damnedest things I ever saw." He remembered himself and touched the brim of his hat, nodding toward Miss Jane. "Apologies for the foul language."

She laughed. "I've heard worse, Tucker."

Butch noted she had used his given name again. "I had

a quick look at those saddled horses you brought in with you. You're right about them fetching a decent price in town."

Miss Jane was still smiling as she looked up at Cobb. "You're always thinking ahead, aren't you?"

"A man has to be thinking ahead if he hopes to survive out here," Cobb said. "And right now, I'm thinking it might be better for all concerned if you would tell the others to get themselves ready to travel. We've still got plenty of hours of sunlight left, and we can make Ennisville long before dark. Get you people in a proper bed instead of a station house bunk."

She touched his arm and moved inside to spread the word to the others.

Cobb and Butch rested one boot on the lower slat of the corral while they leaned on the rail.

Butch said, "I think that girl's sweet on you."

Cobb looked over at the horses. "You really think so?"

"You don't have to be a learned man to see how she looks at you."

"Don't read anything into that," Cobb said. "I was doing something she thought was dangerous and brave. She'd be looking at you the same way if you'd gone instead of me. You can't put much stock in the affections of a woman like that. If you defend her honor in town, she'll be making eyes at you." He held up a finger. "That's a statement, Butch, not a suggestion. I expect you to tread lightly as long as we've got customers. If you're aiming to impress that woman, you'll have to wait until we reach Laramie."

Butch thought he would keep that in mind but doubted any good would come of it. She would have no shortage of suitors in town, and he'd be just another Texan to her there. "You serious about getting back on the road?"

Cobb nodded. "And something tells me you don't think that's a good idea."

Butch pushed himself away from the corral rail. "How'd you know that?"

His partner grinned. "Your tone. Your voice always changes a little when you ask me a question you won't like the answer to. You think we ought to stay on a while to help Ma with the place."

Now that it was out in the open, Butch saw no reason why he should try to be delicate about making his point. "She couldn't run this station by herself if she were ten years younger, which she ain't. It'd be hard enough for Gene to do it, even if he was in his right mind, which he ain't. He started making some sounds on his own after you left, which we took as a good sign. But even if he woke up this very minute, he wouldn't be in any condition to do much for at least a week or more."

"What if he never wakes up?" Cobb asked. "You plan on staying here until the Rapture?"

"Just until someone comes along who can pitch in," Butch said. "It's the least we can do for folks in trouble. They've been mighty good to us since we came to the territory."

Butch disliked the awkward silence that fell over them. He knew Cobb wasn't angry. He was just thinking things over, as was his way.

Butch was glad to have a distraction in the form of young Joe leading the horses from the barn and moving them into the corral with the others.

"That boy's sure got a nice way with animals, doesn't he?" Butch observed.

"He surely does. Why don't you head in to the station and bring me a pencil and some paper. I think I've got an idea that'll work for all concerned."

Butch went inside, found some paper and a pencil on Gene's desk, and brought them out to Cobb. He ignored the many questions Mrs. Wagner fired off to him about when their journey would resume. Cobb was not one to put words on paper often, so when he did, it deserved all of his attention.

CHAPTER 6

Cobb had expected Mrs. Wagner to take his decision poorly, and she had not let him down.

"This is an outrage!" Her chins waggled with anger. "I simply won't stand for it. Joe is just a boy. He has booked passage on your coach. I need him in Laramie with me and my ministry, not left here alone to be corrupted by whatever rabble happen to pass through this godforsaken place."

Cobb held up the piece of paper he had just finished writing. "His seat will be secured on the next wagon heading to Laramie, Mrs. Wagner. My credit's good with any outfit in the territory, and they'll honor it if they have space, which they will."

"It ain't like it's forever," Butch added. "There's bound to be someone along soon. Besides, the boy's anxious to stay. Just ask him."

Young Joe stepped forward. "I really am, Aunt Kathleen. These people need me here."

"Our ministry needs you more," Mrs. Wagner protested. "What kind of a life could he ever hope to have here, even if it were only for a few days. Catering to the needs of an old woman and her invalid son? Why, seeing to those horses alone is too much for him, and I'll not have his fingers worked to the bone for the benefit of strangers. Not when he has a higher, much more noble calling. Besides, I made a promise to his mother, my dear suffering sister Sarah. She entrusted her eldest boy with me to get him away from the drudgery of farm life."

She clasped her black Bible close to her bosom and shook her head with a cold degree of finality that rivaled a winter storm. "I'm afraid it's out of the question, sir. If you feel compassion for these people, leave that ruffian friend of yours behind. He can chew tobacco and spit its vile juices to his heart's content."

Cobb knew Butch had a pinch of chaw in his mouth and motioned to stop him from sending some of it in her direction. "Joe's sixteen, ma'am. Boys younger than him have gone to war and died. I think he can survive a few days of hard labor here. It'll do him some good, and like I said, he wants to do it."

Behind her on the porch, Leon Hunt leaned against a post. "I'll be glad to stay behind, too, if it'll make you feel any better, Mrs. Wagner."

"You?" The pious woman harrumphed. "A former stage actor and reformed gunman? I'd sooner leave poor Joe in the care of red heathens before I put him in your hands. Perish the thought."

Cobb would have liked nothing better than to pull out right now and leave Mrs. Wagner and her objections behind, but he knew she was a talker and would waste no time running him down at the first town she reached. That would be bad for business, and this business was all he and Butch had going for them.

But he could not afford to stand around and argue with her all day, so he decided to force the issue. Cobb stuffed his note in Joe's shirt pocket and began walking back toward the stagecoach. "We're pulling out of here in five minutes. Anyone who wants to come along is welcome. Anyone who doesn't is welcome to stay here and forfeit their seat. No refunds will be available if you do."

Reverend Averill scuttled out of the station building, clutching his heavy bag, and followed Cobb to the coach. "Wait for me. I'm not giving up my seat."

Cobb figured he would not and was glad when Jane had followed him. "I'm coming, too, Tucker."

Butch climbed up to the top of the coach to where the passenger's luggage was stored. "Mr. Hunt already took his bag with him. Anyone else want to stay behind?"

Edward Koppe, who had been standing to Mrs. Wagner's side, fussed with his hat. "Perhaps Mr. Cobb is right. We should be underway. There's still our ministry to consider. We don't want to keep all of those poor souls in need of salvation waiting in a purgatory like Laramie, now do we?"

Mrs. Wagner shot him a glance. "You're more concerned with saving your own hide than anyone's soul, you frightened rabbit of a man."

Koppe ducked his head and looked longingly at the coach. Cobb could see the man did not want to be left behind, but Mrs. Wagner's hold on him was too strong to break.

By the time Cobb took hold of the reins of his new team of horses, Mrs. Wagner had made up her mind. "Well, if Joe and Mr. Hunt are too obstinate to see the error of their decision, I see no reason why the rest of us should waste our time among them any longer." She looked at Joe. "I suppose I have no choice but to leave you in God's hands now."

The boy cringed under her rebuke and looked like he might be on the verge of crying.

As Mrs. Wagner and Koppe scuttled toward the waiting

stage, Hunt stepped down from the porch and placed his hand on Joe's shoulder. "Cheer up, young Hal. Ignorance is the curse of God, but knowledge is the wing wherewith we fly to heaven."

"Who's Hal? My name's Joe."

"Hal was a boy who grew up to be a king," Hunt said, "as I feel you may as well one day."

Koppe ushered Mrs. Wagner toward the stage as she turned and said, "More lunatic ravings from the likes of you."

Hunt bent dramatically at the waist. "Let she who is without sin cast the first stone."

Koppe did his best to crowd her inside the coach and quickly pulled the door shut behind them before Mrs. Wagner changed her mind.

Butch climbed down to the wagon box as Cobb released the brake and let the team move forward to where Hunt and Joe now stood.

"Keep a close eye on Ma and Gene," Cobb said. "It might be a good idea if one of you keeps watch through the night. If there really are some men looking to take those horses back, they're liable to track them here and will be looking for trouble when they do."

"We'll make them rue the day if they do," Hunt said. "We'll be seeing you in Laramie before long. Good luck to you all." He nodded toward the coach. "I have a feeling you'll need it with her."

Cobb snapped the reins as Butch tossed a box of bullets to Hunt, who caught them with both hands.

Butch leaned out over the side as he said, "Something to remember me by, Hunt. Hope you won't have any need for them."

Cobb expected Hunt to offer a final quote from Shakespeare as they got underway, but all he did was wave as they rode out from the station, trailing the horses and saddles of five dead men behind them as they did.

Butch had to hold on as the coach rumbled over pock-marked dirt. "Earlier, right before you boys went to fetch those horses, Hunt called me a 'fallstaff.' What's a 'fall-staff'?"

Cobb did not have the slightest idea. "You can ask him next time you see him."

Judging by where the sun was set in the sky, Cobb figured they had been on the road to Ennisville for more than two hours before Butch finally broke the silence.

"I don't mind telling you that I was mighty impressed by the way you held off that old girl back there. How'd you know she wouldn't stay behind?"

"Words are cheap," Cobb explained, "but I figured the prospect of losing her money would be too much for her to take. I'm glad she finally agreed to come with us. Poor old Gene needs his rest."

"She might've been able to cure him," Butch said. "The way she talks, she might've brought him around if only for him to tell her to be quiet."

"It's because she talks that I was hoping she'd come with us," Cobb admitted. "She'd wreck our business if we'd left her behind. I imagine she'll complain plenty as soon as she gets to Laramie, but her being there at all will be a testament to our service."

When Butch remained quiet, Cobb knew he was chewing over something. He had a decent idea what it might be. "You're annoyed that I didn't tell you about what those dead rustlers said back there. About someone looking to buy the horses they stole."

Butch looked away. "There you go reading my mind

again. One day, you're gonna have to tell me how you do that."

Cobb smiled. "There isn't much of a trick to it. You're like Mrs. Wagner back there. On the rare occasion you're quiet, it gives me time to think of a reason why. And since you've been quiet all the way from the station, I had time to reason out what it was."

"That's why you and me don't play cards," Butch said, "and let that be the last time you go comparing me to Mrs. Wagner. But now that you mention it, I am a bit cross with you about it. You should've told me earlier."

"Why? To give you a chance to argue with me about staying?" Cobb asked. "It wouldn't have done any good. I'm not even sure there's anyone coming for those horses. Hunt was about to shoot that man when he said it. You know how a man's apt to say just about anything when he's looking down the barrel of a gun. He was probably just stalling for time, hoping for a different outcome."

"And if he wasn't?" Butch asked. "If he was telling the truth, then we've just left Hunt and Joe in a dire situation."

Cobb knew that might be the case, but he could not allow a possibility to dictate an outcome. He did not know Leon Hunt well but liked what little he knew about him. Joe had the makings of being a fine man one day if he lived long enough.

But Cobb knew feelings and possible outcomes had no place in the freighting business. "I think there's a chance they might be in danger, but our whole business is at risk if we don't get these people where they need to go. A man low enough to steal a horse and do what they did to poor Del is liable to lie to say anything he thinks might save him. You were a lawman once. You know that."

"That's the funny thing about being a lawman," Butch said. "Just because you leave your star behind doesn't mean it leaves you. Doesn't mean you leave your sense of what's right and what's wrong behind you, either. And I've got a bad feeling that those people are in for a lot of trouble back there. I know it and so do you, Cobb. You're not nearly as cold of heart as you'd like folks to believe. And all the money in the world won't be enough to ease your conscience if I turn out to be right about this."

Cobb was growing annoyed by Butch's insistence, and their fresh team of horses began to feel it. Horses had a way of picking up on the humans around them, and he felt them slow their pace as they tightened up. He snapped the reins again and kept them on the road as he tried to clear his mind.

But his mind would not clear, no matter how much he willed it so. The thoughts Butch had placed there were the reasons why. The possibility of trouble back at Delaware Station began to grow in his mind as they approached the town of Ennisville. They had made better time than he had expected, and there was still a fair amount of daylight left. Enough that he might have entertained the notion of pressing on straight to Laramie, but not now.

"That gate isn't too solid," Cobb said after a while. "Gene and Del should've fixed it years ago."

"And I doubt Hunt and Joe would even think to try," Butch added. "Given what you said about how he took care of those thieves on his own like he did, he might have a chance if they're attacked, but Ma and Joe wouldn't stand a chance. Gene sure wouldn't."

Cobb felt his growing tension travel down the length of the reins, and the horses began to weave. He snapped them again and brought them back to the center of the road.

"You think these saddle horses we're trailing behind

us will be up for a ride back to the station once we reach Ennisville?"

"They looked fit enough when we left," Butch said, "but if they're not, I bet we could talk the livery into lending us some who are."

The more Cobb thought about it, the more certain he grew about what they needed to do next. "We stripped the rifles and pistols off those dead fellas. Five horses and tack ought to bring enough to get us two of the best mounts they have in Ennisville."

Butch took off his hat and flattened down his hair. "Sounds to me like you've made up your mind again."

Cobb let up on the reins and brought the team into a run. The sooner they reached Ennisville, the sooner they could make the return trip back to the station. "Seems like I have."

CHAPTER 7

Fred Haney looked down from his horse at the bodies strewn about the ground. Four of the men had been killed where they'd sat around the fire. Only one had managed to make a run for it, for all the good that it had done him. He had not gotten far.

Fred's brother, Earl, now knelt beside the fifth corpse. "This one is Joe. I recognize him as the one we were supposed to meet. What's left of him, anyhow."

Fred looked out over the grass and saw the droppings of the herd of horses that had once been grazing there. Not too long ago, either. Maybe only a few hours or so before, from the looks of things.

Bill Rogers, one of the Haney gang, said, "It's a bad sign, Fred. I knew we should've gotten here earlier."

"I can see that," Fred snapped at him. "Regret won't do us much good now. The horses are gone, and all we're left with is a passel of dead men with nothing to show for it. The men who wanted those horses won't accept excuses in their place."

Earl rubbed his hands on his chaps as he stood. "Whoever did this took their time picking the bodies clean. Took their guns and horses, too. Saddles. Everything. They didn't even leave us with anything to sell."

Ken Rice cursed. "Savages, whoever they were. As if killing them wasn't bad enough, they had to pillage their remains, too?"

Fred Haney saw no point in reminding his men that the dead were horse thieves and that the Haney boys had planned to buy the stolen horses from them. He decided to speak to his brother instead.

"What do you make of it, Earl? I don't think Gene Bridges could've done this. Not on his own. I've never known him to be a violent man, and Del couldn't have helped him. That doddering idiot can barely hold himself upright. He'd be no match for the likes of Joe and the others. Least not what I've heard of them."

Earl went back to his horse and climbed into the saddle. "Can't tell what a man might do when his livestock's been taken from him, but I agree with you. Whoever did this knew what they were doing." He pointed down at the hoofprints that dotted the ground. "Killing a man is one thing, but keeping a herd of horses together is another. Judging by those prints, I'd say they didn't lose nary a one. No, this wasn't Gene or Del. This was someone else."

Fred usually liked to keep his men well south of this part of the territory, so he was unfamiliar with the land. He asked those with him, "Anyone know if the law hereabouts might've done this? A sheriff with a posse, maybe?"

Buck Hamlin spoke up. "The station is in between towns, Boss. North Branch has a constable, but he'd never ride this far out, even if he knew horses had been stolen. Ennisville is the next closest, but that's Fritz Brickell's patch. He'd be more inclined to take a piece of whatever these boys got for the horses than gunning them down like this. He's never been one for gunplay."

Earl moved his horse next to his brother's. "I care a sight more about where those horses are than I do about who did this."

Fred did his best to remain steady in front of the others. He could not allow them to sense the fear that was spreading in his gut. He knew working for a man like King Charles Hagen would not be easy, but the money had been too good to resist. All he had to do was help bring a few of the last independent stations under Hagen control and he would be a rich man.

But if those horses were back at Delaware Station, Hagen would not care about the cost in human lives. He only cared about getting what he wanted and making an example of those who disappointed him.

Faced with such uncertainty, Fred looked to his brother. "What does the ground tell you?"

Earl looked over the tracks. "I can't read much from this, but it doesn't look like they had a posse with them when they took the horses. There'd be more holes in these boys if there had been more guns around. I'd say this is the work of just two men, maybe three. There's more than a dozen of us, which I wager ought to be more than enough to take on whoever's out there."

Before he died, Fred's father had made him promise to look after Earl. He might be older than Fred by a few years, but whatever Earl had in meanness he lacked in brains. There was a time for fighting and a time for thinking. This seemed to be a fine time for thought.

"I want you to ride on ahead of the rest of us," Fred told his brother. "Head to that station and take a look around. See what you can see from a distance. See if you can't figure out where those horses are. We'll be on the trail behind you. Be sure to take your time about it. There's no use in rushing. Then come back to us and we'll figure out what to do next."

Earl put the spurs to his horse and rode away in the direction the pack of horses had headed. Something told Fred they would find the horses back at the station. Then he would have to figure out a way to get them back. At least he would not have to pay the men who had stolen them. That, he decided, was a good thing.

From his perch atop the station building, Leon Hunt watched young Joe wander outside. He saw the boy looking all over for him and decided to remove the mystery of it. "Look up, Joe. When all else fails, never forget to look up."

Joe shielded his eyes from the setting sun and found Hunt sitting with his legs dangling over the roof. "What're you doing all the way up there, Mr. Hunt?"

"Enjoying the bounty of creation," Hunt said. "You're welcome to join me if you'd like. There's a ladder in the back that leads up here."

The boy ran inside as if he might be rewarded for his efforts with a gold nugget.

Oh, how Hunt envied the boy his youth. He remembered a time when the notion of something new held great promise for him. How he could not wait to escape the doldrums of the Chicago stockyards where he had been raised for the sweeping possibilities of the frontier. He liked to think he had shaken the stench of blood and death from him in all the many years since, but blood and death had found a way to cling to him, anyway. His life may not have been as peaceful as he had once hoped, but it had certainly been an interesting one.

Joe clamored up the ladder and walked across the crooked roof to where Hunt was sitting. "Mind your step,"

Hunt warned him. "Your aunt will kill me if you bust a leg up here."

Joe dropped to his backside and slid to join Hunt on the edge. "What're you doing up here, Mr. Hunt?"

"Your aunt's not around to rap your knuckles over your manners," Hunt said. "When it's just us, you can call me Leon or just Hunt. Most people do."

"How come you're not down there, Hunt?" The boy grimaced at his first attempt at familiarity. "I thought you'd be down there in the overgrowth where Butch was earlier."

Hunt was glad to have the opportunity to impart some of his hard-earned wisdom on the lad. "You know why birds fly, Joe?" He did not bother to wait for an answer. "Not just because they can, but because they don't have a choice. They're not big enough to survive on the ground with the mountain lion or the wolf, so they have to soar above it, all while looking for their next meal, but their quarry doesn't make it easy for them. The mice and snakes and other things they eat stay buried underground until they have to come out and forage for food. Then, they come out at night in the hope the birds won't see them."

Hunt let out a long breath as he allowed his feet to dangle below him. "I figured it would be a good idea to get a different look at things, which is why I'm up here." He pointed out at the land around them. "You can see lots of things high up if you know where and how to look."

Joe looked around, but it was clear he did not see much. "Kind of makes me dizzy." He pushed himself back from the edge. "Makes me feel like I'm about to fall over."

"A man should become familiar with such a feeling if he hopes to make anything of himself in this cruel world of ours. I hope you learn that someday."

"My aunt always warned me you were a strange one,"

Joe confessed. "She said it was wrong the way you quote Shakespeare all the time instead of the given word."

Hunt had always taken a certain amount of pleasure in tweaking the old crone's nose whenever he had the opportunity. She was the type who resented anyone who might have a higher or broader form of reference than her own. She despised what she did not understand, and Leon Hunt had taken great pains to remain a stranger to her.

"To quote the Bard is to quote scripture," Hunt told his young friend. "He drew great inspiration from the Bible. I hope you'll take it upon yourself to read his works one day. It'll do you a world of good."

"I plan to," Joe admitted. "As long as Aunt Kathleen doesn't catch me doing it, of course."

Hunt smiled. "You've just learned your first lesson in strategy, young man. The power of stealth. Well done."

Hunt's smile faded when he heard a great rustling from the overgrowth along the road off to his right. A small flock of birds quickly took to the air and flew away at great speed.

Something had scared them, and Hunt was not sure if he should be scared, as well.

Joe had noticed it, too. "Probably just a coyote or a wolf looking for an easy meal."

"Maybe." Hunt had studied the ground as closely as he could when he had left with Cobb to reclaim the horses. He had not seen any wolf or coyote tracks crossing the road. "But is this one on four legs or two?"

"Never saw a wolf on two legs yet," Joe said.

Hunt kept looking in the direction of the disturbance. "I have." He did not take his eyes from the spot but sought to keep Joe calm. There was no point in unduly alarming him. "How's Gene doing? Has he woken up yet?"

"Not yet, but he's making plenty of sounds. Ma says

she has a feeling he might be getting ready to come out of it."

"That's good. The sooner he's better, the sooner we can get ourselves to Laramie."

"I'm in no rush to get there," Joe admitted to him. "I was hoping to be able to spend some time here with you. I was hoping you could take the time to help me learn how to shoot. With your pistol, I mean. My pa taught me how to shoot a rifle good enough, but we never had the money or the use for a pistol."

Hunt watched a lone bird fly up from the same place where the others had fled. Something there had held its interest far more than a wolf or a coyote could. Something familiar, yet foreign. All the other birds in the area had fallen silent, too.

"I know it might sound funny to a man like you," Joe went on. "About teaching me to shoot a pistol, I mean, but I'd be grateful to you if you did. I was hoping you might be able to teach me after my chores tomorrow. Maybe late morning?"

"Of course," Hunt said. "Tomorrow, if not sooner." Before the boy could ask him more, he urged him to move. "I want you to go downstairs right now and blow out any candles Ma has burning in the building, then lock the front door."

"Why?" Joe backed away from the ledge, quickly now. "Do you see someone out there?"

"I don't know and that's what concerns me. Go on and do like I told you. Leave the back door unlocked. I'll be down in a minute to tend to it myself."

Joe got moving while Hunt remained as still as possible. He only had his pistol on his hip, and whatever was out there was beyond its range. The front gate of the station would not offer much protection from anyone looking to get inside, but it might slow them up enough to give Hunt something to shoot at.

Hunt remained still, watching and listening where he was until he felt the last of the sun's warmth on his back. He heard the branches of the overgrowth move in the dying light and knew the noise was not from an animal. It would have moved on long before now in search of prey.

He lifted his legs over the edge of the roof and moved back toward the wooden ladder in a crouch. The station already provided a worthy target to whoever was out there. He quickly climbed down the ladder. There was much he had to do if he hoped to survive the night ahead.

Cobb stopped his team in front of the Ennisville Hotel on Main Street. Given that it was just after business hours, some of the shops had already begun to close, but the hotel was still very much open for business. Two bellhops came outside to accept the luggage Butch began to hand down to them from the top of the coach.

As soon as Cobb had thrown the brake, Mr. Koppe was outside and helping Mrs. Wagner down from the coach. The two missionaries had already entered the hotel before Cobb could tell them the news. Reverend Averill did not seem interested, either. He slid his heavy bag along the coach floor and kept his head down as he lugged it into the hotel.

Jane offered Cobb a gloved hand, and he helped her climb down from the coach and up to the boardwalk of the hotel.

Cobb said, "Seems like you're the only one of my passengers who isn't in much of a hurry."

"Mrs. Wagner and Mr. Koppe were whispering in each other's ear constantly since we left the station," she told him. "It might've been endearing if they weren't talking about something vile. And they were taking great care to make sure I couldn't hear them, as if I cared about what they were saying. I was only curious because there's not much to do back there and no one to talk to. Reverend Averill always has his nose in a scripture book when he hasn't nodded off."

Normally, Cobb would have been more interested in the activities of his customers, but he had more pressing matters to discuss with her. "I need you to tell the others that Butch and me have to see to something this very evening. We might not be back until tomorrow morning, if not the afternoon. I need you to stall for time. Tell them we had something to do but keep it vague."

"How else could I keep it if you won't tell me?" She searched his eyes. "You're going back to Delaware Station, aren't you? You think there might be trouble tonight."

"I didn't when we left," Cobb confessed, "but Butch and that mouth of his wouldn't shut up about it. Now he's got me worried I might've made a mistake. Just please don't tell the others about it. It won't do anyone any good. In fact, it could cause a lot of trouble for us. We're already well behind schedule."

She looked at the five horses still tied behind the coach. "But how will you get there? All of the animals are tired from the journey. Even I can see that."

"Butch and I will take a couple of fast horses from the livery and double back to check on the station. We ought to be able to make it in half the time it took us to get here. We might even be able to make it before it's dark, or soon after. But I need you to keep things quiet here with the others. Can you do that for me?"

"Of course, I can," she said. "I'll even take anything that Mrs. Wagner throws at me as long as you promise me that you'll be careful."

Cobb thought she looked beautiful in the late afternoon sunlight. He would have given anything to have been able to send someone else in his place so he could stay there with her. But he would never be able to live with himself if something happened to Hunt, Joe, and the others back at the station.

"I promise I'll be safe, and I'll be back as soon as I can. If you decide to take another stage to Laramie, I won't hold it against you."

She smiled. "I like the way you drive a coach, Mr. Cobb. I'll be here when you get back." His breath caught when she placed a gloved hand on his. "And you will come back, I hope. I expect you to return in better condition than when you left."

Having all of her attention on him and him alone caused him to blush. "That's my expectation, too, ma'am."

"And bring Butch back in one piece, too, if you can manage it."

Cobb grinned. "I'll try to keep it in mind."

She bid him a good evening and entered the lobby as the bellhops continued to move the luggage inside the hotel.

Butch climbed down from the wagon box and stood next to Cobb. "I've got to hand it to her, Cobb. I don't think I've ever seen you this smitten over a woman."

Cobb was not sure if he was smitten with Jane, but he was certainly taken with her beauty. "We've got more important things to do than courting. Let's get these horses over to the livery so we can get ourselves back to Delaware Station."

"That's what I wanted to talk to you about," Butch said.

Cobb could tell that Butch was holding something back from him. "Don't tell me you've changed your mind about going. Not after you spent the whole trip here telling me we had to go back."

"It ain't my mind that's changed," Butch said. "It's just that things aren't as clear-cut as they were only a little while ago."

Cobb was beginning to grow frustrated. "You're starting to remind me of Hunt. Throwing a lot of words at something instead of speaking plain. Spit it out, Butch, like it was tobacco."

Butch looked down at his boots. "While I was handing down the luggage from the coach, one of the boys from the hotel told me they thought we were Leo Burke's coach. They were expecting them to arrive this morning, but they sent a wire that they'd thrown a wheel outside of North Branch."

Cobb knew Leo Burke and did not have an opinion on the man one way or the other. He was a competitor, that was all. "That coach didn't reach the station while we were there."

Butch finished the thought for him. "Which means they're bound to reach Delaware Station right about now or before we get there. That means Gene and Ma won't be alone anymore. We might not need to go now."

Cobb found it interesting, but that was all. Still, he was glad Butch had told him about the new wrinkle in an already crumpled situation. "Did this bellhop tell you when the coach left North Branch?"

Butch shook his head.

"They could still be lame outside North Branch," Cobb concluded as he moved to the back of the coach to untie the horses. "They could also ride up on the station while the thieves are attacking the place or soon after."

"It'll mean we're outgunned and outmanned again," Butch said.

That did not bother Cobb. "I don't think we've ever been in a scrape when we had numbers on our side. We'll just have to find a way to face whatever we find waiting for us at the station. Your news doesn't change that, but I'm glad you told me."

"And I'm glad it wasn't enough to change your mind about going."

Cobb undid the knot of the lead line of the saddle horses and began to walk them toward the heart of town. Butch followed close behind, carrying both his Henry repeater and Cobb's shotgun.

As the sun began to dip below the western mountains, Cobb stopped in front of Fregosi's General Store, which was closed. He had planned to trade the animals and tack there. Cobb knew Fregosi would have given him a fair price for everything he brought him, but he had locked up his shop for the evening.

Cobb led the horses toward the livery, which was always open. He only hoped the man who ran the place was an honest man and had a couple of fast horses in the back.

Cobb might have punched the liveryman had Butch not grabbed him first.

"Don't hit him, Boss. We need him."

According to the sign hanging in front of the livery, Jim Thornberry was the owner and proprietor of the Ennisville

Livery and Feed Store, but as far as Cobb was concerned, he was little more than a thief.

Cobb made no attempt to hide his anger. "We just walked in here with five good saddle horses and tack, and the best you can do is offer us a couple nags about ready for the glue pot?"

Thornberry held up a pair of bony hands. "I'm not the one who's in a hurry here, Cobb. You boys are. You can't expect me to lose money on account of your needs, now, can you? You said you want two of my best horses. That's fine. The cost is all five of them horses and all the gear they've got on them, including the weapons. Now, if you're of a mind to wait until morning, I'm sure you can find a better price elsewhere in town. Why, Fregosi down at the general store will be happy to give you something that's more than fair in money or trade. But seeing as how he's closed today, my offer stands. It's liable to be the only offer you get, too."

Cobb walked away from Butch and Thornberry. He hated being over a barrel like this. He hated being at the mercy of another man's greed. He hated giving up prime stock at such a ridiculously low price. He knew he could get a better deal at the general store come morning, but he could not risk the lives of Ma, Gene, and the others over something as petty as haggling.

Cobb wagged a finger in Butch's face. "This is all your fault. If you'd just kept your big mouth shut, I wouldn't be in this mess now. I'd have slept soundly and never given that station another thought."

Butch looked at the straw on the ground. "I told you to let me do the talking here."

Cobb threw a few choice words at him as he went to one of the horses they had brought to Thornberry, took out a gun belt from the saddlebags, and put it on. He had never liked the feel of a pistol on his hip or in his hand, but he was beyond concerns about his own comfort now.

Thornberry raised his chin when he saw Cobb put on the rig. "Our deal was for all the tack, including whatever was in them saddlebags."

Butch stepped between them. "My friend here's not in a playful mood at present. You go back there and pick out two of the best and fastest horses you've got before I turn him loose on your miserable hide."

Cobb's hands shook with rage as he tried to buckle the belt. "I have half a mind to take the difference between what I was fixing to get for these horses and what this land pirate is giving us out of your share of the business."

"You're more than welcome to it if it makes you feel better about things," Butch said. "I've never been one to put a price on something I thought was right."

Cobb was troubled by how few holes were left on the gun belt when he finally had it cinched. "I haven't used one of these things in years. I'm liable to shoot off my foot if I have to use it."

"You'll have your coach gun as consolation. Let's just hope you don't have an occasion to use it."

Cobb did not think his afternoon could have gotten any worse until he saw Thornberry leading out two brown mustangs, fully saddled, from the stalls.

Cobb and Butch were both about to start yelling about the size of the smaller horses, but once again, the livery-man threw up his hands. "You boys are looking for speed, and these two are the fastest I've got. They can run all night without stopping if you need them to. They're too small to pull your stagecoach for you, but they can get you to Delaware Station in a hurry. And they're both two-year-olds. I foaled them myself right here. Sold their mother a year ago."

Cobb took the reins of one horse and led the animal out to the street, where it took him a couple of tries to climb into the saddle. He had not been on horseback in years.

Butch was already on his horse and did not wait for his partner as he began to ride out of the livery in the direction of Delaware Station. Cobb followed, vowing that if he did not break his own neck, he just might break Butch's.

CHAPTER 8

Deciding he had learned all he could by watching the station, Earl Haney rode back along the same road he had taken to find Fred and the rest of the gang. He saw they had stopped less than a mile out from the station.

His brother had never been one for pleasantries, not even when he was in the best of moods, and he was far from a good mood now.

"Well?" Fred asked his brother. "Did you see any sign of the horses?"

"The tracks led me straight back there," Earl said, "but the fence was closed, so I couldn't see them. I heard them well enough. Saw something mighty peculiar while I was there, too. I saw this older fella sitting on the roof of the station building, swinging his legs like he didn't have a care in the world."

Earl and Fred had been to the station a couple of times. Gene and his mother were gentle enough, as was Del, their helper. That was why they knew it would be easy to take back the horses. But neither of the brothers recalled seeing an old man around before or even talk of one.

"That's strange," Fred said. "How old was this fella you saw on the roof?"

"Older than us by a few years or more," Earl said. "Fifty, maybe, but he looked a bit older. He had longish gray hair that came to his shoulders and wore a flat-brimmed hat. Had real sharp features, too. I might've taken him for one of them civilized Indians, but the more I looked at him, I could see he was definitely white. There was just something downright unsettling about him that I can't put my finger on."

"And you say he was just sitting up there?" Fred prodded further.

"Like a bird in a tree," Earl explained, "but he could see a lot from up there, and he was watching all around him. I think he might've spotted me in the bushes. I felt like he was looking straight at me, but he didn't fire off a shot or anything. I saw some kid join him on the roof. I'd put him at about sixteen. And before you ask me, it definitely wasn't Del. They talked awhile before the kid climbed back down and out of sight. This old fella left a bit after he did. Since there was nothing more to see, I figured it was best I came back and tell you all about it."

"You figured right," Fred said. "You did good, Earl."

Earl knew his brother did not like to rush his thinking, so he grew quiet while Fred thought things over. He looked at the other men and quietly willed them to do the same.

Fred turned in the saddle and asked Buck Hamlin, "What do you make of it? You ever hear of an old man and a boy working Gene's station with him?"

"Can't say that I have," Buck admitted, "though it's been a while since I've been in these parts. It could be that Gene hired on a couple of new men to work the place with him and Del. Lots of new stage lines have started up now that the war's finally over, and they're likely to be doing a good business."

Earl knew all about the new stagecoach lines. King Hagen had hired them to bring all the independents in line. The Delaware Station was one of them, though he knew Fred kept that from the men. He did not want them to get greedy by thinking they should get a bigger share of the money Hagen was paying them to run the independents out of business.

Fred looked like he had thought this over enough. "If this old man and the boy worked there before the raid, it would've put Joe's bunch at nearly even when they took the horses. Joe wouldn't move against odds like that. Even if he did, he wouldn't have left anyone alive. No one who was good enough to ride out, kill him, and take the horses back, anyways."

Earl watched his brother puzzle over the facts until Fred said, "No, those two must've come after the deed was done. That old man Earl saw wouldn't have been so re-laxed if they knew we were coming, unless he was as touched in the head as Del, which doesn't seem likely." He looked down at the deep ruts that had been plowed in the road. "I'll bet the old man and the boy were with the same stagecoach that left these marks. There's at least two of them in there, maybe more. I doubt all of them will be men, but it could be enough to give us trouble."

Earl was glad to be able to lend something to the mix of his brother's thoughts. He was not as dumb as Fred or his father had thought. "I saw fresh ruts just like these in the dirt leading away from the station. It stands to reason that the old man and the boy are the only two who stayed behind."

"That's good." Fred's eyes narrowed as he thought, "but it could be bad, too. Could be that they stayed behind to help. Could be they can help Gene and Ma in more ways than just mucking out stalls." He looked at Earl. "You see if that old gate is still as rickety as ever?"

"Didn't pay it much mind," Earl admitted, "but I would've noticed if it was new."

Ken Rice cleared his throat before speaking up. "I don't mean to rush you, Boss, but I think Earl has found out as much as we can by watching the place. I know it's risky going in there, but I think it's time we decide about—"

Earl and each of the other Haney men went for their guns when they heard the hooves of an approaching horse on the road behind them. They only relaxed when Bill, the lookout, called out and said it was him.

Bill brought his horse to a sliding halt between Fred and Earl. "Sorry for the trouble, Boss, but I just saw a stage coming up the road."

Earl could see Fred was encouraged by the news. "How many horses?"

"A team of four," Bill said. "They're moving at quite a pace. And it's real top-heavy with bags of all kinds and sizes, too."

Earl knew that was a good sign for the Haney gang. The coach was either packed with passengers or hauling a few wealthy people. The horses would be good and tired from their pace by now and the stage driver would be less likely to make a run for it with a weakened team.

"You see a shotgun rider?" Earl asked.

Bill shook his head. "If they've got one, he must be inside because I didn't see him."

"Looks like we've got a way into that station, boys," Fred announced to the men. "You all know what to do. Get your kerchiefs on and hide your faces. Our day just got a whole lot better."

* * *

Leo Burke was beginning to think owning his own stagecoach was not everything it was cracked up to be. When he had just been a driver for a larger concern, life was easy. Make the run between stations and towns. Swap out the horses and continue on. Draw pay from a bank at his destination and start it all over again.

At first, Burke had thought the offer to buy his own coach had been too good to be true, and it was beginning to look like it was. Where he had used to think about how he would spend his money in Cheyenne or Laramie, he worried about how much the stations would charge him for room and board for himself and his horses. He had to make sure the hotels knew he was coming and had enough rooms for his passengers.

And the cost of any problems with the coach came right out of his wallet. If they had thrown a wheel when he had been just a driver, the wheelwright would just bill the line. But since he was the one in charge now, they expected cash on the barrelhead. Spending other people's money was much more appealing than spending his own.

The only reason why he was not completely disheartened was the same reason why he had bought his own coach in the first place. King Charles Hagen had put out the word far and wide that he was looking to buy out every freight and coach company in the territory. Burke hoped he would get a similar offer once he reached Laramie, but since throwing the wheel had put him off his schedule, it might drive down the price some. King Hagen was known as a man who appreciated punctuality.

Burke had only become a stagecoach driver because he had not been able to find decent employment elsewhere. He had lost his job at the Green Tree Saloon for drinking more shots than he poured for its customers. He had once had a good head for numbers, but his reputation as a drinker had made it impossible for him to get work as a clerk or a bookkeeper in any respectable business. Driving a stagecoach was the best he could do.

Normally, it was not taxing work, save for the beating his backside took from spending so many hours in the wagon box driving the team. The customers were usually content to spend the entire trip between stations and towns in silence and rarely complained, not that Burke did anything to encourage conversation. He usually had a man riding shotgun with him for most trips of this length, but the man he had hired on had proven useless. He was drunk when they threw a wheel outside of North Branch, and once they managed to fix the wheel after a great deal of effort, the wastrel had decided to crawl deep into a bottle and pull the cork in behind him. Burke had no choice but to leave him behind since they were already behind schedule.

Burke had never been a violent man, and while he accepted that danger and guns were part of the job, he had never been as comfortable around them as he should. Burke kept the shotgun on the bench next to him as he drove the team toward Delaware Station, but when the constant jostling of the coach kept knocking it from the seat, he decided to place it on the floor of the wagon box. Unfortunately, it rattled down there, too, and had almost bounced out of the wagon twice since North Branch. Burke had been forced to keep his foot on it since, causing a constant ache in his right knee and hip. He should have paused long enough to place it back beneath his seat but did not dare risk the time or the damage that further delay might cause to his reputation. He needed every penny of his meager profit to send back home to his wife and children in Missouri.

Burke had not judged his shotgun rider too harshly for

drinking too much back in North Branch, but he cursed the man's drunkenness now as he saw the men on horseback lined up across the road ahead. He began to slow his weary team as four riders broke the line and raced toward him. The kerchiefs hiding their faces left no doubt as to their intention. These were not prospective customers. Not this close to Delaware Station. They were highwaymen looking to rob him, if not more.

Burke continued to pull back on the reins until his laboring team stopped completely. He was no longer worrying about being behind schedule. He only hoped he lived long enough to worry about such things.

Burke had already thrown the hand brake and had his hands raised as the four riders reached the stage. He kicked the shotgun out from beneath his feet and closed his eyes as it clattered to the road below.

Three of the men took hold of the team of horses while the fourth rider came toward him and stopped at the front of the coach. He wore a scarlet red kerchief that was as dusty as the rest of him. He had obviously spent many long hours on a horse.

The man sounded like he was speaking through clenched teeth behind the kerchief covering his face. "You think you're smart for kicking that gun at me, fat man?"

Burke kept his eyes closed and his hands in the air. He had been held up before and knew that the less he saw, the better his chances of survival were. "I didn't reach for it. I was just trying to show you'll get no fight from me."

Burke could hear the smile in the man's voice. "Maybe you're smarter than you look, fat man. Where's the strong box?"

"Right here under my left leg," Burke told him, "but it's empty. I'll get it for you if you promise not to shoot me."

"I don't make promises I'm not sure I can keep." He kept the pistol aimed at Burke. "On your feet."

Burke opened his eyes now as he stood, but looked up at the sky and almost lost his balance. Given his round shape, sitting in the front of the wagon was much easier than trying to stand on it.

The robber lifted the seat and looked inside for himself before letting it close again. "All right. Sit back down and pull the strong box. Hand it to me real slow or my friends here will kill you."

Burke produced the iron strong box and handed it over. "There you go. It's not even locked."

The robber balanced the box on the horn of his saddle and opened it. Empty, just as Burke had said. He tossed it aside and looked up at Burke. "Who're you hauling?"

"A special charter," Burke told him. "A couple of mining bosses on their way to Laramie and their wives. None of them have guns, in case you're wondering. None that I know of, anyway."

"Let's hope for your sake that they ain't."

The man moved his horse back to the coach and kept his pistol trained on the door as he called out to the passengers, "This here is a robbery. Everyone come out of there nice and slow, and I won't have to kill you."

Burke heard the coach door open and looked back to see the two men step out first, their hands up. They were both around sixty with iron-gray mutton chops and expensive suits that looked like they had come from Denver or Chicago. Each man had a well-fed look that rivaled Burke's own. They offered their hands to help their wives down from the coach and the robber allowed it.

The ladies were both dressed in expensive, peach-colored dresses and matching silk hats. They remained close to their respective husbands as they held their gloved hands in the air.

"What a fine-looking bunch of travelers we've got here," the robber laughed. "Give me your names."

Burke heard one of the men say, "Mr. and Mrs. Andre Becquer of the Wyoming Mining Company."

The other man said, "Colonel and Mrs. Louis McBride of the Wyoming Mining Company, you filthy rabble."

Burke shut his eyes. He knew that, despite needing a walking stick, the colonel was going to be a problem. He was a proud man, and his pride might get them all killed.

"Colonel?" the robber noted. "Are you a soldier or were you more of a tent rat during the war?"

"I served with the Army of the Potomac," McBride said proudly. "I was wounded at Antietam."

"I'm impressed, Colonel," the robber said. "It just so happens that you and me fought for the same side. So did most of my men. You're in luck."

"I wouldn't call this luck, you miserable swine," the colonel said. "It's because of louts like you that the war went on for as long as it did."

Burke shut his eyes and prayed to whatever god might be listening that the outlaw had patience.

Burke opened his eyes when he heard one of the three men by the team approach and get down from his horse.

The leader said, "My brother-in-arms here is going to pass his hat among you fine people. You're going to put all your finery in it. Rings, billfolds, necklaces. Even those fine cravats you gentlemen are sporting. Give it all over and don't hold anything back. I'll be searching you later, and I'll shoot one of you if I find any baubles. Go on. Start filling my friend's hat."

Burke remained still while his passengers took off their jewelry and placed them in the outlaw's hat. He was jealous of the haul. He imagined there was more than ten years' worth of wages in there, if not more.

When the hat was almost full, the outlaw tried to take the colonel's silver-tipped walking stick.

McBride's grip held firm. "Unless you intend on carrying me everywhere, a prospect I detest as much as you, I need this to move around."

The leader gestured for his friend to leave it, and the man got back on his horse with the loot.

The leader said, "Go give that to the others. We'll divide it up later as soon as things quiet down."

The man rode off, leaving the leader alone with Burke and his passengers.

The leader said, "Here's what's going to happen next. You nice folks are going to climb back in that coach and sit down like nothing's happened. You'll pull down those leather curtains and enjoy the ride in silence. Do that, and you'll be having a nice meal in the station before you know it. Tomorrow, you'll be in Laramie telling all your fancy friends about how you came up against a band of cutthroats and lived to tell the tale." He gestured with his pistol toward the stage. "Go on. You have your orders. Be quick about it as time's wasting."

Burke watched as the men helped their wives board the stagecoach again. Mr. Becquer went in quietly, while Colonel McBride paused to glare up at Burke. "You, sir, are a spineless coward." He ducked inside and pulled the door closed behind him without waiting for a response.

The leader laughed as he brought his horse alongside Burke. "Don't let that old warhorse trouble you any. You've been smart up to now, and you'll live as long as you go on being smart. Understood?"

"I understand." Burke gathered up the reins of the team.

"I won't give you a lick of trouble. What do you want me to do now?"

"You're going to keep on doing what you were doing. Ride on toward the station like you were fixing to do. Once they open the gate, me and my friends will ride in right behind you. If they ask you any questions once you get inside, tell them you let us ride with you along the trail. Once we're inside, your part in all this is over."

Burke released the hand brake and held the team still. "I'm ready when you are."

But the leader did not look like he was in a hurry. "You ever meet the station manager before?"

"Gene and Ma? Sure. I've known them for years. They're nice people, but they don't have much. You won't get rich by stealing from them. Why do you ask?"

"Ever known them to employ an old man and a boy to help them with things around the place?"

Burke knew he had not. "Del does most of the heavy work. What he lacks in brains, he makes up for in brawn. He can work all day without a word of complaint. Don't know anything about a boy or an old man."

"I'm glad to hear you say that." The leader waved Burke forward with his pistol. "On you go. Nice and easy. Your horses look about done in. No reason to push them any."

Burke cracked the reins and got the team moving again. The men blocking the road parted and allowed the coach to roll by before filling in behind it.

Burke noticed the sun had already set in the western sky, and it was bound to be a long night ahead.

CHAPTER 9

Hunt placed the rifles he had found around the station on one of the beds. It was a sorry state of affairs. Three of the rifles were old Spencers that were long rusted beyond any real use. Hunt imagined they must've been left behind by soldiers who had been glad to be rid of them after the war.

A Henry rifle, similar to the one he had seen Butch Keeling carry, was in decent enough condition. He checked the weapon carefully and was confident it would fire. Unfortunately, he only had ten rounds for it. Just like his revolver, he would have to make each shot count.

He fed some bullets into the Henry and carried it with him when he went to check on the others. Joe was tending the cookstove while Ma sat beside her son's cot.

Hunt tried to keep the concern out of his voice when he said, "How's he faring?"

"A little better," the old woman said as she placed a damp cloth on Gene's forehead. "His eyes are still closed, but I can see them moving around in there. That has to be a good sign, doesn't it, Mr. Hunt?"

Hunt did not take it as any sign at all. He had seen many men kicked in the head by horses who did the same thing only to never wake up. He hoped Gene would be different, even if he would not be able to play any role in whatever fight loomed ahead.

Hunt heard a man's voice bellow from outside. He took his rifle with him as he went to the front door of the station building and saw the gate rattle as someone knocked on it hard.

"Hello in the station. It's Leo Burke. I'm here with some weary passengers. Let us in."

Ma wiped her hands on her apron as she rose from her stool. "That would be Leo Burke. After all that's happened, I forgot his stage is overdue. They must've run into some trouble somewhere along the way."

Hunt motioned for her to remain where she was. "No need to trouble yourself, Ma. Joe and I can take care of them. Can't we, Joe?"

The youth stopped stirring the pot of beans on the stove. He had clearly heard the sound of concern in the older man's voice.

Hunt knew he had to stomp out the fear in Joe before it consumed him. "Don't just stand there, boy. Pull those beans off the flame and go open the gate. There's nothing worse in this world than a pot of burned beans."

Joe did as Hunt had told him and trudged forward while Ma went back to tending to her son.

Hunt pulled the boy close as he ushered him to the door of the station building. "I want you to do exactly what I tell you, understand me?"

"You don't think it's just a stage out there," Joe whispered. "You think it's got something to do with what you saw when you were up on the roof. We can't let them in."

"We've got no way of keeping them out, so we might as well let them in our way. We just might be able to control what happens next."

"How can we do that?" Joe asked as Hunt led him outside. "It's just the two of us in here."

Hunt knew there was not much he could do to keep anyone out of the station, but he had already taken steps to protect the main building. While Joe and Ma had been busy with other chores, Hunt had closed and locked all the shutters from the inside. They were thick and wooden and should hold for a while, but telling Joe about the other things he had done would only upset him.

Hunt projected a calm he did not feel. "You don't need to trouble yourself with that now. I want you to go over there, throw open the latch on the gate, and come running back here as fast as you can. Keep your head down as low as you can when you do it."

Joe's eyes went wide.

"There's nothing to it," Hunt assured him. "Don't look back and don't stop no matter what happens. I'll be right here watching you the whole way, I promise."

Joe looked at the Henry rifle in Hunt's hands. "You'll be watching. With that?"

"I will." The gate was rattling loudly now from Burke's constant pounding. "Get moving. There and straight back. Go!"

Hunt half-shoved the boy out into the courtyard and took a knee in the doorway. He brought the stock of the Henry flush with his shoulder and trained the sights on the fence. He hoped the rifle shot straight if it fired at all. He hoped Joe was as light on his feet as he'd need to be in order to survive.

As Hunt held the rifle still and ready, the steady ache in his left hand abated. He had spent the past hour since his time on the roof laying a trap for possible trouble. He had not worked a hand saw in years.

Hunt kept the rifle trained on the gate as Joe ran over to

it, flicked the bar from the latch, and ducked his head as he ran back to the building as fast as he could.

Hunt saw the fence doors burst open as two riders on horseback charged into the courtyard. One of them aimed a pistol at Joe.

Hunt fired, striking the man in the center of his chest, sending him sprawling backward and out of the saddle.

Nine bullets left.

Joe stumbled as he reached the porch of the building, and Hunt remained kneeling where he was as the second rider rushed a shot that struck one of the porch posts as Joe stumbled inside. Hunt fired and hit the man in the left side of the chest. The injured man managed to remain in the saddle but dropped his pistol.

Hunt levered in a fresh round. *Eight bullets left.*

More riders now flooded into the courtyard, firing wildly at the building as Hunt remained on a knee. As bullets peppered the front of the building, the air grew thick with the dust and the dirt of their impact. Hunt fell backward inside and kicked the front door shut.

Joe helped him back to his feet, and together they placed the heavy bar across the door to keep it from being kicked in.

Ma was on her feet, screaming questions at them through her frightened tears as Hunt and Joe ran through the kitchen and shut the smaller back door. It was not as thick as the front door, but Hunt had planned for that. Joe helped him slide a heavy cabinet over to block it. Hunt picked up a wooden beam he had cut and placed it between the cabinet shelves and the wall.

"They won't be expecting that," Hunt said, already panting from the effort. "They could have a horse give it a kick and it won't budge an inch."

Ma grabbed Hunt by the arms and yelled up at him,

"Why did you do that? Leo Burke is our friend. Why did you shoot him?"

Hunt was glad Joe was there to pull the old woman away. "Nobody shot at Leo, Ma. Mr. Hunt was shooting at the riders who were using him to get in here."

Hunt picked up his rifle and tried to catch his breath. Moving the cabinet had taken more out of him than he had expected. "We're going to need everyone in here to be quiet for a spell. I can't see what's going on outside, so I need to hear it."

Joe eased the weeping old woman back down on her stool while Hunt set about looking for a place to make a stand if and when they finally broke in.

"Leo!" Ma wailed out loud despite Joe's embrace. "Are you hurt?"

"I'm fine, Ma," a man Hunt supposed was Leo answered from outside. "Let us in. I promise that these men mean you no harm."

Hunt went into the sleeping room and looked at the empty beds. He and Joe might be able to flip some of them over to provide some cover. A last-ditch attempt from where they could return fire. It might work, but for how long, Hunt did not know.

Joe tried to quiet Ma as bullets hit the front door, causing the frightened older woman to only wail louder as she draped herself across her son's body.

Hunt yelled to Joe over the sound of gunshots. "Get over here and help me turn over some of these beds so we have a place to make a final stand."

Joe left Ma with her son as he joined Hunt to help with the beds.

* * *

"Set him down easy, boys," Fred Haney ordered his men as they helped Earl down from his horse. The front and back of his shirt was already matted with blood.

The rest of his remaining men had already ridden into the courtyard along with the coach. The fat driver and the passengers were still aboard, but Fred was more concerned about his brother than them.

Fred saw Bill dash to him on foot and kneel beside him next to Earl on the ground. Bill served as the gang's doctor and usually knew how to care for any ailment at hand, including bullet wounds.

Fred didn't even let Bill start looking his brother over before asking, "How bad is it? Tell me the truth."

Bill tore Earl's shirt open and winced at the wound. "It's bad. The bullet's gone straight through him, but I think it's his heart. There's not much I can do for him, but I'll do what I can."

The world spun wildly before Fred Haney as he stood up and let Bill try to save his brother. Fear and rage collided in his mind with enough force to make him dizzy.

Ken Rice was the closest of his men to him. Fred grabbed him by the shirtfront and yelled, "Take some of the others and try knocking down those doors. While you're doing that, I want five men on that roof right away. Tell them to start firing down into them and keep firing until you hit someone. My brother needs a bed, and I don't want to be out here all night."

Rice picked out five outlaws to come with him. Each man took his rifle and followed Rice as he began searching for a way up.

The others were standing around looking at Fred, waiting to be told what to do. The looks of concern in their eyes only served to annoy him. "The rest of you clear up this courtyard. Get your horses in the corral and point every gun you've got on that building. If you see something, call it out and wait for my order. Don't fire until I give the word, no matter what they do. Understand?"

Each man set about following their orders as Fred looked down at his wounded brother. Bill had torn away the remnants of Earl's ruined shirt and had begun to pack the bullet holes as best he could with cotton from his saddlebag. Fred had seen many such wounds during the war and could not remember a single time when the man had survived. He could not let Earl die. Not after all they had survived together. He was the only brother he had left.

Fred felt his hands ball into fists as he looked at the closed door of the building. The entire structure was like a mockery to his fear for his brother's life. Someone had been busy fortifying the place. All the shutters had been shut and probably locked from the inside. He remembered how the front door had been solid and built with thick planks of wood the last time he had paid a visit to the station. He was sure that the heavy bar that was usually propped on the wall beside it must have been brought across it by now.

Going in the front would take a lot of doing. The back door and the roof were clearly his best options.

The old man and the boy had dug in deep. It would be up to Ken Rice and the others to pry them out. And if his brother died before then, Fred would make both of them pay for it. Dearly.

As the men he had chosen followed him around to the back, Ken Rice knew he was liable to be the next man shot if he did not find a way up onto that roof. He looked around the front and the side of the building for a ladder.

He knew there must be one. He remembered Earl had talked about seeing an old man sitting up there as calm as a popinjay earlier.

He led his men around the back and saw a small door that probably led out from the kitchen. He told the others to cover him as he rammed his shoulder into it, but it did not budge. And since Fred had ordered him to get on the roof, not break in, he did not order his men to bust it down.

He found a ladder leaning against the far end of the back wall. Someone had piled a fair amount of hay beneath it. It was probably there to break a man's fall if he fell from the ladder. Without a doctor around within a day's ride of most stations, station managers were known to be a cautious lot. Even the slightest injury could prove to be a death sentence.

Rice ordered one of his men to hold the wooden ladder steady while he and Concho began to scale it. He had just about reached the top rungs when it split apart under their weight. Rice and Concho dropped into the hay, where a fiery pain spread through Rice's legs. He could hear Concho screaming, too, as the others threw aside the remnants of the broken ladder.

Rice's eyes went wide when he chanced a look at his wound and saw the rusted tines of a hay rake sticking up from his legs. He looked beyond his own pain to see Concho had been impaled through the middle by another rake and was beating the ground in agony.

Two of the men grabbed hold of Rice as another one kept his boot on the rake. They lifted Rice into the air, freeing him. He could still hear Concho shrieking when he finally lost all consciousness.

CHAPTER 10

Cobb was annoyed by the sound of the mustangs drinking from the creek. The sky was almost completely dark by now, and he was angry he was not still in the saddle, racing toward Delaware Station as he had planned.

"That horse swindling thief Thornberry told us these horses could run all night without stopping for water. I'm going to drown him in one of his own troughs for this."

Butch remained quiet. "They ran faster and longer than the horses we'd rode in with. Yours got tired because you're almost twice my size. There's nothing wrong with these here animals. We're only a mile or two away from the station as it is. We could tie them up here and walk there if we were of a mind to, but I wouldn't recommend it."

Neither would Cobb. Deep down, he knew his partner was right. The mustangs had performed better than he could have hoped, but he had never been one to allow facts to get in the way of a good rant.

"If we walk there, we have to walk back," Cobb said, "and we'd be left afoot when we got there. I don't aim to get caught flatfooted without knowing what we're up against."

"And yelling about it won't make them drink any

quicker," Butch said. "Neither will you kicking yourself about leaving Hunt and the boy back at the station. You left them for a reason, a good reason, and at the time, you were right. But I also know I feel better about things knowing that the ladies are safe and out of harm's way back in Ennisville."

"Even Mrs. Wagner?"

"Yeah, even her." Butch cut loose with a stream of tobacco juice into the creek. "Though I'd want that old girl right here beside us if this was an oration contest. She could outpreach any parson I've ever heard, and I've heard a few."

"I don't think there'll be much call for oration at the station," Cobb said. "If there's call for anything at all."

"I was working my way around to talking about that," Butch said. "How do you want to take things when we get there? The approach, I mean."

Cobb had spent most of the ride from Ennisville thinking about it and thought he had something close to a plan. "It'll depend on what we find when we get there. I figure we ought to tie off these animals in the overgrowth a bit away from the station and take a long listen. If things seem quiet, we knock on the gate like civilized folks and help ourselves to some beans and biscuits."

"And if we happen upon some trouble?"

"Then what we do next will be entirely up to whoever's causing it." Cobb called the layout of the station to mind. "I figure it'll be best if we avoid the front gate entirely and go through the back door of the barn. I can't remember the last time Gene opened it, but I know it works."

Butch scratched at the stubble on his cheek. "That was my thinking, too. Safest way in. The barn also gives us cover with a wide view of the courtyard."

"As long as no one gets it in their head to throw a lit

lamp in there," Cobb said. "That place will go up like a match head if they do. They'd have no trouble smoking us out then."

Butch hit his thigh in frustration. "There you go ruining a perfectly good plan with dark possibilities. I swear you're the dourest man I've ever met."

"And you've met a few." Cobb smiled. "I know. You've told me."

Cobb's horse lifted its muzzle from the creek. Butch's mustang followed soon after.

Cobb went to his mustang. "Looks like they're telling us they've had their fill."

But Butch did not go to his horse right away. "You know it'll likely mean more killing, don't you?"

Cobb took the horse by the reins and led it away from the stream. "Like I just said, that'll be entirely up to them."

After Cobb and Butch tied their mustangs up outside the station, the screams of men cut through the gathering night. They clutched their long guns and crept through the overgrowth, careful not to snap any twigs or branches that might betray their position.

The screams did not trouble them, for they did not yet know who was doing the screaming. They paused behind the barn and listened closely to understand what was happening inside the station.

Cobb heard a jumble of agitated voices and strained to make sense of them.

"How did you idiots let him get close enough to stick a rake in him?" one man yelled.

"We didn't, Fred." Cobb knew he'd remember the first man's voice belonged to Fred. "They set a trap for us. Someone sawed the ladder half through and had the rakes buried in the hay. We didn't even know they were there until Rice and Concho fell on them."

Cobb burned the names into his memory. *Fred is the leader. Rice and Concho are hurt.*

Another man continued to bellow as Fred shouted, "How's Concho doing?"

"He's dead," another man said. "He died as soon as we managed to pull him off the rake. Those sharp ends cut right through the middle of him. Whoever did it set his trap good."

Cobb knew that had to be Hunt's doing. *Good for him.*

He heard the other man's screams die off as if someone had given him something to bite on or had covered his mouth. "I still want men up on that roof firing down into them, and I want it done now!"

"The boys are working on that, Boss," the man said, "but everything that can reach that high has been busted to pieces. I had Larry sling a lasso up there, but there's nothing for it to grab on to. I think he got hold of a clay chimney, but it broke apart when he put his weight on it. We haven't given up yet."

Fred cursed as he yelled, "Do I have to do all the thinking for you, idiot? Bring one of the horses around and stand on it if you have to. I don't care how you do it, but get moving."

Cobb heard dirt move like someone had gotten to his feet. He could barely make out what Fred said next, but he thought it sounded like, "My brother hasn't given up yet, and he's got a hole straight through his heart. I won't let the rest of you give up, either."

Cobb and Butch exchanged looks. Fred's brother was hurt. Cobb knew that put it at two wounded and one dead, if not more. Hunt was in the station building and probably ready to keep up the fight.

A new voice entered the mix. "What do you want us to do about the folks in the stage, Boss? They're starting to complain, and they want to get out."

Cobb gripped Butch's arm. That was news. There were more civilians in there than either of them had thought. That could change things. It might give this Fred fellow more to watch for.

"They're complaining?" Fred roared. "*They're* complaining? My brother and my men are dying. All they have to do is sit on their backsides, and they're whining? I'll give them something to whine about."

Cobb and Butch heard boots on the compact dirt of the courtyard, and Cobb knew this was their chance to move. There was no other way inside from the back, save for the large wooden doors. With Fred and his men being so close, the slightest squeak from the hinges would be enough to give away their position. Cobb knew timing would be everything.

He heard a heavy pounding, probably on the coach itself, and decided it was time to chance the noise.

"Hello in there," Fred shouted. "Anyone at home?"

Cobb pushed the door in and found enough of a space to get his hand through. Butch joined him in grabbing it but neither began to pull yet.

"There's nothing to be achieved by your theatrics, sir," a man with a commanding voice said. "There are ladies present."

Cobb heard the squeak of a coach door opening, and he began to pull at the barn door. It was not locked, but a pile of dirt that had accumulated at the base kept it from opening. Cobb stopped pulling while he and Butch used their boots to scrape the dirt away as quietly as they could manage.

Cobb heard women gasp, followed by a heavy thud,

then Fred's voice saying, "You want to be in charge so bad, Colonel? Well, here's your chance."

Colonel, Cobb thought. *He's one of the civilians. Was that one woman I heard gasping or two? That would make it four civilians, maybe? The coach driver and a shotgun rider could make it six. How many outlaws with Fred?* There was no way of knowing that without looking for themselves.

"If I were in charge here," the colonel said, "I'd have you and each of your men shot where you stand."

Cobb heard a laugh he assumed was from Fred. "I like your style, pop, so I'll make a bargain with you. You and your fancy walking stick here are gonna saunter on over to the door over there and get those nice people inside to let us in."

Cobb and Butch stopped clearing the dirt when their boots scraped hard ground. Cobb held tight to the door and would not let Butch move it. They had to wait for the right time.

The colonel said, "I'll do nothing that might aid you and put those poor people further in harm's way. I'll not do it, sir. And as you're armed and I'm not, you may do to me what you will."

"To you?" Fred laughed again. "Perish the thought, Colonel. I wouldn't dream about hurting a man like you, a distinguished war hero such as yourself. Now, Mrs. Colonel McBride, on the other hand, is a different matter entirely. She doesn't serve much of a purpose."

Cobb heard a heavy slap as he and Butch began to pry the barn door open. Cobb heard the old wood pop and felt his muscles tense at it took a considerable amount of his impressive strength to get it open a decent amount.

When he did, one of the hinges squeaked.

Butch and Cobb froze but held the door open. Cobb

could see enough through the narrow opening down the length of the barn and through the open front doors. A stagecoach and four-horse team blocked his view of the station building.

Cobb saw Fred had a stout older man pinned against the coach. He took the man to be the colonel.

Fred said, "You have exactly one minute to get them to open that door or I shoot your lovely wife in the head. I've lost some good men here tonight, and I won't lose another if I can help it. Putting a bullet in you or this old hag will help balance the score in my favor. Now get!"

Cobb watched Fred push the colonel forward and deliver a swift kick in the pants for good measure. The blow was hard enough to send the colonel sprawling, causing his walking stick to roll away from him.

Cobb thought some of the other outlaws would laugh at him. They did not make a sound.

Butch surprised Cobb by slipping through the narrow opening between the doors and into the barn.

Cobb tried to pry the doors open wider, but another groan from the hinges made him decide against it. He knew he could not fit between them, so he would have to find another way in. Butch and his Henry repeater were already inside. Going through the front gate was the only option left to him. He took his shotgun and moved off in that direction, hoping that he would be in position before Butch had to start shooting.

Butch was glad all the horses were out in the corral where they belonged and not the barn. One of the milk cows lowed as he crept past it, but no one outside had paid it any mind. They were too busy watching the colonel pick himself up from the ground.

Butch took a spot behind a bale of hay by the open doors of the barn and began to count the number of men Fred had brought with him. He saw one man attending to two others on the ground. The amount of blood he saw on one man's pants and on the other man's chest told him they were out of the fight for certain if they weren't already dead.

Butch looked over the rest of the men he could see in the courtyard and judged there were fifteen with their guns trained on the building. Hunt and Joe had closed the shutters tight. Sawing the ladder up to the roof and hiding rakes in the hay had been smart. Hunt had some fancy moves to go along with his fancy words. Butch hoped to hear more from the actor when all of this was finally over.

Butch watched the colonel use his walking stick to prop himself up as he began to toddle to the front door. If it came down to shooting, he would start with Fred, then continue on toward the right from there. The others might be less likely to be brave when they saw their leader hit the dirt. He imagined he could get three of them before the rest figured out where the shooting was coming from.

He hoped Cobb would be ready to go to work by then, probably from the front. He would be more exposed from there, but that shotgun of his would make up the difference. Maybe drive some of them back into Butch's range of fire.

He and his partner had both been in enough scrapes like this to know planning was useless. Everything fell apart as soon as the lead started flying.

Butch raised his rifle and kept it aimed at Fred, who had decided to watch everything from behind the cover of the coach. He kept his pistol pressed against the belly of a woman Butch took to be the colonel's wife. The concern on her face as she looked on as her husband approached the station made Butch's stomach turn. He did not know how long he would survive once he opened fire, but Butch was intent on making sure Fred died first.

Butch tightened the grip on his rifle as Colonel McBride stood straight as he stepped up to the porch, then rapped his stick on the station door.

"This is Colonel Louis McBride, late of the United States Army and currently with the Wyoming Mining Company. I wish to speak to someone inside this house. I am unarmed and I mean you no harm."

Butch felt some admiration for the colonel. The old boy had sand, despite all that had happened to him.

Butch heard a man's muted voice through the door and recognized Hunt's cultured tone.

"I've been listening to what they've been saying out there, Colonel. I'm sorry about this, but I can't open this door. I know they'll kill me if I do, and I know they'll kill you if I don't. I'm sure I don't have to explain to you the predicament this puts us both in. The weight of my decision is not lost on me."

"I understand your position entirely, sir," the colonel answered, "just as I know these men will kill me and my wife unless you open this door. I don't want you to open it. My wife may die. I, too, may die, but I'd rather her death be by my decision than by the ravings of a mad killer."

Fred stepped away from the coach and thumbed back the hammer of his pistol.

"You asked for it, you old—"

The .44-caliber slug from Butch's Henry rifle slammed into the side of Fred's head. His dead body fell to the other side through the red mist. His pistol discharged only when his hand hit the ground.

The team of horses hitched to the stagecoach screamed

and bucked at the sound of gunfire, sending Burke tumbling from the wagon box as the brake strained to hold.

Butch levered in a fresh round and shot the next man to the right. The bullet punched through his back and knocked him to the ground.

Butch's third shot caught the next man over in the ribs as he turned toward the barn. The impact caused him to spin away.

Butch's fourth shot hit the farthest man to the right in the stomach. Butch's next shot hit him in the top of the head before he crumpled in a heap.

Cobb's shotgun blast boomed through the courtyard as bullets began to strike the interior of the barn. The rounds hit high and wide as Butch dropped to his belly and began to crawl low out from behind the bale of hay as it shook from the impacts of leaden projectiles.

Butch watched the courtyard from between the hooves of the frightened horses as men scattered when Cobb cut loose with another blast. Three men backed up toward the far side of the station building.

Butch propped himself up on his elbows and fired, hitting one in the belly, doubling him over. A second man responded with a shot of his own, but the bullet nicked the hide of one of the stagecoach horses instead.

Butch's next shot fell short of his target, but the one after that caught the man in the leg, bringing him down.

Another outlaw ducked behind the side of the station building before Butch could get him, but Cobb stormed out and brought him down with both barrels of his coach gun.

Butch shifted his aim, looking for more targets as the stagecoach team continued to strain against the brake. He saw Cobb toss his coach gun aside as he drew his pistol and fired twice down into the man Butch had just shot in the leg.

Cobb's face was flush from battle and his beard streaked with blood. "Anyone else want to die here tonight?"

Butch imagined Cobb got his answer when he saw four men on horseback ride away through the open gate.

Butch got to his feet and kept his rifle at the ready as he slowly stepped out from the barn. The team of coach horses had begun to calm down as the gunfire subsided.

A quick glance to his right revealed some men had fallen close to each other on the far side of the courtyard. Butch could see they had caught a blast from Cobb's shotgun. A few more had fallen by the back of the coach near where Fred's corpse now lay in the dirt.

Butch had almost forgotten about Colonel McBride when the coach door flew open and the woman he recognized as Mrs. McBride ran across the courtyard to the station building.

She fell into the arms of her waiting husband. Butch was glad to see the brave old man had made it after all.

Butch looked away from the tender moment when he caught sight of Cobb storming over toward the place where the two wounded men they'd seen before the shooting started were lying. There was no rage in him, though his eyes were wide and terrible. He had seen his friend like this before. He was drunk on bloodshed and eager for more.

"What about you two vermin?" Cobb yelled as he stalked them. "I don't think you've had enough."

Butch knew he was not big enough to tackle his partner off his feet, but he ran to him and wrapped his free arm around him and tried to slow him down. "That's enough, Cobb. Simmer down. They're already dead. Everyone's dead. It's over. We're alive."

He felt Cobb rattle as the wave of his anger ebbed and he began to regain himself.

"You're right," Cobb said. "It's over."

Butch allowed himself to breathe again as he sensed his friend was beginning to return to normal. "Good, because I think we've all had our fill of fighting for one night."

Cobb blinked hard and watched two other passengers heading toward the colonel and his wife.

"That Burke's outfit?"

Burke, who had fallen from the wagon box when the shooting started, waddled over to them as he dusted off his clothes and then he held out a hand to Butch. "Never thought I'd be so glad to see a rival driver. Thanks for saving our lives just now, Butch. You too, Cobb. I held them off as best I could when they jumped us on the road, but there were too many of them."

Cobb pushed past Butch as he closed in on Burke. "You don't look any worse for wear. Looks like you led these boys in here without nary a scratch on you."

Burke laughed as he held his hand out to Cobb. "What was I supposed to do?"

Cobb launched a straight right hand that connected with Burke's nose and knocked him flat on his back.

Cobb made sure to step on the fallen man as he continued on toward the building. "Your job."

Butch followed Cobb toward the station building, whose front door was now open. Ma was inside, welcoming her weary guests.

Leon Hunt stood beside the doorway and began to applaud Cobb and Butch as they approached. "All hail the conquering heroes."

"Looks like you did a fair amount of conquering yourself," Butch said to the actor. "I heard about what you did with those rakes and that ladder. Mighty impressive stuff."

"One should be able to improvise when the need arises, shouldn't one?" The three men shook hands and the actor's act died away. "I didn't think we were going to make it, boys. We all owe you both our lives. Thank you." He bowed at the waist. "I mean that with all sincerity"

Cobb looked back at all the dead men strewn about the courtyard. Butch did not know how many each of them had killed, but such things did not matter just then.

"I hope Joe is limber, because we're going to need his help digging a whole bunch of graves."

Hunt looked out over them. "I wouldn't turn a spade of dirt for the whole lot of them."

Cobb asked, "Shakespeare say that, too?"

"No," Hunt said. "Those are my own words and sentiments. There's an old wagon in the barn. We'll load them upon it and dump them somewhere in the morning. They've troubled us enough for one night." He stepped aside and beckoned them to come in. "For tonight we eat, drink, and be merry."

Butch was not sure about the merry part of what Hunt said, but he had certainly worked up an appetite for himself.

CHAPTER 11

It had taken Cobb, Butch, Hunt, Burke, and Joe most of the morning to load the corpses on the wagon Hunt had mentioned and bring them out to a rocky area away from the main road. They left the wagon there and led the horses back toward the station. Buzzards began to circle high above them as they walked away. Cobb knew the birds would dine well that day.

Cobb would have been happy to walk back to the station in silence, but Leo Burke had other ideas.

"I want to let you know there's no hard feelings, Cobb," Burke said. "About you slugging me last night, I mean."

Cobb did not care. "That's good for your sake because I wasn't planning on apologizing for it."

Burke managed to sound magnanimous about it as he said, "Glad we have an understanding."

Cobb saw Butch look away as he quietly laughed.

Cobb had wanted to leave for Ennisville right after they moved the bodies, but Gene had begun to wake up shortly before they left to dispose of the bodies. So when they got back to the station, he didn't leave just yet. Cobb was anxious to see how he was faring.

The men gathered on the porch while Ma was inside

watching over Gene. Joe surprised them all by announcing, "I don't want to go back with you fellas. To Ennisville, I mean. I want to stay on here at the station to help Ma and Gene."

Cobb had not been expecting that. He would just as soon face down Fred and his men again than consider the prospect of failing to deliver Mrs. Wagner's nephew to her.

"That's out of the question," Cobb said. "Your aunt will skin me and Butch alive if we show up in town without you."

"No, she won't," Joe said. "I've written her a letter explaining my intentions in full. My reasons, too. I'd be obliged if you'd give it to her when you see her."

"Be glad to," Butch said, "provided she doesn't start shooting at us first. Are you sure you want to tweak her nose, son? Station life ain't normally this exciting. It's long days of boredom beside a list of endless chores that need doing rain or shine. Your life is never your own. Strangers traipsing in and out of your home at all hours of the day and night, and some of them ain't too particular about cleaning up the messes they leave behind. You're always at the mercy of the weather and the irregular schedules of some mighty unreliable characters like Cobb and Burke here."

"It doesn't sound all that different from farming in that way," Joe said. "I like it out here, Butch. I like Ma and I think I'll like Gene, too, now that he's woken up. It's good honest work and they need me. My aunt doesn't need me with her in Laramie. She's got souls to save, which is all she's ever really cared about. I can do God's work here as well as I could do it in a big city like Laramie. I'm not promising I'll stay here forever, but I'll be here as long as Ma and Gene want me."

Joe turned to look up at Cobb. "Boys my age are sent

off to war, Mr. Cobb. You said as much yourself to my aunt yesterday. Working at a station for stagecoaches is a lot safer than being a soldier."

Cobb admired the boy's spirit. "The last twelve hours haven't exactly been peaceful."

"I don't need peaceful," Joe persisted. "I just need to be useful and I'm useful right here. I don't think letting me stay here is too much to ask."

Cobb hated being in this position. Mrs. Wagner already despised him, and returning without Joe would not win him any favors with her. But the boy had clearly given the notion plenty of thought, and he did not have the heart to argue with him.

"I hope that letter to your aunt is as eloquent as that speech you just gave us," Cobb said. "It might serve to take some of the venom out of your aunt's stinger."

"It's my life," Joe said. "Not hers."

"That's the style, son," Butch encouraged him. "Old Cobb and me might find ourselves drawn and quartered by your aunt because of it, but I like your spark. Make sure you never lose it."

Cobb could not believe his lousy luck. He had survived cattle drives, stampedes, tornados, and gunmen only to lose his life to an angry missionary woman. In Ennisville, no less.

Upon getting back to the station, Cobb was glad to find Gene was not only awake but also had managed to take some broth Ma had prepared for him. He was weak, but at least he was alive.

"I don't aim to embarrass you, Tucker," Gene said, "but I'll always be grateful for what you did for Ma and me last night." He looked at Butch, Joe, and Hunt, who also stood around his cot. "We're grateful to all of you. We never would've made it if it hadn't been for every one of you."

Butch had never been fond of compliments and said, "You can thank us plenty by taking care of yourself and letting young Joe here do all the hard work for a while. There's no point in pushing yourself to exhaustion. It'll be a long while before you're back to your old self."

Ma took Joe's hand and kissed it. "Thanks for staying on with us, son. Are you sure it won't cause your aunt any worry? She's mighty protective of you."

"I've already given Mr. Cobb a letter that explains everything to her," Joe said. "Think nothing of it."

Cobb hated long farewells, so he patted Gene's foot beneath the blanket. "You take care of yourself, Gene. We'll see you on our next swing through here in about a week or so."

He accepted a hearty hug from Ma that almost broke his ribs and went outside to get the mustangs ready for the trip to Ennisville. Butch and Joe trailed after him, leaving Hunt alone with them to make his goodbyes.

"I don't know why Ma was thanking us," Butch said. "They'd have been dead long before we got here if Hunt hadn't slowed them up like he did."

"Shut up," Cobb scolded him. "Just take their gratitude and leave it at that."

Cobb found the Becquers had already boarded Burke's stagecoach, along with Mrs. McBride. He was surprised to find the colonel waiting outside it, his hands clasped atop his walking stick. "Mr. Cobb, I was wondering if I might have a quick word with you before we depart."

Cobb had no idea what the man wanted to say but went to him, anyway. "Joe, help Butch get our horses ready. We've got a long trip back to Ennisville."

"But the horses are already saddled," Joe pointed out. "There's hardly anything I need to do."

Butch took the boy by the arm and guided him away from the men.

Colonel McBride laughed as he watched them leave. "The innocence of youth, eh, Mr. Cobb. Were we ever that young?"

Cobb was anxious to get back to Ennisville. They were already too late as it was. "What's on your mind, Colonel?"

"I wanted to personally thank you and Butch for saving our lives last night. It's no small thing you did, and I'm in your debt."

Cobb hated being the subject of so much thanks and attention. "No need to thank me, sir. It was just the right thing to do. I'm glad we all made it out alive."

McBride regarded him for a moment. "I take it you don't know who I am."

Cobb only knew what he had overheard in the court-yard the previous night and decided neither of them wanted to relive it. "All I know is that you used to be in the army. The rest is none of my business."

"That's certainly part of who I am, but it's hardly all of it," the colonel said. "I'm also on the board of directors of the Wyoming Mining Company. So is Mr. Becquer. We're both on our way to Laramie to oversee our company's mineral claims in that area. That will put us in opposition to another man I'm certain you've heard of—Charles Hagen."

Cobb did not know much about rich people, but there was hardly anyone in the territory who did not know about King Charles. "I've heard of him. Heard he aims to buy up every stagecoach and freight line in the territory. Butch and me know some people who've sold out to him. Made quite a nice sum doing it, if they're to be believed."

"They wouldn't have to lie about such a thing," McBride said. "Hagen is not a cheap man. He knows what he wants and is willing to pay good money to get it, but I wonder if a man such as yourself would be so inclined, Mr. Cobb."

Cobb was beginning to think the colonel liked throwing around fancy words as much as Hunt. "Inclined to do what?"

"Inclined to sell," McBride asked. "Sell your stage-coach line to Charles Hagen, I mean."

"I haven't thought about it much one way or the other," Cobb said. "If he makes me an offer, I'd be a fool not to consider it. And I might be many things, but I'm no fool."

"I never thought you were. If you agree to sell to him, I hope you'll charge him top dollar. Don't be afraid to be greedy, Mr. Cobb. You only get a bite of this kind of apple once. Ask for more than you think he'll be willing to pay, and you just might find him willing to meet your price."

But Cobb sensed Colonel McBride had not asked to speak to him just to discuss business advice. "And if I turn down his offer?"

The colonel's thick eyebrows rose. "Then you'll find yourself in my shoes. You'll run afoul of him, and Charles Hagen is not used to having his advances spurned. You may even find yourself as his enemy, and he can be a vicious adversary, sir. Most vicious, indeed."

Cobb was beginning to get a clearer picture of McBride's true intentions. "You're fixing to buy me out, aren't you?"

"Not necessarily," McBride assured him. "My company has no need of a stagecoach line. We're in the mining business. We leave matters of transportation to others." He held up a single finger. "But if you refuse Hagen, you'll need a friend. Someone who can help you maintain your business and keep the jackals at bay. Should you find yourself in such a position, please know that I'll be more than happy to help you in any way I can."

The colonel placed his hand on his own bum leg. "I might not be able to move as well as I used to," he said, then tapped his temple with a finger. "But an old soldier always finds a way to fight his enemies." He held out his hand to Cobb. "And I'd be honored to be of service to you and Mr. Keeling in any way I can."

Cobb shook McBride's hand and hoped he would never need to call on him. Men like the colonel and Charles Hagen were like boulders in a rockslide. Once they got moving in a particular direction, they only went one way and did not care about whatever stood in front of them. Life was much simpler if he could just stay away from them entirely.

As the colonel joined the others in the coach, Cobb saw Hunt walking from the building with his black bag in hand. He was not wearing his gun belt.

"You're a hopeful man," Cobb said to the actor. "Stowing your gun rig like you have."

"We're all riding on to Ennisville together, aren't we?" Hunt asked. "I figure you and Butch can protect us from any dangers we might encounter along the way."

Cobb glanced back at the coach and was glad to see the Becquers and the McBrides were engaged in lively conversation. "You'd do well to keep your pistol close, Leon. Some of those boys from last night rode away. They might be looking to jump us somewhere between here and Ennisville. It'd be a shame to get yourself killed after living through what you did."

Hunt looked past the open fence to the land beyond. "If they were the vengeful sort, they would've come back by now. They're off somewhere licking their wounds. I doubt we'll see the likes of them again."

Cobb could not afford to be so optimistic. "They didn't laugh, Leon."

Hunt cocked an eyebrow. "Who didn't laugh?"

"The men," Cobb said. "Last night. You were inside when it happened, so you didn't see it. When Fred gave the colonel a kick in the pants, it was hard enough to send him tumbling over. Not one of the men laughed. They didn't make a sound."

Hunt blinked a couple of times, questioning. "Meaning?"

"Meaning they were focused on the job at hand," Cobb said. "They aren't a bunch of Comancheros or bandits. They knew what they were doing. They had . . ." He searched his mind for the right word, but it escaped him.

"Discipline." Hunt gestured back toward the station building. "I didn't see much of what happened while I was in there setting things up, but I heard almost everything. I couldn't understand what was so unsettling about it, besides the obvious, of course, but now I do. It was that the men were quiet. The wounded cried out, yes, but the men were still. They were focused and waiting for orders until you and Butch showed up. What if those men didn't run away in fear? What if it was merely a retreat?"

Cobb was glad Hunt had been able to put his own thoughts into words. "I hope that's enough to make you think twice about wearing your iron now."

Hunt responded by thrusting his bag at Cobb to hold. He took out his gun belt and quickly put it on. "I'll ride up in the wagon box with Burke while you and Butch ride ahead. I'll keep watching for any trouble I see from behind as best as I can. I'll fire a shot if I do."

Hunt took his bag and climbed up onto the bench. "Let's hope we have a long, boring ride to Ennisville."

Cobb held his tongue, for the only thing hoping had ever gotten him was disappointment.

* * *

Bowsfield shouted over the arguing of the other remaining Haney men. "I say we all simmer down and stay right here until we figure out what to do next."

Ron Bowsfield hated being in charge, but with Fred and Earl Haney likely dead back at the station, someone in the group had to lead. Ted Moeller, Jim Duren, and Ryan Fowler were all in their twenties, which made Bowsfield by far the oldest at thirty-three. It was only natural that it should be him.

"I hate this!" Moeller kicked dirt into the air. They had ridden away from the carnage at the station in such a hurry that each man had ridden his horse to near exhaustion. They had barely had the presence of mind to picket their horses properly before the horror of all they had survived finally caught up to them. By then, it had already been morning.

"We should've just held our ground and fought alongside the others," Moeller yelled. "I can't believe we just up and ran like that."

"That fella barging in with that shotgun like he did kind of made up my mind for me," Duren said. "Bullets and buckshot flying every which way. After I saw Fred get his head blown off like that, what was the point in staying around? We barely got out of there with our lives as it was."

Fowler, a red-headed Irishman, did little to calm their anger. "We ran off like a bunch of scared rabbits while the others stayed and fought. If we'd done the same, we might've made the difference."

"That's just foolish talk," Duren said. "That shotgun would've torn us to shreds like it did the others who stuck. And that second fella with the rifle was picking us off from the barn like we were no better than ducks. What good would've staying done? You saw what happened to Earl and Rice. We should've let those people stay locked up in the house while we took their horses. We had what we'd come for, but Fred had to make a point of it, didn't he? Over Earl getting killed like he did."

"His brother was shot," Moeller said. "You'd want revenge, too, if it was your brother."

"That would depend on which brother," Duren answered.

All the constant bickering was beginning to give Bowsfield a headache. "Enough! I know you boys are young, but you're old enough to know yelling like this won't get us anywhere. Give me time to think about what we're gonna do next."

"Do?" Moeller said. "There's no need to think about it because there's only one thing we ought to do and that's ride down those fellas and finish what Fred and the others started."

Bowsfield knew that was pointless. "Fred went to that station to get those horses he paid those boys to steal. If you want to take another run for them, I'm willing to give it a try, but going up against those two shooters will get us nothing but dead. That man worked that shotgun like it was a pistol. I never saw anyone reload so fast."

Duren said, "That's the way, Ron. We head back to the station and see who's left. Maybe those shooters have moved on by now. If we go in at night, we could get the horses and be out of there without anyone being the wiser until morning."

Fowler was already shaking his head before Duren finished speaking. "The problem with taking them horses is that we have to find someone willing to buy them. In case you're forgetting, Fred and Earl never told us where we were bringing them. Someone would be sure to notice us eventually, and they might raise a posse to take them back.

We had a better chance of fighting them off when we were twenty, not when it's just the four of us now."

Bowsfield waved him off. "I'd sooner take my chances with a posse than against known killers like them. I say we do that, so that's what we're doing."

Fowler's brogue gave his words a sharper edge than any of the others. "And who exactly decided you were in charge. It's not your decision to make."

Moeller picked up a pebble and threw it into the overgrowth. "There still aren't enough of us to move that many horses and keep anyone from taking them off us. A posse could run us down and string us up from the nearest tree. We can't take that kind of risk, but if we ambush that stagecoach, we just might stand a chance. You saw how old those passengers were. They gave over their goods like it was nothing. We won't get much of a fight from any of them."

Bowsfield was about to lose the thread of his own thoughts. "I say we've got no choice but to head south of here where we know the people and the land. See if we can't pick up with another bunch in Colorado. Live to fight another day, just like Fred taught us."

"That's a long way to travel on empty pockets," Fowler said, "unless you've got some money stashed somewhere I don't know about."

Bowsfield wanted to say they had the baubles they had taken from the passengers but remembered he had handed them over to Earl. For all he knew, they were with their rightful owners by now.

"We can hunt what we need along the way," Duren said. "We don't need much."

"Hunt with what?" Fowler asked. "None of us have rifles, just our pistols." He pulled his Colt Walker and opened the cylinder. "I've got four bullets left. What about you boys?"

Duren frowned. "About that many."

Fowler looked at Moeller. "You?"

"With what I've got in my saddlebags? Twelve." He looked at the ground. "I didn't get off many shots."

Bowsfield did not wait for the Irishman to question him. "I've got less than you, which doesn't prove anything except that we're in a bad way. But we already knew that already before you started talking, so just shut your mouth."

"Sitting around feeling sorry for ourselves won't get us anywhere," Fowler said, "and neither will letting the men who did this to us go free."

Bowsfield felt himself lose his grip on his temper. "Do you think Fred or any of the others would care if we got killed instead of them? You saw how he was when he heard that Concho had been killed. He didn't even care that Rice was in agony. He just wanted him to keep his mouth shut so he wouldn't bother Earl any. He was too angry to realize his brother was already dead when we lowered him off the horse. I don't know about the rest of you boys, but I don't owe the memory of the Haney boys anything."

"That may be," Fowler said, "but what do you owe yourself? Spending the next few weeks foraging around out here like a wild animal? Or taking the chance to put our bad fortunes to some use where it'll do us all some good?"

Bowsfield could see that something in Fowler had changed since last night. He was not talking about taking blind revenge anymore. He had moved beyond that and on to something new. Something different. Something more. "Go on."

Fowler did. "You saw those fancy people in the stage-coach we stopped on the road, didn't you?"

Bowsfield had. "Fred had them put all their finery in your hat before you brought it back to Earl. You didn't keep any of it for yourselves, did you?"

"No," Fowler admitted.

"So, he still had the stuff on him when he got killed." Duren threw up his hands. "Which is all the more reason why we ought to go back to the station and get them. It's easy money."

"You're far slower than I thought," Fowler said. "People like the ones we robbed don't forget about their finery so easily. I'm sure they plucked Earl's corpse clean before he was even cold. In fact, I'm counting on it. Because, as far as I'm concerned, that's rightful property of the Haney gang, and as we're the last of it, that means it belongs to us."

Bowsfield saw the madness in Fowler's eyes but was intrigued by his point. "You plan on robbing them all over again, don't you?"

"I do, indeed," Fowler allowed. "It would practically be a sin not to at least consider it. We know how much they have on them and how much we can expect to take. That's not counting whatever they have stowed in their luggage. I aim to take everything worth taking and more." He poked Duren in the chest with his fingers. "And then, when we have the cash lining our pockets, that's when we decide where to head next. Money isn't everything, but it gives us choices we don't have as we sit here now."

When they had first reached the clearing in the woods the previous night, Bowsfield wondered if they would ever agree on anything, but he was not wondering any longer. Fowler's plan had promise. It was almost too good to pass up. It didn't require them to be anything extra, such as horse rustlers, gunmen, or fugitives. All they had to do was remain something they already were.

Thieves.

Bowsfield was glad he could add something to the discussion. "I think I know where that coach will be headed, too. I'm sure it's probably bound for Laramie, but given the night they've just had, they'll be looking for a taste of civilization first. They can get plenty of that and more in Ennisville."

"That's not much of a plan," Duren said. "Towns mean people and people mean law. What if something goes wrong? What if we get caught? What if they see us and recognize us? What if they just start shooting?"

"They didn't see us," Bowsfield assured him, "and if we do this right, they won't see us now. I say we find out where they're staying tonight and rob their rooms. We can be in and out of town before anyone even knows we've been there. And we make sure we stay far away from those two who busted in and shot at us last night."

Moeller nodded. "I've been to Ennisville a time or two. There's only one place in town where a crowd like that would want to stay. They'll be at the Ennisville Hotel. I'd almost bet my life on it."

"That's good," Fowler said as he put his pistol away. "Because that's exactly what you'll be betting. All of us will. But it's also the place where we'll make our fortune."

CHAPTER 12

Butch knew there was nothing that could put Cobb in a good mood quite like striking a bargain.

After taking all the dead outlaws' horses, saddlery, and gear, they had cleared more than they would have received with a full complement of passengers. The Frontier Overland Company was finally on a firm financial footing, and Cobb could not have been happier.

Butch watched as Jane slid her arm through Cobb's as the three of them walked out of Fregosi's General Store.

"Why Tucker," she said. "I think this is the first time I've seen you smile since the first time I met you."

"I guess I haven't had much reason to smile up until now." Then Cobb remembered himself. "Except for meeting you, of course. This journey's been more troubling than I'd expected it to be."

Butch remained a few steps behind the couple. Cobb had pocketed the money Mr. Fregosi had given to him, though Butch was not certain which pocket Cobb had used. And Jane was awfully close to him. Butch wanted to make sure his friend's pocket was not picked by a sporting lady with fast hands. After all, half of it was his money, too.

Still, Butch saw no reason why he should not try to

keep the atmosphere light. "How do you want to celebrate our good fortune, Cobb? Don't tell me by putting it all in the bank. After the trials we've had this trip, I say we owe it to ourselves to live a little tonight."

"The bank's going to be our first stop," Cobb told him, "but you're right about celebrating. We didn't see any sign of the Haney boys on the ride here, our passengers are all up in their rooms, and we've finally got more than two cents to our name. Why, even Mrs. Wagner didn't fly at us when we told her Joe had decided to stay behind at the station."

Cobb must have seen his old friend's frown, for he added, "But don't you worry, partner. The bank won't get all of it. I plan on holding just enough back to give us a night to remember." He patted Miss Jane's hand. "I sure hope you're hungry because you've got quite a meal waiting for you in the best place in town."

Butch kept an eye on the boardwalks on both sides of the thoroughfare as Cobb boasted about how much money he was going to spend that night. And since Cobb did not like saloons or gambling halls, there was no chance that his partner would waste their small fortune on whiskey or games of chance.

Butch knew that on the rare occasions he had known Tucker Cobb to have money, he spent it sensibly, with one exception. He liked to spend big on good meals, which was why Butch was glad they had come into money here in Ennisville rather than in Laramie. Options for fine dining in Ennisville were limited at best, so that should leave a bit over for more than a couple of drinks in the saloon. He had noticed a couple of dining rooms that looked decent, but nothing that would put them in the poorhouse.

Butch paid close attention to the saloons they passed

on their way to the bank. The establishments were doing a sparse business given that it was still the late afternoon, but Butch imagined that was bound to change later that evening. The smaller the town, the faster word traveled, and it would not take long for people to know that Cobb and Butch had come into quite a bit of money.

With a few members of Fred Haney's old gang still running around on the loose, Butch would have to remain vigilant. He doubted the cowards who had run away from the gunfight would come after them in town, but he'd never thought anyone would go to the trouble of stealing a bunch of horses from a stagecoach station, either.

Butch knew the world sure had gone and changed quite a bit in the time since the war, and he imagined it would go right on changing for the foreseeable future. He had noticed that outlaws were often products of their times and doubted Haney's men would be an exception. Anything was possible from such men at any time.

Butch turned and dropped to a crouch and raised his rifle when he heard a man call out to them from behind. "Mr. Cobb! Mr. Keeling! A word, please."

Butch lowered it as soon as he saw the star on the man's chest. He quickly recognized the man wearing it. Fritz Brickell was both the county sheriff and the town marshal for Ennisville.

He was taller and thinner than most, and Butch thought his clothes always looked too big on him. He sported a thin beard and eyes the color of dishwater that never settled on one thing too long.

Cobb and Butch had made the lawman's acquaintance several times when they'd happened through town over the years, but they could hardly be called friends. There had always been something about the lawman that set Butch on edge. Cobb, too. Every lawman had to endure whispers of corruption from unhappy citizens, but the whispers about Brickell were louder than normal.

Cobb and Jane slowly turned as Brickell approached.

"Afternoon, Sheriff," Cobb greeted him. He was still enjoying the afterglow of his good financial fortunes. "What can I do for you this fine day?"

Brickell made a show of acting like he was slightly out of breath, though Butch knew he had not been moving fast enough for that. It was probably his way of taking the sting out of whatever reasons he had for stopping them.

He touched the brim of his bowler to Jane. "Good afternoon, miss. You too, Butch. I was hoping you might excuse us for a moment. I'd like to have a word with Mr. Cobb in private."

"No need for privacy," Cobb said. "Anything you have to say to me, you can say in front of Butch. We're partners."

Brickell glanced at Jane. "And the lady?"

"Is with me."

"Of course." Brickell smiled. "I was just over at Fregosi's General Store. I saw you come into town with a stage that wasn't yours and quite a string of horses behind you. I was hoping you might be willing to tell me where you got them. The horses you sold, I mean."

"I don't see as how that's any business of yours," Butch said. "Cobb's got a bill of sale right there in his pocket."

"The law is my business," Brickell told him. He tapped the badge on his chest with his thumb. "This here star makes it my business. And when an old freighter like you comes into town with horses, tack, and rifles to sell, well, I do my best to find out how he happened to come upon such a bounty. I need to make sure no laws have been broken. We wouldn't want our fair town to be overrun by a criminal element, now, would we? Those empty saddles sure have raised a lot of questions."

Butch had always known Tucker Cobb to be an honest and law-abiding man, but he was also a solitary individual who avoided crowds and preferred to keep to himself when he could. He did not have many friends and had not sought any. In fact, Butch counted himself among the few people who knew Cobb reasonably well, and he did not know all that much about him, save that he trusted him with his life. Sometimes that was enough.

"I came upon them legally," Cobb said. "Out at Delaware Station, which I'm pretty sure isn't in your jurisdiction."

"The matter of whether or not Gene Bridges's place is in my jurisdiction has never been properly settled. But since you sold those horses here in my town, I have the right to ask about how you got them. It ought to be a simple answer."

Cobb cleared his throat, which Butch knew was a sign that his partner was getting annoyed.

"There was some trouble out there yesterday," Cobb told him. "Some thieves stole all their horses. Killed their stable hand in the process. A nice fella by the name of Del. I don't feel right about telling you what they did to him with a lady present."

Brickell scratched at his beard. "Del. He was the simpleton Gene kept around the place to do odd chores and such."

"He was a good man," Butch said, "and someone killed him."

"I didn't say he wasn't," the sheriff answered. "What happened then?"

"Me and one of my passengers tracked the stolen horses to where the thieves were holding them," Cobb explained. "They weren't too happy to see us, and we were forced to defend ourselves. After that, we took the horses and brought them back to the station where they belonged. It was all perfectly legal."

Brickell listened as he ran his hand under his beard. "You said this all happened yesterday. I believe I saw your stage arrive here in town just before dark last night. Why didn't you tell me about what had happened as soon as you got here?"

Butch answered for him. "We didn't have time, Sheriff. The thieves said they were fixing to sell the horses to some men we feared wouldn't be too happy when they found the horses were gone. Cobb and me traded for a couple of mustangs over at the livery and headed back to the station. A good thing we did, too, because there were some men holding the Bridges family and some others hostage. You might say Cobb and me helped free them."

"Traded with what?"

Butch was glad he had an answer for him. Unfortunately, the answer died in his mouth before he said it. He realized he had already said too much.

Cobb said, "We traded the horses we took from the thieves."

"Ah, now I see." Brickell tapped his beard. "Last night, you had dead men's horses to trade and today you have more dead men's horses to sell. Did I get that right?"

"Not the way you just said it, you don't."

"Don't see as there's any other way to say it," Brickell persisted. "You were well within the bounds of the law both times and seem to have profited handsomely from your heroics both times, too."

Cobb's jaw tightened. "What's that supposed to mean?"

"Just trying to get my facts straight, Mr. Cobb," the sheriff said. "You tell me Del is dead—and I'm truly sorry to hear that—but instead of reporting the incident to me, you got fresh horses and went back out, only to come back this afternoon with more than twice the horses you had with you yesterday." He smiled. "That's mighty convenient, don't you think?"

Now Butch was becoming annoyed. "And that's a mighty ugly accusation to make without any proof."

Brickell gestured toward the money bulging in Cobb's pocket. "All the evidence I need is right there in front of me. Fregosi said he paid you handsomely for your work. I take it you're on your way to the bank to make a deposit."

"And what if I am?" Cobb asked.

"I'm afraid I'd have to stop you if that was the case," the sheriff said. "Given that I can't be sure how you came by all of this horseflesh, I'm afraid I can't let you keep it. I'll have to seize it until I have a chance to do a proper investigation. I'm sure you understand."

Jane gasped as Cobb took a step forward between her and the sheriff and said, "I *don't* understand, but you're welcome to try and take it, Brickell."

Butch stepped in front of Cobb to hold him back. It was clear that Brickell would have liked nothing better than to have a reason to throw Cobb in jail. Butch did not want to give him the excuse.

Butch said, "I was a lawman in Texas, Brickell. You need to have evidence of a crime being committed before you take our money."

Brickell laughed again. "Wyoming's a long way from Texas, Mr. Keeling. We do things a bit different here in a civilized part of the world."

"You'll find out how close it is if you try to rip us off."

Brickell's smile faded quickly. "I have every legal right to take your money if I have reasonable suspicion that it was obtained in the course of an illegal act. You've both just admitted to me that you killed men, took their horses, and profited from it. You may have been within your rights to do so, but I have every right to look into the matter. I have no choice but to seize that money until I've had the chance to determine you were in the right." Brickell looked beyond Cobb and Jane as he said, "And my deputies here agree with me."

Butch and Cobb looked around and saw two men standing behind them. They had deputy stars pinned to their shirts, and both of them had their hands on the pistols on their hips.

Butch heard Cobb's knuckles crack as he balled his hands into fists. "Well, this sure is a first. I've never been robbed by a sheriff before."

Brickell held out his hand. "The money, Mr. Cobb, or I'll arrest you for interfering with a peace officer." He smiled at Jane. "You'll spend the rest of the night in jail and miss out on enjoying such pleasant company."

Butch could see that arguing the point with the sheriff would not get them anywhere. Brickell wanted the money and had the men to take it. "Might as well give it over to him, Cobb. The money, I mean."

Cobb dug his hand into his pocket and produced the money. He slapped the wad into Brickell's hand. "I want a receipt for that. I expect to get back every cent once you've finished your *investigation*."

Brickell licked his thumb as he began to peel the bills in the wad in front of them. When he finished counting, he stuck the money in the pocket of his vest, produced a pad and pencil, and wrote out a receipt. "You'll get back every penny coming to you, minus investigation expenses, of course. Enforcing the law is an expensive enterprise, even here in Ennisville."

"But a profitable one, I'm sure," Jane said as she took Cobb's hand.

Brickell signed the receipt and handed it to Butch.

"You should keep this for your records. I wouldn't want any discrepancy on how much you're owed, assuming, of course, I clear you of any wrongdoing."

Butch read the receipt and saw the amount was far less than Fregosi had given them. He glanced back at Cobb but could tell by his partner's expression that he should keep his mouth shut. He pocketed the receipt instead. "Perish the thought."

The sheriff pocketed the pad and pencil. "You said there were other witnesses to what happened at the station last night. I take it they're currently staying in the hotel?"

Cobb said, "The Becquers and the McBrides will be happy to tell you everything that happened. Mr. Leon Hunt was there the entire time, too. So was the coach driver, Leo Burke. Mrs. Wagner, Mr. Koppe, and Reverend Averill were there after the thievery, but spent last night here."

"I'll be sure to add them all to my list," Brickell said.

Jane said, "You can start by questioning me, too, Sheriff. I was a passenger at the station when Tucker and Butch found the horses had been stolen. I'll be happy to give a statement to that effect."

"A witness of unimpeachable character, I'm sure," Brickell sneered. "Your reputation from North Branch precedes you, Ms. Duprey."

Cobb brought his hand back to punch him, but Butch grabbed him and tried to move him aside. "Easy, Cobb, easy. That's what he wants. Don't give him the satisfaction."

The sheriff told his deputies, "Bring the lovely lady with us back to the jail so I can take down her statement. Then head over to the hotel and question the Becquers and the McBrides." He pointed at Cobb and Butch. "I know you boys have a stagecoach line to run, but don't leave town until I give you permission. Your passengers will have to make other arrangements to continue on to Laramie."

Butch had half a mind to let Cobb go. "Is that really necessary, Sheriff?"

"I'm afraid so," Brickell said, though he did not sound like he was. "I'll try to conclude my investigation as quickly as possible, but I'm sure you can understand how long these things can take. You were a lawman in Texas after all, weren't you?"

Brickell beckoned Jane to follow him. "Come along, miss. I'm sure you're anxious to get on with your evening."

Jane followed him as Cobb pulled himself free from Butch's grip. "I'm coming along with you."

Brickell spoke over his shoulder. "I conduct my questioning alone, Cobb. You're welcome to wait outside if you want, but if you step one foot inside my jail, I'll lock you in a cell."

Cobb and Butch remained where they had been stopped on the boardwalk as Brickell escorted Jane toward the jail on the other side of the thoroughfare. The deputies took their time following.

When he was sure they were well out of earshot, Butch said, "That money was less than half of what Fregosi gave you just now. I heard the price you two agreed upon."

"I gave him our poke from our passengers," Cobb said. "Fregosi's money is in my coat pocket, but he didn't know that. He was probably lying about talking to Fregosi, too. He couldn't have talked to him and caught up to us so fast. He was just fishing."

Sometimes, Butch was surprised by how cunning Tucker Cobb could be. "What do you want to do now?"

Cobb began walking toward the bank. "Let's get to the bank and deposit it before that idiot figures out it's not enough for all those horses."

They waited until the others had moved farther up the street before heading toward the bank. Butch knew he would have quite a time keeping Cobb's temper in check. He was calm now because he had a job to do, but after the bank, his pride would start gnawing at him and there would be trouble. He wanted to keep his partner's mind on business.

"We'll have to go back to the hotel to let Mrs. Wagner and the others know that they'll have to go with Burke to Laramie. The sheriff will keep us here a couple of days at least."

Cobb picked up his pace as they approached the bank. "One problem at a time, Butch. One problem at a time."

CHAPTER 13

Bowsfield and his partners had been tracking Cobb and Butch from the street that ran parallel to the thoroughfare. They did not want to risk being spotted by trailing them on the boardwalk.

After seeing Cobb and Keeling's encounter with the sheriff from the safety of an alleyway, Bowsfield gathered the others out of the alley toward the street that ran parallel to the main thoroughfare.

"Did you hear that?" Moeller asked aloud. "That sheriff's a thief same as us."

"Don't sound so happy about it," Fowler said. "A lawman who's as crooked as a dog's hind leg is dangerous to men like us. I don't know whether we should cheer or cry."

Duren said, "If we'd just gone back and grabbed them horses like I wanted, we'd be well clear of this place by now."

Bowsfield had heard enough about Delaware Station. "Shut up. We're passed all that now. A crooked sheriff doesn't change our plans. Those rich folks are still up in the hotel, and that's what's important. When it gets dark and they've all gone to bed, we'll move in and rob them just like we said we would."

Moeller said, "We can't just go busting into rooms at random. We need to know where they're staying. I don't want to kick in a door and face Cobb."

"Or Butch," Duren added.

Bowsfield already had an idea for that. "I want everyone to turn out their pockets. I need to know how much money we have."

None of the others were in a hurry to comply, with Fowler saying, "We came here to steal money, Ron, not spend it."

Bowsfield hated that he had to explain every step to this pack of pups. "They're liable to throw us out on our ear if we walk in there looking like a bunch of broke cowhands. The man at the desk is liable to want to see our money first. I figure that while Fowler here flashes it and chats him up, I'll look over the registry and find out where those rich couples are staying."

"What happens after that?" Moeller asked. "You two go inside, and what are me and Duren gonna do?"

"We're looking for information, not a room," Bowsfield said. "It can't hurt for us to look the place over a little first. I figure we can sneak in the back, rob them folks, then head out the same way."

Bowsfield knew he probably should not lay out his entire plan at first, but since he was talking, it was hard for him to stop. "Three of us will go in while one stays outside with the horses and to keep an eye out for deputies. We rob those old folks, come back down, get on our horses, and make a run for it in the dark. But none of that is gonna happen unless I get a look at the registry first, and that'll take money, so give."

Bowsfield took off his hat and thrust it at them after dumping in three dollars. After the others put in their money, he had almost five dollars.

He scooped out the money and handed it to Fowler. "Flash this to the clerk when we talk to him. You'll get it all back and more after we split our take."

"Don't see why we had to fork it over now," Duren said. "Given how it'll be hours yet before dark. A lot can happen between now and then."

Fowler said, "The whiner here has a point, Ron. If we go to the hotel now, we might catch the clerk unawares. He's liable to forget all about us until well after the deed is done. If we wait until night, it might put him on his guard."

Bowsfield knew he had to give the others something if he hoped to avoid a revolt, so he did not argue with them. "Fine. We'll do it now. Moeller and Duren, you stay back here. We'll come to get you after we've had a look around that hotel and the register."

Duren grabbed Bowsfield's arm as he tried to leave. "Don't forget to come back with our money. It might not be much, but it's all we've got."

Bowsfield fought the urge to backhand the ignorant boy and pulled his hand free instead. Fowler followed him out of the alley and joined him as they tried to look casual as they approached the hotel.

Leon Hunt inhaled the rich aroma of the coffee before he took a sip. The sharp taste hit home, and he closed his eyes in pure delight. Sitting in the lobby , even in a place like the Ennisville Hotel, and drinking coffee from a silver service was his idea of paradise. His years on the stage had taught him how to enjoy the comfort in such surroundings when he could. Luxuries were worth the expense, even on an actor's meager salary. It was all but kindling for the creative fire that burned within him.

His eyes were still closed when he heard a young man out in the lobby say, "Hey, mister. My friend and me might want a room for the night."

Hunt concentrated on the sound. There was something familiar about it, as if he had heard it before. Looking at the man would only clutter his thoughts, so he sat quietly with his eyes closed and continued to listen.

"Rooms mean money," the clerk said, "and we don't take payment in trail dust. If we did, you two look like you could afford the Presidential Suite, assuming we had one."

"We have money" a second man said. "No fear of that. The only question is if this place lives up to our standards. My friend and I have expensive tastes and the money to pay for it."

Some Americans had difficulty distinguishing one foreign accent from another, but not Hunt. He had acted with many from Western Europe, and this second man's brogue was unmistakable. An Irishman, to be sure.

While the clerk explained the qualities of the hotel, Hunt opened his eyes and squinted at the two men. From what he could make out, the clerk had reason to be suspicious. They seemed to have the rough-hewn look of men who had spent the better part of their lives in the saddle. He could see the Irishman's hair was longish and red, and Hunt wondered how much teasing he'd had to endure in his life from his friends.

The first man who had spoken was quieter and clearly older. He was also doing a poor job of appearing disinterested in the hotel's guest registry in front of him. He constantly moved his head and shifted his weight as if bored, though he did not look up from the book or away from it, either.

Interesting.

The redhead put on airs as he looked around the lobby.

"I take it you've got decent food here?" He was clearly not to the manor born but was mimicking what he had seen others do. Hunt recognized a fellow actor when he saw one.

As the clerk told him about the dining options in the hotel and the rest of Ennisville, the Irishman's friend gave up any attempt to look disinterested in the ledger. The man slowly turned the book to get a closer look.

Most interesting, indeed.

Hunt heard the scraping sound as the clerk placed a hand on the registry and the cover graze the wood as he turned it back toward him. "Now, assuming I've answered all of your questions, do you gentlemen want a room or not?"

The Irishman straightened as if he had been insulted. "I'm not sure we like your tone, mister. Do we, Ronald?"

"Can't say as I do." Hunt was sure he had heard that voice before, perhaps at a higher pitch. "I say we ought to go see if we can find a friendlier place to stay."

Hunt decided these two were a curious pair and, as they were about to leave, decided to prod them a little to see what happened.

"Give the lads the benefit of the doubt," Hunt called out to the clerk. "An Englishman is always a fine addition to any establishment. They lend a certain degree of sophistication every time they open their mouths, don't you think?"

The first man had already moved to leave, but Hunt's words froze the redhead in place. He seemed to slowly turn to face Hunt. "What was that you just said, fella?"

Hunt sat back on the sofa. "I was merely extolling the virtues of your homeland, sir. I assure you I meant no offense."

"I'm plenty offended. I'm an Irishman, not a blasted Englishman. You'll live longer if you note the difference."

Hunt allowed his left hand to fall toward the pistol on his hip. The youth had not realized the object of his scorn was armed until then. "Of course. I hear the brogue clearly now. My mistake." He allowed his eyes to remain on the lad. "One I assure you I won't make again."

The first man reached back and pulled the redhead with him as they went outside.

Hunt picked up his cup and saucer and took another sip of coffee. Ennisville might not be as boring as he had feared.

Cobb continued to pace back and forth on the boardwalk across the street from the jail while he waited for Jane to step outside.

"What's keeping her so long? How long should it take to write down a simple statement? She's almost been in there longer than she was at the station."

Butch had chosen to lean against a hitching rail. "It takes as long as Brickell wants it to take. If you keep storming around like this, some Mexican's liable to come along and wave a red cape in front of you."

"I'd have half a mind to charge at it," Cobb said. "We were standing right here when he sent his men to the hotel to question the others. They've been back for more than an hour now. Jane didn't see enough to warrant this much attention."

"The sheriff's bound to have seen you stalking around out here," Butch noted. "He's probably just taking his time to grate on your nerves. The worst thing you can do is give him the satisfaction, and that's just what you're doing."

Cobb knew Butch was right, but he had more on his mind than being wrong. "You know I've never been a patient man. He's got it out for us because he knows we have money."

Butch spat tobacco juice into the street. "There's a lot more to it than that. I think you've gone and developed feelings for that woman."

Cobb knew better than to deny it. He knew what she had done for a living. Everyone in that part of the territory probably knew it, and Cobb did not care. He had never been one to hold a person's profession against them. Some of the worst scoundrels he had ever known had been doctors and lawyers, just as some of the most generous had been the poorest.

A woman's station in life did not always speak to her decency, and neither did Jane's. The way she looked at him may have been the practiced look of a seductress, but she had given it to him, not just anyone. Not to Butch or to Hunt or even young Joe, but to him, and he valued it for whatever it was worth. Right now, it was worth quite a bit to him. He would not have been concerned about her well-being otherwise.

"Of course, I've developed feelings for her," Cobb said. "I'm not blind and I'm not dead. Not yet, anyway."

"Just glad to hear you finally admit it. Gives me hope that you're not entirely a lost cause."

Sometimes Butch chose the worst time to tease him. "Knock it off. I'm busy."

Cobb stopped pacing when he saw the jailhouse door open and Jane step outside.

Fritz Brickell held his hat over his heart as he made his goodbyes. The sheriff made sure he locked eyes with Cobb and offered a smirk before slowly shutting the door.

Cobb could hardly wait for her to cross the street. He began firing questions at her as soon as she joined him on the boardwalk. "Why did he keep you in there for so long? What sort of questions did he ask you? Did he tell you what his deputies found out from the others at the hotel?"

Butch said, "Give the woman a chance to breathe, Cobb. She's hardly been outside for a minute yet. She's been questioned enough for one day."

Cobb knew his social graces left something to be desired, and he forced himself to stop asking so many questions. "I'm sorry about that, Jane. I'm just sorry that he kept you in there for so long on account of me."

"I can assure you I'm made of sterner stuff than that." Jane placed her arm through his as she led him toward the hotel. "It takes a lot more than a talkative sheriff to rattle me, and Fritz Brickell is certainly a man who loves to talk. He's more in love with the sound of his own voice than he could ever be with a woman."

Cobb struggled to tamp down his questions and let Jane tell it in her own time.

She went on. "I know he took your money earlier, but I need to get something to eat. I'm famished, and answering all of his questions was a lot of work. I can pay for my portion of the meal, if necessary."

Butch said, "We're not exactly destitute. Old Cobb's always been a wily one when it comes to money. He squirreled away enough to provide us with a decent meal."

Cobb glared back at him. "That mouth of yours is going to land me in the poorhouse one day."

"A house that pours is just what I need right now," Jane said, "and the stronger the whiskey, the better."

Cobb wanted to kick in the door and throw the sheriff a beating he would not soon forget, but knew that would not accomplish much. "Was it really that bad? What did he ask you all that time?"

"Brickell is quite a character," she told him. "He took down my statement in no time at all. He asked me to explain a few particulars, added them to my statement, then gave it to me to read before I signed it."

Cobb was worried for her. That signature made her statement legal and binding. If Brickell found—or created—another version of what had happened at Delaware Station, he could charge her with lying under oath. "Did you read it over close? Did he add anything to it? Any details that reflected poorly on Butch and me?"

"I'm not a fool, Tucker," she said. "I've seen legal documents before. I never sign something without reading it first. I made sure the sheriff took down my statement exactly as I'd told it to him. After I signed it, I expected to be on my way. But by then Brickell started talking about North Branch and Ennisville and how similar the two towns were to each other. He asked me about people he thought we both knew."

Cobb had feared that Brickell would use the statement as a way to get her to talk about her line of work. "Did he ask about friends of yours?" He tried to think of another word for it. "Acquaintances, maybe?"

Jane looked at Butch. "Is he always like this?"

"If you mean gruff and lacking general manners," Butch said, "then my answer is yes."

Cobb felt himself begin to blush. "How else am I supposed to say it?"

"If you mean business associates," Jane went on, "he hinted at them, but didn't ask me directly about them. He wanted to know how long I was planning to remain in Ennisville, and I assured him we would be leaving for Laramie as soon as he finished his investigation into you.

I should've been out of there an hour ago, but I didn't want to be rude. It was the strangest thing."

Cobb knew there had to be something else. Something Brickell had done or said that had been important, but that Jane might have missed. "What is it?"

"For the entire time we were talking, he just kept on gazing out the window as he came up with another topic to talk about."

Butch slapped Cobb on the shoulder. "See that? He was looking at you. I—"

Cobb had already heard enough from his partner. "If the words 'I told you so' are about to come out of that mouth of yours, you'll be paying for your own meal tonight."

Butch swallowed his words and cut loose with a stream of tobacco juice into the street instead.

Cobb asked Jane, "Did you see him talk to the deputies after they got back from the hotel? I think they went there to take down statements from the colonel and the others."

Jane frowned as she shook her head. "No. I'm afraid I didn't. I saw them hand him papers that could have been statements, but Brickell didn't bother to look at them. He was too focused on me and making you boys wait. I'm sorry I couldn't have found a way to get out of there earlier."

Cobb hated thinking that he had played a part in anything that might have caused her discomfort. "I'm the one who ought to be sorry. If I hadn't ruffled his feathers earlier on the street, he might've gone easier on you. I guess I'm not used to being at another man's mercy is all, even if he happens to be a sheriff."

Jane pulled his arm tighter against her as they walked. "Well, you can make it up to Butch and me by buying us that fancy dinner you promised. Sound like a deal?"

Cobb felt his frustration melt away beneath her warm smile. "Deal. Though Butch here will have to make do with some moldy bread and water."

"As long as they put some whiskey in it first, I'll be grateful," Butch said. "Watching you wear out a hole in the boardwalk back there has given me a mighty thirst."

CHAPTER 14

Later that afternoon, Hunt was glad he had accepted an invitation from Colonel McBride to join him and his friends for dinner in the dining room of the hotel. The idea of refusing such a generous offer never crossed Hunt's mind. A meal always tasted twice as good when someone else was paying for it.

Hunt had dressed for the occasion in his finest black suit and came prepared to entertain them through the dinner. The actor knew he would be expected to perform some kind of entertainment for the evening, and he prepared for this mentally. Actors were accustomed to singing for their supper.

Colonel McBride sat at the head of the table, appearing regal as his guests drank wine and engaged in conversation between courses. Hunt entertained them with thrilling stories of his life on and off the stage. He spoke of the actors he had met, the roles he had played, and the many places he had been. Some of it was even true.

Mrs. Becquer had laughed the loudest and longest at his stories, which only encouraged him to make them even grander and more outrageous. He had never been able to resist the temptation of playing to a friendly audience.

"Come now, Mr. Hunt," she chided him during a rare quiet moment. "You don't expect me to believe that you *really* met Charles Dickens, now do you?"

"I certainly do because I did," Hunt lied. "Or, should I say, he met me. We quite literally ran into each other while he was coming out of Delmonico's one foggy evening, though I can assure you he was in no state to remember it."

Mrs. Wagner, who had been a late addition to the meal, frowned while the others laughed. "Actors. Writers. They're all just drunken wastrels." She scowled at Hunt. "And here I was thinking you were willing to leave all of that behind you when you joined my ministry. I see now that all it took was a few sips of wine for you to slip right back into your decadent ways."

Hunt feigned humility as he bowed his head to her. "I beg your forgiveness, Your Grace. The merriment of the occasion overwhelmed me."

She bristled while the rest of the party enjoyed a hearty laugh at her expense. Even Mr. Koppe had to hide a smile behind his napkin.

The laughter had just begun to run its course as Hunt noticed a man with a sheriff's star on his vest had entered the dining room. The lawman had removed his bowler hat as he slowly approached their table. Hunt felt he was conveying a sense of humility he did not truly feel.

Colonel McBride had stopped laughing when he saw the lawman coming their way. "And just who might you be?"

The stranger offered half a smile. "I hate to interrupt your supper like this, but I'm Fritz Brickell. I'm the sheriff here in Ennisville as well as the town marshal, so you could say I've come here tonight in a dual capacity."

"Ah, yes, Brickell. I remember your name." Hunt saw the colonel was not impressed. "Each of us here have already given our sworn statements to the men you'd sent over earlier this afternoon. They were duly sworn and signed. I have nothing to add to it except to clarify that Mr. Cobb and Mr. Keeling saved our lives. Were they under my command, I would've seen to it that both of them were promoted and given a medal for their brave efforts."

Brickell fidgeted with his hat as he said, "I understand, Colonel, and I'm sorry to have to bother you again so soon, but your statements are the reason why I'm here. I'm sure you're as anxious as I am to conclude this matter quickly so that Cobb and Butch can be on their way."

"As so they should," McBride said. "They should be given a hero's farewell. You should thank them, too, for having restored order where there was none." He reached for and took his wife's hand in his own. "Those two brave men saved our lives."

"I know they did," Brickell persisted, "but the only problem is that some of the statements you and the Becquers gave were almost identical. In fact, I thought they might've been written by the same person until my deputies told me they saw you write them out yourselves."

"There's no cause for alarm in that," Mr. Becquer said. "We all saw the same thing from the same place at the same time, so it stands to reason that our statements would be similar."

Brickell offered a weak smile. "Perhaps, but no two people see something the exact same way. And when my deputies told me they questioned you all as a group while you were at luncheon today, I realized what the problem was. I prefer to get statements from witnesses individually so I can get a clearer notion of what really happened. Something closer to the truth, I mean."

Hunt watched the colonel's dark eyes flash and knew his growing anger was no act.

"Truth?" McBride said as he slowly began to rise. "Truth, you say? Are you implying that our sworn statements are false? That we lied about what we witnessed at Delaware Station last night? That we lied about almost losing our lives at the whim of a murderous outlaw? That my companions lied?" He stomped the floor with his walking stick. "That my wife lied and that I committed perjury?"

Hunt noticed that Brickell, in his defense, readily ceded ground to the colonel. "I'm not saying that at all, sir. I appreciate the horror you survived at Delaware Station, but it's my job to determine what really happened there. In fact, Cobb and Butch's freedom depends on it. I thought that since you say you owe them so much that you'd be happy to answer a few of my questions in private."

Hunt watched McBride's neck begin to redden as his wife touched his hand. "Louis. Remember yourself."

Hunt saw McBride remained rigid. "Do you know who I am, Sheriff?"

"I certainly do, sir," Brickell said. "I know you have a very important position with the Wyoming Mining Company."

"As does Mr. Becquer," McBride added. "We both happen to be attorneys, as well. I don't know what Mrs. Wagner or Mr. Koppe or Reverend Averill told you, but I'm sure it was the truth as they saw it. But none of them were at Delaware Station last night. The members of my party were there, which explains the similarities in each of our statements. We stand by that which we have already said and have neither the desire nor the need to amend them now. I'll take any further claims to the contrary as a personal insult."

The colonel placed one hand over the other atop his walking stick. "There are some men those in your position should not seek to insult, Sheriff Brickell. I assure you I am one of those men."

Hunt could see that the sheriff was not acting when he swallowed heavily. It was clear why McBride had risen to the rank of colonel in the war.

Hunt could not allow the tension that had settled over the dinner to continue without trying to be part of it. "Sheriff Brickell, I must admit that I'm rather hurt that you didn't wish to revisit my statement with me. I was there longer than any of them, including Mr. Cobb and Mr. Keeling."

The sheriff looked down at his hat. "Your statement was elaborate enough, Mr. Hunt. It took you a while to get to the point, but let's just say it's a unique perspective."

Hunt smiled. "If brevity is the soul of wit, then I am content to be a dullard."

The rest of the party laughed, except for Colonel McBride, whose neck was still red as he retook his seat. "You have everyone's statements in full, Sheriff. Now, I'm sure you have other duties to tend to while my friends and I continue our supper in peace. I bid you a good evening."

Brickell stood where he was, clearly not expecting to have been dismissed by McBride so easily.

Hunt felt a small measure of pity for the man and thought of something that might allow him to make a graceful exit with some of his dignity intact.

"Sheriff, I was having my coffee today when a pair of interesting gentlemen stopped by the front desk. I think they might be worthy of your attention."

Brickell looked up from his hat. "That so? What was so special about them?"

"One of them was an American," Hunt said, "while the other was an Irishman."

The sheriff's spirits did not improve. "This is Ennisville, Mr. Hunt. You can't look ten feet in any direction around here without spotting an Irishman."

"This one is easy," Hunt explained. "He has red hair and a surly disposition."

Brickell began to walk away. "Being a surly redhead isn't against the law."

Hunt was not finished yet and wanted to speak his mind in full. "But vagrancy is."

Brickell stopped at the doorway. "If they get drunk and out of hand, I'll lock them up for the night. Thanks for the warning."

Hunt said, "They made like they were interested in renting a room here, but I don't think they were. One of them seemed particularly interested in the hotel's registry."

That had been enough to get Brickell's attention. "Cowpunchers never try to stay here."

"Which was why it struck me odd and why I thought you should know about them," Hunt explained. "After they examined the register, they picked a fight with the clerk and used it as an excuse to leave. It was all rather strange. The clerk out front might be able to give you a better description of them than me."

"There's no crime in not renting a room," Brickell said, "but I'll have my boys keep an eye out for them." He offered a curt nod as he moved away. "I'll let you folks go back to enjoying your meal."

Hunt waited until he was sure the sheriff had probably left before saying, "Now there goes a man who knows how to make a graceful exit."

The dark mood began to crack, and Hunt wanted to set it aside entirely. Tension was bad for the digestion, and they had all just enjoyed a rich meal. Knowing Mrs. Wagner was an easy target, he turned to her and asked, "Come, Your Grace. Tell us how many souls you plan on saving in Laramie. Did you have a specific number in mind or are you content to allow fate to play a role in your ministry?"

They laughed more at Mrs. Wagner's reaction than Hunt's question, which had been the actor's aim. His tools of deception were as sharp as ever.

Later that night, Bowsfield waited for the last window in front of the hotel to go dark before gesturing for the others to follow him. He had already sent Duren to look through the front window of the hotel to confirm that the dining room and parlor were empty. Now that he had returned, it was time to move.

They climbed atop their horses and slowly rode them down the back street of Ennisville. Bowsfield allowed the horses to move at their own pace. Speed would only make noise and noise might draw attention. They needed quiet now. His plan only worked if no one saw them.

They rode down to the edge of town, crossed the darkened thoroughfare, and went up the back street toward the rear of the hotel. All the shops had already closed and the staff at the few dining halls still open were cleaning up. The saloons were doing a decent business but were hardly crowded. That was a good sign. Fewer people around meant fewer problems.

Bowsfield had spent the past several hours since examining the guest register in plotting the theft. Sheriff Fritz Brickell and his deputies were a concern, but from what Duren had reported, they preferred to remain in the jail and play cards. They had patrolled the streets before dark, and Bowsfield imagined they would do so again later that evening, maybe around ten or so. If all went according to plan, the last remnants of the Haney gang would be long done by then.

Bowsfield and the others had been careful to not draw any attention to themselves during the daytime, preferring to hole up in a quiet saloon with a view of the street. They nursed beers while they finalized a plan. Even Fowler had agreed without much debate.

According to the registry, the Becquers and the McBrides had been given rooms at the front on the second floor of the hotel. Closer to the lobby meant fewer steps to climb. Each room had a balcony that overlooked the thoroughfare.

Since the rooms were right next to each other, Bowsfield figured they could hit both rooms at once. Given that McBride had been a colonel, Bowsfield and Moeller would take him and his wife while Fowler robbed the more docile Becquers. Duren would remain in the alley with the horses and keep an eye out for trouble.

Bowsfield slowed his horse to a walk as they reached two buildings away from the hotel. He climbed down from the saddle and handed the reins up to Duren. Fowler and Moeller did the same.

Bowsfield whispered to Duren, "Stay back here with the horses until you see one of us come out with the loot, then bring up the horses."

Bowsfield thought he saw Duren's hand shaking as he took the reins of the three animals. He hoped the boy had not lost his nerve back at Delaware Station.

Bowsfield pulled his kerchief over his face. Fowler and Moeller did so as well as he led them toward the back door of the hotel. He paused to listen for anyone who might be approaching, but hearing nothing, slipped inside. The two others followed.

They took the back service steps up to the rooms. Bowsfield ascended two steps at a time. He was glad they were carpeted, for it blunted any creaking sounds from their weight.

Bowsfield drew his pistol as he reached the second floor and crept toward Room One and Room Two. Fowler remained at the door to Room Two where the Becquers slept while Bowsfield and Moeller proceeded to Room One. He was glad they were the only rooms on the floor. There was less of a risk of anyone making a sound and alerting the others.

Bowsfield and Fowler pressed their backs against the opposite wall as they brought up their legs to kick in their respective doors.

Both doors crashed open at the same time, and Bowsfield moved in on the McBrides. He had his hand over Mrs. McBride's mouth as she began to scream and held his pistol on the colonel as Moeller moved around the bed to silence him.

"Keep quiet and no one gets hurt," Bowsfield whispered. "We're just here for the money, not for blood, but we'll have that, too, if you make us. Now, turn over on your stomachs and bury your faces in them pillows while my friend ties your hands behind you. You put up a fuss or make a sound, you die."

As they had decided in the saloon earlier, Moeller was in charge of binding their hands. He cut pieces of the curtains ties from the windows and used them to gag them and tie their hands behind their backs.

Moeller kept the couple covered as Bowsfield set to rifling through their belongings. He had seen the finery they had handed over to Fred back at the stagecoach, so he knew what to look for. He found most of the stuff on the dresser along with some more jewelry they must have had stowed in their luggage.

Bowsfield took the sack he had brought with him and began to slide everything he could find into it. A gold cigar case caught his eye, and he knew it would fetch a fine price.

He quickly picked through their open trunks but saw nothing of any value except clothes. Since speed was important, he did not want to take the time to look for more. They already had plenty.

He told Moeller, quietly, "Check next door and come right back."

Bowsfield enjoyed the sight of the couple looking humble now that they were bound and gagged like pigs on a spit. The colonel had been a proud man, even after Fred had kicked him to the ground. Too proud to even try to get those people in the station building to open the door to him. He had taken pleasure in defying Fred, even though it would have cost him and his wife their lives.

Bowsfield had no desire to kill them. Knowing the McBrides would have to live with the memory of this indignity was a greater reward. That, and the bagful of loot he was taking with him.

Moeller leaned into the room and beckoned Bowsfield to follow. He might be a hothead, but he knew when to keep his mouth shut when it counted.

Bowsfield pressed the barrel of his pistol against the back of Colonel McBride's head, then bent down to whisper in this ear. "You people best lie still for a while. Would be better if you counted down from three hundred in your heads before you try getting off those beds. I'd hate to see you get yourself killed out of recklessness." He pressed the barrel hard against the colonel's skin. "Or pride."

Bowsfield pushed himself upright and followed Moeller into the hallway. Fowler was already at the back stairs about to head down. His bag of loot was almost full.

Bowsfield glanced in Room Two as he passed and noted the Becquers were not struggling or squirming. He might have thought they were still asleep. What had Fowler done?

The three of them silently went downstairs and outside the back door without a word or a sound from any of them. Just like Fred Haney had trained them. He would have been proud of his men.

Duren rode toward them and brought the horses with him. Fowler and Bowsfield quickly put the loot in their saddlebags, climbed aboard, and began to ride west.

Bowsfield resisted the urge to pull down his kerchief and let loose with a howl of triumph. Their troubles were over, and now they were finally rich!

Bowsfield moved to the front of the group to set the pace. He wanted to put his heels to his mount and send it into a gallop but remembered what Fred and Earl had taught him. That speed caused noise and stealth was their friend. He would wait until they were clear of the town before making a run for it.

He knew the quicker they got away from town, the harder it would be for them to be captured the next day. The sheriff would not be able to raise a posse until the morning, even if he wished to try. He doubted many men in Ennisville would be willing to risk their lives to retrieve some trinkets belonging to a pair of rich couples passing through town.

The group had just reached the end of the street and Bowsfield was about to make a run for it when he saw a lone rider blocking their way. He could see from the burly outline of the man in the moonlight that it was Sheriff Brickell.

He heard one of the men behind him grab for his pistol, and before he could tell him to stop, two more riders emerged from the darkness to surround them. They were Brickell's deputies, and both men had a rifle aimed at them.

Bowsfield's stomach dropped as another one of Fred's lessons came to mind too late. *Never trust an easy score.*

Sheriff Brickell edged his horse toward them and into a patch of moonlight. "I figured you boys might be up to something. I'm glad to see I still have a nose for such things."

Bowsfield did not know how much the sheriff knew, so he played it as he thought Fred would. "If you call heading back to camp after a night of drinking being up to something, then me and my friends are guilty as charged."

"Except you weren't drinking," the sheriff said. "That's the problem. You see, we regard strangers closely here in Ennisville, and you boys were stranger than most. The saloons in these parts don't take too kindly to lightweights taking up tables while they're nursing their beers. It's mighty hard for them to make a living off men like that. Men such as yourselves. It sets them to wondering if you might be up to something besides drinking. That and all that time you boys spent lurking around alleys and such."

Fowler said, "First time I've ever heard a lawman complain about public sobriety."

Brickell ignored him. "I was willing to keep an eye on you boys to see what you were up to. Then, earlier tonight, I had the pleasure of visiting with some nice folks in the hotel. One of them remembered a redheaded Irishman and his friend acting like they wanted a room in the hotel but didn't seem much interested in getting one. Seemed more interested in the registry than a room, which set me and my boys to remembering all those complaints we heard from the saloon earlier that day. A man can learn a lot by listening and watching. You boys would do well to remember that."

Fowler cursed. "That old buzzard on the couch."

Bowsfield swallowed and tried to remain calm. "The clerk had a tone we didn't much appreciate. You can't blame us for being frugal with our money, can you, Sheriff?"

"No reason to be frugal anymore," Brickell said. "Not after the big score you boys just made back at the hotel. I'd wager you four are riding away with a mighty tidy sum."

Duren gagged somewhere behind Bowsfield. The boy always had a weak stomach.

But Bowsfield was surprised by the complete calm he felt despite being caught dead to rights. "What makes you think we stole anything?"

Brickell closed in on him fast enough to make his horse flinch. "Don't get smart with me, boy. The only reason why you four aren't already dead right now is because I want you alive."

Bowsfield said, "I know. You need us for something."

One of the deputies dug the barrel of his rifle in Bowsfield's side. "The only thing the sheriff needs you for is target practice. You mind your mouth when you talk to him."

Bowsfield's pride got the better of him. "Fred told us about you. He told us you'd be more likely to take a cut from them stolen horses we were buying than put anyone in jail. He said you were a reasonable man."

Brickell lowered his head and laughed. "I like your spunk, boy. I certainly do. I might have to kill you on account of it one day, but I like it. I reckon old Fred Haney taught you boys a lot while you were riding with him."

Bowsfield knew the sheriff would not let them go free, but he would not kill them, either. "Fred and Earl taught us to see things as they are," Bowsfield said. "To see people as they are, too."

Brickell looked up to the sky. "Is he dead? Fred, I mean."

"Him, Earl, and the whole gang are dead," Fowler told him. "We're all that's left. The only ones who made it out alive."

The sheriff's eyebrows rose. "I figure that either makes you boys survivors or cowards. You'll have a chance to prove which one you are in the morning." He tossed his thumb over his shoulder. "There's an old house a few miles in this direction. We're going to take you boys there and have ourselves a nice long talk. See if we can't come to some sort of understanding about your future here in Ennisville. See if I have some use for you boys."

"And if we don't want to go?" Bowsfield asked.

"Don't be stupid, boy." Brickell brought his horse about and began to ride away. "We can kill you just as easily out there as we can right here."

Bowsfield did not bother checking with the others before he got his horse moving. They had no choice but to follow Brickell's lead.

Chapter 15

Butch Keeling's endless snoring was not the only reason why Tucker Cobb could not sleep. The notion that his money was in Sheriff Brickell's safe kept him awake.

Cobb looked up at the pattern of the cracks in the plaster ceiling and was reminded of a map of Texas he had seen. He remembered the quiet oath he had made to himself that he would never go on another cattle drive again. Not as a cook. Not as a cowpuncher. Not for any reason except, maybe, if the herd belonged to him. He had been taking orders from other men for most of his life. He hoped he could keep his vow now, but it was not looking promising.

Cobb had always hated being at the mercy of another man's whims, especially when it came to money. Even if he got back every cent from Brickell, which he knew was unlikely, the damage to his reputation was done. He had wanted customers to know they could expect a clean, safe ride with the Frontier Overland Company, but their inaugural trip had proven to be a disaster. A jilted lover, horse thieves, and a band of bandits had ruined the stage line's reputation. Now, a sheriff's greed promised to derail his fledgling business for good.

Cobb had been so preoccupied by his troubles that he

had not realized how quiet it had become in the room until Butch said, "Go to sleep, Cobb. It's late and morning won't come any later on account of your fretting."

Cobb looked across the darkened room toward the sound of his partner's voice. "A minute ago, you were sleeping enough for the both of us, and your snoring's gotten worse. Sounded like you were clearing a whole forest."

"That's on account of it being a fitful sleep," Butch said. "All of your worrying is enough to turn my dreams to nightmares. Swallow your pride and shut your eyes so I can have some peace. A bit of sleep wouldn't hurt you any."

Cobb sat up in his bed when he heard a loud crash through the floorboards. The McBrides and the Becquers were in rooms directly below them. "You hear that?"

"No," Butch said. "I'm asleep."

Cobb pulled the covers aside and slid his legs out over the edge of the bed. Each night, he laid out his pants and boots beside his bed so he could pull them on at a moment's notice.

He strained his ears to listen but heard nothing but muted voices. "It sounded like wood splintering."

"Mr. Becquer looked like he'd had one too many when we came back to the hotel. Maybe the old boy rolled out of bed or walked into a door in the dark. You'll only embarrass him if you go check it out. Go to sleep."

But Cobb knew he would not be able to sleep now that his interest had been piqued. He could always sense when something was amiss, as it certainly was now.

He looked across the room when he heard their door-knob begin to rattle.

Butch sat up in his bed. The pistol he kept under his pillow was already in his hand. Cobb was glad he had been paying attention after all.

Cobb grabbed his coach gun while Butch got out of bed. He crept toward the door as the knob turned and shook. Whoever was doing it was not trying to be quiet about it.

Cobb raised his shotgun toward the door as Butch turned the lock and pulled it open.

Hunt was in the darkened hallway, wearing a bathrobe, his own Colt in hand. He brought a finger to his lips in a silent request for quiet. He then pointed to his ear and down at the floor. He had heard the wood breaking, too.

Cobb set his shotgun on the bed as he pulled on his pants and slid into his boots. Butch did the same, and when they were finished, they followed Hunt toward the stairs. Cobb brought up the rear with his shotgun.

Hunt stopped when he reached the second floor and pointed at both bedroom doors. They were closed but not all the way. Cobb remembered the Becquers and the McBrides had this floor but did not know which couple was in which room. Hunt broke to the right while Butch and Cobb moved to the left.

Butch pushed in the door and moved inside. Cobb saw that Colonel and Mrs. McBride were face down on the bed with their hands bound behind them.

Butch set his pistol on the side table as he began to untie Mrs. McBride. Cobb dumped his coach gun on the bed and began to free the colonel. Upon regaining the use of his hands, the colonel pulled the gag from his mouth and held his sobbing wife, removing her gag, too. "Are you hurt?" he asked her.

The older woman shook her head. "Just a tad frightened is all." She looked up at Cobb and Butch. "The Becquers. They were robbed, too."

Butch remained with the McBrides as Cobb grabbed his coach gun from the bed and ran into the hall. The door to their room was open, but Hunt was nowhere in sight. The elderly couple were still face down on the bed with their hands tied behind their backs.

How could Hunt have been so thoughtless?

But as Cobb went to untie Mr. Becquer's hands, he saw that Hunt had not been thoughtless. There was no hurry to undo their restraints because his skin was cold. Both of them were dead.

Cobb rushed into the hall and headed for the stairs. "You stay here, Butch. I'm getting some help."

He had just reached the lobby as the clerk and one of the bellmen ran up the stairs past him without pausing to question him. He saw Hunt coming back through the front door. His head hung lower than the pistol he had at his side. He looked ten years older than he had only a few hours before.

"See anyone out there?"

"No," Hunt croaked as he sat in one of the plush chairs in the lobby. "But you'd better check to make sure. I'm not feeling up to it."

Cobb went outside and looked up and down the boardwalk. It was deserted.

He ran to the back of the hotel to see if anyone might still be there, but it was too dark for him to see anything. He would not allow that to stop him. After he and Butch threw on some clothes, they would saddle their horses and go after them at first light. The ground was much easier to read from the back of a horse.

He was going to head back inside but decided Sheriff Brickell should be told about what had happened. He jogged over to the jail and rapped on the door. "It's Tucker Cobb. Open up. There's been a murder at the hotel."

He pounded again, but no answer. He went to the window and saw the oil lamp was out and the inside was dark. That was irregular. The sheriff or one of his men should have been in there. *Where are they?*

Cobb was out of breath by the time he made it back to the hotel. It was not a long distance from the jail, but the coach driver was not used to so much running. Hunt was still in the chair like an empty sack. He was not moving. His pistol was on his lap as if it were forgotten while Hunt stared off at nothing.

"You hurt?" Cobb asked him.

"Not physically," Hunt whispered. "Those people were alive a little while ago. The Becquers, I mean. They were both drinking and laughing and enjoying life without the slightest reason to believe that their lives would soon end." A single tear ran down his cheek. "I'd like to think they went peacefully despite the terror they must've felt. At least they were together when they went. They had each other, which is something."

Cobb did not have time for this. "Get up to your room and get dressed. We'll run them down on horseback. Come sun-up."

"What did Sheriff Brickell say?" Hunt asked as Cobb went to the stairs.

"He didn't say anything. He's not around and neither are his men."

"Interesting," Hunt said. "If that's the case, you might as well wait until morning. It's too dark to see anything, and I'm afraid I wouldn't be much good to you, anyway."

Cobb knew this was no time for self-doubt. Not with a bunch of killers on the loose. "Knock it off. You fended off the Haney bunch alone. You won't be alone this time."

Cobb hoped that would be enough to snap him out of it, but it was not. "I'm going blind, Tucker."

Cobb stopped halfway up the stairs. He could hear

Butch and the McBrides talking to the clerk and the bellhop. "You're what?"

"It's been happening slowly for the past few years," Hunt said, "but it's getting worse now. I suppose that's why I fell in with Mrs. Wagner and her ministry. I was hoping for a last chance at redemption while I was still able to do some good." He looked up at Cobb on the landing. "I can see you clear enough, but the rest is all a blur. It's why I don't use a rifle much anymore. No point in it if I can't see what I'm shooting at. It gets a bit better in the sunlight, but not much." He offered a weak smile. "That's not the only reason why we should wait until morning, of course, but it's part of it. You're just as liable to run past them than find them in the dark, and I suspect they're already far from here. The Becquers were both cold, which leads me to believe they've been gone for a long time. Long enough that waiting a few hours until sunrise won't make that much of a difference."

Cobb knew Hunt might be right, but he was wrong about something else. "You're not blind yet and you've still got plenty of life left in you. Get up to your room and get yourself dressed. You sulking down here in a robe won't help any."

Hunt fell silent again and Cobb left him to it. He had to help Butch tend to the others.

Later that next morning, Butch Keeling was reminded why he was grateful to have served the sovereign state of Texas instead of joining the army. He did not think he would have enjoyed being the subject of a senior officer's wrath, especially if that senior officer was Colonel McBride.

There was no doubt who was in charge as he watched the colonel focus his anger on Sheriff Brickell in the dining room of the Ennisville Hotel. "Mr. Cobb informs me that he went to the jail to report the horrors that had happened here earlier this morning, but you were nowhere to be found." He gripped the handle of his walking stick tightly. "I demand to know where you were."

"Where I usually am at that time of the morning," Brickell said. "On patrol around town. People prefer to break the law when they don't think anyone will see them do it."

"All of you?" the colonel asked. "At the same time? Leaving the jail unguarded."

"There was no reason to guard it because we didn't have any prisoners," Brickell said. "My men were off duty getting some much-needed rest while I was looking in on the town. I'm sorry I wasn't there to talk with Mr. Cobb, but I'm here now."

Butch saw the colonel's neck redden before his wife placed her hand on his arm. She gestured toward the lobby, where men from the funeral home were carrying the earthly remains of the Becquers past the doorway.

Butch looked away. He felt guilty about not listening to Cobb when he had heard the first sound. He had thought his partner was just hearing things. If they had moved then, the Becquers might still be alive and the men who attacked them dead.

Brickell remained quiet for a few moments until the bodies had been carried to the wagon outside. "Me and my men aren't taking this lightly, Colonel. We understand what happened here, and we're determined to find the men who did this."

Butch heard the hint of an excuse coming in his voice. "But?"

The sheriff glared at him. "What was that, Keeling?"

"There's a condition coming," Butch said. "Go on. Spit it out."

Brickell traced the inside of his mouth with his tongue before saying, "But we need to keep perspective here. While the loss of the Becquers is certainly a tragedy, it seems to me like the robbers didn't mean for any harm to come to them. Why, Doctor Garver couldn't find any bruises on them. He thinks they both died as the result of weak hearts, which was understandable given the strain they were under." He quickly added, "The strain you and Mrs. McBride suffered, too."

The colonel slammed the tip of his walking stick down on the floor. "My wife is my concern, not yours. The Becquers died during the commission of a robbery, sir. If this was the army, the charge against them should be murder."

"But this isn't the army," Brickell said. "This is Ennisville and I'm its sheriff." He looked down at his notepad. "I see here that you and Mrs. McBride report that the two men who robbed you were wearing kerchiefs over their faces. You can't remember the colors or anything peculiar about their person. Is that right?"

Mrs. McBride said, "We were woken out of a dead sleep, Sheriff. You can't expect us to see so many details in the dark. Especially when they were so quick to bind our hands behind us."

The sheriff offered her a tender smile that made Butch's skin crawl. "I didn't say you should. I'm just pointing out that, unless we find the stolen items in their possession, it's going to be difficult to find the men who did this. Perhaps the Becquers got a better look at them, but they aren't here to tell us. I wish they were. I mean that."

Beside him, Butch could feel Cobb's annoyance building. "You and your men kept us from following the tracks behind the hotel this morning," Cobb said. "Why?"

"I saw those tracks myself," Brickell said. "Saw them going in several different directions. Lots of people use the back streets for all sorts of things. I needed you here to give me your statement, not out chasing hoofprints." He held up his pad. "And I was right because your information was important."

Hunt, sitting next to the colonel at the head of the table, cleared his throat. He had changed out of his robe but was dressed more plainly than usual. He had not bothered with a collar for his white shirt. "What of the information I gave you last night, Sheriff. About the redhaired Irishman and his friend who were looking to stay here? Were you able to find them?"

The Sheriff tucked his pad away in the inside pocket of his jacket. "Didn't have the chance to look."

Butch noticed the way Brickell's eyes shifted. He had not even bothered to look.

Colonel McBride said, "I heard Mr. Hunt's descriptions last night, Sheriff. I would have thought you might've given the matter your full attention, especially in light of what's happened here."

"Maybe those men had something to do with this, Colonel," Brickell said, "and maybe they were just a couple of cowboys who'd rather spend their money on whiskey and women than a decent night's sleep. I promise I'll look for them today while I look for the men who robbed you and your wife."

"And killed the Becquers," the colonel added.

Brickell got to his feet and straightened out his jacket. Butch could see he did not like getting grilled by the old man. "I know you've all been through a grueling evening, but I think it would be best if you all continued your journey on to Laramie. There's not much you can do here, and while I think the men who did this are long gone, I can't guarantee your safety. I've already spoken to Mr. Burke about it, and he's getting his team of horses ready as we speak. He'll be happy to help you gather your belongings whenever you're ready."

The colonel used his walking stick to steady him as he stood. "Are you ordering us out of town, Sheriff?"

"I'm only recommending what I think is best for all concerned," Brickell said. "There's enough room in the coach for you and Mrs. McBride, Miss Duprey, Mrs. Wagner, Mr. Koppe, Mr. Hunt, and Reverend Averill. You're welcome to stay here if you'd like, but I can't spare the men to guarantee your safety." He glanced over at Cobb and Butch. "I'm afraid they'll have to stay here a bit longer than they'd planned since I haven't had the chance to look into what happened at Delaware Station yet. And since the Becquer deaths take priority, they'll have to wait."

Cobb was about to say something, but a slight elbow from Butch made him swallow it. He answered for Cobb. "Whatever you think is best, Sheriff."

Brickell made his goodbyes but did not seek to shake hands before he left.

Colonel McBride was frowning when he retook his seat. He glared down the length of the table at Cobb and Butch. "Well, gentlemen? Are you as disappointed in the sheriff's report as I am?"

"You could say that, sir," Cobb answered.

Hunt added, "He was lying about the Irishman. I saw a change come over him as he denied looking for him. Perhaps it's just my old actor's instinct, but I have a feeling he knows exactly who it is."

Butch had the same feeling but decided to keep it to himself. There was not much to be gained by sharing such an opinion.

The colonel tapped his walking stick on the ground as he thought it over. "I never liked that fellow from the first time I laid eyes on him last night, and my opinion hasn't changed after this latest meeting." Again, he looked at Cobb. "Since it appears you boys will be here for a while longer, I'd like to make you a proposition. Put your time here to use by holding Brickell's feet to the fire. I'll pay your hotel bill and double whatever money he confiscated from you if you agree to look for Mr. Hunt's redheaded stranger and accomplice. Find them and bring them to justice. Send word to me in Laramie, and I promise you'll have the full backing of the Wyoming Mining Company and all of its considerable resources at your disposal. I make the same offer to you, Mr. Hunt. Your help will be indispensable in this, since you're the only one among us who knows what they look like."

Butch watched Hunt shift in his seat. Something was bothering him, and it wasn't his backside.

The actor said, "I'll be glad to help in any way I can, Colonel. I may not have known the Becquers for long, but I grew fond of them in a short amount of time. You may rest assured of my best efforts."

The colonel tapped his walking stick with finality as he stood. "Then the matter's decided. I feel much better knowing you three will be here to keep Brickell honest." He offered his arm to his wife, who took it as they left the dining room. "Mrs. McBride here will let the others know of our agreement. We'll be ready to leave within the hour. We'd feel better about things if you were there to send us off."

"We'll be there," Butch said.

This time, the three of them stood while the McBrides left and took the stairs up to their room.

Butch felt he could finally breathe. "That old man's got some years on him, but he's still quite a force, ain't he?"

Hunt crossed his legs and pawed at his mouth. "Indeed."

Butch was still bothered by the way the actor reacted when the colonel asked him for his help. "I don't see why you're all fidgety all of a sudden. You weren't lying about seeing that Irishman and his friend yesterday, were you?"

"You're quite perceptive, aren't you?" Hunt's left eyebrow rose. "I wasn't lying, but I'm afraid it's not as simple as that."

"Leave it alone, Butch," Cobb cautioned. "We can talk about this later."

But Butch did not want to wait until later. He'd already had his fill of surprises for one day. "We might as well talk about it now. Did you see those boys or not?"

"In a matter of speaking, yes."

"In a matter of speaking?" Butch repeated.

Then he began to remember some of what he had seen since they had first picked up Hunt and the others back in North Branch. How Hunt had stumbled getting into the coach even though it was an easy climb. How he had said he did not need a rifle when going after the horse thieves. Cobb's story about how Hunt had killed them with a pistol instead. There were other flashes of memory, too, and all of them led him to the same conclusion.

"You can't see too good, can you?"

Hunt's face tightened. "Like I just said, you're very perceptive."

Butch had been confident in their chances up to that moment, but this changed everything. He held up three fingers on his left hand. "How many?"

Hunt looked away. "I won't perform tricks for you like a dog in a show."

"This ain't no show," Butch insisted. "How many?"

"Three." Though he did not sound sure of his answer.

"A fine guess," Butch said. "How far can you see? And don't lie to me, damn it, because this is important. You don't have to show off for the colonel and his friends anymore."

"I'm not showing off for anyone," Hunt protested. "You two are clear enough, but I can't read the titles of the books on the shelves behind you." He held up his own hand and stretched out his arm. "I can see clear as day at this distance, but anything closer is a little blurry."

Butch figured that explained why he had trouble getting into the coach back in North Branch.

Cobb tried to stop him from stepping away from the table, but Butch needed answers. "Where were you sitting when you saw those boys yesterday?"

"On the couch against the wall over there," Hunt said. "I heard the Irishman's brogue and saw his red hair. I saw his friend looking down at the registry instead of at the clerk. I can see outlines of people, but not their features. I can see movement if the light's good, but not details."

Butch walked over to the couch and saw it offered a clear view of the front desk twenty feet away. He picked up a pillow from the couch and slammed it down again in anger. "That's just great." He saw Cobb was looking at him. "How long have you known about this?"

"Since last night when he told me," Cobb said. "I didn't know anything before he mentioned it. It's not important, anyway, Butch. He doesn't have to see these fellas to identify them. He can remember their voices."

"A redheaded Irishman with a brogue ain't much of a description."

"But it's all we've got," Cobb said, "and it'll be enough for our purposes, won't it, Hunt?"

"If I can hear them," Hunt said, "I can find them, for where one is the other is sure to be close. My eyes may be failing me, but there's nothing wrong with my hearing."

Butch had always prided himself on never allowing his temper to get the better of him. It was why he and Cobb had always gotten along so well. It was clear that Hunt could not be blamed for losing his vision, and Butch could not blame him for keeping it quiet. He had been brave when it counted and had earned his respect.

"Sorry I lost my temper, Leon. I don't lose it often."

"I'm glad," Hunt said, "though your concerns are valid. All I can promise is that I won't be a hindrance to you in any way. I'd be on that coach to Laramie if I thought otherwise."

Cobb stood up and stretched his legs. "We'd best get ourselves outfitted to give the others a decent send-off. I hate the notion of losing my fares to that idiot Burke, but it looks like I don't have much of a choice."

Cobb went left to go upstairs to their room first while Butch remained back with Hunt. The actor said, "You don't have to worry about me, Butch. I can manage well enough on my own without any help from you."

"I know you can, but I figure you could use an apology from me. I should've been kinder when I learned about your eyes. I was taken by the news and reacted poorly. I shouldn't have done that."

Hunt would not hear of it. "You weren't chastising me about using the wrong fork at dinner, Butch. You're relying on me to be able to hit what I shoot at. Your cause for concern is valid and your apology is unnecessary. Though I have a feeling we're going to have to keep a close eye on your partner upstairs. Cobb's already straining against Brickell's leash, and it hasn't been a day yet."

Butch knew handling Cobb would be a problem all its own. "For a man who's supposed to be losing his sight, you sure do see a lot."

Hunt urged Butch to leave the dining room first. "Let's just hope all of us see what we're supposed to see."

CHAPTER 16

Cobb kept his coach gun in hand but at his side as he, Butch, and Hunt stood on the boardwalk to wish their passengers a good trip.

Sheriff Brickell and two of his deputies were there as well but had the good sense to stay a good distance away while they watched the boarding.

As expected, Mrs. Wagner was first out of the hotel. Burke had already loaded her luggage on the top of the wagon.

"I suppose we'll have the displeasure of your company before long in Laramie, Mr. Cobb?"

"Butch and I will be there as soon as we're allowed to get underway," Cobb told her. She did not respond but took the hand Hunt offered her as she went inside.

"I trust you'll have a pleasant remainder of your journey, Your Grace," Hunt said. She pulled her hand away and moved deep inside the coach. Mr. Koppe followed, doffing his hat and smiling weakly as he passed them.

Reverend Averill was next. He was still carrying his heavy satchel with both hands and stumbled as he stepped across the hotel's threshold. He pitched forward and fell to the boardwalk as his parcel fell, too. Cobb and Butch grabbed him before he fell on his face, but his bag landed with a muted clank. The bag remained buckled and shut, but the sound was unmistakable.

Hunt toed the bag with his boot and looked at the reverend. "Sounds like you've been hauling some golden knowledge all this time."

Reverend Averill recovered his balance and quickly lifted his bag. "That's no longer any of your concern."

But Hunt did not step aside to let the man pass. "The safety of these people is my concern, and if you're holding what I think you're holding, the lives of everyone on this coach is at risk because of it."

"That's impossible," Averill said, keeping his voice down. "No one knows what I've got in here."

"Don't be so certain," Hunt said. "Are you even a reverend?"

"Of a sort," Averill said, lifting his head in defiance.

Hunt blocked his way. "Well, I've been a sort of outlaw at various times in my life, so let me give you a word of advice. Tuck that bag away and don't lay hands on it until you reach Laramie. And once you're there, you'd better take it straight to the bank or to whomever is going to buy it from you. It's hard to keep a secret in a big town. Harder than you think."

Cobb watched Hunt step aside and let Averill climb into the coach on his own. Butch tapped his partner lightly with his elbow and nodded toward where Brickell and his men had been standing. All three of them were gone.

"When did that happen?" Cobb asked out of the side of his mouth.

"Right after Averill's bag of gold hit the boardwalk," Butch said. "I think they were close enough to have heard it for themselves."

Cobb knew that if the sheriff had heard the bars clanking together, the lives of everyone on the stagecoach were in danger. He went to Burke, who was up in the wagon box waiting to get underway. "I think it might be a good idea if you put off your trip a while longer, Leo. Wait until the afternoon. There'll still be plenty of light left for you to get to Laramie before dark."

"Nonsense," Colonel McBride said as he stepped from the hotel with Mrs. McBride on his arm. "We're all mighty anxious to get to Laramie as soon as possible. There's no sense in delaying things any longer."

Cobb knew Burke would do whatever the colonel told him to do. He whispered his concerns to him. "It seems Reverend Averill has been lugging around bars of gold in his bag all this time, Colonel."

"Unless he's taken a vow of poverty," the colonel said, "I fail to see how that concerns the rest of us."

"Sheriff Brickell disappeared after the reverend fell," Cobb explained. "I think he might try to make a play for Averill's gold. I don't trust him, sir."

"Neither do I." Colonel McBride opened his coat and revealed an ivory-handled Remington pistol. "I'll be ready for any men foolish enough to try their luck with us. I'm a good shot, Mr. Cobb. Any men who cross us will rue the day they were born. I was caught flatfooted by highwaymen once. That won't happen a second time."

Cobb wished the six-shooter would be enough but doubted it would. He made his excuses to the McBrides and ran off toward the jail. His stomach dropped when he saw Brickell and one of his two deputies heading inside. He wondered if the other deputy had already been dispatched to lay a trap for the stagecoach on the trail.

Cobb called out to the sheriff before he went inside the jail. "I need a word with you, Sheriff."

Brickell stopped in the doorway while the deputy went inside. "Need's a mighty strong word, Cobb. What's wrong?"

He knew it was madness to tell the man he suspected of possibly attacking the coach about his desire to protect it, but he did not have a choice. "I'm concerned about sending that coach out unguarded, Brickell. I'd feel a whole lot better about it if you'd let me send an outrider with it to assure safe passage."

Brickell sneered. "Let me guess. You're recommending yourself for the job, and you promise you'll come right back after seeing them on to Laramie."

Cobb was glad to disappoint him. "I was thinking Butch could do it. I'd stay here until you're done with your investigation at Delaware Station. Butch would come back after they were in sight of Laramie."

The sheriff gave the suggestion some thought. "I don't trust Butch any more than I really trust you. But I'll be glad to send my two deputies to ride with them for half the way if it'll make you feel any better about things."

Placing Brickell's deputies in charge of protecting the coach was like asking a fox to guard a chicken coop. "I'd feel better if you'd let Butch do it. He's had plenty of experience with this kind of thing before."

"Yeah," Brickell agreed. "Too much experience for my taste."

The sheriff looked inside the jail and called his other deputy to come out. Cobb did not know this one's name, but he was as tall and lean and forgettable as the sheriff's other deputies. "Chance, I want you to catch up to Dean Sprout. I want you both to ride with the wagon to the edge of our jurisdiction and come straight back. See to it that no harm comes to the stage or its passengers. Understood?"

Chance nodded that he did. "I might be able to catch up to Jerry before he leaves the livery if I make a run for it."

The deputy ran off in the direction of the livery, leaving Cobb and Brickell alone on the boardwalk. "That make you feel any better, Cobb?"

"I won't feel better until I ride out of here."

Brickell looked down at the coach gun at Cobb's side. "And I'd feel a lot better if you kept that cannon stowed in your room."

"Any law against carrying firearms in town?" Cobb asked. "I didn't see anything posted anywhere."

"We frown on it," Brickell said, "but you're not breaking any laws. Just be careful where you bring it. Word about your tendency to cut men down has spread all over Ennisville. I'd hate to see you caught up in another misunderstanding."

"I'm sure you would," Cobb said as he turned to head back to the hotel, "but there aren't many misunderstandings when I'm holding Old Betsy here. I don't put her to work without a good reason."

Cobb returned to the hotel to find the colonel was still waiting with Hunt and Butch outside the coach.

"I spoke to the sheriff," Cobb told him. "He's sending two deputies with you as far as his jurisdiction. It's not ideal, but it ought to get you a good piece closer to Laramie. It's all flat, clear land from there. It'll be hard country for anyone to jump you out there." He looked up at Burke in the wagon box. "You keep an eye on the road ahead of you, Leo. If you see anyone blocking your way, turn around and head back here."

Burke said he would, and Cobb lowered his voice to the colonel. "Keep that hogleg in hand the entire trip, sir. I don't trust Brickell's men any more than I trust Brickell himself."

"Your suspicions are well placed." The colonel shook his hand. "I'll handle any trouble that arises."

Hunt helped McBride into the coach as Jane Duprey stepped outside. She was wearing a deep green dress Cobb had not seen before. She carried a matching parasol to shield herself from the sun. Cobb liked to think she had worn the dress for him.

Hunt took off his hat to her. "You're a vision, Miss Duprey. Simply a vision. Wyoming's answer to Helen of Troy."

Jane smiled. "I don't know if that's a compliment, Mr. Hunt. I don't think things ended too well for the Trojans who took her."

"That depends on which histories one chooses to read," Hunt replied.

Butch said, "I don't know much about Troy, but I know Ennisville will be a mighty dull place without you in it."

She touched Butch's arm before collapsing her parasol and joining Cobb in the shadow of the coach. "I sure wish you'd let me stay here with you and Butch. I don't like leaving you with things like this."

Cobb did not like the idea of setting her on a trail where the men who had killed the Becquers might be waiting to attack them, but it was the safest gamble. "Brickell won't let anything happen to you while they're with you. Just help the colonel keep a sharp eye out once his men leave and you'll be fine." He only wished he believed that.

Jane looked away, and he thought he saw a tear in her eye. "I'll be expecting you to pay me a visit as soon as you reach Laramie."

Cobb took her hand in both of his. "You can bet your bottom dollar on that."

He helped her up into the coach and pushed the door shut. He told Blake, "Don't stop until you get to Laramie. Your horses are fresh and rested, so they should make it easily."

Burke released the hand brake and snapped the reins, sending his team forward toward their destination.

Cobb looked after them, hoping Jane would offer him a wave as they sped out of sight. It did his heart good to see that she did.

Deputies Ned Chance and Dean Sprout raced past the hotel and ahead of the stagecoach to lead them out toward the end of Sheriff Brickell's jurisdiction.

When they were far enough ahead of the wagon, Dean asked his partner, "You're sure that's what the boss told you? That he doesn't want us to rip off the stage?"

"That's what he told me," Chance said. "Right in front of Cobb, too."

"But the gold," Dean said. "We heard it clank in that preacher's bag when he fell. I can't see him wanting to pass up an easy payday like that."

"He's never been one to explain himself to us, and I didn't have time to ask him back there," Chance said. "You ought to ride ahead and tell Bowsfield and his friends to forget about stopping this coach. Tell 'em they'd best head back to the sheriff's house and wait to hear from him."

Chance had worked with Dean for more than two years by then. He had never known him to take his time about carrying out an order, but he was in no hurry now. "We're getting close to where they're supposed to be waiting for us. You'd better get moving."

"What if we don't," Dean suggested. "What if we go ahead with the plan as is and rip off these people?"

Chance did not like what he was hearing. "You might be willing to go back to the boss and admit you defied him, but I'm not."

"Who says we have to go back at all?" Dean asked aloud. "We've got ourselves a nice robbery all set to go. Why ruin a perfectly good plan? I say we not only let it happen, but we also help it along. We take that preacher's gold, plus anything else the others have on them and high-tail it for Laramie or Cheyenne. We'd be long gone before Brickell even knows what happened."

Chance was aware that he had never been known for his intelligence, but even he could see the madness in the idea. "Those people know who we are, Dean. They've seen our faces. They'd tell everyone that we were the ones who did it. Brickell would have wanted posters on us all over the territory before supper. Don't talk stupid."

Dean continued to ride on. "They can only tell people if they're alive."

Chance had made a lot of money helping Sheriff Brickell bend the law, but no one had ever lost their lives because of it.

Dean interrupted his thoughts. "And before you go thinking you're above murder, think again. That old couple died last night because of what Bowsfield and the others did. We're just as guilty for taking their loot off them."

"That's different," Chance protested. "That was an accident. Ripping off a bunch of thieves after a job is one thing. What you're talking about is just plain, old-fashioned murder, and I won't take any part in it."

"If you're happy taking the boot from Brickell for the rest of your life, be my guest. But I've got bigger plans for myself than being a deputy for the rest of my days. If it wasn't for that preacher's gold, I'd be inclined to let them go, but this quit being about what Brickell wants the second we heard them bars rattle on the boardwalk back there. They're all old and washed up, anyway. They've lived their lives. Why shouldn't we? You know I'm right."

That was the trouble. Chance knew Dean was right. How many times would they be this close to a bag of gold so ripe for the taking. Even if the reverend was only carrying silver bars, it would be a good payday for them. There was something to be said for having money of his own. Enough to give him a fresh start in life somewhere besides Wyoming.

But that new life could not come at the cost of others. Nothing good could ever come from cold-blooded murder.

"Not all of them are old," Chance offered. "Miss Duprey is still young enough."

"Which is why I was thinking we save her for ourselves," Dean replied, grinning. "Maybe we could—"

Chance had heard enough. He leaned forward in the saddle as he dug his heels into the flanks of his horse and sped away from his former partner. First, he had spoken of murder, now he was considering abduction. It was beyond his capacity to ignore. If Dean would not ride ahead to call off Bowsfield and his partners, then Chance would have to do it. He had been watching when the old colonel showed Cobb his revolver before boarding the coach. He would probably be able to fend off Dean if he had to. The old soldier still had some grit to him.

Chance remained low in the saddle as his mount finally reached its top speed as it crested the hill and came down the other side. He saw the old Brickell house slumped in front of a cluster of trees off to his left. The farmhouse looked menacing enough at night, and the sunlight did little to soften its appearance any. He knew Bowsfield and the others would be among the overgrowth on either side of the road, ready to surround the coach as it approached their position, just like Brickell had ordered the previous night.

But that had been before the lawmen knew about the reverend's gold. Before Dean had decided to make himself a wealthy man.

The wind had been roaring in Chance's ears when he felt the hot fire of a bullet cut through the right side of his back and chest. A second bullet struck him in the lower left of his back, and the impact was enough to shove him out of the saddle as his horse raced on.

Chance tumbled through the overgrowth and down a slight hill, rolling until a rotted tree stump broke his momentum. He felt himself beginning to fade as more bullets struck the ground around him but missed. Chance heard Dean riding past him while he felt himself growing weaker. His entire body now ached as he tried to check himself for bullet holes. He knew of the one in his chest and in his lower back. Were there others?

He listened for the sound of the coach coming to a halt, but heard it rumble past him on the road above. Had the driver not been paying attention? Hadn't he seen Dean gun him down?

Then he remembered back to the hill and how he had been shot on the other side of it. Burke may not have seen him fall, only both deputies riding ahead, perhaps to check the trail.

Chance tried to call out to them but could not draw enough air in his lungs to be heard over the sounds of the team and the coach they pulled behind them. Everyone was riding into a trap, and there was nothing he could do about it.

As the darkness finally reached up to claim him, he accepted that he could not even help himself.

CHAPTER 17

Colonel McBride had been keeping his eyes on the window when he felt the coach begin to slow. He remembered the last time Burke had slowed down and the terror that ensued after that.

"What seems to be the trouble?" he shouted up to the driver. When Burke did not respond, he leaned out the window and saw five men approaching on the road.

Staying in the coach would only limit his options, as it had outside Delaware Station. If he was marked to die, he would be sure to take some of the attackers with him.

"All of you get on the floor right now," the colonel ordered as he opened the door and leapt outside. His wounded leg cried out in protest, but he held on to the wagon wheel as he pulled himself behind the coach. Miss Duprey grabbed the coach door and pulled it closed.

McBride removed his hat as he moved to the left side of the coach and then chanced a quick look beyond it. He saw one man out front, flanked by two men on either side of him. The others were wearing kerchiefs to hide their faces, but the lead rider was not. He recognized him as one of Brickell's deputies. Since the man was not covering his face, he was not worried about being recognized.

He was not counting on allowing anyone to survive the attack.

McBride would be happy to disappoint him.

He remained behind the coach, waiting for the men to come within range of his pistol.

He heard the deputy say, "I guess you must know the drill by now, Burke. Hands up where I can see them."

The colonel's blood ran cold when he heard the driver say, "You'll get no trouble from me."

He heard the deputy laugh. "Ain't that the truth."

He heard gunmetal scrape leather just before a single shot rang out.

The team of horses bucked as Burke fell out of the wagon box and dropped to the ground. McBride's training and instinct caused him to break cover. He hobbled out from behind the coach and fired when the team lowered their heads.

His shot passed between the heads of the two horses in front and struck the deputy in the throat, causing the wounded man to grab at his wound.

One of the men on the left rushed a pistol shot, which hit the coach just above McBride's head. The colonel lost his balance and fell behind Burke's corpse, but the fat man's bulk provided him decent cover. He stuck his pistol out across Burke's belly and fired up at the robber who had shot at him. The bullet hit the man just below the breastbone and sent his horse bucking.

One of the three remaining riders managed to get control of his horse as he aimed down at McBride. His shot hit Burke in the belly as McBride stretched out his right hand and squeezed the trigger.

The shot missed the rider but caught his horse on the top of the head. The animal shuddered before dropping, giving the man enough time to spill from the saddle before he was crushed beneath its weight.

The throat-shot deputy fumbled with his reins as the outlaw, now afoot, knocked him from the saddle and took his horse from him. He joined his three other companions as they brought their horses about and quickly rode off in the direction from which they had come.

McBride ignored the pain in his leg and the screams from inside the coach as the sound of his own blood roared in his ears. He had not known combat since he was wounded, but by God, the thrill of it had found him now.

He pulled himself onto his feet and tucked the pistol into its holster. He swung his weakened leg straight as he struggled to pull himself up into the wagon box. Too many steak dinners and late-night cigars served to make it more of an effort than he remembered, but he hauled himself up into the box. The back of the bench and the seat were still splattered in Burke's blood, but McBride was beyond caring about such things now. Four men had tried to kill him and his wife. He would have to kill them before they rallied and tried it again.

He had never driven a coach before but understood how they worked. He released the hand brake as he gathered up the reins and snapped them hard to get the team moving. The frightened animals responded, eager to get away from the death that littered the ground around them. Their hooves trampled the deputy just before the wagon wheels rolled over him. The women in the coach screamed, though he doubted one of them was his wife. She was likely the only one of the passengers encouraging the others to keep their heads.

He watched the four riders in front of him look back, their eyes growing wide with fear at the sight of the horses and coach tearing after them. McBride caught the metallic taste of blood that was not his own and imagined he must look like a mad coachman driving the team after them. He took the pistol from its holster and resisted the urge to crack off a shot at the fleeing robbers. They were on the edge of his range, and he needed to make every shot count.

His heart leapt in his chest when he watched the cowards dash to the right side of the road and gallop off toward the east. He watched them tail off again to the south, back the way they had come, where an old farmhouse stood alone amid the overgrown countryside.

It was over. He had won. Again.

McBride cracked the reins and cut loose with a mighty holler. It was not as fierce as the rebel yells that had once haunted him on the field of battle, but it was his own.

The colonel had slowed the pace of his team gradually as they continued to race on toward Laramie. He had no idea how far they were from the town but imagined the road would lead them there. He had not noticed any signs along the way but remembered Cobb's description of the land when he had been talking to Burke. It was flat and devoid of any trees or rocks that could afford cover to bandits or thieves.

The colonel brought the team to a complete stop and threw the hand brake to give the beasts a rest. They had certainly earned it.

"We'll stop here to rest for a while," McBride called back to the passengers. "Anyone hurt?"

Both doors of the coach flew open, with Jane stepping out on the left side to help the others down. Mrs. Wagner bolted from the right and got sick on the side of the road.

He was glad to see his own wife step around to the

front, but the blood on the front of her dress made him gasp.

Martha McBride held her hands up to him. "Don't go getting yourself into a tizzy over nothing, Louis. I'm fine, but Reverend Averill wasn't so lucky. One of those first shots struck him in the back. He passed on a little while ago."

The colonel placed his knee on the bench as he kept an eye on the road behind them. He did not think the gang had been chasing them all this time, but he wanted to be certain.

"Mr. Koppe hurt?" he asked.

"He's tending to Mrs. Wagner now. He deserves a medal for his efforts."

"As do you, Colonel," Jane said. "You saved our lives back there. You were very brave."

Mrs. McBride glanced at her. "I don't think Mrs. Wagner can stand to have the reverend's corpse ride all the way to Laramie with us. See if Mr. Koppe can help you pull his body out of the coach. The colonel can't do it and I'm not very strong. Be a dear and try, will you?"

Jane said she would and walked around to the other side of the coach, where Koppe was tending to Mrs. Wagner.

McBride kept his pistol at his side, scanning the horizon for any sign of riders. The road stretched back a fair ways from where they had stopped, and he was sure he could see anyone approaching on horseback. He only hoped the horses had sufficient rest before the gang tried another attack.

He felt the hairs on the back of his neck begin to stand the way they did whenever danger was near. He looked down at his wife and caught her glaring up at him.

"What?" he asked her.

Martha McBride's mouth was a thin line as she folded

her arms. He had been the recipient of that look many times over the course of their long marriage.

"What?" he asked again.

"Don't you 'what' me, Louis McBride. You know 'what.' You had no business pulling a stunt like that back there."

He had been afraid that was the reason for her anger. "I couldn't just sit there and let us get held up again. We all would've wound up like the reverend if I had."

"What if they'd only wanted money? What if you'd gotten yourself killed over nothing."

For once, he knew this was an argument he stood a good chance of winning. "The one who was leading them was one of the deputies. He wasn't wearing a mask. That meant he wasn't planning on letting any of us live." He rubbed his sore leg. "I think I acquitted myself quite nicely for an old man."

"A foolish old man," Martha added. "I didn't leave Chicago to come out to this godforsaken wilderness just to be left a widow on account of you."

"Of all the things in this world that might conspire to kill me, cowardice isn't one of them."

"No, but that damnable pride of yours just might." She produced a handkerchief from her sleeve and held it up to him. "Wipe that blood off your face. You look like a mad Scotsman from a history book."

The colonel's joints popped as he bent to take the handkerchief. "I am a mad Scotsman, by God and by blood. And don't you forget it."

His wife smiled despite herself. "Never let it be said that Louis McBride still doesn't know how to show a lady a good time."

McBride laughed, too, as he began to wipe the dried blood from his face. "I never promised you a dull life, Mrs. McBride."

"No, but sometimes, I'd welcome a little dullness."

McBride looked at the handkerchief to see if it had removed any of the gore but saw that it had not. He decided to leave it there. Let the good people of Laramie see what he had done. It would be good for them to see the sort of man they would be dealing with. It might help avoid any misunderstandings in the future.

A dull ache began to settle behind Cobb's eyes as he walked back to the hotel. He, Butch, and Hunt had decided it would be best to split up in their attempt to find any trace of the thieves who had killed the Becquers the previous night. As saloons rivaled barbershops as places where gossip could be overheard, the three men had picked one saloon apiece. Cobb had chosen the Shooting Star as his place to start. He had given them some of the money he had held back from Brickell to buy drinks—and hopefully information—from the locals about the two strangers.

All Cobb had to show for his efforts was several stories about Ennisville, a few unsavory rumors about Sheriff Brickell, and a mild hangover from all the beer he had been forced to drink while listening to it all.

Cobb was glad the shades in the hotel's parlor had been pulled down when he found Butch already waiting for him. But Butch grew concerned when he saw Cobb's condition.

"What happened to you?"

Cobb went to a chair and sat down. "I'm not used to drinking while the sun's still up. My head is pounding something awful."

Butch poured him some coffee from the silver pot. "I warned you that all that decent living was going to catch up to you sooner or later." He placed the cup in front of

Cobb, then took a seat on the nearby couch. "You find out anything?"

Cobb shut his eyes in the hope it would keep the room from spinning. "Yeah. Ennisville has secrets. Brickell is a crook, and the ones who killed the Becquers were a band of Chinese fugitives from the railroad."

"Glad I'm not the only one around here who only heard nonsense," Butch said. "I listened to a guy tell me who did it, but the more he drank, the more his story changed. Turns out he was looking to cause trouble for some Irishman who took this saloon girl's affections from him."

Cobb sighed heavily as the pain in his head began to subside. "Serves us right for thinking we could play at being lawmen. This town doesn't trust strangers."

"I've never met one that did," Butch admitted, "but it was a noble effort and we ain't sunk yet. Hunt hasn't come back yet, so maybe he's found a nugget out there somewhere."

Cobb hoped he had. It would be nice to have something to show for their efforts besides a midafternoon hangover.

Both men looked up when they heard Hunt whistling a tune to himself as he strode into the lobby. His flat-brimmed hat was tipped forward at a rakish angle, and his cheeks had the glow that often accompanied the consumption of significant amounts of whiskey.

Butch said, "Looks like you've had yourself quite an afternoon."

"I certainly have." Hunt lowered himself into a chair. "Our friends made quite a spectacle of themselves while they were killing time before killing the Becquers."

Cobb forgot about his headache. "Tell it in plain English, Hunt. Skip the gingerbread and spindles you put on most things you say."

Hunt removed his hat as he crossed his legs and tossed

the hat on his foot. "It appears the men I saw were only half the gang. There were four of them, with one of them being a redhead. They spent half the day in the Ennisville Saloon, then went on to the Shooting Star."

That had been the bar Cobb had visited. He knew they had been hiding something. "Go on."

"They didn't drink much," Hunt told them. "Only two beers apiece in the entire time they were there. They kept to themselves and seemed more interested in looking out the window than joining in any friendly conversation. They offered only one-word answers to the bartenders when prodded and left when they began to attract too much attention. They haven't been seen since a little while before the robberies took place."

Cobb felt his hopes dash with the ending of Hunt's brief tale. "That seals it. None of us found out anything new. A day wasted."

"All is not lost," Hunt cautioned. "I did uncover a pearl among the pigs." He leaned forward and looked out into the lobby to make sure the desk clerk was not listening. "Sheriff Brickell knew about them long before I mentioned them at dinner."

Cobb and Butch exchanged glances, with Butch saying, "How do you know?"

"The bartender at the saloon told me he didn't like the looks of them," Hunt said. "Didn't like how they were taking up a table and preventing drinking men from using it. He said he made a point of complaining to Brickell about them and the sheriff had one of his deputies look for them." He shrugged. "I know it's not much of a detail, but it shows that Brickell already knew about that redheaded Irishman before I mentioned it to him that night. Maybe it means something. Maybe it doesn't."

Cobb thought it meant quite a bit. "Brickell might be

crooked but he's nobody's fool. He should've realized the bartender and you were talking about the same men. And I'd just bet he did."

Butch folded his hands together on his lap. "That's where my thinking takes me, too. And it's a dangerous place."

Cobb took his pipe and tobacco pouch from his pocket and began to pack the bowl. The pipe often helped him organize his thoughts, and he needed all the help he could get. "It makes sense. Remember how I went looking for Brickell and his deputies right after we found the McBrides and the Becquers? He was nowhere to be found. Neither were any of his deputies."

"If I remember correctly," Hunt added, "he claimed to be elsewhere in town on patrol."

"Yeah." Cobb flipped his pouch closed and pocketed it before fishing out a match. "Two hours later. This town isn't big enough to take two hours to cover." He thumbed a match alive and brought it to his pipe. "But he'd have plenty of time to watch the redhead and his friends rob those two couples and wait for them when they made a run for it."

Butch took off his hat and tossed it on the cushion beside him. "We know how fond he is of helping himself to other men's money. He ripped us off, so it stands to reason he'd do the same to this Irishman and his friends."

Hunt took his hat from his shoe as he leaned forward in his chair. "That would also explain why he didn't want us tracking them the next day. Do you think he has them?"

His bowl lit, Cobb waved the match dead and tossed it into the fireplace. "He knows where they are, either above ground or in it. And since I've never known him to be a wasteful man, I'd bet he's got them stashed someplace. Maybe not here in town, but close by."

"If he had them here in town," Hunt said, "I'm sure my new friends at the saloon would have mentioned it. You boys are more familiar with this area than me. Any ideas where he could be hiding them?"

Cobb drew the tobacco smoke deep into his lungs before slowly exhaling it through his nose. "Could be. He'd want them close so he could keep an eye on them, but not close enough to risk them being spotted. And if they're still alive, he'll put them to use. The question is how?"

Butch said, "There's an old farmhouse a couple miles out of town we always pass on our way to Laramie. I never saw any sign of someone living in it, but it's not exactly a ruin. It could make a good spot for the redhead and his boys to hole up for a while."

Cobb remembered the house, a washed-out structure with vines running up its walls as if the ground were slowly trying to reclaim it. "That's the same route Burke took with his stage just now. They'd roll right past it if they kept to the road."

Hunt looked at the two men. "Burke strike you as the type to go his own way?"

Cobb and Butch were on their feet at the same time, with Cobb saying, "Hunt, you'll stay here while Butch and me get our mustangs mounted. I want to ride out and have a look around that farmhouse with my own two eyes."

Cobb wanted to see if Burke's coach had been attacked but did not want to breathe life into the unthinkable.

CHAPTER 18

As the three men left the hotel, Cobb heard Sheriff Brickell call out his name from the middle of the thoroughfare.

Cobb stopped as he turned, conscious of keeping his coach gun aimed at the ground as he did. "You've got a bad habit of yelling at folks when their backs are turned, Brickell. That's a dangerous habit to have."

"That's because you always seem to be running off to one place or another whenever I need to talk to you." The sheriff approached them slowly with his hands behind his back. Cobb noticed his pistol was still holstered on his hip. "Mind telling me where you boys are going in such a hurry?"

Cobb said, "Just out for a quick stroll around town."

Brickell grinned. "Guess you have a need to clear your head of all that whiskey I heard you boys drank today. I'll admit I was surprised to hear it. You boys don't strike me as the type who drink during working hours." He glanced at Hunt. "As for you, well, no one expects your kind to be sober at any time of day. Being an actor and all."

Hunt bowed slightly at the waist. "'Good wine is a good, familiar creature, if it be well used.' And my compatriots and I have put it to good use today."

Brickell rocked up on his toes. "If I didn't know better, I might think you boys have designs on my job. Well, it just so happens that I have some good news for you. It's time for you to get back to work."

The sheriff tossed a sack of money to Cobb, who gathered it against his chest as Brickell said, "You're free to go. You too, Hunt. I took a quick ride out to Delaware Station earlier this morning, and your account matches what Gene and Ma told me. I've got no reason to hold you any longer, so I'll be expecting you to be on your way."

Cobb felt the sack of money in his hand. "Doesn't seem to be any lighter than when I handed it over to you yesterday."

"I waived the fees," Brickell said. "Seeing as how your time here in Ennisville has been a trying one, I figured it was the least I could do. But now that I don't have any hold on you, I'll be expecting you three to be on your way. Within the hour."

Cobb handed the money to Butch as he took a step closer to the sheriff. "Why the sudden rush?"

"I figured you boys would be anxious to be on your way and get on with your stagecoach business."

Butch pocketed the sack of money. "What's the real reason?"

"I don't like you," Brickell admitted. "I don't like either of you. I don't like the way trouble seems to follow you wherever you go. I don't like the way you're digging all over town like a hound on a scent. And I don't like anything about the three of you. The sooner you move on from here, the sooner this town can go back to being a sleepy little stop on the stagecoach line. Blood's bad for business, boys, and you have a way of attracting it."

Cobb knew it did not matter why Brickell was letting

them go. He had returned the money without taking any of it for himself. Cobb should count himself lucky.

But he knew that men like the sheriff were not generous. They only gave up what they did not value. If he passed on helping himself to Cobb's money, it meant he had something bigger to cash in already in hand.

Cobb was about to say something, but Brickell silenced him by holding up a single finger. "Don't push your luck, Cobb. You still have to run passengers through here on your way to and from Laramie, so keep your mouth shut. I gave you back your money and your freedom. A wise man knows when good enough is as good as it's going to get. Go back upstairs to your room, collect your things, climb aboard your coach, and drive away." He nodded over at Hunt. "And take this curiosity with you when you go. Ennisville has enough drunks already."

Butch grabbed Cobb's arm and pulled him back a bit in the direction of the hotel. He always had more sense when to stop than his partner, and Cobb did not resist.

But Leon Hunt stood face to face with Brickell in the thoroughfare. "If it's all the same to you, Sheriff, I think I'll stick around town for a while longer."

Cobb watched Brickell's eyes narrow. "I told your friends to clear out of here, and the same goes for you."

"You certainly have, but I'm afraid the matter is a bit more complicated than you realize. You see, I accepted a commission from Colonel McBride to investigate what happened to his good friends, the Becquers. Cobb and Butch have a stagecoach line to run, so I can't expect them to stay, whereas I am in between engagements at present. I'm going to remain in Ennisville and see what I can turn up on my own. I owe the colonel and the Becquers that much."

Brickell took a step closer. "It's not your place to investigate anything around here, Hunt. That's my job, so you'd best be on that coach when it pulls out if you know what's good for you."

Hunt stood straighter. "Why, Sheriff Brickell. I could be forgiven for taking that as a threat."

"You can take it any way you want as long as you take it with you when you leave," Brickell said, seething. "The colonel's promises might not be worth as much to you."

Cobb pulled his arm free of Butch's grip. "What's that supposed to mean?"

Brickell quickly remembered himself. "You know how rich folks are. The farther away they get from a problem, the less interested in it they become. In a day or two, he'll be fat and happy in Laramie and the Becquers will be a distant memory. It might be for them, but it won't be for me. I'll get to the bottom of it, and when I do, I'll see to it that they hang."

Cobb had sensed something was off about Brickell as soon as he had called out to them on the street. It was not until that moment that he realized what it was. "You going to do it alone?"

"If I have to."

"Where are your deputies, Brickell? They're usually around to back your play. How come they're not with you now?"

Butch joined in. "Come to think of it, I haven't seen them around all day. They should have been back by now."

The sheriff threw up his hands and walked away from them. "I've got better things to do than argue with you three in the middle of the street. You've got forty-five minutes to get out of Ennisville, boys. If you're not on your coach, you'll be in my jail. Get moving."

Cobb glanced back at Hunt, who had not moved. "You still thinking about staying?"

Hunt smiled. "The thought of leaving never crossed my mind. I'm an actor, after all." He pointed at Brickell, who was still storming back toward the jail. "And I seem to have an eager audience for my performance."

After Cobb and Butch had stowed their meager belongings in the boot of the coach, the liveryman helped them hitch up their team in preparation for making the push on the final leg of their journey.

"I hate rolling into Laramie empty like this," Butch said, "but we've got some prospective customers waiting for us there. That is, if Burke or some other outfit hasn't wooed them away from us first."

Cobb was normally the more business-minded of the two, but not that afternoon. Leaving Ennisville like this felt like a defeat, and although he tried to avoid competition and contests whenever he could, he had never been fond of losing. "This whole thing stinks."

The liveryman tried to look busy as he helped with the horses, but Cobb could tell he was listening.

Butch came to him and lowered his voice as he said, "Save your griping for the road. This livery's got ears."

Cobb grumbled as he climbed up into the wagon box. "I never saw one that didn't."

Butch took the money from the sack to pay off the liveryman and joined Cobb in the wagon box. The two mustangs they had purchased followed on a lead line at the back. Cobb released the brake and steered the team toward the Ennisville Hotel, where Hunt was standing on the boardwalk waiting to bid them goodbye. He was glad to see Hunt had taken to wearing his pistol on his left hip. It was liable to be the only friend he had in Ennisville once Cobb and Butch left.

"You sure I can't change your mind about staying," Cobb said. "There's no shame in it. We can always come back later. It's not a long ride."

"There may be no shame in leaving," Hunt answered, "but there's no reason for it, either. I seem to have struck a sour chord with the sheriff. I'd like to understand why. Besides, Mrs. Becquer laughed at my jokes during her last dinner, and I feel as though I owe her something for her patronage." He laughed at himself as he looked away. "Who am I kidding? I'm an old man who goes a bit blinder every day, but I'm a burr under Brickell's saddle. I like making him uncomfortable. If I can do some good in the course of making him uncomfortable, all the better. It's not like I've got anything else to do."

Butch said, "You've got Mrs. Wagner and her ministry waiting for you in Laramie."

"Mrs. Wagner is a religious force unto herself," Hunt observed. "Her zeal rivals only that of the apostle Paul. I doubt she'll even miss me."

Cobb could see there was no point in trying to talk him out of staying. He tossed a thumb back toward the livery. "If things get too hot for you, they've got plenty of good horses back there. I've got a line of credit with the owner, so don't be afraid of putting one on my tab and hightailing it to Laramie if the need arises."

Hunt stepped forward and offered his hand up to Cobb. "You're a good man, Tucker Cobb. I'll see you soon." He looked at Butch. "Keep an eye on him for me. This territory needs good men like him. And you, my frontier Falstaff."

"I still don't know what that means," Butch admitted, "but I've chosen to take it as a compliment."

"You take it as it was intended, sir." Hunt took off his hat with a great flourish. "Farewell to thee, you gentle gentlemen. May the road to Laramie be a straight and calm one."

Cobb snapped the reins and got the team moving again. They rumbled along the thoroughfare and past the jail. Sheriff Brickell was outside, watching them carefully. He did not offer a wave but peered into the coach and frowned when he found it empty.

When they reached the end of town, Butch said, "I sure hope Leon knows what he's doing by staying behind like that. Brickell doesn't like him much."

"Brickell only likes what makes him money," Cobb said. "Keep your Henry ready. Something tells me this isn't over yet."

Cobb figured he had spent the better part of his adult life driving a team of horses for one purpose or another. As a younger man, he had driven the chuckwagon for many a drive that brought cattle and horses to markets all over the country. He had later been a freighter and a coach driver for other outfits in Colorado and, later, Wyoming.

A man who had done so much driving in his life tended to develop a sense of the land around him. He learned to pay attention to what he saw and what he did not see. The road could tell a man much if he knew how to listen and what to look for.

As he judged they had traveled just a mile or so out of Ennisville, Cobb saw the faded farmhouse in a peaceful pasture to his right. But the road before him showed evidence of recent chaos.

The ruts in the road left behind by Burke's coach became crooked once it reached this spot, and deep divots in the packed dirt showed something had happened there. Something unexpected.

Butch spoke what Cobb was thinking. "This doesn't feel right."

Cobb eyed the tall grass on either side of the road for a hint of what had gone wrong. "No. It doesn't."

He pulled the team to a halt when he saw the tall grass to his left broken and the ground around it disturbed. He held onto the reins as he stood up to get a better look around and saw a man lying on his side against a tree stump down a slight incline from the road.

Cobb secured the brake and jumped down to investigate. Butch grabbed up his rifle and remained with the coach. He could see much more from up there.

Cobb half-stumbled, half-slid his way down toward the fallen man. He used the tree stump to steady himself as he looked over the man's injuries. His eyes were half-open and vacant, proving that he was dead. Cobb pressed two fingers against his neck but could not feel a pulse.

"He alive?" Butch called down from the stagecoach.

"Nope." Cobb moved the dead man's arm to get a better look at his injuries. "Looks like he's been shot. Twice in the back. Bullets look like they came out the front."

"You recognize him?"

Cobb moved away some of the dirt and grass that covered his face and peered down at him. "Looks like he's one of Brickell's men." He pushed the man over onto his back and saw the deputy's star pinned to his shirt. "Just found his badge. He's one of Brickell's boys." Cobb pulled the star from the shirt, tearing it. He did not think the dead man would mind the indignity of a torn shirt.

"How long?"

Cobb pocketed the star and began to make his way back up to the road. "His limbs are only just getting stiff, so I'd say he's been dead since the morning. Right around the time when Burke's stage left town."

When he reached the road, he slapped his hands clean on his pants and tried not to think about what the dead deputy might mean for the prospects of Jane and the other passengers. He asked Butch, "See anything ahead from up there?"

He saw Butch squinting into the distance. "Looks like there's a couple of shapes in the road up ahead. I don't take them for deer carcasses, so—"

Cobb ducked behind the coach when he heard a rifle shot echo across the flat land that surrounded them. Butch did not jump down to join him on the ground, but instead slid onto the top of the stagecoach. Without the burden of baggage up there, he had a good place from which to return fire.

"You see where that came from?" Cobb shouted up to his partner.

"From the farmhouse over yonder," Butch answered. "I just caught a puff of gun smoke from the porch."

Cobb pulled himself up to the wagon box, lifted the seat, and took out his coach gun just as a bullet struck the seat inches from his head. He fell and landed hard on his back but managed to keep hold of the gun.

Cobb groaned as he sat up. "That come from the same place?"

"Yep." Butch fired once. A yelp rose from the direction of the farmhouse. Cobb looked in that direction and saw a red stain on the porch wall that had not been there before. As usual, Butch had hit his mark.

Cobb knew they could not remain in the middle of the road like this for long. Whoever was shooting at them was good with a rifle, and it would only be a matter of time before he started aiming at the horses. Cobb knew they would be stranded here if he did. "You see anyone else over there?"

"No, but there's one less of them than they started with," Butch said. "What are we gonna do, Boss?"

Cobb thought quickly. He knew better than to believe in coincidences, which meant these men must be the same ones Hunt had spotted in the hotel in Ennisville. That meant there were at least two of them out there but possibly more. Even with one dead, they were still possibly outgunned, and a team of horses pulling a coach was not exactly fleet of foot. Whoever was shooting at them would have plenty of time to draw a careful aim on Cobb or Butch or one of the horses. Even if they survived the resulting wreck, he and Butch would be stranded with little cover and no possibility of help. He knew the next stage was not scheduled to come by for another two days at the earliest.

Another shot sailed high overhead, and Butch responded with a shot of his own. "I think I winged him, but I don't know if he's dead. He's hiding behind a woodpile by the house. What are we gonna do here, Boss? They'll start aiming at the horses next."

Cobb stood up and looked over the top of the horses. The farmhouse stood about a hundred yards away. The only cover he could see were the tall weeds that would betray their position if they tried to approach it that way.

No matter how he tried to slice it, there was only one way out of this and that was straight ahead.

"Keep a sharp eye," Cobb said as he pulled himself up into the wagon box and gathered up the reins. "Get yourself flat because we'll be moving fast."

Cobb released the brake and snapped the reins, sending the already nervous horses into a gallop. He kept his eyes on the road as the coach hurtled forward along the road.

He kept his foot on his coach gun in the well of the box and his head low as another shot sounded from the farmhouse. Butch cracked off two blasts in response, and the pace of the team did not falter.

Bile rose in Cobb's mouth when he saw the bodies of two men in the middle of the road, both crushed beneath the wheels of a coach. One of them was clearly Burke. His girth made him easier to spot.

The other man was face down in the dirt, and while Cobb could not be certain, he wondered if he was Brickell's other deputy.

Butch fired three times in rapid succession as they raced by the farmhouse and continued on at speed. Now that the body of the coach was between him and the farmhouse, he sat up straighter as he kept the team on the road. Butch cut loose with a final shot before dropping down beside him on the wagon box.

Cobb spoke over the sound of the hard-charging team of horses. "They coming after us?"

"Let 'em come," Butch said as he began to feed fresh rounds into his rifle. "They won't get any closer than they are now."

Sometimes Cobb wished his partner could simply answer a straight question. "I didn't ask if you could hit them. I asked if they were coming after us."

"Didn't see any horses about," Butch said. "Probably had them in the barn." He looked behind them. "And no one's coming after us, either."

Cobb was grateful for that much at least. "How many of them were there?"

"Two that I saw," Butch reported. "Could've been more inside, but they didn't come out when the shooting started, so I can't say for certain. I might've seen some smoke rising from the chimney, but I was a bit too taken with other things to swear to it."

Cobb knew the team of horses could not keep up this breakneck pace forever, so he began to pull on the reins to bring them to a gradual stop. "Burke's dead. Saw him in the middle of the road. Saw another fella next to him but couldn't make out his face. I think he might've been one of Brickell's deputies."

"Too bad it wasn't Brickell himself." Butch rested the butt of the rifle on his leg. "But if they really were his men, it kinda changes our thoughts of him, doesn't it? He wouldn't send two good men to die just for a couple of trinkets from some rich folks, now would he?"

Cobb was not so sure. He did not think it was that simple. Life rarely moved in a straight line, and the two deputies could have gotten themselves killed for any number of reasons.

"I'm more concerned about us being alive," Cobb said. "The rest is Brickell's problem."

"Let's just hope it doesn't become our problem, too."

CHAPTER 19

Sheriff Fritz Brickell watched the shadows grow long across the jailhouse floor and knew something was wrong. His deputies should have been back hours ago with some kind of report about robbing the coach. His old family farmhouse was only a few miles out of town, so what was the delay? He doubted any of the passengers could have put up much of a fight. He did not know the mettle of Fowler and the other rustlers, but Chance and Dean were good men. The only one of the passengers who might have put up a fight was Colonel McBride, but that old warhorse was no match for his deputies.

He had to find some reason for why they were delayed. Tucker Cobb and Butch Keeling had left hours ago, more than enough time for Chance and Dean to have put the coachmen out of Brickell's misery. He had taught the boys how to lay an ambush personally. He had no doubt that the coachmen had both been killed before they realized they were being attacked.

But the nagging voice in the back of his mind kept at him. *If everything had gone fine, why hadn't they come back yet?*

He got to his feet and went outside to check the road

again, as if watching it might bring them back sooner. He looked in the direction of the farmhouse, but there was no sign of them. Just a thin haze of dirt blown up from the road out of town.

He looked in the opposite direction and heard the saloon sounds begin to pick up throughout the small town. They were getting ready for the evening, and Brickell wondered if his men would be back in time.

He looked at the Ennisville Hotel and saw Leon Hunt sitting on the bench on the boardwalk. His faded black suit looked almost shiny in the light of the afternoon, and his long legs were crossed in front of him. His head was down as though he was sleeping, but Brickell sensed the man was awake. Listening. Watching. There was more to the old actor than just fancy words and an affected manner. The way he carried himself revealed there was something of the killer about him. The way he wore his gun tied down to his left leg. The butt of the pistol was always within easy reach whenever he wore it, and Brickell could see he was wearing it now.

Hunt had a way of working his way under a man's skin and was not afraid of getting a man's ire up. He never spouted words to hear himself talk, but always watched their impact, like he was measuring their reaction. Brickell was not afraid of him—he had not been truly afraid of anything since boyhood—but he would do well to remain on his guard around Hunt. He was sure more than a few graves had been filled by men who had done otherwise.

Thoughts of death and dead men led him back to his concern about his missing deputies. He decided enough time had passed since Cobb had left for him to head to the farmhouse to take a look for himself. He would learn nothing by remaining alone in the jail and worrying.

He untethered his bay from the hitching rail in front of

the jail and climbed into the saddle. As he brought the horse around, he took a quick glance back at Hunt to see if he had noticed him, but the actor had not moved. He wondered if the man might have died. Brickell would count himself fortunate if that were the case.

He allowed his horse to move at its own pace along the road, paying attention to the marks in the dirt. Two stagecoaches had rumbled through that day, and the road bore the deep scars of their heavy wheels. He began to wonder what fate the passengers had met and if they had suffered much before death found them.

He had given Fowler and the others specific instructions about how to attack the coach. Chance and Dean would lead Burke's coach into the trap, ensuring that they slowed down long enough for the outlaws to rush them. The deputies would help Burke to drive the coach across the rugged land to the barn beside the farmhouse. There, they could easily dispatch the passengers and their driver without fear of being seen. He had ordered them to not hurt the Duprey woman, as he wished to save her for himself. He had designs on becoming more than just the sheriff of Ennisville, and a handsome woman on his arm—not to mention in his bed—would be a welcomed asset. He knew her reputation and doubted she would balk at the arrangement. Women such as her rarely allowed something like murder to get between them and life's comforts.

He allowed himself to think about his future as he rode upon the rise of the road. This was the spot where the deputies were to begin to put his plan into action. They would race ahead of the coach to let Fowler and his men know they were coming. And once the stage had crested the hill, they all would quickly surround it and hold the frightened people at gunpoint before leading them to their end.

He wished he had been there to see the starch knocked out of Colonel McBride. The pompous fool had deserved a bit of humbling before he met his maker. He was only sorry he had not been able to mete out the punishment directly, but his duties in Ennisville were more important. Someone had to keep an eye on Cobb, Keeling, and Hunt lest they decided to check on their friends.

Cobb and Keeling. Brickell would delight in their death almost as much as he would Colonel McBride's. They had a great deal of arrogance about them for coachmen, Cobb worst of all. Brickell imagined his formidable size and strength had been enough to keep most men from challenging him, but no man was bigger than a bullet, particularly when it was being fired by men who knew how to shoot. Chance and Dean knew how to shoot. They were good men and loyal.

Getting rid of Fowler and the others would be easy enough. He would dump them in the same grave as the others. No one would come looking for them, and few would miss them. When the McBrides were found to be overdue in Laramie, Brickell was sure his friends at the Wyoming Mining Company would come looking for him. They would probably dispatch a company of Pinkertons out of Chicago to start the search, but they would not find them. Months were likely to pass before they got around to looking for them, and Brickell would stall them when they did. The ground would reclaim their graves by then, and any trace of them would be gone from the earth. He would have Averill's gold, not to mention whatever price he could find for the valuables from the McBrides and Becquers in Laramie. He would be sure to split whatever he received with Chance and Dean, too. He needed friends for where he was going, and they would be the rocks on which he built his career.

But there was still the question of what to do with Leon Hunt. It would have been much easier if the old actor had just agreed to leave town with Cobb and Keeling. They all would have been dead and in the ground by now, but Hunt would not budge. Brickell would have to find a way to take care of him in his own time. He could probably convince a couple of the drunks in the saloons to do the deed for him. He would take great delight in deciding a fit ending for the troublesome troubadour.

As he reached the top of the hill, Brickell pulled his horse up short. He had expected to see the road continue on toward Laramie, but found it littered with dead bodies. The road was pockmarked with ruts left by coach wheels and divots caused by the hooves of frantic horses.

He urged his bay forward and found Chance's body off the side of the road against a rotted tree stump. His front was a mess of dried blood, and the flies had already found him. Chance had worked for him since he had been a boy, and Brickell quickly looked away from him.

He rode on toward the two bodies in the road. The corpses of Burke and Dean had been mangled by the coach wheels and trod under by what looked like more than one team of horses. He gripped the reins tightly. *How had this happened?*

He stood up in his stirrups and looked around for any explanation of what he saw. The land told him nothing, except when he looked at his family's neglected farmhouse. There, on the porch, he saw a splattering of blood on the wall.

Brickell drew his pistol and moved his horse off the road and toward the house. The bay stepped carefully along the weedy ground, and he urged it to continue on. He stopped about twenty yards away when he saw Fowler's body on the porch. His rifle lay beside him and his shirt had been ripped open. The young fool had torn at his own clothes to find the wound in the center of his chest.

Out of the corner of his eye, Brickell saw a trail of blood beside the pile of wood that led into the house. He did not know if any of the bandits were inside, and he did not want to risk getting shot while he found out. He remained on horseback as he called out, "This is Brickell. Who's inside?"

"It's Bowsfield," one of the men shouted out to him. "Get in here quick. Duren and Moeller are hurt bad."

Brickell had sprung enough traps on men in his time to know that rushing killed more men than being careful ever did. He climbed down from his bay and wrapped the reins around a porch post. He kept his pistol in hand as he slowly stepped up on the porch. The wood was rotted in certain places, so he chose where he stepped carefully.

He kicked in the rotting door and stood back in case one of the outlaws began shooting at him.

The front room of his old house was full of cobwebs with dust strewn along half-broken furniture. The plaster walls had cracked and flaked many seasons ago, coating the room in a thin layer of gray powder.

Off to the left, he saw Bowsfield tending to two men on the floor. He recognized one of them as Duren. He had been shot through the throat and appeared to be a few hours dead.

Bowsfield focused his efforts on Moeller, who was gasping loudly to breathe. A bullet wound in his upper chest was the reason. Despite having used some rags he had managed to find around the abandoned house, Bowsfield had been unable to stop the bleeding.

The young outlaw struggled to keep his friend sitting upright while he kept pressure on the wound. But the bullet had passed straight through him, and Bowsfield did not have enough rags to cover both holes. Brickell had seen such wounds before and knew Bowsfield's efforts were pointless. Moeller was slowly suffocating and would only get worse.

"Don't just stand there!" Bowsfield yelled up at the sheriff. "Help me."

Brickell needed Bowsfield's help first. "What happened here? Both of my men are dead."

Bowsfield's hands shook as he tried to keep pressure on Moeller's chest wound. "That stagecoach wasn't nearly the easy pickings you told us it was. The coachman gave up soon enough, but McBride came out fighting. He shot my horse out from under me and shot Duren there in the throat. You didn't tell us anyone beside the driver would be toting a firearm."

Brickell had not known the colonel had been armed, but one old man with a pistol should not have been a match for six young men in their prime. "How'd Chance get killed?"

Bowsfield tried to keep Moeller upright although he began to succumb to his injuries. "I saw Dean shoot him, but don't ask me why he shot him because I don't know. Dean rode on to where we were and told us to follow him. As soon as we got close, McBride started shooting at us. Shot my horse out from under me, then shot Duren here in the throat. Dean shot the driver, then he got himself shot, as well. We barely managed to get out of there with our lives."

Brickell did not believe him. "That doesn't explain why Fowler's lying dead on my porch and your friend is gasping for air. Don't tell me an old man with a bad leg did all that."

"He didn't," Bowsfield said. "McBride's stage took off while we were trying to regroup. We rode back here after they left to tend to Duren's throat, but he died right after we carried him in here."

Brickell took a step back as if he had been struck. "You mean you didn't even go after the preacher's gold?"

"Didn't know about any gold," Bowsfield answered. "Couldn't have gotten close enough to get it even if we had. McBride had us rattled and anything on that coach went with him."

Brickell struggled to make sense of what had happened. Chance and Dean were dead, and he did not have anything to show for it. Not even the preacher's gold. All because of a stubborn cripple with a pistol?

"What happened with Fowler and Moeller?"

"Fowler kind of went crazy after Duren died. We were in here trying to figure out if we should come to tell you about what had happened when we heard a coach coming down the road."

"That would've been Cobb and Butch," Brickell said.

Bowsfield continued with his story. "He and Moeller took their rifles and ran outside. I tried to cover them from the doorway. That coach was still a fair distance away, and I told them to wait, but they were both out for blood. Fowler shot first from the porch, but Butch shot back and hit him dead center in the chest. Moeller here was over by the woodpile, but he got dropped next. The coach took off and I dragged Moeller in here. I know I can save him, Sheriff. Run back to town and fetch us a doctor. He's young and he's strong. He's held out for a long time like this."

Brickell felt embarrassment and rage wash over him. Embarrassment that he had given these fools a simple plan to follow and they had still managed to come away with nothing to show for it. He was angry that he had lost two good men and was left with a half-dead outlaw and a use-less one to take their place. The gold and the woman he had been counting on to give him a fresh start in life were long gone for Laramie. He still had the loot Bowsfield and the others had stolen the previous night, but it was cold comfort when compared to a bag full of gold.

Bowsfield's voice cracked when he yelled, "Damn it, Sheriff. Moeller's dying. You have to do something!"

Brickell knew exactly what he had to do.

He raised his pistol and shot Moeller in the head, then Bowsfield. Both outlaws dropped to the floor, thus solving all of his problems.

His work done, he holstered his pistol and began to head back outside. An explanation of what had happened had already begun to form in his mind. With the passengers of Burke's coach still alive, he would have to concoct a story that would match what they had seen, which was exactly what he began to do.

When the two deputies he had sent to guard the stage-coach did not return, Brickell had decided to ride out to see what had happened to them. Dean must have thrown in with the thieves and shot Chance during the robbery. Colonel McBride put up a brave fight and repelled the attack, saving the passengers from harm. Cobb and Butch stopped a second attack from the farmhouse and escaped with their lives.

When Brickell happened upon the scene, he naturally checked the farmhouse and was ambushed by the last surviving outlaw, who was now dead. Justice had been served, and Fritz Brickell's hide had been saved.

If he told the story the right way, Brickell thought, he just might come out of this a hero. It was practically the truth, and there was no one left to call him a liar.

He stepped outside and saw Leon Hunt waiting for him atop a horse. He recognized the paint gelding as one of the horses the livery allowed visitors to use while they were in town. Hunt looked as if he had been out for a quiet ride in the countryside, save for the pistol in his left hand.

"You've been mighty busy, Sheriff."

Brickell did not know how much the aging actor had seen or heard, so he played it safe. "How long have you been lurking out here, Hunt?"

"Long enough to learn the truth," Hunt said. "I found your deputies and Burke up on the road. Looks like your plan to get the reverend's gold failed. I've spent all morning wondering why you suddenly decided to let Cobb and Butch leave town. Now I know why. You figured your men would still be up for blood after finishing off McBride and the others. You thought they'd ride right into your trap. Sounds to me like you thought wrong."

Brickell had not heard his version of the story aloud, and he decided Hunt would be a good audience, especially since he would not be alive for much longer. "What makes you think you heard anything at all?"

"'False face must hide what the false heart doth know'," the actor said. "A fellow by the name of William Shakespeare wrote that a long time ago, but the sentiment still holds true."

"Shakespeare ain't here," Brickell said. "I am and I didn't have any hand in what happened here today. I rode out here, found my men dead, and killed the man who did it." He smiled. "Some might call me a hero after what I did today."

"They won't call you anything but what you already are. A lying thief and a coward."

Brickell placed his hand on his pistol, but Hunt did not react. He did not even flinch or raise the pistol in his left hand. In fact, the actor was not looking at the sheriff at all despite their standoff. *Why?*

"That's the truth of what happened, Hunt, and there's

no one to call me a liar, least of all your friends. I'm sure they'll back up my story when they reach Laramie. Even you won't be able to call me a liar then."

"I guess you haven't been listening," Hunt said. "I already have."

Brickell grabbed the butt of his pistol and began to lift it slowly, silently. Hunt did not react. It was almost as though he could not see him.

He continued to quietly slide his pistol from the holster. "We don't have to be enemies, you know. Ennisville is a good town. You and me could work it together if you decide to stay. I can work the law angle of it, and you, with your fancy words and the way you are, could charm some well-heeled visitors into investing in the place. We could make the town as big as Laramie if we do it right." His pistol was clear now and flat against his right leg. "I know we could do it if you help me."

"You mean we could be partners." It was a statement, not a question.

"If you prefer to think of it like that. We don't have to be enemies."

Hunt's head tilted toward Brickell, though he still was not looking at him. "Perhaps not, but with what I know, we'd never be able to fully trust each other. It'll come down to us squaring off against each other eventually. I'd rather get it over with now and skip the dance. Never been much of a dancer."

Brickell knew if he killed this man now, he would always wonder if he could not have done more to talk him out of it. A man like Leon Hunt on his side could come in handy somewhere down the road. He had seen what regret could do to a man and wanted to spare himself the trouble on those long nights to come when doubt would visit him.

"Think long and hard about this, Hunt. I don't know

what you think you heard, but it's your word against mine."

Hunt grew even more still than he already was. "Good thing this isn't a court of law and I'm not a lawman. Justice comes in many forms, and the Becquers have not received their fair share. Not yet."

Brickell had his answer.

The sheriff heard the gunmetal of his pistol clack as he finally began to raise it.

Hunt shot him four times through the chest before Brickell knew what happened. He staggered back to the steps of the porch and fell on them. His gun slipped from his hands as he began to paw at his wounds.

Hunt remained on his horse. "Like I said, there's nothing wrong with my hearing."

Brickell felt panic rise in him as he watched his own blood begin to spread on his shirt front. Everything he had done since boyhood had been a bid to escape this house and its cursed land. The stingy soil that refused to yield a decent crop. The grass that livestock of any kind refused to eat. Now he was about to meet his end on the very steps he had fled so long ago.

He used whatever remaining strength he had to lift his head to see the man who had killed him. "I didn't kill that old couple."

"Perhaps," Hunt said, "but you let them die, and that's almost as bad."

Brickell tried to reply, but a wet cough racked his body and his strength finally left him. He felt his head rest on the porch, and his eyes settled on its roof. There was a hole in it that allowed him to look up at the sky. His last thought was one of gratitude as he breathed his last.

* * *

When he heard Brickell's last gasp, Hunt climbed down from the saddle and went to where the sheriff now lay. He paused to listen for a final death rattle, but all he heard was the wind in his ears. He placed his hand on his chest and felt no movement. Sheriff Brickell was gone.

He took the star from Brickell's shirt and held it. It felt odd in his hand and was not as light as he had thought it would be. There was heft to it, as there should be. The weight of such responsibility should be heavy to any man who decided to wear it. The burden often caused some to buckle. Men like Fritz Brickell were a testament to that.

Hunt closed his fingers around the star. He had never played a lawman before, not even on the stage. He wondered if it might become his last great role. He was willing to give it a try. He doubted he could do a worse job than Brickell had, and he might actually be good at it.

He pinned the star on his lapel and went back for his horse. He would have quite a story to tell when he returned to Ennisville, and he was nothing if not an easy mark for a good tale.

As he began to ride back to town and doubt about what he had done and what he was now setting out to do began to creep into his mind, he found some comfort in something the Bard had written long ago.

Time is the justice that examines all defenders.

CHAPTER 20

Colonel McBride was more tired than he let on when he pulled the stagecoach to a stop in front of the Laramie Hotel that afternoon. The excitement of the morning had left him as quickly as it had visited him, and he felt the worse for it. His leg ached from the effort of climbing into the wagon box. His arms and shoulders ached from hours gripping the reins and keeping the horses on the move. His lower back was sore from sitting on the bench, and he had almost nodded off twice during the journey.

He ignored the confused looks he drew from the towns-people as the coach rumbled through town. He knew his face was still stained with blood and his clothes were ruined by mud, so he imagined he made quite a sight. As he threw the hand brake, he was glad their journey was finally at an end.

His wife and Miss Jane were out of the coach and eager to help him as he inched his way down to solid ground. A clerk from the hotel scuttled out to greet them, but the colonel ordered him to leave them alone. Mrs. Wagner was already halfway out of the coach when he asked her to go back inside.

With Mrs. Wagner and Mr. Koppe seated inside the

coach, the others gathered around the open door. The colonel reached in and pulled Reverend Averill's bag toward him. He opened the satchel and removed the books, revealing four gold bars beneath it.

"I thought I heard something strange when the reverend fell getting into the coach," McBride said. "I figured it was gold and I was right."

"Good heavens!" Mrs. Wagner exclaimed at the sight. "No wonder the poor reverend struggled to lift it. I had no idea he was carrying such a parcel."

But McBride had no sympathy for the dead man. "He struck me as more of a man of ledgers than a man of God, Mrs. Wagner. There's probably an employer somewhere back there who's wondering where all of his gold went."

Mr. Koppe could not take his eyes off the bars. "Then we must make every effort to ensure it's returned to its rightful owner at once."

McBride had no patience for such decency. "I'm not much of a lawyer, but there's an old Scottish saying that possession is nine-tenths of the law, Mr. Koppe. The same rule applies here and now. Even if we knew who this belonged to, which we don't, I wouldn't hold out much hope of it reaching him. We've got it now, and we're going to put it to a good use that benefits all of us."

McBride replaced the books on top of the bars and shut the satchel as Mrs. Wagner glared at him. "I hope you're not saying what I think you're saying, Colonel McBride. Theft is theft, no matter how many hands are in the deed, and I imagine you already have quite a bit of money already."

"I do, but you don't," McBride said, "and neither does Miss Duprey here. The only people who know about this gold are us. While I don't know how Averill came upon it, I know how we're going to use it." He had given the matter a lot of thought on the road from Ennisville, and his mind was made up. "Mrs. Wagner here gets two bars for her ministry, while Miss Duprey gets the other two bars to do whatever she sees fit."

He was glad to see a protest die on Mrs. Wagner's lips. Since the colonel had put it like that, she looked differently on the prospect of keeping the gold.

Jane touched his arm. "Are you sure about that, Colonel?"

"As sure as I am that you'll do more with it than that rat Averill ever could." He closed the satchel and slid it aside. "Martha and I will have it brought up to our room with the rest of our things. Tomorrow morning, we'll sell it somewhere here in town and split the money between you. I'll see to it that you get a fair price. Of course, if you'd prefer to keep the bars yourselves, you may, but in my experience, a fair price today is better than a better price later."

Jane said, "But what about Tucker and Mr. Keeling. It doesn't seem right that they shouldn't benefit from this, too. Not after saving our lives like they did."

"I'll see to it that they receive a sizable reward for their efforts, but I'll be happy to discuss the matter with them once they arrive here in Laramie. Let this be the last we speak of it until tomorrow. The fewer people who know about this, the better for all concerned. Agreed?"

They all agreed.

McBride stepped back to allow Mr. Koppe to exit the coach, and they both helped Mrs. Wagner down.

The colonel accepted his walking stick from his wife as they walked into the hotel together. He told the desk clerk, "There's quite a lot of luggage to unload, so you'd better have someone see to it immediately. There's a satchel in the back that should be brought up to our room with the rest of our belongings. Mrs. McBride here will help you sort everything out."

"Mrs. McBride?" the clerk said. "Then I suppose that makes you Colonel McBride from the Wyoming Mining Company."

"I should hope so," McBride said. "Now, have someone see to those bags. I'd like to be up in my room sometime before midnight."

The clerk dashed off to find some men to get the luggage, leaving McBride and his wife alone in the lobby while the others milled around out on the boardwalk. "You certainly are full of surprises today, Colonel McBride. I can remember a time when you would've kept all that gold for yourself. You're getting awfully generous in your old age."

McBride smiled. He never feared becoming too conceited around her. His wife always found a way to cut him down to size. "Think of it more as philanthropy, not generosity. King Charles Hagen won't take too kindly to our arrival in Laramie. He hates our company and how it might give him a run for his own mining interests in the territory. We'll be needing some friends here, and those two ladies are forces to be reckoned with. We'll need them on our side in the days and weeks ahead."

Martha's expression soured. "You never could let a nice moment sit, could you?"

The colonel spotted a chair in the lobby where he could sit without being forgotten by the clerk. "I don't make the rules, my dear. I just live by them. And bend them to my will when I can. I may not always be so lucky."

Since they did not have any passengers, there was no reason for Cobb and Butch to stop at the hotel, so they went straight on to the livery instead. Russ Sprout, the livery owner, ambled out to greet them when they stopped in front of his establishment. He still had the same unruly white beard he had worn since Cobb had first met him years before.

"We sure are getting our fill of coaches today," Sprout said when Cobb and Butch climbed down from the wagon box. "Laramie's getting to be a lively place all of a sudden."

Cobb saw Burke's coach sitting behind the livery stables. "Looks like the others reached town earlier. How were they faring when they got here?"

"Mighty poorly," Sprout said. "From what I heard tell of it, Leo Burke got himself killed and they lost a reverend to bandits. Losing a preacher to bullets is bad luck, but Colonel McBride wouldn't hear of it. He fought them off single-handedly with just a six-shooter and plain, old-fashioned meanness. He took up the reins and drove the team here all by his lonesome."

Cobb had already seen what had happened to Burke on the road from Ennisville. "What about the ladies who were traveling with them. Were they hurt?"

"Not that I heard," Sprout said, "but don't go by me. I'm just repeating what folks have been saying. They came to get me to take the coach away after they took the bags from it. Don't know what I'm gonna do with it, but I expect I'll be able to sell it for a decent sum. King Charles has been buying up every line he knows of, so maybe I'll be able to convince him to take it off my hands. At least the horses are fresh." He looked over the team that had brought Cobb and Butch to town. "Fresher than this lot, leastways."

Butch went to the back of the coach and took out their

bags. "You hear anything about what happened to us in Ennisville?"

"Can't say that I have," Sprout admitted, "though I'd be glad to hear it after you boys get yourself settled. It'd be kinda nice to get something straight from the well instead of hearing it watered down in the telling like I usually do. Will you boys be staying here or at the hotel? I've just laid down some fresh hay in the stalls if you're of a mind to want them. Got a few empty stalls at the moment, and you're welcome to take your pick."

Cobb had never been one to turn down a roof over his head, but after the long day they had experienced, a delicious meal and a decent bed might be worth the expense. He also wanted to check on Jane to see how she was doing. "Thanks for the kind offer, Russ. We'll try our luck at the hotel, but we'll be back to let you know."

Never one to allow his guns to stay unattended, Cobb took his coach gun from beneath the seat and accepted his bag from Butch. His partner also carried his rifle and bag with him as they made their way toward the hotel together.

Butch looked over the street as they walked. "Is it me or are there more people in town than the last time we were here."

Cobb had been too consumed with concern about Jane to have noticed it, but now that he looked, he saw Butch was right. "Looks like Laramie's gone and made itself into a proper town. I imagine the whole territory will spruce itself up now that the war's over."

"All that fighting had to go somewhere," Butch said. "I'm glad folks are putting their efforts to good use."

"Amen to that," Cobb said, which reminded him of what Russ Sprout had just told them about the reverend. "Sounds like Averill got himself killed."

"Sure does," Butch agreed. "Wonder what happened to all those bars he was carrying. Gold or silver, it sounded like he was lugging quite a sum to my ears."

"Mine, too," Cobb said, "but guessing about it won't help any. Let's get to the hotel and see if the colonel or the others are around."

Butch grinned. "You mean Miss Jane."

Cobb did not mind Butch's teasing on the subject. "Last I checked, she was one of the others."

They found the Laramie Hotel off the main thoroughfare on a side street from where City Hall was being built. It promised to be an impressive stone structure once they finished it. Cobb watched the workmen scramble across the scaffolding as the top of the building rose just above it. The twelve steps leading up to the main entrance had been laid since the last time they had been in town, and work had begun on the wall that would enclose the courtyard that led to the new jail in the basement. He had been a free-ranger long enough to hate seeing walls going up, but he supposed they were the price of progress.

They entered the lobby of the hotel and were immediately greeted by a scowl from Mr. Herman, the fussy head clerk. Cobb had often wondered if the man had a neck as his head seemed to rise from the starched collars he preferred to wear. His head itself was a bald, smooth shape that reminded Cobb of a lily bulb.

"I was wondering when you two wastrels would show up," Herman said. "The rest of your party checked in several hours ago."

Herman had never had any love for either of the coachmen but reserved most of his dislike for Butch. Unfortunately for Herman, Butch knew it and never passed up the opportunity to annoy the man. He set his bag on the high counter, causing a significant amount of trail dust to rise up as he did and causing the clerk to cough.

"Good to see you, too, Hy." Butch smiled. "I was beginning to think you might've forgotten about old Cobb and me, seeing as how we haven't been here in a while."

"How could I forget?" Herman coughed. "They just finished patching up the bullet holes in the ceiling from your last visit."

"I had no part in that revelry," Butch protested. "That was just a couple of drovers out of Tennessee who couldn't handle their whiskey and were anxious to prove their prowess with a pistol."

"Indeed," Herman said. "Anyway, I'd like nothing better than to turn you away, but unfortunately, I won't have that pleasure. Colonel McBride has made arrangements for you. A week's stay. Paid in full, including meals."

Butch slapped Cobb on the back. "See that? We go into business, and we've already got friends in high places. I thought the old boy liked my charming personality and manners."

"Quite." Herman turned the ledger so Cobb and Butch could sign it. "Sign your names or make your mark. Our new owner demands an accurate accounting of all our guests."

"I can sign my name as well as I can say it," Butch said as he took the pen from the inkwell. "Mama always wanted her boys to be able to sign their names proper-like."

Cobb had always enjoyed the pleasure his partner took in making the clerk uncomfortable. "You've got a new owner? I thought Mr. Leek would never sell this place. Always figured they'd have to carry him out of here on a bier."

"Mr. Leek is a sensible man," Herman intoned, "and the

new owner made him quite a generous offer. Mr. Hagen is not known for his frugality."

Cobb closed his eyes. He should've known. "That would be King Charles Hagen, I guess."

"Your guess is correct, for once," Herman said. "He insists on keeping a close eye on all of our guests. His man was here earlier today to examine the register personally."

Cobb opened his eyes. "Let me guess. That would be John Bookman."

"The very same," Herman confirmed. "He saw your names and took note of them." Herman went to the wall of wooden cubbyholes behind him and selected an envelope. "He returned an hour later and left this for you." The clerk held it out to him but did not give it to him. "I'll be happy to read it to you if you need."

Cobb plucked the envelope from him. "No, thanks. I can read better than Butch can write his name."

Butch finished signing the register and replaced the pen in the inkwell with great ceremony. "You'll have to read pretty good to beat that signature, Cobb. Take a gander at it. A thing of beauty, even if I do say so myself."

Cobb opened the envelope and read the letter, even though he was fairly certain of what it would say. As he read it, his suspicions were confirmed. "Looks like we've been invited to his ranch up in Blackstone tomorrow. Says here he's most anxious to speak to us." Cobb put the letter back in the envelope and pocketed it. "Five will get you ten that he wants to talk about buying us out."

Herman folded his hands on the counter. "You'd do well to consider his offer. As Mr. Leek could attest were he here, Mr. Hagen is quite generous. But alas, Mr. Leek is not here. He's in San Francisco, where I understand he's thriving in a new establishment all his own."

"Bully for him." Cobb took the pen and signed his

name below Butch's flourishing signature. "Is the food here still lousy, or has Mr. Hagen improved that, too?"

"The Laramie Hotel has been redone from top to bottom per Mr. Hagen's exact instructions. You'll find everything in here is much improved."

Cobb stuck the pen back in the inkwell. "Except for the help."

Cobb and Butch flinched when a rebel yell cut through the air from the saloon in the back of the hotel.

Herman pursed his lips. "Quite."

Butch laughed. "Glad to see this place hasn't gone and lost all of its character. What do you say to a drink, partner? I don't know about you, but I'm parched."

Herman handed Cobb a key. "You're in room number ten, two flights up. It's not exactly a suite, but I'm sure you'll find it comfortable enough for your purposes."

Butch pulled his bag off the counter and tucked his rifle in the crook of his arm. "Let's stow this stuff in our room and commence with the revelry. If we're going to be meeting with King Charles, I aim to have a decent hangover when we do."

"Tucker! Wait a moment."

Cobb lost all feeling in his legs when he heard Jane Duprey call his name as she stepped out from the dining room. Colonel and Mrs. McBride were right behind her.

"We were just talking about you over dinner." Jane rose on her toes and gave Cobb a peck on the cheek before putting her arm through his. "We have so much to tell you about the trouble we faced when we left Ennisville."

Cobb's mouth ran dry. Jane had taken great pains to clean herself up and put on a new blue dress that made her eyes sparkle. He did not want to talk about stagecoaches and journeys and death. He would have been content to just stand with her and take in her beauty. "No need to tell me, Jane. We saw it all and worse when we rolled through that stretch."

"The bodies you saw only tell half the tale." The colonel stomped the end of his walking stick defiantly on the floor. "Road agents attacked us, killed Burke, and might've killed us, too, if I hadn't managed to repel them."

"We saw your handiwork on the road, Colonel," Butch said. "That was some mighty fancy shooting."

The colonel did not accept Butch's praise. "One of the men I killed was a deputy from Ennisville. I don't remember his name."

"Dean Sprout," Cobb said. "We saw him next to Burke in the road. Or what was left of them."

Mrs. McBride brought her hand to her mouth and Cobb felt bad about it. "Forgive my frankness about it, ma'am. I meant no offense."

"No need to apologize," the colonel's wife said. "I was there and saw it all with my own eyes. The colonel saved our lives by running off the bandits and driving us here. Did you encounter them later when you left Ennisville?"

"Trouble of a different sort," Butch said. "Looks like some of the men who attacked you still had plenty of fight left in them because they came at us, too. We took some fire from that old farmhouse off the road."

Jane looked up into Cobb's eyes. "Were you hurt?"

"Didn't get a scratch." Cobb patted her gloved hand. "Butch was too good a shot for them. He killed at least one and maybe a second, though we didn't stick around to find out for certain. We just got here a little while ago."

Again, the colonel stomped his walking stick in approval. "I'm glad to see it. I was wondering how long you two planned on being in Laramie. I'm sure you're anxious to get back on the road."

Butch could see Cobb was too taken with Jane to

answer, so he did the talking for them. "Can't say that we've given it much thought. For the moment, Cobb and me are just interested in whiskey and having a roof over our heads. Tomorrow will be time enough to think about the future."

Colonel McBride looked over his shoulder as some of the patrons in the saloon began singing a bawdy version of "Old Dog Trey." "I may have a proposition to make to you boys in the morning, but I'd like to sleep on it first before we discuss it. Would either of you mind if I called on you tomorrow morning? After you've had sufficient rest, of course."

Cobb did not have to ask Butch for his opinion, for he knew what his answer would be. "We'd be fools not to listen to you, Colonel. Just don't make it too early. I don't know what condition we'll be in come dawn."

"I'm not the early riser I used to be," McBride answered. "And whatever condition you'll be in, you've earned the right to it. Until then, I bid you all an enjoyable evening."

The older couple wished the three of them a good night and made their way up the stairs.

Cobb realized the three of them were standing in the middle of the lobby and asked Jane, "Any idea on what he wants to talk to me about?"

Jane smiled as she shook her head. "No, but I know he's quite fond of you. Both of you. I'm sure that whatever he wants to talk about will be pleasant. Far more pleasant than dealing with Mrs. Wagner. We saw her inside just now. She and Mr. Koppe arrived in the dining room just as we were leaving. The trip here didn't do much to take any of the starch out of her. She's boiling over with fire and brimstone, more now than ever."

Butch looked back in the direction of the dining room.

"Good thing for us there's other ways to get into the saloon. I'm not in the mood to have my wicked ways called into question this evening."

Cobb knew that Butch was anxious to get to the saloon, but he was enjoying Miss Jane's company.

"Butch and me were gonna put our stuff in our room, then head down to the saloon for drinks. I'd be happy to meet you later if you'd like."

"I'll be fast asleep as soon as my head hits the pillow," she said, "but tomorrow would be better. Lots of good things will happen then. You'll see. Don't ask me more or you'll ruin the surprise."

She popped up on her toes and gave him another peck on the cheek before gathering up her skirts and walking up the stairs. "Don't let him drink too much tonight, Mr. Keeling. You both have a big day tomorrow. You don't want to be sick for it."

Butch joined Cobb in watching her go up the stairs to her room, with Butch saying, "Laramie's a funny place. A few minutes ago, we were worried about Charles Hagen ruining our lives. Now, a mining boss wants to talk to us in the morning. It's so that a man doesn't know how he should feel from one minute to the next."

But Cobb knew better. "That's not Laramie. That's just life."

CHAPTER 21

Butch could barely contain his excitement as he and Cobb went back downstairs to the saloon. He had not had himself a decent time since long before North Branch, and he was due to live a little. North Branch was a sleepy town, and the events that transpired in Ennisville had not allowed him to properly relax.

He knew Cobb could use a break, too. He was always given to brooding too much, a condition Butch feared would only worsen with Miss Jane Duprey around. It was clear that his partner had developed feelings for the woman. Feelings that Butch doubted would be reciprocated now that she was in Laramie. Like Cobb usually did, she had her mind more on business than love. His friend did not care about much, but when he did, he gave it his all. Butch knew Cobb was bound for heartache, and Butch also knew he would be there to help pick up the pieces after it happened.

He ran his hand along the butt of the pistol he had insisted on carrying with him as they entered the saloon. While the rest of the place had fancy furnishings and new rugs, he was glad to see that Hagen had left the drinking room relatively intact. The wooden bar still bore the familiar gouges and burns from unattended cigarettes. The tables where men gambled and drank were still crooked on sawdust floors, and the mirror behind the bar still had a crack in the corner of it. Some men had different ideas of heaven, and this was Butch Keeling's version of it.

He could see Cobb was still preoccupied with Hagen's note, and he made it his mission to help him forget about that for a few hours. "Come on, old man. I'll let you buy me a drink or five."

"I'm not old and it's our money," Cobb said. "You're buying yourself a drink."

"I know, but as long as you're the one to put the money on the bar, it'll make me feel better."

Cobb found a free spot at the bar and ordered a bottle of whiskey from the bartender. Butch allowed the drunken laughter and tobacco smoke to seep into him, and he felt the endless miles on the road melt away.

Until he heard a man say, "I don't care what that fat old woman says. The last thing this town needs is another Holy Joe showing up and spouting off about sin."

"You can say that again," another man agreed. "She wasn't off the coach for an hour before she started preaching at us. I wouldn't have believed it if I hadn't seen it with my own two eyes and heard it with my own ears."

Butch hoped Cobb had not heard it but could tell by the rigid way he was standing that he had.

He tried to distract Cobb by pointing at the new whiskey bottle on the bar, but Cobb pushed past him and approached the loudmouth. "What was that you just said?"

The man turned and took his time looking Cobb over. Tucker Cobb was not exactly tall, but he was taller than most, and what he lacked in height, he made up for with a thick neck and arms and rough hands that were big for a man his size. Of all the words he had heard used to describe his friend over the years, *friendly* had never been one of them.

"What's it to you?" the loudmouth asked. "I wasn't talking to you."

"You were talking loud enough for me and everyone else to hear it," Cobb said. "Interrupting our drinking time. I'd like to know why."

The man set his glass on the bar and turned to face Cobb full on. He was bearded and taller than Cobb by half a head or more but was not nearly as wide. "Not that it's any of your business, but I was talking about this preacher woman who threw us nasty glances when we were walking in here before. Not only did she look at us like we were dirt, but she started calling us sinners who ought to repent for our ways. She kept on about demon rum and the ruin of whiskey. But don't worry about it none. We gave her a piece of our mind, didn't we, Boyd?"

Butch saw Boyd move next to his partner. "We surely did. Her and that old scarecrow she had with her. They'll mind their words the next time they find themselves around Hagen men."

Butch winced as he reached for the whiskey and poured himself some. He might as well get his drinking in before Cobb lost his temper.

"You boys are Hagen men," Cobb repeated. "What do you do for him? Shine his boots?"

The other men standing around them grew quiet as they paid attention to what was happening.

"We do anything he needs doing," Boyd answered. "We run his cattle, tend to his horses. Even work his mines when there's call for it, but keeping nosy fellas like you in line is our specialty. We put Holy Joes in their place for free." He took a step toward Cobb. "You a Holy Joe, mister? You don't look like a Holy Joe to me."

The first loudmouth smiled. "Don't be silly, Boyd. This man's a coach driver. So's his skinny friend with him. This here is Tucker Cobb and Butch Keeling. The last of the independents. That is, until tomorrow. Then we'll see who's shining the king's boots."

Cobb backhanded the man across the jaw, dropping him to the floor.

Boyd reached for his pistol but stopped when he felt the barrel of Butch's revolver under his chin.

"I wouldn't do that if I were you," Butch cautioned him. "The clerk out at the desk told me they just finished patching up a hole in the ceiling from the last time I was here. I'd sure hate to make them do it again so soon."

Cobb stood over the fallen man. Butch knew his friend would stay on an enemy until he was distracted, which was why Butch thrust his glass against Cobb's chest. "Leave it alone and pour me another. Cowing braggarts is mighty thirsty work."

The men around them backed away as the gamblers at the table grew quiet.

Cobb took the glass and poured him more whiskey.

Butch enjoyed the look of fear in Boyd's eyes. "Now, you're gonna reach down with your left hand, unbuckle that gun belt, and let it fall to the floor. Then you and your friend here are gonna find another place to drink. You've worn out your welcome here. If you behave yourselves, I'll bring your rig back to you when we come to visit your boss in the morning."

Boyd spoke through clenched teeth. "And what if I don't?"

"Then you won't be having much use for it, and I'll be happy to add it to my collection."

Butch noticed the men by the door move out of the way and was glad to see Sheriff Rob Moran cut through the crowd. He was tall and dark haired with sharp features and narrow eyes, and Butch knew he was every bit as formidable as he looked.

"That's enough of that," Moran said. "Butch, put that thing away before someone gets hurt."

Like most men who spent any considerable time in Laramie, Butch knew Moran was not a man to be defied. It was not just because of the star on his chest but also because of the sort of man he was. Butch lowered the pistol and quickly holstered it.

Moran grabbed the fallen loudmouth by the shoulder and helped him to his feet. "On your way, Reavis. You too, Boyd. The party's over for you two, at least in here. Go drink somewhere else."

Boyd rubbed the spot under his jaw where Butch had pressed his barrel. "I'm not giving over my gun no matter what this horsewhipper says."

"And you won't have to if you leave now," Moran said. "If you don't, you'll both be spending the next week in jail."

Boyd held his ground until Reavis grabbed his arm and pulled him along. "These two aren't worth a week's wages. Let's go. There are plenty of other places where a Hagen man can drink in this town."

Moran watched the two men leave before he turned his attention to the rest of the saloon. "You all can go back to whatever you were doing when I walked in here. The show's over."

The saloon gradually became noisy again as Moran went to the bar and helped himself to Cobb's glass and the bottle of whiskey. "Since you're not having any, it'd be a shame to let this go to waste." He poured himself a drink and toasted Butch. "Good to see you boys again. I can see you're still as shy as ever."

Butch downed his own shot, which only deepened his desire for another. "I swear, keeping Cobb alive is worse than a job."

"He was asking for it," Cobb said. "He was running down a friend of mine."

Moran drained his glass and quickly filled it before refilling Butch's. "I'd give you some advice if I thought it would do you any good. Laramie's changing, boys. It's not the same town you remember."

"We haven't been gone that long," Cobb said.

"Things change quicker than we'd like," Moran told him. "In some ways it's good and in some ways it's not. King Charles made a lot of money during the war, and he's making even more of it now. He's chosen to spend it right here in Wyoming, which is no small thing. He's got a lot of men on his payroll now. More than he used to."

"I've heard," Cobb said. He did not seem interested in whiskey anymore, not that he ever was. "He's bought up all of our competitors, and I guess he aims to buy us out, too, come tomorrow."

Moran swallowed his whiskey. "I thought I'd heard something about you boys starting up your own stage line. Heard it a week or so ago. I didn't believe it at first. You boys aren't slackers, but you're not exactly the business types. You're a bit rough around the edges for that kind of work." He poured another drink but left it on the bar. "Guess I was wrong."

"You're not the only one who's wrong around here," Cobb said. "If Hagen believes we're selling to him, he's got another think coming."

Moran drummed his fingers on the bar as he considered it. "There's no law that says you have to sell out to him. Then again, there's no law that says he has to be happy about it, either. He doesn't get many refusals these days, so I hope you boys know what you're in for if you cross him."

Cobb flexed his hand. "It's Hagen who doesn't know what he's in for."

Moran smiled. "Tucker Cobb can always be counted on to ignore reason. What about you, Butch? How wide's your independent streak these days?"

"I'm with Cobb." He placed his glass on the bar and re-filled it himself. "Where he goes, I go."

"Loyalty," Moran said. "I admire that. I really do."

Cobb placed his hands on the bar. "How's your inde-pendent streak faring these days, Sheriff."

Moran stood up straight. Butch saw no threat in it, other than the threat a man like Moran always posed. "Butch is loyal to you. I'm loyal to the law. Always have been, and Hagen buying up everyone and everything in sight hasn't changed that. He doesn't own me or my men. No one does, just like nobody's above the law. If you decide to buck him, that's your right. And as long as you don't break the law, I won't have anything to say on the matter."

Butch had figured he would say something like that. "What if Hagen breaks it."

"He won't," Moran said, "but if he does, you be sure to come let me know. Just be careful not to stray too far from him while you're on his land tomorrow. You tweaked Reavis and Boyd's noses pretty hard here tonight. They've got a lot of friends on that ranch, and you don't have any. I won't be there to stop them if they try to get even, and I won't be happy if I hear you two have tried to settle any scores. Blackstone is out of my jurisdiction."

"We'll be sure to keep that in mind," Butch said as he poured himself another drink. "Sure you won't stay for an-other one, Sheriff?"

"Nope. I've said everything I came here to say." Moran

tapped Cobb on the chest. "Hold on to that temper of yours tomorrow, Tucker. I like you and I'd hate to see you in trouble. Not from me, but from him."

Cobb's jaw tightened. "Seems like everyone has to mind themselves except me."

"That's because you're more formidable than most." The sheriff slapped Butch on the back. "Keep an eye on him for me. I'll be around if you need me."

Cobb watched the sheriff leave as easily as he had entered while Cobb poured his friend a drink. "Have this, will you? Your brooding is dampening the atmosphere."

Cobb slid the glass toward him but did not drink it. "I hate bullies, Butch. I always have. You know that."

"Tonight, the sum of my knowledge can be found at the bottom of this here bottle," Butch said. "Drink up. Tomorrow promises to be a trying day."

Cobb picked up the glass and drained it. "It certainly does."

CHAPTER 22

When Butch woke early the next morning, he was disappointed that he only had a dull headache and a dry mouth to show for the previous night's efforts. The fight in the saloon had dampened his enthusiasm for whiskey, and considering Cobb's dark mood at the time, both men had decided it would be best if they turned in early.

It was not Cobb's snoring in the other bed that had kept him awake that night. It was Butch's concern over Cobb's well-being in the days to come. He fretted over how his friend would react once Jane Duprey threw him over for someone else. She had not come to Laramie to find love or for the scenery. She was a sporting woman who was good at her trade and needed to make the most of her looks while she still had them. Butch did not resent Jane for it any more than he might blame a rabid dog for trying to bite him. Natural inclinations were hard to overcome, be it in an animal or a human being.

The previous night down in the saloon, Butch had watched Cobb knock that cowboy flat for talking poorly about Mrs. Wagner; a woman he did not particularly like. Butch did not dare think about what Cobb might have done had they been making crude comments about Jane

Duprey. He imagined he and Cobb would be sitting in Sheriff Rob Moran's cell right now awaiting trial for murder.

Butch would push Cobb to get on their stagecoach and leave Laramie as soon as possible. The less time they spent in town, the better for everyone.

He grabbed the pistol he kept under his pillow when he heard a loud rapping on the door. "Cobb? Butch? It's Colonel McBride. I have an important matter to discuss with you."

Butch had forgotten that the colonel had asked to see them in the morning.

Although his loud snoring might have made people think otherwise, Tucker Cobb was a light sleeper, and he woke immediately. He shook the sleep from his eyes as he swung his feet out of bed and gestured to Butch to open the door.

Butch kept his pistol ready as he opened the door only a few inches. When he saw McBride was alone, he opened it all the way and allowed the colonel inside.

"You're a careful man, aren't you, Mr. Keeling?"

Butch shut the door. "Cemeteries are filled with a lot of careless ones. And it's early enough in the morning for you to call me Butch."

"Then Butch it shall be." McBride sat on the edge of Butch's bed and looked over the still-groggy Cobb. "While I was down at breakfast earlier, I heard you boys had yourselves quite an evening in the saloon last night."

Butch slid his pistol in the holster of his gun belt, which was slung on the back of a chair. "Not the kind we'd been hoping for. Sorry you and your missus had your breakfast ruined by talk of it."

"On the contrary," McBride said. "Martha is something of a gossip maven herself. She finds it entertaining. I heard the sheriff made an appearance. I was wondering what you may have talked about."

Cobb yawned as he ran his fingers through his matted graying hair. "He stopped me from pounding a loudmouth cowpuncher into dust, but I don't think he just happened to be there. Charles Hagen left a note for us with the clerk. He wants us to see him up in his ranch in Blackstone. Had his man John Bookman deliver it to us."

"Bookman." McBride repeated the name as though it were a curse. "The king's shadow. Are you planning to go?"

"Would be rude not to," Cobb said, "though I'm sure I already know what he wants to talk about. He wants to buy us out, just like he's bought out every other outfit in the territory."

"That's where my thinking on the subject leads me, too." The colonel placed both hands atop his walking stick. "I noticed Leon Hunt didn't come with you. I suppose he decided to remain behind in Ennisville."

Butch answered while Cobb yawned again. "He said you paid him to look into who killed the Becquers and he wanted to give you your money's worth. Maybe he had other reasons, but that's the one he gave us."

"He strikes me as a capable man," McBride said. "A bit theatrical, perhaps, but capable. I look forward to hearing from him soon. But before you go to pay adoration to His Holiness, I was hoping you boys would be interested in a bit of light work."

Cobb stretched his limbs. "How light?"

"Escorting Mrs. Wagner, Miss Duprey, and me to and from the bank." He looked at both men. "You recall the distinct sound you heard back in Ennisville when the late Reverend Averill tripped getting into the coach."

Butch had almost forgotten the reverend had been killed. "I remember how expensive it sounded."

"Four gold bars worth," McBride told them. "I examined it personally after his unfortunate demise during the attack. I've decided the found money should be divided equally between Mrs. Wagner's ministry and Miss Duprey's business interests. It seems only fair."

Butch initially did not think it was entirely fair but remembered that he and Cobb still had plenty to last them for the next few months. The notion of gold always affected men differently.

"Sounds like a good idea," Cobb said. "What does it have to do with us?"

McBride told him. "I'd like you to escort us to and from the bank. I've never been a man who put much faith in the discretion of bankers, and word is liable to spread quickly that the ladies have come into a considerable amount of money. Your presence with us during the transaction would help tamp down any interest in our activities from some of the more curious, less noble elements in town."

Butch wanted to put a finer point on it. "You want us to guard you."

"As you guarded us in Delaware Station and in Ennisville," McBride said. "In return, I pledge to guard you from a different kind of threat. The one posed by King Charles Hagen himself."

Butch and Cobb traded glances before Cobb asked, "How do you figure?"

"I've known Charles Hagen for quite a long time," the colonel explained. "Our paths crossed before the war, and we've been at odds ever since. He tried to buy his way in to the Wyoming Mining Company, and I took steps to make sure he was kept at bay. I have every confidence that he would've robbed the concern blind and for his own benefit. There are only two kinds of people in his world. The Hagens and everyone else. I believe there's more than enough money to go around for everyone and had no desire to allow the concern to become subservient to his whims. He's resented me for it ever since."

Butch said, "I still don't see why that's got anything to do with us."

"Hagen is a glutton, sir. He consumes businesses and money and people, not because he needs them but because they're in his way. Because he can. He's done it to all of your competitors, and he'll do the same to you if you allow him. If you don't mind working for him, you can allow him to do the same to you. While I know we've only been acquainted with each other for a brief time, you both strike me as the kind of men who value independence. That's what I'm prepared to offer you now if you want it."

Butch said, "Working for Hagen and working for you turn out to be about the same thing to me."

"It would be an agreement in name only," McBride said. "Charles Hagen is a predator and, like most predators, thrives on taking advantage of vulnerable prey. Or at least prey that seems vulnerable. Should you decide to decline his offer, which I'm certain will be generous, you can tell him you've decided to come work for me instead. That should ensure that he'll leave you alone."

"It also might make him angry," Cobb pointed out. "Especially if you two hate each other like you say you do."

"He'll be angry with you anyway if you decline his offer," the colonel said. "I'm in no position to order you to tell him this, of course, I'm simply giving you the option of being able to use my name and influence on your behalf. He'll be less inclined to trouble you further if he believes I'm on your side. Men like Hagen only understand one thing, gentlemen. Force. I should know because I am the same way."

Butch could not see what Cobb was thinking, but knew he would not want to discuss it in front of the colonel.

Cobb began to pull on his pants. "When were you thinking about bringing the ladies to the bank?"

"They're finishing their coffee in the dining room as we speak," McBride said. "They can wait a while longer if you agree to escort us."

"You'd best head down there with them while I splash some cold water on my face," Cobb said. "Butch and me will be down in a bit."

Butch opened the door for the colonel and closed it behind him when he left. "Well," he asked his partner when they were alone, "what do you make of it?"

Cobb poured water from the pitcher into the wash bowl and dunked his head in it. He brought it back up after a few seconds and grabbed a towel to wipe his face dry. "You feel like working for a king?"

"I could if the money was right," Butch admitted. "It'd be kinda nice not to be poor for once. You?"

"I've been trying to avoid thinking about it since we bought the coach," Cobb admitted. "Even if he buys us out, we'd still be working for him for less money than we could stand to make on our own. He wouldn't pay us as much as he paid Mr. Leek for this hotel, so it wouldn't be enough to live on for the rest of our lives."

"That depends on your definition of *living* and where you live," Butch pointed out. "I know a few places in Mexico where we could live pretty well on a little bit of money."

"That depends on your definition of *pretty well*," Cobb answered. "It could last us just enough to carry us into old age, when we'll be too old to work. I don't aim on being an old pauper gringo in Tijuana, and I don't think you want that, either."

Butch could always count on Cobb to take the good out of an idea. "No, I reckon not."

Cobb dried his face and tossed the towel aside. "Looks like we're always going to be under somebody's thumb, Butch. It might as well belong to someone who likes us."

Butch began to pull on his pants. "I reckon you're right."

Cobb noticed how Jane did not accept his arm when he offered it to her on the street. She preferred to walk with Mrs. Wagner behind the McBrides on the way to the bank. Butch carried the reverend's satchel with the gold bars.

Butch carried the satchel one-handed but was struggling with the weight. "How come I'm always the one who has to carry things around here?"

"You're the youngest," Cobb said.

"By only a couple of years," Butch protested. "And you ain't exactly ready for a rocking chair yet. That cowboy from Hagen's ranch can attest to that."

Cobb had almost put the incident entirely out of his mind. "Thanks for reminding me. We'll probably be seeing him in Blackstone today."

"Him and all of his friends," Butch added. "I'm not worried about it, though, and neither are you."

"No, I'm not."

Cobb kept an eye on the people they passed on the street as they walked. He had never seen the thoroughfare so crowded with wagons and riders threading their way through traffic to different areas of town. Freighter wagons of all sizes hauled goods of every description, and all of them bore the Hagen name on the side. King Charles could never be accused of being subtle about his plans.

Every storefront Cobb could see was occupied with some kind of business, and the boardwalks were full of people heading from one place to another. None of them paid much attention to the small procession of strangers heading for the bank.

Cobb remained outside the bank while Butch carried the satchel full of gold inside for the others. After several minutes, an elderly bank guard in an ill-fitting uniform stepped outside and told him, "You can't stand here like that, mister. You have to move on. We don't allow people to loiter in front of the bank. It don't look good and it ain't secure. You can wait inside or somewhere else, but you can't do it here."

Had he been in a worse mood, Cobb would have told him the sight of a skinny old man in a uniform did not make the bank look exactly secure. But Cobb was still groggy from a lack of coffee that morning, and he found it easier to just move elsewhere. Not everything in life had to be an argument.

Cobb stood in front of a barbershop next door. He glanced inside and saw all four chairs were full. Men were standing, looking for a seat to open up while they waited for a cut and a shave. He ran a hand along the stubble on his face and decided he could use a shave himself. He wondered if he might have enough time to get one before he and Butch headed up to the Hagen spread. A clean-shaven look might improve his odds with the wealthy man.

He turned when he heard the small bell over the door of the barbershop ring and saw John Bookman step outside. Hagen's foreman always struck Cobb as the kind of man who was decent at just about anything he tried but excelled at nothing. He could fix a fence, rope a cow, or move a herd of horses adequately enough, but not enough to be considered great at it. He wore a pistol on his hip, and while he would never be confused for a gunfighter, he usually hit what he aimed at. If it needed doing, Bookman was the one. His plain and forgettable face rarely betrayed emotion, and that moment was no exception.

"Morning, Cobb." Bookman did not offer his hand and neither did Cobb. "You waiting for a cut and a shave to make yourself presentable to Mr. Hagen?"

Cobb knew he could not tell him he was there with Hagen's rival, the colonel. "Just out for a bit of fresh air."

"I figured you'd still be sleeping after all the hell you raised last night in the saloon."

Cobb grinned. "So, the little pig ran back to the farm and squealed to you about me slapping him down. I knew he'd be a whiner."

"They didn't say anything about it," Bookman answered. "They didn't have to. There were lots of men who saw what you did, and there's no shortage of men who are loyal to us. They're smart enough to know that King Charles is a good man to have on your side."

"Us." Cobb laughed as he repeated it. "You make it sound like you and Hagen are partners. That's funny. Men like Hagen don't have partners, John. They have relatives and people who work for them. You're just the hired help, same as those two idiots from the saloon."

"The world's changing," Bookman said, "and Laramie's changing right along with it. Things aren't as black-and-white as they used to be. The war changed that. It changed the boss, too. He knows he can't get to where he wants to be on his own and he needs men who can help him. Men like me. Men like you, too, if you're smart enough to see it."

Cobb did not want Bookman to be there when Colonel McBride and the ladies left the bank. Butch was sure to be with them, and Bookman would know it was not a coincidence. He might have been a Hagen lacky, but he was no fool and would understand the significance of Cobb being with Hagen's rival.

"You might as well run along and finish your errands for your boss, Bookman. Butch and me will be on our way within the hour."

"The only errand I have in town is you," Bookman said. "I was about to head over to the hotel to wake you up, but running into you like this saves me the trip. Let's go."

Cobb did not want Bookman seeing the colonel, the ladies, and Butch together, but he did not want to leave without Butch knowing where he was going. His partner was liable to jump to all sorts of conclusions and act accordingly.

"I'm waiting on a lady friend to finish her business in the bank. You can go fetch your horse. I'll be along as soon as I'm done here."

"That so?" Bookman enjoyed the information. "Must be something wrong with her if she's shown any interest in you. I think I'll stick around a while and see what she looks like. Should be a sight for the ages."

Cobb was too concerned about the colonel and the ladies to give Bookman's insult any notice. He saw the bank door open a bit, only to close again without anyone coming outside. He was relieved when Butch came out alone.

Butch looked annoyed as he came over to them. "Every time I get to forgetting why I hate banks so much I find myself in one and I'm reminded of it all over again." He sniffed the air and looked at Bookman. "You smell pretty, John. Just come from a cathouse?"

Bookman looked him over, then looked at the bank. "This the lady friend you were talking about, Cobb? Looks like a Laredo mule to me. Smells like it, too."

Butch took a step toward the man. "I'm out of Dallas, you ignorant—"

Cobb cut off the war of words before it started. "Looks like Jane's still busy inside."

Butch followed his partner's lead without skipping a beat. "You know how she is when she gets talking to strangers. She's liable to be in there for another hour or more. Told me that we should head on back to the hotel, seeing as how we have ourselves an appointment with the king." He cut loose with a stream of tobacco juice that narrowly missed Bookman as it reached the street. "We can talk to her later."

Bookman's eyes moved to Cobb. "You sure you don't want to wait for her? Never let it be said that I got in the way of true love."

"You couldn't get in the way if you tried." Cobb pushed past Bookman and started walking to the livery to get their mustangs. Butch and Bookman followed together. Cobb was glad Colonel McBride had not led the ladies outside without checking the street first. It would have made his tough conversation with Charles Hagen much less friendly than it already promised to be.

CHAPTER 23

Tucker Cobb could not remember the last time he had ridden through Blackstone but knew it had been quite a while. He had trouble recalling how long it had been, not because of any problem with his memory, but because the town was an easy place to forget.

Unlike Laramie or even Ennisville, Blackstone had always seemed like an afterthought to him, a place that had been built out of a current need more than a specific plan or vision. Some buildings were narrower than others, and the windows, especially on the upper floors of the taller buildings, were not lined up correctly. Some buildings were too close to each other, while others were too far apart. They looked like they had been built by men distracted by something else.

Cobb was not sure if this was due to poor craftsmanship or if it was due to the settlement of the buildings into the muddy ground.

Every building was made of wood, save for the jail, which was a squat stone structure at the end of Main Street. Cobb noticed a swollen man sitting in an old chair in front of the jail. His faded pants were secured by ratty suspenders over a filthy shirt. A jug was on the ground next to him as he peered out at the riders on their way to Blackstone Ranch.

"Who's that old fella sitting in front of that jail over there?" Butch asked aloud. "He looks like the town drunk."

"That's because he is," Bookman said from the front. "He also happens to be the sheriff. That's Randall Bonner."

Cobb recognized the name. It had meant something once. "Looks like he's fallen on hard times."

"A man's times are what he makes of them," Bookman said. "He fell into a bottle a few years ago and hasn't found a way out of it since. He's not good for much, but we don't need him for much. The boss keeps him on out of pity." He glanced back at Cobb and Butch. "He feels the same way about you boys, come to think of it."

"I'm as sober as a parson," Butch said, "and so is Cobb here."

"Sounds like you boys know some mighty uninteresting clergy," Bookman said.

Cobb remembered Reverend Averill and his golden bars. Butch continued riding. "You'd be surprised."

Cobb followed Bookman past the town and up an incline toward the Hagen ranch. The main house spread out along the hilltop and dominated the town. It was a wood and stone structure that had been built to convey a sense of power to anyone who saw it at a distance. In that, it succeeded as far as Cobb was concerned.

They passed between two large stone columns that flanked the road and forced the men to ride single file. Bookman spoke as they rode through them. "This is where Blackstone gets its name from. When the boss found this land, he saw this great big boulder on this hillside. He wanted to put his house up there where the ground is flat, but the only place for any kind of decent road is right through here. He wouldn't let anyone just blow it up, but the boulder cracked when the men started working on it. You can see the result here. Makes for a handy cattle shoot to count heads while we bring them to market. He's had to shore it up over the years when cracks appear, but it gets the work done."

Cobb could have done without the history lesson. He only cared about one aspect of the feature. "Guess this is the only way in or out back to Laramie?"

"No," Bookman admitted, "but it's the most direct way. It'll take you a good hour to ride around it. The slope on either side is muddy and full of holes. We filled them in with sand over the years, but I wouldn't ride through it. Horse could break a leg and its rider a neck. Even the livestock know better than to try it when we're bringing them to market."

"Animals are funny that way," Cobb said. "They always know how to sense when danger's around."

"Guess that's why they taste so good," Bookman said. "The cattle, I mean. Never developed a taste for horseflesh myself. What about you, Butch? I imagine horse is about all a man can hope for back where you come from."

"Can't say as I have ever had it," Butch answered. "We always had enough beef around to overcharge you Northern boys for it."

Cobb had no time for banter as he kept his eyes on the land. He noticed how it changed as they got higher up the slope. It was a long, sloping road that got flatter as they got to the top. He knew the ranch house was on the edge of the property, with the grazing pastures for horses and cattle stretching for miles out behind it. He remembered hearing that a man could ride for the better part of a day before he could even see the end of Hagen's land. Cobb was sure the rancher had only bought more of it in the years since.

Cobb and Butch followed Bookman up the slope and over to a hitching rail in front of the main house. Cobb looked for any sign of the two men from the saloon the previous night but was glad he saw no sign of them. He doubted they would be waiting for them in the main house, as King Charles was known to be a stickler for etiquette. Having his hired hands under his roof was not exactly proper.

Bookman stopped in front of the rails and climbed off his horse. Cobb and Butch did the same, then wrapped the reins around the rail.

Bookman stepped up on the wide porch that spanned the length of the house but motioned for Cobb and Butch to remain where they were. "There's a few rules you boys need to follow before you come inside."

"Rules?" Butch spat a stream of tobacco off the hilltop. "What kind of rules?"

"If you need to use the privy, you'd best do it now. Mr. Hagen doesn't allow guests to use his facilities. The house enjoys indoor plumbing, though you boys won't have any cause to use it."

Cobb had seen toilets before, so the concept was not completely foreign to him. "We'll both be fine."

Bookman moved on to his next point. "I'll be bringing you in to Mr. Hagen's study. You'll sit down and wait for him to talk to you. You won't get up, you won't walk around, and you're not allowed to wander off into other parts of the house. If he offers you some refreshment, you can either accept it or decline it, but you're not allowed to ask for it. Even the slightest violation of any of these rules will end the meeting and you'll have to leave immediately. We clear on that?"

Cobb winced when Butch asked, "Who's gonna make us leave?"

Bookman said, "That would be me."

Butch scratched his chin. "You can try."

Bookman pointed at him. "No spitting into the fireplace, either. There are plenty of cuspidors in the den, and you're expected to use them. If you don't or you miss, the meeting is over."

"I'll be sure to keep that in mind," Butch said, "but I'm liable to forget myself and just spit it in your eye if you stand too close."

"Consider us told." Cobb gestured toward the front door. "Let's get this over with."

"Just one more thing," Bookman said. "No sidearms in the house." He held out his hands. "You can leave them in your saddlebags or give them to me. Either way, you'll get them back when you leave."

Cobb still was not in the habit of wearing a gun and had almost forgotten he was wearing one now. He handed over the pistol and motioned for Butch to do the same. He did so with great reluctance.

Now that the guests were unarmed, Bookman beckoned them to follow him inside.

Cobb had seen the house from a distance but had never stepped foot inside. Judging by the grandeur of the place, it was clear that King Charles intended to live up to his nickname. A wide set of stairs rose through the center of the main hall and split into both wings of the house. A sparkling chandelier was suspended from the high ceiling, and there was not a hint of candle wax anywhere on it.

Bookman set their pistols on a table in the hall and led them to the oak-paneled study where Charles Hagen was seated at a heavy wooden desk, furiously writing on a piece of paper. Behind him, expensive drapery flowed from large windows that offered an expansive view of the valley below.

Bookman quietly gestured for them to sit on a cowhide leather couch that faced the great man while he worked. Cobb had seen King Charles Hagen many times in Laramie over the years, but always from a considerable distance. The millionaire's appearance never changed. He always sported a full head of gray hair and dark, deep-set eyes that smoldered in their sockets like charcoals. He had a regal posture, which Cobb supposed explained why men had taken to calling him a king. He never slouched, not even on horseback or on those rare occasions when Cobb had seen him drinking in a saloon with friends. Cobb rarely found himself intimidated by any man, but Charles Hagen gave him pause.

Bookman stood beside Hagen's desk but did not interrupt him or make any effort to introduce them. Hagen was deep in thought as his pen moved furiously across the paper.

Cobb saw Butch looking around them for something and remembered he still had a chaw of tobacco in his mouth. He spotted one of the cuspidors Bookman had told them about by the fireplace. Butch leaned over, picked it up, and placed it between his boots before using it to catch his tobacco juice.

Bookman's face reddened as Hagen did not look up from his writing. "If you missed, there'll be more than tobacco stains on that rug."

"I don't miss," Butch said.

"Neither do I." King Charles set his pen aside, picked up a blotter, and rocked it on the paper. "We all know why I sent for you, so there's no point in being coy about it. I want to buy out your stage line. I know it's new, but I can see you two have promise."

"How can you tell that?" Cobb asked. "You haven't even looked at us yet."

Hagen set the blotter aside and glared across his desk at them. His eyes were as dark as Cobb remembered and were framed by iron-gray brows. He was a formidable looking man, but Cobb did not look away and neither did Butch.

"I'm proposing a seventy–thirty split in profits with the seventy percent going to both of you. You run it, keep the lion's share of the profits. I cover all expenses."

Cobb knew any offer too good to be true usually was. "But you tell us what to do."

"What to haul, who to haul, and where to haul it to."

"And what not to haul," Butch added.

King Hagen's eyes narrowed. "You're smarter than you sound, Texas. I won't ask for much and I won't ask often. You'll get paid regularly whether you run or don't. Play it smart and you two will be rich in no time."

"Minus thirty percent?"

"Sometimes a man has to spend money to make money." Hagen sat back in his chair as he handed the paper to Bookman. "It's all right there in writing and plain as day. I'm not asking you to sign it now. Take a day or so to think about it. Bring it back to Laramie with you and have a lawyer look it over for you if you'd like."

Cobb said, "I'll just bet Laramie's full of lawyers just champing at the bit to defy you."

Hagen grinned. "It's not like that. Any man who knows the law in any part of the country will read that over and tell you the same as I'm telling you now. That it's all legal and completely aboveboard. You boys got in the right business at the right time. You ought to know a good thing when you see it, especially from the driver's box of a wagon."

Cobb watched Bookman place the paper on the table in front of them but did not touch it. Neither did Butch, who said, "That's a mighty fine bit of handwriting you've got there, Mr. Hagen."

"It reads even prettier than it looks," Hagen said. "I'd sign it right now if I were you. A man never can tell what will happen if a deal sits too long. A bird in the hand and all that."

Cobb had spent many miles with his partner. They had enjoyed many a conversation over a cook fire in the wilderness. They had survived stampedes and storms and rough terrain and faced down more than a few dangerous men.

But Cobb knew they had never gone up against anyone who was as dangerous as Charles Hagen. He had not been able to build a house like this by simply being good with numbers. The fine house they were in right now had been built on the bones of men just like them.

Cobb thought he knew what Butch would say, but he had to be sure. This was too important. "What do you make of it?"

"Same thing you make of it." He spat into the cuspidor between his feet. "Tell him."

That was all the assurance Cobb needed. "We sure do thank you for the generous offer, Mr. Hagen, but I'm afraid we have to turn you down. Me and Butch have been working for someone else our entire lives. Now that we've finally got a stake in something we can call our own, we're not looking to give it up just yet."

Hagen did not move. He did not even blink. "Eighty-twenty. Same rules, only more money."

"You could go up to a hundred and our answer would be the same." Cobb stood up and, after moving the cuspidor aside, Butch joined him. "We know your time is valuable, so we won't waste any more of it. We'll be going back to Laramie and leave you in peace."

"Sixty-forty," Hagen said. "Your stubborn nature just cost you twenty points."

Cobb had figured this would be how it went. "I'd rather have a hundred percent of something than sixty percent of nothing."

Hagen sat back and folded his hands across his flat stomach. "The price just dropped to fifty-fifty. Don't be stupid, Cobb. I'll be happy to wreck your business for nothing. Drive off your business. It won't be hard to do. That mess in Delaware Station will scare off some folks. A bad word from me will take care of the rest. And if that doesn't work, I'll have five coaches follow right behind you wherever you go. Any price you offer your passengers, they'll beat it. Not to mention there won't be a hotel in the territory that'll let you stay there if I tell them not to."

Butch said, "Cobb and me are fond of sleeping out of doors or in the coach if we have to."

"And what a fine coach it is," Hagen said. "It'd be a shame if something happened to it, like catching fire or your team getting poisoned. Horses are such delicate animals, aren't they? They eat the wrong thing and all sorts of things can happen. A coach isn't much good without horses to pull it."

Cobb felt his temper begin to build. "We're not that easy to run off. You'd do well to remember that."

Bookman stepped between them and the door. He did not place his hand on his pistol, but it was near it. "I hope you don't think Colonel McBride will do you much good. I heard you two got close, which is understandable, seeing as how you saved his life and all. Too bad about the

Becquers, though." He offered a smile. "I hope you boys don't blame yourself for that. Nobody's perfect."

Cobb should have known Hagen would have heard about that. "Guess you were in the barbershop when you saw me and Butch escort him and the ladies to the bank."

"I already knew about it before I went to the barbershop," Bookman said. "Wyoming's a small place if you know the right people. Just like it can be an awfully lonely place if you don't have friends to help you. And if you two walk out that door right now, you'll find out just how lonely it can be."

Butch moved beside Cobb. "We might be forgiven for taking that as a threat."

"Take it as it's intended," King Charles said. "As a fact of life. An act from God."

Butch pulled Bookman's gun from its holster and slammed it against the man's head before Cobb had seen him move. He pushed the stunned Bookman back to the window as he aimed the gun down at Hagen and squeezed the trigger.

The hammer struck an empty chamber.

Butch kept the pistol aimed down at the wealthy man, who, to his credit, had not even flinched.

"I love how these cowboys always leave the chamber under the hammer empty," Butch said, "but I'm sure this next one's got some kick to it. What do you say we find out together?"

Cobb watched Hagen's black eyes blaze. "You drop that hammer, my boys'll hear it. You'll be roped and gelded before you reach the black stones."

"My partner and me ain't so easy to kill," Butch said. "You'll find that out the hard way if you try us, and so will any man foolish enough to come gunning for us or our business."

Hagen slowly shook his head. "I think that hot Texas sun baked all the sense out of your head, Keeling. The world's not nearly as simple as you make out. Why do you think that station got robbed? Because the Haney boys woke up one day and got it into their head to steal some horses from a flea-bit station in the middle of nowhere? Do you think those horses getting stolen just before you got there was a coincidence? That my idiot son just happened to be in North Branch when you were there? You think all of that's just a stroke of bad luck?"

Cobb felt the room begin to tilt. *No. It couldn't be.*

Hagen laughed. "Luck doesn't exist outside a gambling parlor, boys. I make my own luck. You two are the last of the holdouts. Everyone else has sold out to me, and every station, too. If you want to shoot me now, go ahead because it won't make a lick of difference. My boy will take over within a week, and you'll go right back to being marked men. He'll hunt you down to the Cape Horn of Chile if he has to. Not because he loves me, but because he's a Hagen. Because you're in our way and no one walking this earth has ever stayed there for long."

Cobb felt sweat break out along his brow and down his back as it felt like the walls were about to close in on him. He did not want to believe everything he had heard, but he thought there was no way Hagen could have known all that so soon. He had to have known it before. Cobb needed to get out of there before he got sick.

He placed a hand on Bookman's pistol and lowered it. "Let's go."

Butch walked backward as Cobb went to the hall to pick up their guns.

Hagen's laughter followed them. "Be sure to give Miss

Jane my regards and tell her I expect her to open her house in a week. My boys are lonely and in dire need of company."

Cobb stopped walking and slowly turned to face him. "What did you just say?"

Hagen slowly rose from behind his desk. "You heard me. Why do you think she came to Laramie in the first place? For her health? You have no idea how the world works, do you, Cobb? Well, you're about to find out. My way."

Cobb started for him, but Butch blocked his path. "Not here and not now, Boss. Let's get our stuff and go. He ain't going anywhere."

Hagen's laughter followed them out to the hitching rail, and Cobb could have sworn he could still hear it as they rode through Blackstone.

CHAPTER 24

In the sheriff's office back in Laramie, Cobb held his head in his hands while Butch finished telling Rob Moran about their visit to Blackstone.

"At least you didn't kill him," Moran said. "I know it doesn't feel like it now, but that only would've made things worse for you two."

It had been hours since they had left Hagen, and Cobb still had trouble getting his mind around it. "Do you think he was just lying to get under our skin for turning him down? Could all of that be true?"

Moran's chair squeaked as he sat back in it. "I've never known him to lie. Cheat and steal, maybe, but he usually tells the truth. It's not all that far-fetched if you think about it. He's trying to button up everything with wheels in the territory, so he gets a piece of everyone and everything that comes here. It stands to reason that he'd go after the stations, too."

Butch was more animated than Cobb. "You mean he had those Haney boys rob the stage? And kill the Becquers, too?"

"Of course not," Moran said. "You know how quickly these things can get out of control once they start going.

Someone gets their head busted or their pride hurt, and it takes on a life of its own. He was driving you boys just as sure as he drives every head of cattle through that stone gate of his. He was figuring you'd come limping into Laramie begging to sell."

Cobb rubbed his temples to make the growing ache go away. "He figured wrong."

"Seems that way," Moran admitted, "but it's not too late to reconsider. Life's difficult enough out here without a man like Hagen gunning for you."

"It's too late for that," Butch said. "We didn't exactly part on the friendliest of terms."

"You might not be able to go," Moran allowed, "but I'll be happy to smooth things over on your behalf if you want." Cobb began to protest, but Moran spoke over him. "I said if you want. I'm not telling you what to do either way. You don't want to sell to him, don't."

Cobb hated to ask his next question, but it could not be avoided. "And what if he burns out our coach or poisons our team? What'll you do then?"

"Investigate it," Moran said, "and if I can prove he had a hand in it, I'll bring him in."

Butch looked away. "Don't make me laugh."

Moran glared at him. "I never joke about the law, Butch. But questioning him is a lot different than arresting him, and I wouldn't count on catching him lurking around the livery with dry hay and a match. If he does it, he'll have it done. My guess would be far away from here, too. He's in no hurry and has nothing but time."

Butch scratched his chin. "No offense meant, Rob. I'm not myself today."

"It's not every day you find yourselves staring down a man like Hagen," Moran said. "I don't know how long you boys were planning on staying in Laramie, but if I were you, I'd take the first fares I could get and be on your way. Make as much money as you can before he poisons the well against you. There's only so much me and my men can do to protect you."

"We don't need protecting from the likes of him," Cobb growled.

"We all need protection from the likes of him," Moran said, "including me. What about Colonel McBride? I understand he likes you boys. He can help."

Cobb's temples began to ache again. Moving people from one town to another was supposed to be simple. He did not like having to make so many considerations just to run a stagecoach line.

"The colonel's a miner with concerns of his own," Butch said. "He likes the notion of annoying Hagen now because it suits him, but I expect he'll get tired of it soon enough, not that I could blame him."

Cobb could see that Moran was getting restless and knew it was time for them to go. He had a whole town and county to look after and not just the concerns of a couple of mule skinners with a poor choice of enemies. Like Colonel McBride, he had more to worry about than their well-being.

Butch stood with him when he decided it was time to leave. "Thanks for listening, Rob. It means more than you know."

The men shook hands. "Put some distance between you and Hagen, boys. He might just let you boys get away with this once he's had a chance to cool down."

Cobb saw no reason to argue with him. Moran had not seen the look in Hagen's eyes or heard the tenor of his laugh. He had, and he knew they had made an enemy for life.

By the time they made it out to the street, the sun had already begun to set over Laramie, and Butch decided it was time to try to lighten his partner's mood. He had seen Cobb disturbed before. He had even seen him angry enough to kill a man in blind rage, but he had never seen him as disheartened as he was now.

"This ain't just about Hagen, is it?" he said. "This is over what he said about Jane."

Cobb let out a long breath. "It's not all of it, but part of it."

Butch had thought that was the case. "It's not like she lied about it. She always said she was coming to Laramie to open a place of her own. You knew what she was. You didn't think she was coming all this way to open a dress shop, did you?"

"I didn't think anything," Cobb said as they walked across the thoroughfare. "That's what's bothering me. I didn't think to ask. I didn't think at all. I just felt."

"No harm in having feelings," Butch said. "Some might call it a virtue."

"I don't know what to call it, but it's no virtue. Stupidity is more like it. She's been with us since we picked her up in North Branch. We did an awful lot of talking around her. She'll probably spill it all to Hagen or Bookman."

"Don't be so sure," Butch said. "She's got money of her own now, remember? She's not beholden to Hagen, at least not as much as she used to be."

"Two gold bricks aren't much against a man like Hagen." Cobb pulled off his hat and wiped his brow with his hand. "He could build a house out of all the gold bricks he's got and still have enough left over to buy the whole territory."

"He'd have done that by now if he could." The more Butch talked, the more certain he became that their circumstances might not be as dire as they both believed. "My old pa used to say you can tell a lot about a man by the enemies he makes. That cuts both ways."

Cobb waved him off. "Sometimes I think you just talk to hear the sound of your own voice."

But Butch could sense he was on to something. "Think about it. Let's say Hagen is a man of his word. Let's say he puts a lot of time and money into trying to ruin us. Some folks are liable to get scared off by him, sure, but not everyone likes him, and it'll make them wonder what's so special about us. Not everyone likes Hagen, and there'll be more than a few who'll probably like to show him up by throwing some business our way."

Cobb's face softened a little. "Sure, but not nearly enough to keep us in business."

"I ain't done yet," Butch said. "We're also a thorn in his side. We matter to him, which means we can bother him. Every run we make will push that thorn deeper in him. And we both know what happens if you leave a thorn in you for too long."

Cobb's brisk pace slowed. "It swells up and makes you sick."

"That's right." Butch was glad Cobb was coming around to his way of thinking. "The longer it stays in there, the worse it gets. That's us. A couple of thorns that'll work their way in so deep that Hagen will just decide to leave us alone."

"Or pull us out and throw us away," Cobb countered, "and then we'll be worse off than we started."

"Don't sell us short," Butch said. "You just stick with me and my way of thinking, and we'll get through this better than ever."

Cobb put his hat back on his head. "If we have to live by your wits, we're liable to starve to death."

"That ain't likely," Butch said. "My old pappy's wisdom is enough to see us through any travail or tribulation this side of the Old Testament."

"Maybe I should've had him as a partner instead of you."

"That'd be hard, seeing as how he's been gone, lo, these many years."

Cobb looked at him. "Last week you told me he was in the Oklahoma Territory."

"That's as good as being dead for a Texan." Butch saw they had already reached the Laramie Hotel. He was less concerned about the building than he was about whom he saw standing in front of it.

Jane Duprey was wearing a new dress Butch had not seen before. It was powder blue with a veiled hat to match. Her face had white powder on it that only served to give her skin more of a glow than it normally had. She was quite a vision after a long and trying day.

When he heard Cobb's breath catch, he knew his partner had seen her, too.

Butch hung back a couple of steps and let Cobb move ahead. He took off his hat as he said, "You look really nice, Jane. What's the occasion?"

"A friend and her husband have invited me for dinner." She smiled up at him. "I'd thought about asking you to come with me, but the clerk said you haven't been in your room all day. I haven't seen you since the bank. You were already gone by the time we were ready to return to the hotel, but the colonel wouldn't tell me why." She looked at Butch. "He never told me what you said to him that made us stay inside for a bit."

Butch looked away. Since Cobb was the one who had feelings for her, he should speak for both of them.

"We were busy," Cobb said. "Had a meeting with a friend of yours."

Her smile remained. "That couldn't be. I don't have many friends in Laramie."

"He knows you. Nasty fella. Owns half the territory. Says he owns you, too. Charles Hagen."

Jane slapped him and did not look like she regretted it. "No one owns me, Tucker. Not Charles Hagen or you or anyone else."

Cobb did not touch the growing red spot on his face. "But he's the reason why you're in Laramie, isn't he? He brought you here."

"He offered to set me up in business," she said, "and you know what kind of business I'm in. But I don't need his money anymore after today. Not after the colonel sold that gold to the bank."

"I'm sure you got a good amount for it," Cobb said, "but it won't be nearly enough. Hagen wants you working for him, and he won't stop until you do. Men like him always get what they want."

Butch saw Jane searching Cobb's face, but not in the kind way she used to have. "He tried to buy you out, didn't he? He's been buying up every stage line in the territory, and you turned him down, didn't you?"

Cobb simply nodded.

"I see," she said. "And you don't think I have enough backbone to turn him down like you did?"

"Butch and me are in a different business," Cobb said. "We might have a chance if we keep moving, but you can't do that. You're a sitting target for him, and he'll grind you down until he gets his way. We both know he will. He doesn't like to lose because he hasn't lost much."

Butch watched a carriage with shiny brass fittings pull up to the boardwalk and stop beside Jane and Cobb. A caped driver in a black stovepipe hat climbed down and opened the door for her.

"Evening, Miss Duprey. I've been sent to take you to dinner."

Butch saw a subtle change come over Jane Duprey. He saw the affection she'd had for Cobb only seconds before fade into something closer to disappointment. There was a permanence to it that made him feel bad for his partner.

Jane drew herself upright. "You've lost something, too, Mr. Cobb. More than you know."

She accepted the driver's hand as he helped her up and into the carriage, then shut the door before climbing aboard. He used a thin riding crop to get the horse going. Jane kept facing forward as she rode away.

Butch went to his friend, who had not raised his head since Jane had slapped him. Butch did not know whether Cobb had been right or wrong for speaking to her in such a manner, but not everything in life could be easily boiled down to such distinctions. Certainly not matters of the heart. "I'm sorry about that, Cobb. I truly am."

Cobb put his hat back on. "Guess some men are just meant to be bachelors."

"There's plenty of women out there. You just have to find the right one for you."

Cobb let out a heavy breath. "Can't do anything about it now, I guess, but there's plenty we can do for ourselves. Come on. I've got an idea."

Butch did not know what his partner was thinking, but whatever it was, they would do it together.

CHAPTER 25

Boyd and Reavis did not mind riding in near-total darkness. They had gone to Laramie from the Blackstone Ranch enough times in daylight to know every inch of the road. Both men were confident they could have made the trip blindfolded.

Boyd was the first one to speak since leaving the ranch. "You think Mr. Bookman was right about us having enough whale oil to burn that coach?"

"It's kerosene, not whale oil." Reavis held onto the jug full of kerosene as they continued on toward town. "I've never known him to be wrong about such a thing before. Have you?"

Boyd thought about it for a moment. "That's the trouble with a man like Bookman. Even when he's wrong, you can't speak of it out of fear he'll lose his temper."

"Well, you don't have to worry about him being wrong about this," Reavis assured him. "That stagecoach ain't very big, and it won't take much to burn it whole." He shook the jug and heard the flammable liquid slosh around inside it. "Once we pour some of this on some dry hay, it'll go up like kindling."

"We just have to make sure we're ready to ride as soon

as we strike the match," Boyd said. "Mr. Bookman said we're on our own if we get caught."

Reavis did not need Boyd to remind him of the foreman's warning. He knew why Bookman had picked them for this job. There was bad blood between them and Cobb and Keeling. If anyone caught them setting fire to the coach, Bookman would be able to let the blame rest on their heads, to say that they were trying to get even for what had happened in the saloon the night before. The ranch or Mr. Hagen or even Bookman would not take responsibility, even though Reavis was sure Mr. Hagen had ordered it done. Bookman never would have ordered it done without permission. When it came to Mr. Hagen, Bookman was as skittish as Boyd.

"We didn't have to do this, you know," Boyd said as they rode along. "We could've had him pick someone else to do it instead."

But the idea of turning it down had never entered Reavis's mind. It would have meant leaving the ranch and never working again in Wyoming. He liked the ranch and counted Boyd among one of his best friends. If keeping his job meant he had to burn the coach of two men he did not like, it was a price he was glad to pay.

"If we'd said no, we'd be sent on our way come morning, and you know it."

"I guess," Boyd said. "You think we can do it? Get away with it, I mean."

In the year they had been working together, Reavis knew Boyd had an unhealthy preoccupation about winding up in jail. It was not that he was afraid of breaking the law or amending his behavior. He was just afraid he would get caught.

Reavis just wanted to reach Laramie as soon as possible and get it over with. "I guess we're about to find out."

* * *

Upon arriving in Laramie, Reavis was glad to see it was a quiet night in town. The streets were empty, which he took to be a good sign. The fewer people outside, the less likely someone might be able to identify them after the fire.

Reavis led them down a side street that took them directly to the livery. He dismounted when he got about half a block away but gestured for Boyd to remain in the saddle. "You stay mounted and in the mouth of that alley over there. After I set the fire, we need to be ready to move slow until we reach the edge of town, understand? Running right off will just make folks take a closer look at us. We can hightail it out of here as soon as we hit the edge of town. Got it?"

"Got it," Boyd repeated. "What do you want me to do if I see something while I'm waiting?"

Reavis had thought of that. "I won't be gone but a minute. Try to stay out of sight and wait for me. But if you see Moran or one of his deputies, give them a loud greeting so I can hide what I'm doing. I ain't afraid of getting locked up, but there's no reason to make it easier on them."

Before Boyd could ask any more questions, Reavis took the jug of kerosene and headed down the alley that led to the livery. Rooming houses were on either side of the alley. They were wood, just like the livery, and he only then realized that setting fire to Cobb's coach could burn down not only the livery, but these houses, too. Maybe even the whole town. Laramie was proud of its fire brigade, but dry straw burned as well as any kindling. He had not thought of the animals who lived in the livery, not to mention the people who lived near it.

Reavis wished Bookman were there to tell him what he

should do, but he remembered Bookman had been specific about what he wanted done. He knew the town and must have thought about the risks of a fire. He remembered that Bookman did not make mistakes.

He found the stagecoach parked alone behind the livery. He was encouraged that a thick tarp was draped over it. Maybe someone would see the fire and call out the brigade to keep it from spreading.

Reavis went to the covered coach and lifted the side of it, exposing one of the doors. He pulled it open, set the jug on the ground, and began to scoop up dry straw and throw it into the compartment.

He stopped when he heard something click behind him.

It was not one of his joints. It was the unmistakable sound of the hammer of a gun.

"Stop what you're doing and turn around real slow, mister." Reavis recognized that Texas drawl as belonging to Butch Keeling. "One false move and I'll send you straight to hell."

Reavis still had a big handful of straw. He thought he knew where Butch was but needed to be certain so he asked, "Should I just drop this?"

"I don't care if you eat it," Butch said.

Reavis quickly turned and threw the straw in the direction of the voice as he dove toward it.

But the straw missed its mark as he saw Butch had taken a knee and was aiming a pistol directly at his middle. The coachman fired three shots into his chest. He pitched forward and fell to the hay. The last thing he saw was some sawdust being kicked in his face as Butch backed away.

Upon hearing the gunshot echo through the alley from the livery, Cobb grabbed Boyd's shirt and pulled him off the horse. The younger man landed hard on his chest, and Cobb heard him gasp as the wind escape from his lungs. He pressed both barrels of his coach gun hard on the back of Boyd's neck and pulled the pistol from Boyd's holster. Cobb called out to Butch, "What happened?"

"Reavis here did something stupid," Butch said as he stepped out into the alley. "It was also the last thing he did on this earth."

Cobb tucked Boyd's pistol in his belt. He was glad to see his friend had not been harmed. "Help me get this one up and moving."

Each of them grabbed a shoulder and pulled the cowpuncher to his feet.

"Your friend died for nothing," Butch said as he took Boyd by the collar. "Don't go making the same mistake."

Russ Sprout rushed out from his livery and into the alley with an old Colt Walker in his hand. "What's going on out here? I heard shots."

"Simmer down, Russ," Cobb said. "We caught this fella trying to set fire to your livery. You'll find a friend of his over by the coach. His name is Reavis and the one we've got here is called Boyd."

"We weren't doing anything of the kind," Boyd said as he struggled to break free of Butch's grip. "Reavis just went in there to make his water when these two jumped out of the dark and tried to bushwack us."

Butch pushed Boyd against the wall. "He was looking to relieve us of our stagecoach by relieving that jug he was toting of its kerosene or whale oil. He was fixing to set a fire, Russ. You'll find a jug near the body in there."

Boyd twisted his head to look at the liveryman. "Anything you find in there is what these two put in there. They were looking for an excuse to kill old Reavis after he showed them up in the saloon last night, and now they've gone and done it. Don't let 'em get away with it, Mr. Sprout. Get the sheriff to lock these two up for murder."

"No need to get the sheriff," Rob Moran said as he and one of his deputies entered the alley from the street side. "I'm right here. You can let him go, Cobb. He's my responsibility now." He took hold of Boyd and pushed him over to his deputy. "Sherwood, take him back to the jail and lock him up. I'll be over to charge him once I'm finished here."

The deputy left with the prisoner as Butch began to tell the sheriff all that had happened.

But Moran stopped him before he got too far. "I like to see something for myself and hear the details later. Come with us and stay quiet. You too, Cobb."

Cobb was concerned by Moran's tone. "We under arrest too, Rob?"

"You're not on your way to a cell, are you? For now, you're just a couple of citizens doing your civic duty. If that changes, you'll know it."

Cobb, Butch, and Russ Sprout followed the sheriff into the area behind the livery. Cobb saw that the tarp over the stagecoach had been moved and the door was open. Needles of hay littered the steps of the coach, and the jug Butch had mentioned was on the ground beside the corpse. Reavis was on his side, his arm cradling the three holes in his belly.

Moran knelt beside the dead man and felt at his neck for a pulse. Finding none, he took the jug, removed the cork, and sniffed it. He flinched at the harsh odor and put the cork back in the jug. "Don't know what that is. Could be kerosene. Could be from a still."

Cobb and Butch traded glances but remained silent while Moran continued his investigation.

The sheriff stood and looked inside the coach, then examined the tarp. "You put this here, Russ?"

"That's my tarp," the liveryman said, "but I didn't put it there. It was folded up in the corner."

Moran looked at Cobb. "You boys put it here, didn't you?"

"I did," Butch admitted.

"Why'd you go and do something like that?" Russ asked. "Earlier, you said you boys were fixing to leave in the morning. Why go to the bother of covering it for such a short amount of time?"

Moran pulled the tarp completely off the coach and let it fall to the ground. He had found the answer. "Because it's not their coach."

"That's right." Cobb failed to see the problem. "After our meeting with Hagen didn't go so well, Butch and me figured he might pull something like this. That's why we moved our coach for safekeeping."

Butch added, "This here is Leo Burke's coach, the same one Colonel McBride drove into town yesterday."

Russ Sprout scratched his chin as he looked up at the coach. "That was mighty smart thinking, boys. I didn't even see you move it. Guess I must've been at supper when you did it."

"You were," Cobb confirmed, "but don't worry. We'll pay you for the night's boarding before we leave."

Russ was pleased to hear it. "Mighty kind of you boys."

"Mighty dumb is more like it," Moran said. "Russ, I'm going to need you to head over to the jail and have Deputy Blake take down your statement. I've got to talk to these two for a bit. We'll keep an eye on the place until you get back."

The liveryman was flustered at the prospect of being part of such official proceedings. "A statement about what?"

"About what you heard and what you saw," Moran said. "The truth. It's the easiest thing to remember. Go on, now."

Russ mumbled to himself as he went to obey the sheriff's command.

Moran placed his hands on his hips as he looked at the two coachmen. "You boys have really done it this time. You might've been clever enough to put a noose around your own necks."

Cobb had not been expecting to hear that. "We stopped a man from setting a fire that could've burned the whole town to the ground."

"We ain't expecting a medal," Butch added, "but a bit of thanks would be nice."

Moran matched his glare. "I'm not in the habit of thanking murderers."

CHAPTER 26

"Murderers!" Cobb shouted. "We didn't murder anyone."

"We were defending our property," Butch said.

Moran slowly shook his head. "That's the problem. You were too clever. Where'd you stash your coach and team?"

"Behind that old warehouse down the street from City Hall," Cobb said. "We wanted it to be close so we could get to it if we needed to."

"So, this coach here doesn't belong to you," Moran pointed out. "It didn't even have a tarp on it until you placed it there before you hid in wait for Hagen's men. You used this coach as bait. Putting that tarp on it proves you were looking for an excuse to shoot Reavis. That's something the law calls premeditation, Butch. That makes it capital murder, and you can hang for it."

Cobb might have thought the sheriff was joking if Moran had a sense of humor. "Butch stopped him from setting a fire. Who cares if it was our coach or not?"

"The law cares," Moran said. "You moved your coach and animals, so you had no legal right to be here. Russ could even charge you with trespassing if he had a mind to. Maybe I could look past it if Reavis was still alive, but seeing how he's not, that complicates things. And not in your favor."

Butch was getting as worked up as Cobb. "We told you about our run-in with Hagen earlier, Rob. You didn't do anything about it. And Reavis rushed me when I shot him. Those holes are in the front of him, not the back."

"And Boyd's still alive," Cobb added for good measure. "They'd both be dead if we came here with murder on our mind, wouldn't he?"

"Maybe," Moran allowed, "or maybe Russ came out here before you could kill Boyd, too. I know that's how Mr. Hagen's lawyer is going to see it. He's liable to get the county attorney to see it the same way when he puts it to a jury."

Cobb made a practice of not panicking, but he felt the cold tide of panic flow through him now. "You mean to arrest us for what we did here tonight?"

Butch placed his hands on his hips as he cursed, then said, "I can't believe this."

Moran's hand went to his gun. "You'd do well to stay away from that hogleg, Butch. As a matter of fact, I'd feel a whole lot better if you unbuckled your gun belt and let it drop to the ground." He looked at Cobb. "You, too, Tucker. Set that coach gun against the wall and drop that pistol in your belt on the ground."

Cobb did as he had been told as Butch unbuckled his belt and placed it on the ground. Then Cobb asked, "We would've been better off letting them burn the place, wouldn't we?"

Moran relaxed a bit now that the two suspects were unarmed. "I didn't say that. I'm not going to arrest you boys, either, though I probably should. For your own good."

Cobb asked, "How would putting us in a cell be for our own good?"

Moran gestured down to Reavis. "You think that idiot and his friend did this on their own. Hagen ordered them to do it or had Bookman do it for him. They're probably on their way into town right now to either gloat or make it plain that they had no part in this. When they find out you killed one of their men, they'll be howling for your heads. And Hagen draws a lot of water in Laramie. A lot more than either of you."

Cobb pulled off his hat and ran his hand over his head. He felt like he was trapped in a nightmare and could not wake up. "So, you're letting us go but without guns to defend ourselves."

Moran picked up Butch's gun belt and tucked Boyd's pistol into his pants. He cracked open Cobb's shotgun and handed the shells back to him. "I want you two to go back to your room in the hotel, lock the door, and stay there until I come to get you. It might be tonight. It might not be until morning. I'm going to have one of my men put a chain around your coach wheels so you can't leave town. I heard you've got a couple of mustangs here with Russ, but I'm going to tell him you can't have them or any other horse until I say so."

Butch said, "Let's say you're right about Hagen and his men coming to town. What's to keep them from setting a fire to our coach now that they know where it is? You might not tell them, but Russ might. He heard where we stashed it."

"I'll have it brought over to the courtyard at City Hall. It'll be safe there. I want you two out of my sight and in that hotel until I come get you. If I see you two even use the privy out back, I'll lock you both up. That clear?"

"It's clear enough," Cobb said.

"You ain't exactly a subtle man," Butch said. "We'll stay in our rooms for as long as you say, but you'd do well to make sure no one fixes to come bother us while we're there. Cobb and me won't have much of a welcome for anyone looking to cause trouble."

Moran stepped forward and pointed a finger at Butch. "I'll have a deputy camped outside your room all night. If there's any trouble to be had, he'll take care of it before either of you can."

"I wouldn't bet my life on it," Cobb muttered.

The sheriff slowly lowered his finger as he turned to face Cobb. "What did you just say?"

Cobb knew Moran and his deputies were braver and more honest than most lawmen he had met in his life. They were certainly better than Fritz Brickell back in Ennisville. But dealing with a criminal—even a stone-cold killer—was much different than tackling a powerful man like Charles Hagen. Such men had a habit of getting their way without worrying about consequences.

Cobb knew there was no point in arguing that point with Sheriff Moran. Not in the alley behind the livery with a corpse at their feet. "I said I'll sleep better knowing it. That you'll have a deputy watching over us, I mean."

The sheriff grunted and sent them on their way.

Cobb could not blame Moran for not believing him. He had never been much good at lying.

Back in their room at the hotel, Cobb and Butch told the whole story to Colonel McBride. About their meeting with Hagen and Bookman. About how Hagen had been responsible for the horse theft at Delaware Station. About Jane's true loyalties and about how they were now facing a murder charge for preventing Leo Burke's carriage from being burned to the ground.

The colonel's face had remained blank once he had

finished encouraging the men to tell their tale. He had sat calmly, his chin resting on his hand on the knob of his walking stick as he listened throughout, taking down each detail in his mind. His expression did not betray any emotion until Cobb told him about Sheriff Moran ordering them to remain in their room.

Colonel McBride's right eyebrow arched when Cobb finally grew silent. "And that's it? That's all of it?"

"I'd say there's quite a bit to it as it is," Butch answered, "and none of it's good."

"I wanted to make sure you gentlemen hadn't left out any details," McBride said. "Details are important if I aim to plan a course of action to save you two from your present difficulty."

Cobb really had to admire the older man. He had found his taste for the rough stuff on the ride from Ennisville, and he was looking to remain in the fight at all costs. "I appreciate the effort, Colonel, but Butch and I can handle ourselves in a fight."

"Not this kind of fight." He looked at the pistol on Butch's hip. "Do you think you'll find a way out of this predicament with guns or rifles? You can't punch or shoot your way out of this one, boys. Your only weapon is your mind. That's the only way a man can ever hope to beat someone as cunning and ruthless as Charles Hagen."

Cobb almost felt foolish under the colonel's glare, even though it was his and Butch's lives that were at stake. "What do you think we should do?"

The colonel stood alone and with little effort, using his walking stick to balance himself. He nodded at Butch's waist, where his gun belt should have been. "I'm no lawyer, but I'm a fairly decent negotiator, and it seems to me that this deal hinges entirely on Burke's carriage." He began to pat the pockets of his jacket but stopped when he found a small notebook. He pulled it out and quickly flipped it open to the last blank pages. He removed a pencil from his pocket and handed it to Butch. "You, sign your name on this paper. Cobb, you sign right below his."

Butch was about to do it when Cobb stopped him. "What are we signing. This page is blank."

"I know," the colonel said. "That's because I haven't had the time to figure out what you'll be signing yet. Just sign like I told you or your lives won't be worth the lead in that pencil he's holding come morning, if not sooner."

Cobb saw no reason not to trust McBride, so after Butch signed his name, so did Cobb. The colonel took back the notebook and pencil and began to leave their room. "If anything happens between now and sunrise, don't hesitate to come up to my room and get me. I doubt Martha and I will be able to sleep tonight, anyway. We've much to do."

Cobb followed McBride to the door to show him out. One of Moran's deputies was standing guard in the hall. It was the same one he remembered seeing in the alley behind the livery. "What's your name, son?"

"Deputy," the guard said, "and I ain't your son."

Cobb had meant nothing by it. "What's your last name?"

"Sheriff. Deputy Sheriff, which is just about all you need to know about me, mister. Now, shut the door and go to sleep while you still can, because tomorrow, you won't have such nice arrangements."

Cobb closed the door and leaned against it. He and Butch had survived a few close scrapes in their time, but he was not sure they would get out of this in one piece.

"I think we might be in some real trouble this time, Butch. I think we're boxed in."

"We ain't nearly as boxed in as you think. We've got them out in the open right where we can see them." Butch reached behind his pillow and pulled out a pistol. Not the one he had handed over to Moran in the alley. This was the one he had taken from Bookman in Hagen's ranch house.

"I'd forgotten about that," Cobb admitted.

"Good thing I didn't." Butch opened the cylinder and checked the five bullets individually before taking one more from his saddlebag, then flicked the cylinder shut again. "I know it's only one gun in the face of a dozen or more, but I'll sleep better knowing it's under my pillow."

Cobb sat on the edge of his own bed. "Who can think about sleep on a night like this?"

"We don't sleep because we're tired," Butch said as he pulled off his shoes and stretched out on his bed. "We sleep when we can. We're gonna need our rest for tomorrow."

The brass lamps installed at the four corners of the coach burned bright as Hagen and Bookman rode into town.

Bookman held the rifle between his feet as he rested his head against it. The cold of the gun metal helped quell his turning stomach. He had always been uncomfortable in such enclosed spaces. He could ride a horse all day and night without trouble, but rocking back and forth inside the coach only made him nauseous. He would not have ridden in one now if his employer had not insisted.

"What's the matter with you?" Hagen glanced over at him. "You look like you're about to be sick."

Bookman knew his boss rarely missed anything. "I'll be fine. Just not much for close quarters like this."

Hagen grunted in understanding. "That's because you're an open sky man, just like I was when I first came here years ago. Dragged my family lock, stock, and barrel from a comfortable home in Denver to a canvas tent on the top of a wind-scoured valley. I made something of the place, though. Something of myself and my name, too."

Bookman watched Hagen look out the window of the coach as if the old rancher could see into the past. "It was a different country back then, John. I know there's no shortage of old-timers like me who'd be all too glad to tell you about how tough life was for us. How the summers cooked us and the winters froze us, and how the Indians hid behind every bush and rock on the hunt for our hair." Hagen smiled at his reflection. "But life was easier back then because a man had to be willing to fight for what we wanted. Fight the land and the elements and the livestock mostly. The Indians were peaceful enough if you didn't rile them. Sometimes I think it was easier because we were younger, but the fighting doesn't stop just because a man's bones set to aching or he gets a few more lines on his face. The fighting only gets harder if you've built something worth defending, and that's why we're riding into town tonight, John."

Bookman sat uneasily in his seat. "I work for you, Mr. Hagen. You tell me what to do and I do it. No matter the day or the hour."

"A thing is easier to do if you know the reason for it, John, which is why I'm telling it to you now. I'm not asking for permission or even your blessing. I'm just explaining it to you on account of what Cobb and Keeling represent. I wouldn't blame you for wondering why I care about a couple of cut-rate mule skinners who defy me. I'm not coming down hard on them on account of greed. I'm doing it to make an example of them. Today, it's just the two, but in a month, there'll be ten. Maybe even twenty. Men will quit their routes, change their names, and move away just to get out of our agreement."

Bookman realized he was speaking before he could

stop himself. "A lack of drivers for the freight and coaches will drive up the price, and you can always find other men to work them, sir."

"I know that," Hagen agreed, "but I shouldn't have to. Today, it's the coach drivers. Tomorrow, maybe it's the miners who spout off against me. Or you cowboys."

Bookman took that last notion as something close to an insult about how he handled his workers. "Any man who speaks out against you on your ranch will answer to me."

"Which is why we're headed into town now," Hagen explained. "If Reavis and Boyd managed to burn down that coach without getting caught, then we've made the trip for nothing. But since neither of them strike me as astute criminals, they're either in a grave or a cell right now. Since their actions can reflect poorly on the ranch, I want to nip that kind of talk in the bud. Moran will be looking to punish someone for it, and we must make sure it isn't either of us. If they keep their mouths shut, I'll see to it that they're released."

Bookman knew Hagen had left out another strong possibility. "What if they're both dead?"

"Then it'll be up to us to see to it that they're remembered as the honored dead," Hagen said. "Good men who were hunted down in the prime of life by a pair of no-good interlopers who had a grudge against me." The rancher grinned. "Cobb and Keeling are worthless as they are right now, but by the time I'm through with them, they'll be seen as a couple of blood-thirsty pirates."

There were times when Bookman wished he had been born a smarter man. It would have been nice to view the world the way men like King Charles Hagen did. Seeing men not as human beings but as a deck of cards where their value was determined by the other cards in your hands at the moment.

And there were other times, such as that moment, when he was glad he was just a ranch foreman. Kicking horses and cranky cattle and surly cowhands gave him more than a challenge. Life was much easier when you just had to follow another man's orders and not worry about the consequences.

But this trip into Laramie was different. Bookman knew they might be facing consequences that neither of them was prepared for. "You know Laramie is different than Blackstone, Mr. Hagen. Sheriff Moran won't be easy to win over to your side."

Hagen continued to look out the window. "Then I suppose we're lucky that I enjoy a challenge."

CHAPTER 27

After a few hours of tossing and turning, Cobb had just managed to fall asleep when he heard the commotion out on the street. By the time his feet hit the floor, Butch was already at the window with Bookman's pistol in hand.

"What's going on out there?" Cobb whispered as he hobbled barefoot to the window.

"From what I can see," Butch said as he stepped aside, "looks like King Charles has stepped down from his throne to grace us with his royal presence. Brought his coach and everything. I think that's John Bookman with him, too."

Cobb looked out the window and saw a brown coach with brass fittings parked in front of the hotel. The thoroughfare was empty, save for Moran, Hagen, and Bookman. A fourth man, the driver of the coach, sat in the wagon box with a riding crop he looked willing to use if he had to.

"I've seen that driver somewhere before," Cobb observed.

"That would be Pete Rigney," Butch said. "He used to ride with the Hammond outfit out of Nebraska. We played cards with him a time or two."

Once again, Cobb found himself admiring his partner's memory. "Used to cheat, if I remember correctly."

"You do," Butch confirmed. "If there's a shortcut to be taken, Rigney will find it and take it." He raised the window as he said, "Looks like an animated conversation. Might as well hear what they're talking about."

Cobb cocked an ear and heard Moran say, "I'm telling you for the last time, Mr. Hagen, that Cobb and Keeling are my responsibility, not yours."

Hagen stamped his foot on the packed dirt of the street in annoyance. "But why are they in a hotel room while one of my men is dead and the other is in a cell? You claim to be a fair man, Sheriff. Does that seem fair to you?"

"Because no one's sworn out a complaint against Cobb and Keeling yet," Moran explained, "but your man Reavis got himself killed while in the commission of a crime. He was fixing to burn down a coach he thought belonged to Cobb and Butch while Boyd stayed with the horses and kept an eye out. Your man didn't even dispute it until later."

Bookman took a step closer to the sheriff. "You mean you believe the word of a pair of coachmen over Mr. Hagen here?"

Moran held his ground, both with his feet and with his words. "I do since what they told me lines up with what I saw. And what I smelled, too."

"Smell?" Hagen scoffed. "You're not some bloodhound, Sheriff. What does smell have to do with anything? Especially behind a livery of all places."

"Because I found a jug of kerosene next to that coach Reavis was fixing to burn," Moran said. "I smelled the stuff on Boyd when I took him in. I didn't smell it on Cobb or

Keeling. That's what made me believe them, not their story."

Cobb was enjoying watching Hagen grow angry at the sheriff's defiance. He saw him push his hat farther back on his head as he said, "But you said it wasn't their coach. You said they had moved it and their team elsewhere. They weren't there to protect anything. They were simply waiting for some of my men to come into town and attack them. The rest of it is a lie, pure and simple. It's so plain that even a blind man could see it."

Moran put his hands on his hips and looked directly at Hagen. "Why would they do that?"

"Because we had words earlier in the day," Hagen said. "I was kind enough to invite those two ruffians into my home and make them a fine offer on their business. They thanked me by insulting me and assaulting Mr. Bookman here."

"I wouldn't call it assault, sir," Bookman interjected. "More like a lucky punch I didn't see coming."

Moran shook his head. "I wasn't talking about that. I'm talking about why, of all the places in town, that they'd wait to jump your men by the livery. If they'd done it on the street or in a saloon, I might be inclined to believe you. But something made those boys move their rig and their horses from the livery, and I think it was a threat from you that did it."

Butch elbowed Cobb in the ribs. "Rob Moran's a pleasure to watch, ain't he?"

Cobb waved him quiet as he watched the scene down on the street play out.

He saw Hagen square up to Moran as he said, "Business isn't always a polite affair, Sheriff. Sometimes it becomes heated, especially during a negotiation. Any disagreement between us should have remained between us. And none of this changes the fact that those men weren't guarding their property. The coach in question didn't belong to them. They just used it as bait to attack two of my best men, and no amount of word-twisting on your part will prove enough to change that."

"Hold it!" Cobb heard a man call out from the hotel entrance. "Not so fast, you scoundrel."

Cobb and Butch almost bumped heads as they craned their necks to see who was joining the conversation. When they saw it was Colonel McBride in a bright blue bathrobe, they ducked back inside and pulled on their pants and boots. This was something they had to see for themselves.

They both reached the door at the same time, with Cobb opening it first. Butch raced past him without being stopped, and Cobb realized Deputy Sherwood Blake was no longer guarding their room. He must be downstairs backing up his boss on the street.

Butch bolted down the stairs as Cobb followed. Butch was stopped at the front door by Blake, who said, "Not so fast, Keeling. You and Cobb ain't free yet. Get back to your room."

"With all this racket?" Butch said. "They're talking about our lives, so we're staying right here."

Cobb moved past the curious clerk at the front desk and stood behind his partner. He looked beyond the deputy to see Colonel McBride showing a long piece of paper to the sheriff.

"It's all written down right there, Sheriff," McBride said. "Clear and legal. Mr. Cobb and Mr. Keeling signed a contract with the Wyoming Mining Company back in Ennisville two days ago. They, along with a fellow named Leon Hunt, were working as my agents to determine who killed my fellow board members, the Becquers, while they slept in the Ennisville Hotel. Mr. Hunt decided to keep searching while the rest of us came here to Laramie."

Cobb knew they had not signed a formal contract in Ennisville but remembered how the colonel had asked both him and Butch to write their signatures in his notebook earlier that night. Cobb had not understood the colonel's reasoning then, but he was beginning to understand it now.

Hagen scowled as he looked down at the document, standing next to Moran. "A contract signed in Ennisville has no bearing on what happens here. This is Laramie, McBride."

"The contract has no end date," the colonel said. "It's still valid as far as the Wyoming Mining Company is concerned, which is all that matters."

Cobb saw Bookman move behind Moran and the others and drift toward the hotel. He saw a fresh pistol on Bookman's hip.

Blake saw Bookman, too, and said, "That's far enough, John. Keep your distance."

Bookman ignored him and kept his eyes on his boss, whose face was almost scarlet with anger.

"I don't care if they're working for the president of the United States himself," Hagen shouted, "it still doesn't justify them shooting down my man in cold blood. It wasn't even their coach they were protecting!"

"No," McBride agreed. "It was mine." He produced a second piece of paper from his robe and handed it to the sheriff. "Leo Burke signed over his coach to me before we left Ennisville. I was going to make the same offer to Cobb and Keeling, but we were all anxious to get to Laramie and time did not allow for it. As you know, Leo was killed on the way here and I was forced to drive the coach to town. You'll see that this contract is every bit of valid as the one having Mr. Cobb and Mr. Keeling as my agents."

"I don't believe this!" Hagen snatched at the second document, but Moran held it out of his reach. "This is all a might too convenient, even for you, McBride."

"It's perfectly legal," the colonel answered. "I ought to know. I'm an attorney. I don't believe you are, though."

Hagen seethed. "I've employed enough of them over the years to understand the law, sir."

"Then you should have no problem understanding that this document is valid."

Moran squinted as he read the contract over in the dim light from the coach's brass fittings. "It might very well be, Colonel, but I have no way of knowing if this signature is genuine. I knew Leo Burke, but I never saw his signature."

Cobb thought they were sunk until the colonel produced a ticket from his robe pocket. "This is the ticket Mr. Burke signed for us when we boarded his coach in North Branch. You'll see the signature here matches the one on the agreement, with a few variations, of course. He signed the agreement on a desk in the hotel, whereas the ticket was signed as we got on the coach. I'll be happy to leave it with you if you wish to verify it independently."

Cobb kept a close eye on Butch, hoping he would not allow his enthusiasm to give up the game. He was glad his partner seemed to be keeping his emotions in check.

Hagen whisked off his hat and pointed down at the documents in Moran's hand. "You can't believe any of this. If this was true, why didn't he file it when he first arrived in town?"

The colonel leaned on his walking stick. "My wife and

I were out of sorts after our coach was attacked. The loss of Mr. Burke and Reverend Averill affected us deeply. We had more on our minds than a simple business transaction. But given the spectacle you've put on here tonight, I'm glad I still had them in my possession. For once, my forgetful nature served a higher purpose."

Hagen stormed away from them before turning back to the group. "Moran, if you—"

"That's *Sheriff* Moran to you, Hagen," Moran yelled, "and you're not in Blackstone anymore. You're in Laramie, and in my town, you'll behave yourself or you'll wind up in the cell right next to Boyd."

Moran refolded the papers and placed them in his back pocket. "Here's what's going to happen next. Hagen, you and your men are getting in your coach and heading back to your ranch. You're going to stay there and out of Laramie while I take a long, hard look into this."

Colonel McBride said, "My wife and Miss Duprey will be happy to attest to everything I just told you here tonight, Sheriff."

Moran turned to the colonel. "You're going back up to your room and staying there. I'll be by to talk to you and the ladies in the morning after I've shown these papers to a judge." He pointed at Cobb and Butch. "I'm pulling Deputy Blake off your room, but I'm ordering you two to stay in the hotel until I tell you otherwise. If I let you go, and that's not a guarantee yet, I want you both out of town as soon as I do it. I won't care where you go as long as you're out of my sight for a while." He looked over each of the parties. "Have I made myself clear?"

Cobb felt John Bookman's eyes boring a hole through him as he said, "Looks like not everyone agrees with you, Sheriff."

It did not take long for them all to see Bookman and where he was looking.

Moran said, "I told you to get back in the coach with your boss, Bookman. Go on."

But Bookman held his ground. "I've got a man dead, and you're just going to let the men who killed him get away with it on account of some words on a scrap of paper?"

"No one's getting away with anything," Moran said. "Get moving while you—"

Cobb saw Bookman reach for his pistol as Butch drew the gun he'd taken from Bookman earlier from under his shirt. He had it in hand before the foreman had cleared leather.

Cobb rushed forward to drop Bookman with a single hard blow to the jaw.

As Bookman fell to the street, Sheriff Moran and Deputy Blake drew their pistols and aimed them at Butch.

Blake was closest and had the barrel of his gun flush against Butch's temple. "Don't go doing anything stupid, now."

"This is all just a great big misunderstanding, boys." Butch tucked his index finger behind the trigger and allowed the gun to flip down so the butt faced the sheriff. "I took this here iron off Bookman this afternoon. I was just trying to give it back to him before he left is all."

Blake took the pistol and tucked it in his belt as he holstered his own. "Yeah, I bet that's what you were doing."

Moran stepped over Bookman and told Cobb, "You knocked him out, so you get to put him in the coach. Hagen, you get in on the other side." Hagen went to obey his orders while Cobb hauled Bookman up and easily carried him to the coach. He laid him on the floor and slammed the door on his head with a satisfying thud.

Moran got out of the way of the four-horse team as he told the driver, "If I find out that you stopped anywhere between here and your ranch, you'll personally answer to me."

Cobb watched the driver release the brake and cracked the crop to bring the team to a trot before they turned around and headed back in the direction of Blackstone.

Moran coughed as the dust from the coach began to settle in the street. The colonel bid them all a good evening before moving back inside the hotel, leaving Cobb and Butch alone with the sheriff and his deputy.

Moran said, "I hope you boys know how lucky you are to have a man like the colonel in your corner. Hagen might be a sidewinder but he was right about you staking that coach as bait. And I know a judge or two who might agree with him if these papers McBride gave me don't convince them."

"They're the truth," Cobb said, "and the truth's got nothing to fear from the law, now does it?"

Moran laughed as he looked away. "You'd best have a plan on where you're going by this time tomorrow, because I want you gone when I cut you two loose." He beckoned his deputy to follow him, which he did.

But not before Blake offered Butch a word of warning. "I noticed you're mighty fast with a pistol, Keeling. You're almost as fast as me, but not quite."

Butch answered, "Let's hope neither of us have to find out for certain."

Blake touched the brim of his hat and joined his boss as they walked back to the jail.

Cobb went back into the lobby, where he found Colonel McBride sitting on the bottom steps of the stairwell. He had looked pink and robust out on the street but looked tired now.

"I can't thank you enough for what you did for us just now, sir," Cobb said. "You got us out of a pretty bad mess out there."

The colonel motioned for them to be quiet and looked over at the night clerk at the desk. "Excuse me, young man, but could you brew us up some tea? It'll help us all get to sleep."

The clerk offered a simper. "I'm sorry, colonel, but the kitchen is closed for the night."

"Good heavens, man," McBride bellowed. "I'm not asking for a four-course meal and all the trimmings. I'm asking you to boil some water for tea. Do it so I can speak to these men in privacy, you imbecile."

The clerk offered his apologies and disappeared into the back reaches of whatever lay behind the desk.

The colonel looked up at Cobb. "You've got to be more careful about what you say and to whom you say it, Tucker. Anything you say can be used against me later."

Cobb blushed at the admonishment. "Yes, sir. I will."

"And no need to thank me, either. It's Mrs. McBride you ought to thank. Those contracts were my idea, but she's the one who put the signatures to paper. She's quite an artist, my wife."

"Mrs. McBride." Butch scratched the stubble on his chin. "I didn't figure her for the devious type."

"We prefer to think of it as being creative," the colonel said. "She's had to put that creativity to use in the past. Like Hagen said just now, business is not always pleasant. There comes a time when the facts have to be bent to meet a desired outcome. Moran won't find enough to overturn them, don't worry, but you boys should make plans to make haste come the morning. Whatever Hagen may have thought about you before tonight, you can rest assured he has a much lower opinion of you now. The best remedy for that sort of thing is time and distance."

The colonel began to stand up, and both men helped him. "And now that I've done my good deed for the evening, I think it's time for me to get back up to my room. I don't want to risk that idiot clerk's tea. He's liable to burn it while he's preparing it."

The colonel shook hands with Cobb, then Butch. "You boys don't have to worry about that contract, either. I won't be looking to enforce it. As far as I'm concerned, it expires tonight."

"We don't need a piece of paper to remind us that we'll always be in your debt," Butch said. "Though I've half a mind to ask if you've got any other good things stashed in that pocket of yours."

The colonel looked him up and down before heading up the stairs. "And I have half a mind to have you committed to an institution. Good evening, gentlemen."

Cobb and Butch remained in the lobby, waiting until they were certain Colonel McBride had made it up to his room before they began walking up the steps.

Butch let out a heavy sigh as he said, "Well, we'll never be able to say the first week of the Frontier Overland Company was a dull one, will we Cobb?"

Cobb found himself thinking about all that had transpired that week. They had left North Branch with a rebuilt coach, a new paint job, and a few passengers bound for Laramie. Along the way, they had found murderers, thieves, a Shakespearean actor, and, if Jane's disposition toward him softened, perhaps love.

Tomorrow, they would be heading out with an unknown future and the most powerful man in the territory as their bitter enemy. But their fate, just like their new stagecoach line, was their own.

"You can say that again, Butch, but I think we ought to pack before we try to go back to sleep tonight. I think we've worn out our welcome in Laramie."

"Don't let it trouble you, Cobb. They'll forget all about it by the next time we roll through here."

Cobb doubted that would be the case, but it was too late to argue. Not even with his partner and friend.

TURN THE PAGE FOR AN EXCITING PREVIEW!

A giant grizzly on a killer rampage
terrorizes a small ranch community—and lures
legendary mountain man Smoke Jensen
into the deadliest trap of all: the human kind . . .

**JOHNSTONE COUNTRY.
HUNT OR BE HUNTED.**

The bear seems harmless—at first. Just a lost and
confused grizzly poking around Big Rock.
Then the killings begin. A horse wrangler is mangled.
A rancher mauled. Then a bartender in the heart of
town is found clawed to a bloody pulp. Now every
man in Big Rock is taking up arms to hunt down the
beast before it strikes again—which worries the local
sheriff. He's afraid this amateur hunting party could
turn into a mass funeral real fast. So he asks
Smoke Jensen to help keep everyone calm and
contain the panic. Unfortunately, it's too late.
The panic is out of control. And the hunt is on . . .

While the gun-toting locals head for the hills in search
of the bear, a ruthless gang of bank robbers ride into
the half-empty town—armed to the teeth.
Then a professional wild game hunter shows up
offering to kill the grizzly—for a price. If that wasn't
enough, a traveling medicine man claims the bear
is part of his act—and wouldn't hurt a soul.
Smoke Jensen isn't sure what to believe or who to
trust. But one thing is certain: where there are jaws,
claws, and outlaws, there will be blood . . .

National Bestselling Authors
William W. Johnstone and J.A. Johnstone

DARK NIGHT OF THE MOUNTAIN MAN

On sale wherever Pinnacle Books are sold.

Live Free. Read Hard.
www.williamjohnstone.net

Visit us at www.kensingtonbooks.com.

CHAPTER 1

It was safe to say that Nelse Andersen had been drinking when he encountered the bear. Every time Nelse drove his ranch wagon into Big Rock to pick up supplies, he always stopped at the Brown Dirt Cowboy Saloon to have a snort or two—or three—before heading back to his greasy sack outfit northwest of town.

Smoke Jensen happened to be in the settlement that same day, having come in to send some telegrams related to business concerning his ranch, the Sugarloaf.

A ruggedly handsome man of average height, with unusually broad shoulders and ash blond hair, Smoke stood on the porch of Sheriff Monte Carson's office, propping one of those shoulders against a post holding up the awning over the porch.

The lawman was sitting in a chair, leaning back with his booted feet resting on the railing along the front of the porch. His fingers were laced together on his stomach, which was starting to thicken a little with age.

At first glance, neither man looked like what he really was.

Smoke was, quite probably, the fastest and deadliest shot of any man who had ever packed iron west of the Mississippi. Or east of there, for that matter.

As a young man, he'd had a reputation as a gunfighter and outlaw, although all the criminal charges ever levied against him were bogus. Scurrilous lies spread by his enemies.

These days, he was happily married and the owner of the largest, most successful ranch in the valley. In fact, the Sugarloaf was one of the finest ranches in all of Colorado. Smoke was more than content to spend his days running the spread and loving Sally, his beautiful wife.

Despite that intention, trouble still had a habit of seeking him out more often than he liked.

At one time, Monte Carson had been a hired gun, a member of a wolf pack of Coltmen brought in by one of Smoke's mortal enemies to wipe out him and his friends.

It hadn't taken Monte long to figure out who was really in the right and switch sides. He had been a staunch friend to Smoke ever since, even before Big Rock had been founded and he'd been asked to pin on the sheriff's star.

Pearlie Fontaine, another member of that gang of gunwolves, had also changed his ways and was now the foreman of the Sugarloaf. Smoke couldn't have hoped for two finer, more loyal friends than Monte and Pearlie.

Or a finer day than this, with its blue sky, puffy white clouds, and warm breeze. Evidently, Monte felt the same way, because he said, "Sure is a pretty day. Almost too pretty to work. What do you reckon the chances are that all the troublemakers in these parts will feel the same way, Smoke?"

"They just might," Smoke began with a smile, but then he straightened from his casual pose and muttered, "or not."

Monte saw Smoke's reaction and brought his feet down from the railing. As he sat up, he said, "What is it?"

"Hoofbeats. Sounds like a team coming in a hurry."

Monte stood up. He heard the horses now, too, although

Smoke's keen ears had picked up the swift rataplan a couple of seconds earlier.

"Somebody moving fast like that nearly always means trouble."

"Yeah," Smoke said, pointing, "and here it comes."

A wagon pulled by four galloping horses careened around a corner up the street. The vehicle turned so sharply as the driver hauled on the team's reins that the wheels on the left side came off the ground for a second. Smoke thought the wagon was going to tip over.

But then the wheels came back down with a hard bounce and the wagon righted itself. The driver was yelling something as he whipped the horses.

Monte had joined Smoke at the edge of the porch. "What in blazes is he saying?"

"It sounds like . . . *bear*," Smoke said. "Is that Nelse Andersen?"

The wagon flashed past them. Monte said, "Yeah, I saw him drive by a little while ago, not long before you showed up. Looked like he was on his way back to his ranch."

They watched as the wagon swerved down the street and then came to a sliding, jarring stop in front of the Brown Dirt Cowboy Saloon. Nelse Andersen practically dived off the seat and ran inside, leaving the slapped-aside batwings swinging to and fro behind him.

"Well, I have to find out what this is about," Monte said. "He can't be driving so fast and reckless in town. He's lucky he didn't run over anybody."

"I'll come with you. I'm a mite curious myself."

By the time they reached the saloon and pushed through the batwings, Andersen was standing at the bar with a group of men gathered around him. A rangy, fair-haired man, he had a drink in his hand, which was shaking so badly that a little of the whiskey sloshed out as he lifted the glass to his mouth.

The liquor seemed to steady him. He thumped the empty glass on the bar and said, "It was ten feet tall, I tell you! Maybe even taller!"

One of the bystanders said, "I never saw a grizzly bear that tall. Close to it, maybe, but not that big."

"This wasn't a regular bear," Andersen insisted. "It was a monster! I never saw anything like it. It had to weigh twelve hundred pounds if it was an ounce!"

He shoved the empty glass across the hardwood toward the bartender and raised expectant eyebrows. The bartender looked at Emmett Brown, the owner of the place, who stood nearby with his thumbs hooked in his vest pockets. Brown frowned.

A man tossed a coin on the bar and said, "Shoot, I'll buy him another drink. I want to hear the rest of this story."

Brown nodded, and the bartender poured more whiskey in the glass, filling it almost to the top. Andersen picked it up and took a healthy swallow.

"Start from the first," the man who had bought the drink urged.

"Well, I was on my way back to my ranch," Andersen said. "I was out there goin' past Hogback Hill, where the brush grows up close to the road, and all of a sudden this . . . this *thing* rears up outta the bushes and waves its paws in the air and roars so loud it was like thunder crashin' all around me! Scared the bejabbers out of my horses."

"I think it scared you, too," a man said.

Andersen ignored that and went on, "I thought the team was gonna bolt. It was all I could do to hold 'em in. The bear kept bellerin' at me and actin' like it was gonna charge. I knew I needed to get outta there, so I turned the team around and lit a shuck for town."

Emmett Brown had come closer along the bar. "You had a gun, didn't you? Why didn't you shoot it?"

Andersen tossed back the rest of the drink and once again set the empty firmly on the bar.

"I didn't figure that rifle of mine has enough stopping power to put him down. I could'a emptied the blamed thing in him and it might've killed him eventually, but not in time to keep him from gettin' those paws on me and tearin' me apart." Andersen shuddered. "I wouldn't'a been nothin' but a snack for a beast that big!"

"I still say you're exaggeratin'," claimed the man who had said he'd never seen a grizzly bear ten feet tall. "You just got scared and panicked. Maybe it seemed that big to you, but it really wasn't. It couldn't have been."

Andersen glared at him and said, "Then why don't you go out there to Hogback Hill and see for yourself? I hope that grizzly gets you and knocks your head off with one swipe o' his paw!"

"I don't cotton to bein' talked to like that—" the man began as he clenched his fists.

"That's enough," Monte Carson said, his voice sharp and commanding. "You're not going to bust up this saloon because of some brawl over how big a bear is."

Enthralled by Andersen's story, the men hadn't realized that Smoke and Monte were standing at the back of the crowd, listening.

Now they split apart so that the sheriff and Smoke could step forward. Nelse Andersen turned from the bar to greet them.

"Sheriff, you better put together a posse and ride out there as fast as you can."

"Why would I do that?" Monte asked. "I can't arrest a bear. Assuming there really is one and that he's still there."

"You don't believe me, Sheriff?" Andersen pressed a hand to his chest and looked mortally offended.

"Those do sound like some pretty wild claims you're making."

Smoke said, "I've seen some pretty big grizzlies, but never one that was more than ten feet tall and weighed twelve hundred pounds. I think you'd have to go up to Alaska or Canada to find bears that big."

"Well, Smoke, no offense to you or the sheriff, but I'll tell you the same thing I told Hodges there. Why don't you ride out there and have a look for yourself? A critter as big as the one I saw is bound to have left some tracks!"

Smoke exchanged a glance with Monte and then said, "You know, I think I just might do that. Especially if you come along and show me where you saw him, Nelse."

Andersen swallowed hard, opened and closed his mouth a couple of times, then he nodded and said, "I'll do it. I got to go home sometime, and I'll admit, I'll feel a mite better about travelin' on that stretch of road if you're with me."

"I'm ready to go if you are." Smoke looked at Monte again. "Are you coming?"

"No, I'd better stay here in town," the sheriff said, adding dryly, "since I don't really have any jurisdiction over bears. But you'll tell me what you find, won't you, Smoke?"

"Sure," Smoke replied with a chuckle.

One of the bystanders said, "How about the rest of us comin' along, too?"

"Might be better not to," Smoke said. "A big bunch might spook that bear and make him attack, if he's still out there."

The real reason Smoke didn't want them coming along was because he knew how easy it was for a group of men to work themselves up into a nervous state where they might start shooting at anything that moved. That could lead to trouble.

A few men muttered at the decision, but Smoke was so well respected in Big Rock that no one wanted to argue with him. He and Andersen left the Brown Dirt Cowboy, but not until Andersen cast one more longing glance at the empty glass on the bar and sighed in resignation.

Smoke's horse was tied at the hitch rail in front of the sheriff's office. He swung into the saddle and fell in alongside the wagon as Andersen drove out of Big Rock. The Sugarloaf was located off the main trail that ran due west out of the settlement, but Andersen followed a smaller trail that angled off northwest toward the small spreads located in the foothills on that side of the valley.

As they moved along the trail, Smoke chatted amiably with the rancher, who was a bachelor, well-liked but not particularly close to anybody in these parts. Andersen asked after Sally, as well as Pearlie and Cal Woods, another of Smoke's ranch hands. He didn't seem to be affected much by the whiskey he had consumed. Smoke had heard that Andersen had a hollow leg when it came to booze, and now he was seeing evidence of that.

They covered several miles before Andersen pointed to a rugged ridge up ahead on the right and said, "That's Hogback Hill."

"I know," Smoke said. "Good name for it. It looks like a hog's back, sort of rough and spiny."

Andersen was starting to look apprehensive now. "That brush on the right is where I saw the bear. He must've been down on all fours in it. When I came along, he just reared up bigger'n life. I really thought he was gonna eat me."

Smoke's sharp eyes scanned the thick vegetation they

were approaching. "I don't see anything moving around in there," he said. "Or hear any rustling in the brush, either."

"I didn't see or hear anything out of the ordinary until suddenly he was right there, no more than twenty feet from me. He's a sneaky one, that bear is. He was layin' up, waitin' to ambush me."

Smoke tried not to grin as Andersen said that with a straight face. The rancher appeared to believe it. Smoke supposed he ought to give the man the benefit of the doubt. As far as he could recall, Andersen didn't have a reputation for going around spreading big windies.

"We'll be ready, just in case," Smoke said as he pulled his Winchester from its saddle scabbard under his right leg. He laid the rifle across the saddle in front of him.

A moment later, Andersen pulled back on the reins and brought his team to a stop. "This is it," he said. "This is the place." He pointed into the brush. "Right there. I'll never forget it."

Smoke studied the bushes and listened intently. There was no sign of a bear or any other wildlife, other than a few birds singing in some trees about fifty yards away.

"I'm going to take a closer look," he said.

"Are you sure that's a good idea?"

"I don't think there's anything in there." Smoke swung a leg over the saddle and dropped to the ground, holding the Winchester ready in case he needed it. He had spotted something that interested him, and as he moved into the brush, using the rifle barrel to push branches aside, he got a better look at what he had noticed.

Quite a few of the branches were snapped around the spot where Andersen said the bear had been, as if they'd been broken when something large and heavy pushed through the brush. A frown creased Smoke's forehead as he spotted something else. He reached forward and plucked a tuft of grayish brown hair from a branch's sharply broken end.

That sure looked like it could have come from a bear's coat.

Smoke moved closer, pushed more of the brush aside, and looked down at the ground. Some rain had fallen about a week earlier, so the soil was still fairly soft, not dried out yet.

After a long moment, he turned his head and called, "Come here, Nelse."

"I ain't sure I want to," the man replied. "What did you find?"

"Better you come take a look for yourself. There's nothing around here that's going to hurt you."

With obvious reluctance, Andersen set the brake on the wagon, wrapped the reins around it, and climbed down from the seat. He edged into the brush and followed the path Smoke had made.

When Andersen reached Smoke's side, Smoke pointed at the ground and said, "Take a look."

Andersen's eyes widened. He breathed a curse as he peered at what he saw etched in the dirt.

It was the unmistakable paw print of a gigantic bear.

CHAPTER 2

"So he was telling the truth? There really is a monster bear roaming around out there?"

Monte Carson sounded as if he were having trouble believing what he had just said.

Smoke, straddling a turned-around chair in the sheriff's office, said, "We only found three tracks, and they were scattered some. I couldn't tell from them exactly how tall the varmint is, but they were deep enough that I can say he's pretty heavy. Might go a thousand pounds."

"So not as big as what Nelse claimed, but still a mighty big bear."

"Yeah," Smoke agreed. "I don't recall ever seeing one that big around here."

"What did you do with Nelse?"

"Rode with him back to his ranch." Smoke smiled. "He didn't much want to travel alone. He kept looking back over his shoulder like he was afraid that bear had climbed into the wagon with him."

"Then you came back here instead of heading home?"

Smoke nodded. "Sally's not expecting me back at any particular time. I thought it would be a good idea to let you know there was some truth to what Nelse said. There was a good-sized bear within a few miles of town earlier today. The tracks prove that."

The broad shoulders rose and fell in a shrug as Smoke continued. "Of course, that doesn't mean it's still anywhere around these parts. When you watch bears moving around, they look like they're just lumbering along, but they can move pretty quickly when they want to."

"Yeah. Kind of like runaway freight trains."

"Anyway, this one has had enough time to cover some ground. He could be a long way off by now."

"Or he could be wandering around the edge of town." Monte sighed. "I'm going to have to warn folks, Smoke. They need to be on the lookout and especially keep an eye on their kids."

"I agree, but I wish there was some way to avoid a panic."

"It was too late for that once Nelse Andersen started guzzling down whiskey and spewing his tale," Monte said. "You know some of the fellas who were in the Brown Dirt Cowboy have already started spreading the story by now."

"More than likely." Smoke rested his hands on the chair's back and pushed himself to his feet. "Let folks know that first thing tomorrow morning, Pearlie and I are going to try to pick up that bear's trail and find out where it went from Hogback Hill. If it left this part of the country, then people can stop worrying about it."

"And if it's still around here somewhere?"

"Pearlie and I will find it and drive it on out of the valley if we can."

"What if it won't leave?"

"Then we'll deal with it," Smoke said with a note of finality in his voice.

* * *

For such an apparently huge creature, the bear proved to be surprisingly elusive. Smoke and Pearlie found its tracks leading north from Hogback Hill the next morning and followed them for a while, but the trail disappeared when it entered the rocky, mostly barren foothills at the base of the mountains in that direction.

When they finally reined in and admitted defeat after casting back and forth among the hills for several hours, Pearlie shook his head disgustedly and said, "We need Preacher with us. That old boy can follow a trail better'n anybody who ever drew breath."

"I can't argue with that," Smoke said. The old mountain man had been his mentor and like a second father to him for many years. It was said he could track a single snowflake through a blizzard. "There's no telling where Preacher is, though. He could be anywhere from Canada to old Mexico."

Pearlie rubbed his beard-stubbled chin and said, "We're liable to have folks from town roamin' around out here on the range lookin' for the critter, figurin' they'll shoot it and be acclaimed as heroes, but more than likely they'll accidentally shoot each other."

"I know," Smoke said, nodding, "but I'm hoping the bear actually has moved on and that as time goes by without it being spotted again, people will forget about it. It may take a while, but things ought to go back to normal eventually."

"Maybe." Pearlie didn't sound convinced. "Problem is, when folks get worked up about somethin', all their common sense goes right out the window."

Smoke couldn't argue with that statement.

* * *

Three days later, a middle-aged cowboy named Dean McKinley was following one of his boss's steers that had strayed up a draw. Water ran through there any time it rained very much, but that dried up quickly, sucked down by the sand underneath the rocky streambed.

The iron shoes on the hooves of McKinley's horse clinked on those rocks as he rode slowly, swinging his gaze back and forth between the draw's brushy banks.

McKinley had heard about the bear. Another cowboy who rode for the same spread had been in the Brown Dirt Cowboy that day and had brought back the tale of Nelse Andersen's run-in with the giant beast.

As far as McKinley was concerned, Andersen was a loco Scandihoovian who drank too much, but the story had had the ring of truth to it.

The last thing McKinley wanted to do was run into a grizzly bear while he was out there alone on the range.

Maybe the smart thing to do would be to turn around and hope the steer found its way back home, he told himself.

Then the blasted critter had to go and bawl piteously, somewhere up ahead of him. To McKinley's experienced ears, it sounded like the steer was scared of something.

He hesitated for a couple of heartbeats, then muttered a curse under his breath and dug his bootheels into his horse's flanks, sending it loping forward.

He had just rounded a bend in the draw when something loomed in front of him, moving his way fast. McKinley couldn't hold back a startled yell as he tugged hard on the reins and brought his horse to an abrupt stop. His other hand dropped to the butt of the revolver holstered on his hip.

Then he realized it was the steer charging toward him, wild-eyed with fear. McKinley jerked his mount to the side to get out of the way. The steer's run was an ungainly thing, but it was moving pretty fast anyway as it charged past him.

"What the devil?" McKinley muttered as he twisted in the saddle to look behind him. The frantic steer disappeared around the bend, heading back the way McKinley had come.

The cowboy was still looking back when his horse let out a shrill, sudden, terrified whinny and tried to rear up. McKinley hauled hard on the reins to keep the horse under control as he looked in front of him again.

Twenty yards away, from around another bend, came the bear.

The creature was enormous, even on all fours. To McKinley's eyes, it seemed like the bear was as big as the horse he was on, maybe even bigger.

And it was coming fast toward him, panting and growling.

"*Yowww!*" McKinley cried as he realized what was happening. The steer had fled in blind panic from the bear. Now it was his turn. The massive beast had already covered half the distance between them by the time McKinley got his mount wheeled around and kicked it into a run.

The horse took off like a jackrabbit, so fast that McKinley had to reach up and grab his hat to keep it from flying off. He didn't really care about the hat. Grabbing it was just instinct.

The bear was so close that McKinley could hear its breath rasping. He thought he could feel the heat of it on the back of his neck, but that was probably just his imagination. The cow pony, once it got its hooves under it, was running fast and smooth now.

Unfortunately, a bear could run just about as fast as a horse. That was what McKinley had heard. It appeared to be true, but as he glanced back over his shoulder, he saw that the bear wasn't gaining on him, either.

It might come down to which animal tired first or whether the horse tripped.

If they went down, McKinley knew, it would be all over.

He suddenly remembered that he had a gun on his hip. He knew better than to think a Colt would stop a huge grizzly bear, but he clawed the iron out of leather anyway and triggered it behind him without looking. Maybe the racket would make the bear stop, if nothing else. He pulled the trigger until the hammer clicked on an empty chamber.

A bellowing roar sounded. McKinley looked back and saw that his desperate ploy might have worked. The bear had stopped and reared up on its hind legs. It swatted at the air with its massive paws and continued to roar.

At the same time, the racing horse was putting more distance between it and the bear. McKinley clung to the saddle. They swept around another bend, and he could no longer see the bear.

Of course, it could resume the chase, if it wanted to, but with each stride, the horse put the huge, hairy menace that much farther behind.

Even so, McKinley didn't heave a relieved sigh until the draw petered out and he emerged onto open range again. He reined in, turned his mount, and looked back.

No sign of the bear.

The monster had gone back to wherever it had come from, McKinley thought.

The steer he had followed up the draw stood about fifty yards away, cropping calmly on grass as if nothing had happened. McKinley glared at the steer for a moment and then shook a fist at it as he called, "Next time you go wanderin' off and find yourself on the menu for a bear, I'm gonna let the dang thing have you, you blasted cow critter!"

The next day, Smoke and Pearlie were leaning on one of the corral fences, watching as Calvin Woods cautiously approached a big gray horse.

"He's givin' you the skunk eye, Cal," Pearlie called to his young friend. "Don't trust him."

"I wasn't planning on it," Cal replied. "But I'm not gonna let some jugheaded horse think he's gettin' the best of me."

"Now, I don't know why he'd think that," Pearlie drawled, "just 'cause he's already throwed you half a dozen times today."

Cal scowled over his shoulder, then turned his attention back to the gray. He spoke softly to the horse as he reached out with one hand. The gray blew a breath out, making his nostrils flare, but he didn't shy away as the young cowboy stroked his neck.

"All right now," Cal said. "You and me are gonna be friends, horse. You just take it easy." He lifted his left foot, fitted it into the stirrup. "No need to get spooked. I'm not gonna hurt you."

He grasped the reins and the horn and lifted himself into the saddle. His eyes were wide with anticipation as he settled down in the leather.

The gray didn't budge, just stood there calmly.

"Well, son of a gun," Pearlie breathed. "Maybe the boy's done it."

Equally quietly, Smoke said, "Look at the way that horse's tail is flicking."

From atop the gray, Cal said, "See, I told you I'd—"

The horse exploded underneath him.

The gray was a sunfishing, crow-hopping, end-swapping dynamo as Cal yelled in alarm and clung to the saddle for dear life. It was an effort that was doomed to fail. Only a handful of seconds elapsed before Cal sailed into the air and came crashing down on the ground inside the corral.

The horse bucked a few more times as it danced across the corral, seemingly celebrating its triumph.

"Are you all right, Cal?" Pearlie called.

Cal groaned, sat up, and shook his head groggily. He had lost his hat when he flew out of the saddle. He looked around for it, spotted it, and started to crawl toward it on his hands and knees.

"You'll get him next time," Pearlie said, then added under his breath to Smoke, "or not."

Smoke smiled. He was glad that Cal wasn't hurt and admired the young cowboy's determination, but something else had caught his attention.

"Rider coming," he said with a nod toward the trail that led to the Sugarloaf from the road.

Pearlie squinted in that direction and then said, "That's Monte, ain't it?"

"Yep," Smoke replied. He turned away from the corral and started toward the ranch house, intent on finding out what had brought the lawman out there.

Sally must have sensed somehow that company was coming because she came out the front door onto the porch as Smoke walked toward the house. She wore an apron over a blue dress, and her thick dark hair was pulled back and tied behind her head. She'd been cooking, and she dusted flour off her hands as Smoke approached.

She was the prettiest woman he'd ever seen. The smartest, bravest woman he'd ever known. The former Sally Reynolds had been a schoolteacher when he first met her up in Idaho. It was her students' loss and his gain when she'd agreed to become his wife.

"Did you know Monte was coming out here today?" she asked.

"Nope," Smoke replied. "He must have news of some sort."

It probably wasn't good news, he mused. Otherwise, he would have waited until the next time Smoke came into Big Rock to talk to him.

Monte loped up and reined in. Sally smiled and said, "I hope you're in the mood for some nice cool lemonade."

"That sounds like the next best thing to heaven," he replied. "I'm much obliged to you."

Pearlie had followed Smoke from the corral. He took the horse's reins from Monte when the sheriff dismounted.

"I'll take care of this ol' boy for you, Monte."

"Thanks, Pearlie."

Smoke said, "Come on up onto the porch and sit down."

Sally had gone back into the house. She returned a few moments later carrying a tray with a pitcher and three glasses on it. She poured lemonade for all of them, then joined Smoke and Monte in the wicker-bottomed rocking chairs on the porch.

"What brings you out here, Monte?" Smoke asked after taking a sip of the cool, sweet beverage.

"That bear again," Monte said.

"The giant bear Nelse Andersen saw?" Sally said. "Smoke told me about it."

"It's been spotted again?" Smoke asked.

"More than spotted. It chased Dean McKinley and nearly got him."

"McKinley . . ." Smoke repeated as he tried to put a face with the name. "Puncher who rides for Bart Oliver's Boxed O brand?"

"That's right," Monte said. "He followed a steer up a draw, and that bear nearly got both of them."

The Boxed O was a small outfit bordering the foothills to the northwest, five or six miles from the Sugarloaf. Bart Oliver, who owned the spread, worked it with his two teenaged sons and a couple of hired hands, one of whom was Dean McKinley.

"McKinley wasn't hurt?"

Monte shook his head. "No, he was able to get away on horseback."

"He was lucky, then. Bears are mighty fast when they want to be."

"Yeah. McKinley said he emptied his six-gun at the beast. He probably missed with all his shots, and even if he didn't, a .45 slug wouldn't do more than annoy a grizzly unless you hit it just perfectly."

"Not likely from the hurricane deck of a running horse, especially when the fella pulling the trigger was probably scared to death."

"No probably about it," Monte said. "McKinley still looked pretty shook up when he came into town and talked about it this morning."

"So now folks are all worked up about the bear again," Smoke said. "I sure was hoping it had moved on."

Almost a week had passed since Nelse Andersen's encounter with the bear. Phil Clinton, editor and publisher of the *Big Rock Journal*, had printed a story about it on the paper's front page that was picked up and reprinted by one of the Denver newspapers, so it was doubtful that anybody in this whole part of Colorado hadn't heard about the giant bruin.

But after a few days of hunting parties going out to search for the creature with no success, most of the interest had died down.

This latest development would change all that.

"I'm hoping you'll agree to try to track it again," Monte said. "I'm going to issue an order for everybody in the valley to stick close to home and stay out of the way so you can find the bear and deal with it."

"Kill it, you mean?" Sally said, with a slight frown of disapproval.

Monte shrugged. "I'd be fine if the varmint just wasn't around these parts anymore, but I don't know how you'd guarantee that. Even if you drove it off a long way, it could come back. They can range for hundreds of miles."

"First thing is to find it," Smoke said. "I'm certainly willing to try again. I'm not sure you'll be able to get people to stay home, though."

"It'll be easier if I can tell them that you're on the trail. They'll want to give you a chance to succeed. I appreciate you taking on the chore, Smoke."

"I'll do my best."

Monte drank some of his lemonade and then sighed. "I hope you can get him. Andersen and McKinley were lucky. That luck probably won't hold up. Sooner or later . . ."

"Sooner or later, somebody who runs into that bear is going to wind up dead," Smoke said.